THE FATED SKY

TOR BOOKS BY MARY ROBINETTE KOWAL

THE GLAMOURIST HISTORIES

Shades of Milk and Honey
Glamour in Glass
Without a Summer
Valour and Vanity
Of Noble Family

Ghost Talkers

THE LADY ASTRONAUT SERIES

The Calculating Stars
The Fated Sky

THE FATED SKY

MARY ROBINETTE KOWAL

A TOM DOHERTY ASSOCIATES BOOK ✶ NEW YORK

This is a work of fiction. All of the characters, organizations, and events portrayed in this novel are either products of the author's imagination or are used fictitiously.

THE FATED SKY

A Tor Book
Published by Tom Doherty Associates
175 Fifth Avenue
New York, NY 10010

www.tor-forge.com

Tor® is a registered trademark of Macmillan Publishing Group, LLC.

The Library of Congress Cataloging-in-Publication Data is available upon request.

ISBN 978-0-7653-9894-9 (trade paperback)
ISBN 978-0-7653-9893-2 (ebook)

Our books may be purchased in bulk for promotional, educational, or business use. Please contact your local bookseller or the Macmillan Corporate and Premium Sales Department at 1-800-221-7945, extension 5442, or by email at MacmillanSpecialMarkets@macmillan.com.

First Edition: August 2018

Printed in the United States of America

0 9 8 7 6 5 4 3 2 1

For my niece Laura Olafson,
who boldly goes.

Our remedies oft in ourselves do lie,
Which we ascribe to heaven: the fated sky
Gives us free scope, only doth backward pull
Our slow designs when we ourselves are dull.
What power is it which mounts my love so high,
That makes me see, and cannot feed mine eye?
The mightiest space in fortune nature brings
To join like likes and kiss like native things.
Impossible be strange attempts to those
That weigh their pains in sense and do suppose
What hath been cannot be: who ever strove
So show her merit, that did miss her love?
The king's disease—my project may deceive me,
But my intents are fix'd and will not leave me.

—Helena, *All's Well That Ends Well*,
William Shakespeare

THE FATED SKY

ONE

IAC HEAD WARNS ABOUT CUTS IN BUDGET

By JOHN W. FINNEY

Special to The National Times

Aug. 16, 1961—Horace Clemons, head of the International Aerospace Coalition, warned the United Nations today that any cuts in the "minimal" space budget would make a manned Mars landing in this decade impossible. He also cautioned that any extension in the timetable of the Mars program would increase the cost of the First Mars Expedition, now estimated at $20 billion. As a result of the $600 million cut made by the United States Congress in this year's budget, he said the IAC has had to sacrifice the "insurance" that had been built into the program "as a hedge against unforeseeable or intractable technical problems" and to delay crucial experimental flights in the Cygnus spacecraft.

Do you remember where you were when the *Friendship* probe reached Mars? I was getting ready to return from the moon. I'd been up in *Artemis Base* for a three-month rotation, flying geologists from our tiny colony out to different survey sites.

While we were all called astronauts, only a handful of us were also pilots, by which I mean glorified bus drivers.

The rest of the two hundred "citizens" came and went, depending on their area of expertise. Only fifty or so were "permanent" residents in the underground bunkers we called home.

Along with half the population of the base, I skip-walked in the light gravity through a buried gerbil tube called "Baker Street" toward "Midtown." With no atmosphere to protect us from the cosmic rays hitting the moon, we'd scraped up a layer of the moon's surface and buried the tubes in regolith. Aesthetically, the outside of the base looked like a decaying sandcastle. The inside was mostly smooth rubber, occasionally punctuated with light wells, aluminum supports, and pressure doors.

One of the doors hissed open, and Nicole hopped through, holding the handle. She pulled the door closed behind her and dogged it shut.

I spread my legs to kill my momentum as I landed from my last skip. She'd rotated to a position here on the last ship and it was darn good to see her. "Good morning."

"I thought you were Earthbound." Like me, Nicole was wearing a light pressure suit, and had the rubberized safety helmet tethered at her waist like a gas mask from the war. It wasn't much, but in case one of the tubes was breached, it would give us ten minutes of oxygen to get to safety.

"I am, but I wasn't going to miss the first Mars probe landing." I was currently on rotation as a copilot for the small shuttle from the base to IAC's *Lunetta* orbiting platform. It wasn't much more than a space bus, but the big ships like the *Lunetta*-to-Earth, Solaris class, were all piloted by men—not that I was irritable about that or anything. I patted the carryall that hung over one shoulder. "Heading straight to the *Lunetta* rocket after this."

"Say hello to a hot shower for me." She joined me in skip-walking down Baker Street. "Do you think we'll see Martians?"

"Not likely. It looks almost as bleak as the moon, at least from the orbital pictures." We reached the end of Baker Street. The delta-pressure gauge on the panel by the door read lunar normal 4.9 psi, so I pumped the rachet handle to open it. "Nathaniel says he'll pull out his own eyeteeth if there are Martians."

"That's . . . graphic. Speaking of, how is he?"

"Good." I pulled the door open. "He's been making noises about . . . ah . . . rocket launches."

Laughing, Nicole slid into the Baker Street-Midtown airlock. "Honestly, you two are like newlyweds."

"I'm never home!"

"You should get him up here again to visit." She winked at me. "I mean, now that private quarters are an option."

"Yeah . . . You and the senator should probably put a little more thought into how well the air ducts carry sound." I started pulling the hatch shut.

"Hold the door!" In Baker Street, Eugene Lindholm bounded toward us with loping strides. If you've never seen someone move in low gravity, it's sort of like mixing the grace of a toddler skipping with the ground-eating stride of a cheetah.

I pushed the door open wider. He corrected badly and cracked his head on the frame as he came through.

"Are you okay?" Nicole caught his arm to steady him.

"Thanks." He pressed a hand against the ceiling as he caught his balance. The other hand held a sheaf of papers.

Nicole glanced at me before she moved over to the door into Midtown. I nodded and dogged the Baker Street door shut, but she didn't open the next door.

"So . . . Eugene. As someone who flies with Parker . . ."

She gestured at the papers in his hand. "I don't suppose you want to 'accidentally' drop some of those?"

He grinned. "If you're hoping for duty rosters, all I've got are recipe clippings for Myrtle."

"Drat." She opened the hatch and we headed into Midtown.

Wafting in from the pressure difference came a scent rare on the moon, loam and green and the soft scent of water. The center of the colony had a broad open dome that allowed in filtered light, which nurtured the plants growing here. It was our first really permanent structure.

The areas along the walls had been partitioned into living quarters. Sometimes I wished I were still berthed here, but the newer pilots' quarters were conveniently located by the ports. Other cubicles had been erected for offices and our one restaurant. There was also a barber shop, a second-hand store, and an "art museum."

The very center held a tiny "park." By "park," I mean it wasn't much bigger than a pair of king-sized beds, with a path through the middle. But it was *green*.

What did we grow in this carefully ameliorated soil? Dandelions. Turns out, when properly prepared they are tasty and nutritious. Another favorite, prickly pear, has beautiful flowers that turn into sweet seedpods, and flat pads that can be roasted or baked. It turns out that many of nature's weeds were well suited to growing in nutrition-poor soil.

"Hot dog." Eugene slapped his thigh. "The dandelions are in bloom. Myrtle has been threatening to try her hand at dandelion wine."

"By 'threatening,' you mean promising, right?" Nicole bounded past the raised beds. "Oh, Elma, also say hello to a dry martini for me when you get home."

"I'll make it a double." I had thought that Nathaniel and

I would be some of the first settlers on the moon, but with the *Artemis Base* established, the agency had turned its attention to settling Mars, and he had to stay on Earth for planning purposes.

Mars consumed everyone's conversations at the IAC. The computers sitting over their equations. The punch card girls keying in endless lines of code. The cafeteria ladies ladling out mashed potatoes and green peas. Nathaniel, with his calculations . . . Everyone talked about Mars.

And it was no different on the moon. On the far side of Midtown, they had brought out a giant four-foot television screen from the launch center and erected it on a sort of podium. It looked like half the colony was here, crowded around the TV.

The Hilliards had brought a blanket and what looked like a picnic lunch. They weren't the only ones who were turning this into a social occasion. The Chans, Bhatramis, and Ramirezes had also set up on the ground near the podium. There weren't any children yet, but aside from that, it was almost like a real town.

Myrtle had a blanket set up too, and waved Eugene over. He smiled and waved back. "There she is. Want to join us, ladies? We've got plenty of room on the blanket."

"Thanks! That would be lovely."

I followed him over to the blanket, which looked to have been quilted together from old uniforms, and settled down with Eugene and Myrtle. She'd trimmed her hair from its bouffant into something more suitable to the moon, mostly because aerosols were not a great thing to have in space. She and Eugene had volunteered to be some of the permanent residents. I sorely missed them when I was on Earth.

"Hey!" A voice from the front of the crowd cut through the murmur of conversation. "It's starting."

I rose onto my knees to see over the heads of the folks

in front of us. In grainy black and white, the TV showed a broadcast from Mission Control in Kansas, though we were getting it with a 1.3-second delay. I studied each image, looking for Nathaniel. I loved my job, but being away from my husband for months at a time was challenging. Sometimes I thought that quitting and going back to being a computer would be appealing.

On the screen, I could see Basira working away on equations as the teletype coughed out pages. She drew a strong line under a number and lifted her head. "The Doppler signature indicates that the two-stage separation has occurred."

My heart ratcheted up, because this meant that the probe was about to enter the Martian atmosphere. Or, rather, it had entered already. The weird thing was that all the numbers she was getting from Mars were twenty minutes old. The mission had either already succeeded or failed.

Twenty minutes old—I glanced at my watch. How much time did I have before I had to be in the hangar?

Nathaniel's voice came over the television and I inhaled with longing. "Atmospheric entry in three, two, one . . . Speed 117,000 kilometers. Downrange distance to landing site is 703 kilometers. Expected parachute deploy in five seconds. Four. Three. Two. One. Mark. Awaiting confirmation . . ."

The entire dome seemed to hold its breath, leaving only the constant low hum of fans to stir the air. I leaned toward the screen, as if I could see the numbers coming off the teletype or help Basira with the math. Though, in truth, it had been four years since I'd been in the computer department or doing anything more complicated than basic orbital mechanics.

"Confirm parachute. Parachute has been detected."

Someone let out a whoop in the dome. We weren't down yet, but oh—it was close. I wrapped my fingers in a corner of the quilt, clutching it as if I could steer the probe from here.

"Awaiting confirmation from the spacecraft that retro-rocket ignition has occurred." Still, Nathaniel was talking about an event that had happened twenty minutes ago, while I was listening to his voice from 1.3 seconds ago. The vagaries of life in space.

"At this point in time, we should be on the ground."

Please, oh, please let him be right. Because if they failed to land that probe, the Mars mission would come to a sudden and grinding halt. I looked at my watch again. He should be announcing confirmation of the landing, but the seconds just ticked by.

"Please stand by. We are awaiting confirmation from the Deep Space Network and the *Lunetta* relay station." Nathaniel wasn't on the screen now, but I could picture him standing at his desk, a pencil gripped so tightly in his fist that it could break at any moment.

A tone sounded.

Beside me, Nicole inhaled sharply. "What is that?"

The tone repeated, and Mission Control dissolved into cheering. Nathaniel's voice rose as he fought to be heard over the din. "What you're hearing, ladies and gentlemen, is the confirmation tone from our Mars probe. This is the first broadcast from another planet. Confirmed. *Friendship* has landed, paving the way for our manned mission."

I jumped to my feet—we all did—and forgot about gravity. Laughing and soaring awkwardly through the air, I cheered for the success of the *Friendship* probe and the team who had planned the mission.

"You're late." Grissom glowered at me as I swung into the pilot's lounge by the port. He had his travel duffel resting by the bench and drank from a sip-pack of coffee.

I glanced at the wall clock. "By thirty seconds."

"That's still late."

He was right, but no one else was there to notice, and launch wasn't for another two hours. "And you're still ugly."

"Heh. I figured you were watching the landing?" He passed me our flight plans to review as we walked to the ship. Grissom grumbled a lot, but he was as much of a space junkie as I was.

I nodded, flipping through the pages of burn times and rates, attitude and velocity. We'd spend three days making the transit to *Lunetta,* during which time there wasn't much to do but monitor gauges. Heck, even the slow pressure increase from moon base psi to *Lunetta*'s standard psi was automated. "There's not anything to see yet, but I just wanted to . . . I don't know. Be there."

Grissom grunted. "Yeah . . . I watched the moon landing the same way."

Silence hung between us for a moment with the reminder that I had been on that mission three years ago. It had turned me into something of a celebrity, which was part of why I probably enjoyed life on the moon a little more than life on Earth. I didn't have to deal with fans. Usually.

"Did you watch it? The Mars landing, I mean."

"Nah. Listened to it on the radio." He shrugged as we reached the corridor leading to our ship. "Spent some time with my girl before heading out. They're rotating me down to the Brazilian spaceport for a month to train on the new ship."

"The Polaris class?" I whistled when he nodded. "Confirmed, jealousy."

He snorted. "It'll take a week for me to even stand, I've been up here so long. The training itself won't take more than two weeks."

"Still. The specs on it make it look like a dream. Plus Brazil beats Kansas." I stopped at the hatch to the pilot cabin for the taxi and checked to make sure the delta-pressure gauge was at 4.9 before opening the hatch. There was always a chance that there wasn't a ship on the other side, even though we were at the right port. "A vertical landing will make everything so much easier when going home."

"Won't be as smooth as the moon lander." He shrugged. "I'm fond of the glider myself. Get to see more on approach, but this won't be as weather dependent, and with the hurricanes getting worse . . . On the other hand, I don't mind the extra days in orbit waiting for a hole."

"Sure, but that's because you're a wimp about gravity acclimation." I ducked into the compact pilots' compartment. The limp artificial gravity on *Lunetta*'s rotating section was one-third that of Earth—just like Mars—and made a good transition for people coming back from the moon. "I'm hoping for good weather when we head down. Can't wait to get home."

"Then maybe you should have been on time."

I stuck my tongue out at him, laughing, and we got down to the business of our preflight check. One of the nice things about a takeoff from the moon is that there are far fewer variables than on Earth. Without any atmosphere to speak of, we didn't have to deal with weather or wind or anything, really, except a little bit of gravity.

The passenger compartment behind us could hold twenty people. Most flights, it was completely full of specialists who were rotating back to Earth after whatever project they'd come up for had finished. The cargo hold, likewise, would be filled with personal luggage, science experiments, and our very few export items. For instance, one of the geologists had begun carving moon rock, and her sculptures were selling for astonishing amounts back on Earth. Myrtle's "moon quilts" from recycled fabric also fetched enough to finance all three of their sons through graduate school. The arts were surprisingly alive and well in space. I'd even joined in with a sort of paper sculpture made from old punch cards, but hadn't quite gotten up the gumption to try to sell them.

Even people on Earth who didn't like the space program got all excited by anything coming from the moon. I guess if you spend millennia romanticizing a place in myths and legends, it takes a while to wear off.

Grissom and I had flown together often enough that we had the preflight check down to a routine. Not that we skipped any steps. Routine or no, weather or no, we were still sitting atop what was basically a bomb.

It's funny . . . the way you can get used to anything.

Two hours later, we'd finished our checklist, and the passengers were all strapped into their seats. Grissom looked over at me and nodded. "Let's light this candle."

The engines whispered to life, nearly silent on the airless surface of the moon. We lifted off and in that acceleration I felt weight again, as if the moon wanted to pull me back down to it. Below us, the gray-and-brown craters fell away, washed in the flames of our exhaust.

I said you can get used to anything. I might have lied.

Arriving in low Earth orbit and docking with the orbital station, I was a pilot astronaut: even sitting in the copilot seat and mostly handling navigation calculations, I was intimately involved in the procedure. Grissom and I handed off our ship to the replacement pilots, who were heading out for their three-month stint on the moon, and drifted inside.

Leaving *Lunetta*, I was just another Earthbound passenger dropping out of orbit. So far, the International Aerospace Coalition had yet to staff any women as pilots on the big orbital rockets. It wasn't official policy that we weren't allowed to pilot them, but when I inquired, I always got something along the lines of how they wanted to use my expertise "where it's most valuable." Since the lady astronauts had gotten into the corps on the strength of our computing skills, it was hard to get them to let us sit in a different seat.

I floated into the passenger compartment with the rest of the Earthbound folks. While *Lunetta* had artificial gravity in the spinning outer ring, the center remained stationary for docking purposes. It made handling luggage easier and harder at the same time. It weighed nothing, but also had a tendency to wander off if you didn't strap it down. I wedged my bag into the small compartment beneath my seat and tightened the tie-down straps before shutting the compartment door.

"Elma!" In the aisle floated Helen Carmouche, née Liu. She wore her dark hair pulled back in a ponytail and the ends floated above her head.

"I didn't know you would be on this rocket." Grinning, I pushed myself up to hug her, almost overshooting the mark—I'd gotten used to having at least the moon's microgravity—but Helen hooked a foot under a rail like a zero-g pro and caught me.

Remember what I said about how you can get used to anything? This did not feel much different than running into her on a streetcar or train.

"We need to do some Earthside training." She eyed the couch next to me. "May I?"

"Absolutely!" I swung up to let her pass beneath me. "How's Reynard?"

She laughed as she tucked her bag into the compartment. "He says he has repainted the living room. I dread to see it."

I pulled myself closer to the "ceiling" to let other passengers through. "Color choice or skill?"

"Two words: Martian. Red. But how would he know?" She shook her head, yanking on the tie straps with practiced ease. "We don't have pictures from the surface yet."

"It could be worse. It could be regolith gray."

"Neutral may be better." She closed the hatch of the luggage compartment with a click. "How's Nathaniel?"

I sighed, without meaning to. It just slipped out. "Good?"

She straightened, catching herself on the seat. "That not sound good."

"No, no. He's fine. Everything is fine." I pulled myself down to my seat and began strapping in. As I worked the shoulder straps into place, I could feel Helen staring at me. "It's just hard being gone so much. You know how it is."

She settled into the seat next to me and patted my hand. "At least we are going home."

"I'm sorry—I shouldn't complain, not about a three-month separation." Helen was on the Mars mission team, so she had been training for fourteen months, and when the expedition left next year, she and Reynard would be separated for another three years. "I honestly don't know how you're going to do it."

"It would be harder, I think, if we had been married longer." She winked. "Keeps honeymoon going. You know? When I come home . . ."

"You have ignition?"

"All thrusters firing."

Overhead the speakers crackled into life. "Ladies and gentlemen, this is Captain Cleary. We will push back from the station in a moment, and should have you back on Earth at the Kansas Astrofield in about an hour."

Routine. I'd made the trip between Earth and the moon about a dozen times. On each trip things became a little more polished. A little more . . . normal. It really wasn't any different now than a cross-country train trip. Except, of course, for everything.

A slight clunk reverberated through the ship as the locking mechanism released from the station. Outside the tiny porthole, fireflies seemed to eddy as the frozen condensation on the spacecraft's skin came out of the station's shadow and into the light of the sun. The frost flurried around us, luminescent against the ink of space.

I keep trying to say that this is nothing more than a routine, but the truth is that it is magic. Around us the great arc of the station swept in dizzying circles. If I hadn't been strapped in, I would have leaned forward and pressed my face against the window.

"There!" Helen pointed to something just out of sight ahead of us. "The Mars fleet."

The ship vibrated and began a slow rotation, coming around into position for dropping out of orbit. As it did, the three-ship fleet designed for the First Mars Expedition panned into view. Against the ink-black sky, the two passenger ships and the supply ship stood out as irregular cylinders, the passenger ships long and slender, girdled with a centrifugal ring like the space station. Someone had likened the ring to an . . . adult toy, which told me two things: one, that I was more of a prude than I thought I was, and two, what that particular item must look like and how it might function. I had yet to ask Nathaniel about it, because I wasn't sure if I wanted to know if he knew what it was.

In any case, if you did *not* have experience with such things, the ships were an innocently beautiful sight. "You know . . . there are times when I'm a little jealous of y'all."

"Eh." Helen shrugged. "I'll be doing math all the way there and back."

"Why do you think I'm jealous?" I rolled my eyes. "I'm basically a bus driver."

"On the moon."

"True. And I love it, but . . . it's not very challenging." I could have gotten on the Mars mission if I'd wanted to, but the truth is that Nathaniel and I had been talking about children. "I'm thinking about retiring as a pilot and maybe going back to the computer department."

Helen is the queen of the disdainful snort. "And go back to flying a Cessna?"

"Or doing training for incoming astronauts. I'm just . . ." Bored. "I want to focus on my marriage."

Helen gave me one of her patented sniffs. She really is a master of those little noises of disbelief. I was saved from the full brunt of her scorn when the rocket shuddered as the captain fired the deorbit burn.

Behind us, someone whimpered a little. Helen glanced over her shoulder and leaned closer to me. "Just wait until we hit the entry interface."

"Must be their first return to Earth." I did not glance back. Grandma had always said that when someone was embarrassed, the cruelest thing you could do was stare at them, and I understood what they were feeling. Even with training, there was nothing like the real thing, and it was going to get a lot worse before we got down.

Helen and I chatted through the first half hour, catching up on life in space. Then a piece of popcorn began a slow fall from someone's bag. That first sign of gravity was our indication that we'd fallen far enough toward Earth for the atmosphere to be slowing us down.

Outside, we began the slow process of heating up to 1,649 degrees Celsius. Outside the windows, the air began to glow orange with streamers of superheated atmosphere whipping past us in a wake of plasma. What's funny is how quiet it gets during this part of the descent. We aren't in enough atmosphere to cause vibrations, and are basically a big glider, so there's no engine noise. But even quieter are the astronauts inside, watching the spectacle of reentry. It never gets old.

The captain banked the ship in the first of a series of long S curves to kill some of our speed. The g-forces grabbed at us, pulling me down into my couch. It was only two G, but after months at one-sixteenth, it felt as though I were buried in mud.

The g-forces continued to rise, pressing me into the side of my couch. I waited for the captain to pull us out of the turn into the next part of the S curve, but the rotation continued. This was not routine.

And being stuck in the passenger compartment, there was not a darn thing I could do.

TWO

CYGNUS 14 LANDS OFF COURSE
AFTER ERROR OR A GLITCH

By STEVEN LEE MYERS

KANSAS CITY, KS, Aug. 20, 1961—One of the Cygnus class spaceships that ferry astronauts from the International Aerospace Coalition's *Lunetta* space station back to Earth landed about 260 miles past its intended target today, officials said, after a technical malfunction or piloting error during its fiery descent. The spaceship is a variant of the ones used almost since the program's inception, but the ship that landed today was a new version, making its first trip with modified rockets and control systems that had been intended to ease its descent and landing.

My arms weighed five thousand pounds, and a Clydesdale sat on my chest, drumming the walls with its hooves. I dragged my eyes open to see why no one had chased it off, and was rewarded with a regolith gray field. Not the moon. No . . . the chair in front of me. Groaning, I turned my head but stopped as nausea grabbed my stomach and squeezed it.

At some point, the g-forces must have gotten high enough to make me pass out. I don't know how the captain had managed to set the rocket down—or for that matter, what had gone wrong—but we appeared to be miraculously alive.

The pounding continued, though the Clydesdale was simply the weight of my body under Earth gravity for the first time in three months. The air stank of vomit and urine. Slowly, I turned my head to check the life-support telemetry panel. All signs were earth-normal, but until they opened the door, we were still in an airtight can, and protocols had to be observed.

Next I turned to check on Helen. She was still out, which wasn't surprising, but otherwise appeared unharmed.

I closed my eyes, taking slow controlled breaths through my mouth while we waited for the recovery team to come aboard. They were taking an extraordinarily long time. On the other hand, I didn't know how long we'd been down or what else they had to deal with. Maybe one of the landing wheels had caught fire, or who knows what.

Finally—and it's a little embarrassing that it took this long—I realized that the pounding was coming from the hatch. It must be jammed. As much as my Southern training made me want to stand up and try to help, years of astronaut training brought the protocol checklist to the front of my mind.

Smell of smoke? None. Oxygen? Confirmed. Injury? I was fine, Helen was fine . . . I opened my eyes and very carefully turned in my seat to look around the cabin. The other passengers were whey-faced or green, but no one seemed to be in unexpected distress. A Black man across the aisle with a crooked nose—one of the geologists from the Mars team, what was his name . . . ?—anyway, he caught my eye. "Should we help with the door?"

I did *not* shake my head. "They've got the tools. We're safe, so we'll let them do their job."

He nodded and immediately went gray-green, swallowing

hard. I winced in sympathy. Anytime you changed gravity environments, sudden head movements were nauseating.

Leonard Flannery—that's right. We'd had a nice conversation about the Loire Valley at Helen and Reynard's wedding. He'd been appalled that I hadn't gotten to taste any wine there back when I was ferrying planes during the war.

Vindicating my choice to stay put, the hatch opened with a hiss of changing pressure. The distant roar of our T-38 chase planes rumbled through the cabin. Sunlight and fresh air tumbled in, along with the scent of burnt rubber, raw earth, and, underneath all of that, freshly mowed grass. I closed my eyes again, because goddamn it, I was not going to weep over greenery.

"Nobody move!" A gun cocked, metal on metal.

My eyes snapped open of their own accord. Crowding through the hatch, six men in hunting camouflage held rifles trained on us. They were a mix of Black and white and tones in between, wearing various forms of masks over their faces. One had a balaclava, which masked everything but the fact that he was Black. Another with a sunburnt tan had a bandana tied over his face like a comic book bandit. A third had a gas mask. The rest wore dust masks from a construction site.

How had they gotten past security at the IAC with—Oh. Wait. The chase planes were still circling. No telling where the captain had needed to set down, but my guess was that we weren't in Kansas. I had no protocol or routine for this.

Beside me, Helen groaned.

"Hey! Shut up!" One man wearing a balaclava and armed with a gun and a heavy Brooklyn accent charged down the aisle to point his weapon at Helen.

She snapped her head up and immediately vomited. Like the pro that she was, she managed to turn her head so that it didn't hit me, though bile spattered her own thigh. It set off a wave of retching from other parts of the cabin.

I swallowed hard, keeping my jaw clenched. Who knew that years of dealing with anxiety-fueled vomit would come in handy? Still, my heart labored against the stress and the gravity load as the Brooklyn man turned his gun toward each new sound. Behind the mask, his brown eyes were pinched and angry. "What the . . . What are they sick with?"

Behind me, someone gagged. Another of the men said, "Don't lift your mask! You don't want to catch it."

"Space germs."

It was probably not the best choice to laugh, but a single "Ha!" escaped. It bounced around the cabin and drew all eyes to me. But, honestly . . . space germs? It sounded like something out of a radio serial.

"You think that's funny?" Brooklyn pushed closer to me, pressing the gun against my temple. The metal made a cold indention in my skin, grinding against the bone. "You think poisoning the Earth is funny?"

"No, man. Don't do this." Leonard leaned against his straps. "You know how this will look. Don't—"

"Shut it." Brooklyn pointed his rifle at Leonard. "I don't have time for an Uncle Tom. You're part of the problem, and we aim to stop it."

"Hey!" The man with the gas mask strode forward with proper military bearing, his gun held down at an angle. Even muffled behind a filter, his voice resonated like a drill sergeant. "Sick or not, the clock's ticking. We aren't going to get another chance like this, so—holy shit. You're the Lady Astronaut."

Of all the times to encounter a fan, I had not anticipated it happening at gunpoint. Still, it gave me a script of sorts.

I knew how to talk to fans. Even with the gun held to my temple, I smiled at the new man. Behind the lenses of the gas mask, he had muddy hazel eyes with a dark mote in one. "You must be a fan of *Mr. Wizard*."

"My daughter loves the show." His eyes softened for a moment, but then he shook his head, shoulders tightening. "Doesn't matter. Except . . ." He thumped Brooklyn on the upper arm. "She'll do. They'll pay attention to her."

"I thought we wanted the pilots."

"Well, we can't fucking get to them, now, can we? Cockpit is sealed solid. But she's a genuine celebrity. A national treasure. They'll—"

In the distance, sirens wailed, growing louder by the second. Brooklyn straightened, staring back at the door. "Shit. That was fast."

"What did you expect, doofus?" My fan reached out and grabbed my arm, trying to haul me out of my seat without undoing the shoulder straps.

"Let me help?" I held my hands carefully where they could see. "There are a lot of buckles."

He grunted, stepping back to give me space. With leaden fingers, I fumbled with the shoulder straps. The weight of the Earth pulled me down, and even the straps weighed a thousand pounds. It didn't matter how much time I spent in the gym on the moon, the first week on Earth was always Hell. All the while, the sirens dopplered closer to us.

From his seat, Leonard said, "Please. Don't use a white woman as your hostage. You know how this is going to go down."

For a moment my fan hesitated, then he shook his head. "They won't care if we use a Negro as a hostage. The Lady Astronaut, though? That'll get their attention."

When I shrugged off the second shoulder strap, my fan grabbed my arm again and hauled me to my feet. I leaned my weight on him and grabbed the seat back in front of me, while my brain tried to figure out what to do with all this extra weight. I struggled to support myself as the cabin spun wildly around me. Vomiting seemed like a plan.

"She—" Helen's voice cut off behind me. But, bless, her, she started again. "She will be dizzy. Go slow if you do not want her to vomit on you."

My stomach was already empty, because I avoid eating before a flight. Still. I stalled, trying to get my bearings. "What do you want me to do?"

"You're going to stand in the door and give our demands." Brooklyn shoved me down the aisle, and I staggered as my feet dragged through the gravity.

My fan caught me before I went down. "Just do as we say, and no one has to get hurt."

"Sure. Of course." Catching my breath got harder. From exertion or fear, I'm not sure. Maybe both. I leaned on my fan as we made our way to the rocket hatch.

The passengers all seemed to be awake now. Once upon a time, I'd known everyone in the astronaut corps, but now I only knew half of them on sight, and some of them seemed only vaguely familiar. Still. I knew Helen, Leonard, and Malouf would all be good in a pinch. Over by the door, Cecil Marlowe from engineering fiddled with his shoulder straps like he was thinking about getting up. Ruby Donaldson, with her blond pigtails, looked like a child, but had been a doctor on the front lines during the war.

What must the pilots be doing up front? Presumably, they were conscious and aware of what was happening, or at least knew that someone other than the rescue team was aboard. There was an intercom to the back, but not a camera. If I were them, I'd be listening in right now, trying to get more information. I'd be piping it to Mission Control, too.

I cleared my throat. "What did the *six* of you want me to say?"

Brooklyn stopped me at the end of the aisle. "Tell them there's problems here on Earth. Leave space alone until you get the Earth fixed."

I nodded slowly. They were Earth Firsters, which I should have guessed sooner. Most of them tended to be refugees from regions that had been hit hardest in the aftermath of the Meteor. The fellow from Brooklyn had probably lost everything, and, being Black, had been left to rot in the ruins of Brooklyn. "Okay, but you don't need everyone here in order for me to give a message . . ."

"You'd like that, wouldn't you."

"It would be kind." Beyond the door, rescue vehicles pulled to a stop, lights flashing. It was a local ambulance and three fire trucks, not the IAC. One of them stopped sideways so I could read "Madison County" on its side. "Where are we?"

"Alabama."

"Okay . . . well, it will take a while for someone from the IAC to get here." Even with chase planes and radar trackers letting them know where we'd set down, they would still have to travel. "Since some people aren't well, why don't you let them off to go with the ambulance? It would . . . it would isolate any space germs."

One of the men peeked out, then pulled his head back in. "EMTs are heading this way."

"Stop them." My fan jerked his chin, gas mask canisters wobbling with the movement.

Taking a breath, the man at the door poked his rifle out

and fired it into the air. The sound ricocheted in the cabin, filling it with violent echoes. He shouted out the door. "That's close enough!"

Brooklyn shoved me forward. His thumb dug into the flesh above my elbow, but his grip was the only thing keeping me upright.

My fan glanced at me. "You're going to tell them that we want a news crew here. And the president. And Dr. Martin Luther King."

"And the head of the UN," one of the bandanaed men said. He had the darkest skin of the bunch and an unexpected British accent. I knew other black Brits, but had thought the Earth Firsters were all Americans.

"You know . . . you know that's not going to—" Not going to happen, but I caught myself before being too blunt. "That's not going to be fast."

The Brit raised an eyebrow. "The ambulance got here fast."

"The ambulance is local." I wasn't sure what to do here. My training was in mathematics and piloting spaceships. What I knew about hostage situations was formed entirely from films, and I was fairly certain *Suddenly* wasn't a good model. None of these men were going to mistake a cap gun for a revolver. I had no way to electrocute them. Heck, I could barely stand. Keeping them calm and cooperating seemed like the only way forward. "I'll tell them, but I just want to make sure you're prepared to wait."

"You aren't in a position to tell us what to do," the Brit said.

"I understand. I'm only trying to make sure you have the information you need. It's a five-hour flight from Kansas to here. Okay? That's all I'm saying." Actually, it was more like two hours, but I figured having extra time wouldn't hurt . . . I mean, they could load the president into a T-38 and get him here in twenty minutes, but that seemed crushingly unlikely. I turned toward the door, squinting at the unfiltered sunlight. "They'll ask why you want to talk to them."

"That can wait until they're here. Right?" My fan gestured to the door. "News crew, the president, Dr. King, and the head of the UN. You say nothing else. Got it?"

Brooklyn charged back down the aisle and aimed his rifle at Helen. "For insurance."

The only thing keeping me upright was adrenaline and the fact that I had spent decades learning to mask anxiety. Inside my suit, my skin felt too tight and my knees shook with each racing beat of my heart. Somehow, I was able to nod and step to the door.

I braced my hand against the door frame. My fingers trembled, which undercut my attempt to display confidence. The firemen were standing near their truck, clearly consulting about what to do, while the ambulance driver had his radio out, talking to someone. One of the firemen saw me and nudged another.

I inhaled to shout our captors' instructions. That deep breath of unfiltered air, laden with dust and pollen and burned fuel, set off a coughing fit. Clutching the doorframe, I bent double. Not from the force of the coughs, but just to keep from passing out. Someone rested a hand on my back, and another on my arm, bracing me.

"You okay?" My fan crouched down, using the doorframe as a shield.

I nodded, and regretted it. Clamping my jaw shut, I swallowed hard and waited for the spinning to stop. "Help me stand? Slowly."

He nodded, gas mask bobbing with the movement, and helped me straighten. Leaving a hand on my arm, he stared at me with those muddy hazel eyes until I drew a more cautious breath. The EMT had come closer while I was coughing, as if he couldn't help himself.

I focused on him, a young white man in his early twenties, with frizzy blond hair that had writhed out of its pomade. "These men would like a news crew, and to speak to the president, the head of the UN, and Dr. Martin Luther King, Jr."

"Who?" A fireman with shoulders like a bear, freckles spattering his pale cheeks, stepped away from the group. "What do they want?"

I glanced to the side, and my fan shook his head. "Tell them they'll find out when the president gets here."

Which, if I knew the government, meant never.

Down the aisle, Brooklyn still had the rifle trained on Helen, so I repeated the message before stepping back out of the sunlight. "May I sit down, please?"

I'd half expected them to say no out of spite, but my fan led me back to my seat. Brooklyn lowered his gun as we walked toward him and Helen slumped, as if the gun had been a gantry holding her up.

Much as I wanted to drop into my seat, I lowered myself carefully. My fan helped me, as if I were an old lady and not a hostage. I cleared my throat, and would have given a lot for water. "I thought we could talk through what you want me to say when the president gets here. You mentioned problems on Earth . . . ?"

My fan exchanged a look with Brooklyn and then behind me as well, presumably checking in with our other captors. Across the aisle, Leonard leaned a little toward us, listening. At some point while I was in the front, he'd undone his shoulder harness.

Narrowing his eyes, my fan studied me. I don't know what he saw, but he eventually nodded. "People on Earth are getting left behind. All the money is going into the space program instead of cleaning up the mess that the Meteor left. People crowded into apartments. Refugees that still, after ten years, can't go back to their homes because the insurance companies just say 'Act of God!' and that the governments are 'allocating resources' as needed." His brows lowered with a scowl. "As if we can't see where the resources are being allocated. As if we don't know whose neighborhoods are being left out."

I spent so much time in the space industry and working with people who understood, intimately, what was happening to the Earth's climate that it was easy to forget that many people had much more immediate needs. "If the climate keeps warming the way the meteorologists think it will, we'll all be in trouble, unless we've established homes on other planets. It's . . . The space program *is* for the people of Earth."

"Please. We've seen this before. Space will be for the elite and everyone else will be left behind."

I shook my head. "No. That's not how it's going to work."

"Look. Around."

I did, turning my head with care so I didn't add to my malaise. Our captors had spread out so that two stood at the back of the cabin. Three were at the door, leaving my fan with me. All of the passengers had a greenish-grey tinge, though whether that was from gravity or the situation, I couldn't say. Probably both. Helen had her hands folded in her lap and was wearing the set expression that consumed her when she played chess or did computations. Leonard had his hands tucked into his armpits, sucking on his lower lip while he watched us. Ruby Donaldson's right knee jiggled, and Vanderbilt DeBeer was chewing on the cuticle of his thumb.

"Okay. Everyone looks miserable."

"Look again. How many people look like me?"

I glanced at Leonard, across the aisle, and he winced. I swear, someday I will not be so slow to figure these things out. On a rocket full of astronauts, we had one Black man, a Taiwanese woman, and thirty white people. Or twenty-nine and a Jew, depending on how you counted me. "I can't say that you're wrong . . ."

"But you're going to try to anyway." He shifted the gun in his grip.

"It's the early stages of the program." People had this glamorous view of the space program created by shows like *Buck Rogers,* and it just wasn't like that. "Look . . . I live on the moon six months out of the year. We have no running water. My bed is a sleeping bag. No alcohol—" Mostly. Nothing palatable, at any rate. "All the food is tinned. And an error could kill everyone in the colony. Currently you need to have a very specific set of skills to go into space. I think everyone here has a master's or a doctorate."

My fan leaned down, eyes tight behind his gas mask. "And you're making the assumption that Black people don't."

Across the aisle, Leonard cleared his throat. "Some of us clearly do—" He stopped as my fan spun on him.

With a jerk of his gas mask, my fan grunted. "Let's hear what you have to say, Uncle Tom."

Leonard rolled his eyes. "The kinds of degrees they are looking for take more than hard work. They take money and connections. Mind you, this is a bone-headed stunt you're pulling, but I agree with the why of it."

Here's the thing about spaceships: They are airtight. Even with the hatch open to the muggy air of Earth, we did not get a lot of circulation. It was August. In the South. And remember that thing about people vomiting everywhere thanks to the descent?

Four hours into our wait, the heat and the smell just kept getting worse. Normally by this point we would have been floating on waterbeds at the IAC's acclimation center. Instead, we were forced to sit upright, under full Earth gravity, in a sweltering room filled with the miasma of human ejecta.

Helen reached over and put her hand on my leg, then she began tapping her forefinger. Brilliant woman that she is, it was Morse code. I rested my hand on hers as if we were comforting each other and tapped back an affirmative.

In a string of long and short taps, she spelled out: USE GERM FEAR

Tapping the back of her hand, I asked: HOW

I PLAY DEATH. She paused and looked at me out of the corner of her eye. YOU TALK

Oddly, I knew that she could "play death" well. There's this thing in astronaut training called a "death sim" where we simulate what happens when an astronaut dies. Usually, the astronaut whose sim card comes up "death" just sits out the rest of the sim, but Helen had acted out her death scene, complete with an alarming rattle, and then just hung around, limp in the creepiest way possible.

Goodness knows if it would work, but there was no way that the president would come . . . and no telling what these men would do if he didn't. I sat up, looking around for my fan. His name was Roy, which I only knew because Brooklyn had asked him where the bathroom was.

Roy was probably the only person who was remotely comfortable on the ship, because of his gas mask. I lifted my hand to get his attention and, wonder of wonders, he came right over. "I have been thinking about your goals, and I have a suggestion."

"I can't wait to hear this."

In one of the most heroic acts I've ever seen, Helen leaned forward, whipping her head sharply, and vomited onto Roy's shoes. All of the actions we avoid to keep from vomiting when we first come back to Earth, and she'd done them in rapid sequence with brilliant precision.

Roy stumbled back, knocking into Leonard's seat. Even behind the gas mask, his face was twisted with revulsion.

The other captors went onto high alert instantly, rifles rising to point toward us, even while they tried to figure out what was going on. Helen raised her hand, shaking, and croaked, "Space . . ." She coughed. "Germs."

And then she collapsed, limp across my lap. Even knowing it was coming, I still recoiled in genuine shock. Then I put my hand at her throat, where her pulse was fast and hard. Looking up to Roy, I tried to will him to believe me. "She's pretty bad."

Behind Roy, Leonard leaned forward in his seat. "Do you think anyone is going to listen to you if you let a rocket full of astronauts die? You think Dr. King is going to support that?"

With my hand still on Helen's neck, I begged, "Please. As a show of good faith, let the people who are the sickest off the rocket."

"Giving up our leverage, you mean?"

"An act of compassion like letting people who aren't well get the medical attention they need can only help your case." It didn't look like he was folding. Not even a little. "I'll stay here as your go-between."

Dawn Sabados from comms dry-heaved then, and it broke the composure of one of the lightskinned men wearing a bandanna. He shook his head at Roy. "Come on . . . Before we all catch it."

Safely behind his gas mask, Roy turned to look at each of his compatriots. Brooklyn had a hand clapped over his nose, even with the balaclava. He pulled his hand away long enough to say, "Do it."

"Okay." He reached down to grab my arms. "You need to tell them what's happening."

I eased Helen off my lap. She stayed as "dead" as she had in the sim, letting one arm droop to the floor. Roy helped me to my feet and the room swayed, graying around me. I clenched something—the seat back, I think—until I was steady enough to stumble down the aisle.

Before we got to the door, I paused and turned to Roy. "The EMTs will need to meet them as they come out. Most will be too weak to stand."

The Brit looked up from where he leaned against the doorframe, rifle at ready. "Two by two?"

Roy nodded. "No heroics."

"Understood." I walked to the door. The Brit had to reach out a hand to steady me. The sun had dipped in the sky, painting everything a beautiful golden color, punctuated by the red and blue swirling lights of emergency responders. The ambulances had multiplied, and there were police cars as well. The protestors had their news crews now. It looked like all three networks, plus multiple radio stations, had come out to set up shop.

Not too close, though, because they were all behind the military cordon that had formed around the rocket. When I stepped into the doorframe, all the guns raised to point at me. I had to swallow before I could speak. "They want to let some of the astronauts out, as a show of good faith. Two at a time. EMTs can come forward to meet the astronauts."

And then they hauled me back from the door. My knees went out from beneath me and I fell to the floor of the rocket. The Brit grabbed me, hauling me to my feet, and the sudden change . . . Well. I passed out.

When I woke up, it was just me and the protesters on a ship reeking of vomit and fear.

THREE

EARTH FIRST PROTESTERS ABOARD SPACESHIP FREE 31 OF 32 HOSTAGES "AS A GESTURE"

By DAVID BIRD

MONTGOMERY, AL, Aug. 21, 1961—Earth First protesters seized an opportunity when the spaceship *Cygnus 14* landed off-course, and stormed the craft, taking 32 astronauts hostage. Earlier today they released, "as a gesture of good faith," all but one of those astronauts. The remaining hostage, Dr. Elma York, known as the Lady Astronaut, is still being held until the protesters' demands are met, and has been serving as their means of communication with officials.

Hour ten. The ship was dark, lit only by the observation lights the rescue team had set up outside. My vestibular system hated being back on Earth in full gravity. I was ill, and even weaker than I had been when we'd first landed. Despite my best efforts, I'd fainted two more times after they had me walk to the door to make another demand for the president, the head of the UN, and Dr. Martin Luther King, Jr.

They weren't going to come. I knew that. It was only a matter of time before the Earth Firsters understood it too. President Denley had a reputation for ordering his troops to fire on civilians in the Korean War. I didn't think he would bend for these men.

In between trips to the door, I sat in one of the vacant seats near the front of the rocket with my head against the neck restraints, and tried to nap. Even at 2 a.m., sitting in the dark, I was too tense to sleep, but while my eyes were closed, the protesters were freer about their conversation.

"Bloody hell. I'm hungry." That was the Brit, whose name was Lysander. He was married to Brooklyn's sister, who was Roy's cousin. It had become clear that this whole thing wasn't really planned. The men had been hunting, seen the rocket come down, and all their anger from the past ten years boiled over into action.

"You think you can get them to bring us some food?" Brooklyn shook my shoulder.

I waited until he shook me a second time before opening my eyes. Again, I was using film tactics, figuring it might help to pretend to be weaker than I was. Not that I could really be much weaker. "Hm?"

Pointing to the door, Brooklyn repeated himself. "Tell them to bring us some food."

Roy shook his head. "Don't be an idiot. They could poison anything they send us."

"So we ask for cans." Brooklyn shrugged. "Can of SPAM and a loaf of bread. We can make sandwiches."

At the word "SPAM," my stomach made a desperate leap for my throat. I tried to swallow it back into place. "May I go to the restroom? I think I'm going to—" I pressed a hand over my mouth. "Please?"

Roy got a hand under my arm and hauled me to the restroom. It was optimized for space travel, with a vacuum toilet and a bar to hold you in place. On Earth, the gravity feed worked just fine.

I staggered in and shut the door, leaning against it for a

moment, before sinking to my knees and being wretchedly sick. I hate vomiting. It left me panting, and weak on the floor of the tiny room.

Roy pounded on the door. "You done?"

"Almost!" The thought of having to stand again and walk all the way back to my seat tied my limbs to the floor and—

Gunfire.

I'll admit it, I shrieked. Outside the bathroom, all I could hear was the harsh blast of shotguns peppered with the bright percussion of assault rifles. And men shouting.

Yes, I cowered. Yes. I was terrified. I'd been in World War II, and while I was never supposed to see combat, the fact is that some days . . . some days my ferry missions had me flying into besieged locations. I knew what was happening out there, and I would be an idiot not to be afraid when all I had between me and death were the walls and the plastic door of the restroom.

I crouched down, wrapped my arms around my head, and tried to make myself as small a target as I could. That's it. That is the sum total of my heroics—just trying not to get shot.

The guns stopped.

"Clear!" echoed from one male voice to another, until one stopped outside the restroom door. He tried the handle. "Dr. York? Sergeant Mitchell Ohnemus with the UN."

"Yes. Just a moment." I wiped my eyes and used the wall to lever myself up to standing. I might cower on the floor, but I was not going to be rescued there. It took a couple of tries for me to get enough coordination to work the lock.

Outside, the scent of cordite lay over vomit and urine. I hadn't thought the rocket could smell worse, and yet it did. The young UN soldier had freckled white skin and lashes so pale that he must have been a natural blond under his helmet. “Ma’am. Are you all right?”

“Thank you. Yes.” I held out a hand. “But I’ll need some help walking.”

Roy writhed on the floor, bleeding from the upper chest. From between the seats, another arm stretched across the carpet as if in supplication. Someone groaned, thank God—not that he was in pain, but that he was alive.

It shouldn’t have come to this. Strange as it might seem, I think if the president had come, they really would have just let me go. If he’d come. But that was never going to happen.

It took another four hours for them to clear me through medical and a debriefing. And then . . . Let me describe to you the wonders of a shower after three months of linen towels and dry shampoo. People who have never been in space do not understand what a luxury water is. I sat on a stool under the falling water in the shower attached to my room at the acclimation center. The droplets pelted my head, finding their way through my hair to trickle down my face, my neck. Liquid warmth wrapped around me, sliding with sensuous glory down the length of my limbs.

I would have to go through another, longer debriefing, but for the moment, I could just sit in the shower. Leaning forward, I rested my elbows on my knees and let the water cascade against my back in a many-fingered massage. Outside the bathroom, an attendant waited to help me to the waterbed that would support my aching limbs tonight. Much as I wanted to stay under the shower forever, there would be more showers later. And baths. Oh . . . to submerge myself in the tub and let the warm water take the weight and support me.

Meanwhile, I was being rude to the attendant. Sighing,

I turned off the water and pushed the call button. The door opened as if she had been waiting with a hand on the knob and—

Nathaniel stood in the door. He smiled, and it was like meeting the sun. "You needed some assistance, Madam Astronaut?"

I stretched my seventy-pound arm out for him. "Someone might need to help me towel off."

"I can do that." Already barefoot, Nathaniel walked into the shower room and took my hand, leaning down to kiss me. Sure, they'd let us talk on the phone after they'd pulled me out of the rocket, but until this moment he had still seemed like a hypothetical ideal.

My husband's hand was warm and familiar, from the permanent pencil callous at the first knuckle of his index finger, to the dry tickle of the blond hair on its back. His lips against mine were warm and a little chapped, but with such familiar contours that I melted against him. When you haven't seen your beloved in three months, that first moment back together—the touch. The smell. Just the orbital influence of his presence made me feel as if I was no longer lost to sidereal motion.

Oh, I was still too tired to stand on my own, but the world was right again. "I've missed you so much."

"This is the first time I've literally worried I would never see you again." He leaned forward to grab the towel off the stand.

"I was never in any real danger." I grimaced with the weight of memories. "Aside from the reentry."

His jaw went slack with surprise. "Elma. You were held hostage by six armed men."

"Well . . . yes. But they weren't going to shoot me." Maybe I was delusional, but their anger had never really been directed at me. "They were a bunch of guys out hunting and they saw an opportunity to act and took it."

"So they were impulsive."

"Determined." I squeezed my eyes shut, remembering Roy's eyes above his mask when he spoke about his daughter. "They had families. They just wanted a better world for their kids."

I know the silence of my husband's disagreement. He inhales as if he is going to speak, then stops breathing for a moment. Nathaniel let that held breath out, running the towel down my back. "Well, I can't wait to get you home again."

If we were at home, I would have asked him what he disagreed with, but I was exhausted, so I let Nathaniel change the subject. "Tell me what's new?"

"I bought a new rug." The towel followed the path down past my hip to my thigh. "Actually, Nicole Wargin picked it out, but I used my hard-earned cash."

"Is it possible to have soft-earned cash?"

"Yes? If you lie down all the time?" The towels followed the contours of my body as he talked, like he was trying to reassure himself that I was real.

"They won't let me lie down long." I'd have today to rest, then tomorrow my physical therapist would start whipping my vestibular system into shape to reacclimatize me to Earth's gravity. Thank God, it didn't take as long as it did my first couple of times. The process wasn't pleasant, but they'd have me out in a week. "What color is it?"

"What? Oh. The rug. It's, um . . . reddish? With a pattern." He chewed his lower lip for a moment. "It goes with the pillows on the couch."

I narrowed my eyes at him. "Hm . . . Well, Nicole has excellent taste. What prompted the purchase?"

He folded the towel. "Last time, you had trouble with the smooth floors. I thought traction might help."

Such a sweet man, my husband. "I could wear shoes in the apartment."

"I know, but you like being barefoot." Nathaniel hung up the towel, with a line of concern between his brows. "It's a nice rug. Honest."

I laughed, which felt alarmingly good. I'd just survived two different potential deaths, to say nothing of living in space, and we were discussing rugs. "I believe you." I took his hand and looked to the door. "Help me to bed?"

Ever so carefully, Nathaniel eased me up. I stopped him with my arms around his neck and leaned in. His arms came around me, pressing gently at the aching spots on my spine. He felt so good. Just the warmth of him, pressed against the full length of my body.

My eyes burned, and I had to close them to keep the longing inside. His hand traced the curve of my spine, down to my buttocks, and back around to my waist. He squeezed gently and stepped back, still supporting me. With a sigh, I let him help me into my hospital gown and then across the short distance to the waterbed.

My feet burned where my calluses had dropped away, so it felt like I was the Little Mermaid walking on knives. Funny thing was that I had calluses on the tops of my feet, from anchor rungs, and my toe tips from pushing off in the skip hop. But my heels? Soft and delicate as a baby's.

I settled on the bed slowly and let him help me swing my legs up onto it. With a sigh that sounded like I was deflating, I leaned back into its support. God, I was tired. The waterbed helped, but nothing on Earth is comfortable after living in microgravity.

Patting the area next to me, I slid over to make room for Nathaniel on the edge of my narrow waterbed. He settled next to me carefully, so that the bed didn't slosh me around too much, and curled up against me. Nathaniel ran a path back and forth along my collar bone, raising heat down to my core.

"Myrtle is talking about making dandelion wine." It was just noise to fill in the space between us. Being gone so long . . . there are so many words and thoughts bottled up that it's hard to know where to start, or what I hadn't told him. "And after the raisin experiment, I'm pretty sure that everyone—"

"Wait. Raisin experiment?"

"Oh. Right. Sorry, I couldn't tell you about that without Ground Control catching on. That giant store of raisins that got sent up? She rehydrated them, and managed to get a fermentation going."

"She made wine?" The waterbed quaked with his laughter. "On the moon?"

"Alcohol is an important part of a viable community."

Nathaniel kissed my cheek. "I'm sure it is. How was it?"

"Cough syrup and turpentine."

That got a whistle. "Wow. And you know moon wine would sell for thousands here on Earth."

"Well, Henri Lemonte distilled it and made a respectable brandy out of it." I wrinkled my nose. "And by respectable, I mean that it mixed well with juice. And by well, I mean you could barely taste it."

"I'm surprised she didn't try fermenting the apple juice."

"People wanted that. The raisin shipment was at the request of Olga Baumgartner, but she got pregnant and had to go back to Earth early." I shrugged as best I could lying down.

"Yeah . . . I heard about that." He sighed. "Someone's going to have to be the first to stay up there, if we're going to have a self-sustaining colony."

"Who wants their kids to be test subjects? There was enough of a foofaraw when we started breeding rabbits on the moon." The animal rights activists had been furious, but, to quote my grandma, there's good eating on a rabbit. "The bunnies we've brought back down have been miserable. Who would want to doom their kid to never coming back to Earth?"

"The way things are going, they might not want to."

I sighed, nestling deeper against him. That was exactly what Roy and his friends had been scared of, that there would be an exodus from Earth that wouldn't include them. And they were right: someone would wind up getting left behind, either because of resources, or politics, or just sheer stubbornness.

There didn't seem to be a good answer.

Of all the things I miss while in space, you would not expect the Monday morning staff meeting to be one of them. I suppose it's not strictly true that I miss the *meeting*, but it's a chance to catch up with friends and colleagues. Also, coffee and donuts.

A week after returning to Earth, I walked into the meeting feeling much steadier on my feet. The din of forty or so people chatting over the aforementioned coffee and donuts gave a lift to my step. The astronaut corps had gotten huge, so this was just one department: the pilot astronauts. We're "elite," which really just means that we do more training and—let's focus on the important thing—get better donuts.

Benkoski saw me first and hooted, "The Lady Astronaut has landed!"

Elite does not equal dignified. My face must have gone as red as a signal flare. I was not the only woman in the room, and yet somehow that moniker had stuck. People crowded around me, grinning and clapping me on the back.

Malouf handed me a steaming cup of coffee. "You. Were. Amazing. Space germs . . . Ha!"

"*Helen* was amazing. Space germs were her idea."

"True." He toasted me with his own cup of coffee. "But I already complimented her, and you're the one who stayed on the rocket."

Clemons strode into the room, which freed me from being the center of attention, as everyone scurried to grab chairs. Leonard and Helen must be getting similar attention over in their Monday meeting with the rest of the Mars group. On the other hand, a lot of them had been on the rocket, so maybe they'd already talked it all through. I was just happy to get back to the business of space.

Before I sat, I snagged a donut. I wound up sitting between Sabiha and Imogene. Whatever Clemons started saying never made it past my first bite of donut. Let me tell you . . . deep-fat frying is not a thing you can do in space. A donut is such a humble food until you really contemplate it. The glaze had begun to crystallize as the donut drew the moisture out of the sugar, leaving a sweet shell that separated as I bit into it, to reveal a delicate interior. Sugar and yeast and butter and God . . . God was in the donut.

Imogene leaned over and murmured, "Does Nathaniel know you make that face outside the bedroom?"

I snorted and then choked. The meeting ground to a halt as Clemons stared at me, while I cleared my throat. Face flaming, I took a sip of coffee and cleared it again. "Sorry. Gravity."

As if that were reasonable, Clemons nodded and carried on. Funny thing: The director of the IAC has never been in space. He has a bad heart valve and probably wouldn't survive liftoff. Which really got back to the point that Roy and his friends were making, that space was only for a certain percentage of the population. Many people would, of necessity, get left behind. It would be like a self-selecting eugenics program which . . . honestly, the horror of that hadn't occurred to me until now.

But what choice did we have? I mean, yes, people were trying to ameliorate the runaway greenhouse effect, but by the time we knew if those efforts had failed, it would be too late to establish colonies. Sighing again, I put the donut down and pulled my binder forward, flipping through the handout to see what my assignment was.

Clemons continued at the front, going through the agenda and talking to each group about their tasks. As I turned the pages, my brow started to furrow, and by the time I got to the last page, it seemed set to split my head. My name wasn't on any of the pages.

One of my responsibilities when I'm on Earth is to help train colonists for the moon. All the astronauts have to take turns doing this. Each "class" of colonists is assigned a pair of astronauts who accustom them to what they need to understand to survive on the moon. I'd been expecting to be assigned a new class, but—

"York. Good job with the protesters. We're giving you and the other astronauts who were on that flight an extra week off to deal with the press." That was not the reward that he seemed to think it was. With a puff on his cigar, Clemons closed his agenda. "That's it, everyone. Get to work. York—stay put for a moment."

Smiling, I nodded, but a groan pressed against my throat. I hated press junkets. Sabiha patted my shoulder in commiseration. "Tell him that you need to help me refresh on the moon bus sim."

"Thanks." I pushed my chair back and stood to meet Clemons. "I don't think he'll let me off so easily."

"Worth a try. And it's true, too."

I laughed, doubting that. Sabiha had more flight hours than I did, but I appreciated her effort to give me something less in the public eye to do. After gathering my binder, I walked up to the front table. "You wanted to see me, sir?"

"Yes." He puffed on one of his ubiquitous cigars, letting clouds of smoke surround his face like water in zero-g. "Malouf! Close the door on your way out."

Shit. That . . . that sounded like I was in trouble. *2, 3, 5, 7, 11* . . . I'm sure it was nothing.

"York . . . You impressed a lot of people during the hostage situation." Clemons lowered his cigar. "A lot of people. The public relations blokes are clamoring to get their hands on you for interviews. Are you up for that? I don't want to send you out if you still need time to acclimate."

"Thank you, sir." There's no astronaut or pilot who will admit to infirmity if they can help it. As much as I hated the press junket, I knew its value to the space program. "Whatever I can do, I'm happy to."

"Good . . . good . . ." He tapped the ash from his cigar into the glass ashtray on the table. "Here's the thing. The space program has been facing some difficulties, and the men who took you hostage represent that. People who don't understand the importance of the program are pressuring the government to pull our funding."

"I'm aware of some of the concerns."

He nodded. "So we need some good publicity. Someone that the people look up to. You . . ." He sighed. "You remember how you told me, years ago, that we needed women in the space program early to make it seem safe?"

Where the heck was this going? Clemons looked as worried as I'd seen him in years. "Yes, sir."

"You were right. I was dead wrong."

Words blew away from my head like an airlock voiding into space. "Um. Thank you?"

He snorted, a smile softening his broad face. "People like you. They trust you. So . . . for the sake of the space program, I want to ask you to be the face of the IAC, and, specifically, to join the First Mars Expedition."

FOUR

HURRICANE CARLA DEVASTATES TEXAS

GALVESTON, TX, Aug. 28, 1961—Hurricane Carla, with wind velocities reaching 173 miles an hour, ranks as one of the eight worst reported on the Texas coast since 1875. Men, women, and children fled before the storm in a mass evacuation, one of the greatest such exoduses since the Meteor struck in 1952.

All this serves as a reminder that though man may reach for Mars, there are still natural forces on this Earth that he neither understands nor is able to prevent or control. Every second, a hurricane releases at least ten times as much energy as the Meteor released over Washington, D.C. Or, to put it another way, during its lifetime, a hurricane unleashes as much energy as 10 million atomic bombs. This awesome fact should serve to stimulate a certain sense of humility in the face of nature.

I gave Clemons a firm "I'll think about it" and walked out of the conference room, down the hall, to the stairs, across to the engineering wing, and straight into Nathaniel's office. He looked up from a set of plans on the drafting table with a smile.

The smile dropped to the desk with his pencil. "What's wrong?"

37, 41, 43 . . . I shut the door carefully . . . *47, 53, 59* . . . As carefully, I inhaled and folded my hands neatly together as my mother had taught me. "Clemons asked me to go to Mars."

"What?"

"He said that there were funding issues?" My body seemed to be five feet in front of me, down a long tunnel. "Nicole had mentioned something about it too, on the moon."

"Yeah . . ." Nathaniel pulled out a worn Eames chair, beckoning to me to sit at his desk. "President Denley is—he hasn't made any public statements, but according to Clemons, he's apparently considering gutting the space program, despite our agreements with the UN."

I sank onto the leather seat, which creaked with my weight. "That would be . . . Clemons told me that he wanted me as 'the face of the IAC' to get out in front of public opinion." I stared at my hands, which were tight with anxiety. "He even said he was wrong for blocking women in the space program, and that I was right about needing us to prove that space was safe."

Nathaniel whistled. "I didn't realize things were getting that bad."

"My exact reaction."

He leaned down and opened his desk drawer. Inside was an eagle I'd started making out of punch cards the last time I was home. He bent down to pull it out, so I couldn't see his face when he asked, "Do you want to go?"

"I don't know." Past Nathaniel, a fan sat on the edge of his desk, oscillating back and forth to try to cool the room. "I mean . . . Mars. But it's three years."

"Minimum." He set the eagle, my tiny brass sewing scissors, and a pot of paste in a neat row next to me. "If it were only three months, would you want to go?"

"Yes. Obviously."

His gaze lifted up to me. "And if I weren't in the equation? But it was still three years?"

I inhaled slowly and let it out again. "Yes. Probably. I don't know. I'd miss Tommy's graduation. And Aunt Esther's hundredth birthday." I needed something to do with my hands before I wrung them into pieces. Which is why, no doubt, Nathaniel had pulled my eagle out of his drawer. I reached into the trash for a discarded punch card. It shook a little as I pulled it out. "It's just . . . Clemons wants me to be out in front."

"So a lot of press conferences." He winced, knowing my . . . idiosyncrasies.

"Yeah. *And* I would also be playing catch-up to the rest of the team. They've been training for fourteen months already." It was mad to even consider it, but that same yearning that got me into the space program in the first place jumped up and down and tugged on my heart like a five-year-old pointing at the circus. I could go and see and explore and fly under a different sky and . . . "Would *you* go?"

"Yes. If I could do this . . ." He waved a hand toward his desk. Papers stacked in the untidy angles of his midproject mind. A model for one of the second Mars Expedition ships stood in a corner. ". . . from space. But I'm not ready to go yet."

"It's not a permanent move."

"And I want to wait until it is . . ." He sat forward again, blue eyes sharp with concentration. "That's the difference between us. A round trip would be three years of me not being able to do what I love. And three years of you doing exactly what you love."

"And three years away from you."

"But if I weren't in the equation . . . you'd go."

"You're not a variable to be eliminated." I lined the punch card up with the rest of the eagle, and the little holes winked with light as it slid into place. If only words fell so easily. There had to be a path through this conversation that wasn't circular. "It was hard enough on the moon, with only three months apart. And there, we could talk occasionally and send letters."

He waved a hand as if that wasn't a concern. "The program has a teletype set up for spouses and a dedicated radio channel. Granted, there would be an increasing delay, but we'd be able to talk. Look . . . you were thinking about retiring. Tell me why again."

I sighed, but this is why I'd come to him. I mean, besides the fact that he was my husband and this was a decision that would affect him directly. Nathaniel helps me understand myself better, sometimes just by the questions he asks. "A bunch of reasons. The ferrying I do . . . it's basically driving a bus. Granted, a bus in outer space, but it's still—it's . . . I want to matter. Which is incredibly vain and self-centered, and I know that I should be grateful just to have a job, and . . ."

Nathaniel cleared his throat, looking at me with his brows raised.

I stopped and closed my eyes. Goddamn it. I was never going to get over the feeling that I needed to apologize for wanting to excel. *2, 3, 5, 7, 11, 13* . . . "I want to make a difference." Lightning did not strike me down. I opened my eyes and concentrated on the eagle's talons, but moved to the hard bit buried in the heart of the conversation. "But then . . . If we want to start a family . . ."

He picked at a loose thread on the knee of his trousers. "It can wait until you come back."

"Can it?" I sighed, snipping the excess card away to flutter down to the desk. We kept putting children off, and there were solid reasons, but if I went . . . "The radiation. The time in space and what it will do to my bones, even with the amelioration efforts. I might not be able to have children when I come back."

"If you can't—if that's not a solvable problem, then the human race is a dead end anyway." Nathaniel rubbed the back of his neck, staring at the floor. "Sorry. That's a little blunt. But . . . okay. Let's say you retired from the space program. What would you do?"

I opened my mouth, and it was as if the inhalation of breath brought with it a view of that future. I would work in the computer department again until I got pregnant. Then they would fire me. I would cook, and clean, and raise our child until they hit a certain indeterminate age, and I would start to volunteer for charitable organizations, as my mother had done. I would matter, but in a very small, very narrow sphere. Mathematics. Flying. Space—those would all be closed doors. "Well, damn."

Nathaniel snorted. He leaned forward and put a hand on my arm. "Would you be happy?"

I wanted both. Why couldn't I have both? But he was right. I didn't want to give up space flight. Sure, I was a glorified bus driver, but it was a job filled with beauty that I couldn't get on Earth. Mars was still up in the air, but . . . "No." I reached for another punch card so that I did not have to see his face as I admitted my selfishness. "I want children, but the life I want wouldn't be fair to them. If it's not Mars, it will be something else that catches my attention and my time."

He inhaled, as if he were going to say something, and then held his breath. I did not push on whatever it was he had decided not to say, instead concentrating on my paper crafting. I say that, but as the bird continued to take shape under my fingers, it was clear that I was answering his silence, because I layered punch cards to create an egg held between the eagle's talons.

His chair creaked as he finally leaned back. "Okay. So children are out of the equation. That simplifies things. Do you want to go?"

"I don't know." Three years. Three years away from this man, who understood me so well that he did not question or try to convince me that I was wrong. Unlike in space, here my tears could fall, but the eagle in my hands was still blurry.

Nathaniel pulled it out of my grip, gently, and then folded me into his arms. In hindsight, I suppose the eagle I'd made answered all his questions.

It was in flight, but had its head turned to the side as though it were looking back over its shoulder. It had an egg clutched in its talons. The symbolism was a little blunt, but clear.

Even after talking with Nathaniel, I was still unsettled and had no idea what answer to give Clemons. Since my husband still had work to do, I pretended to be fine, which he allowed, but clearly didn't believe. I headed out into the hall to go back to the astronaut wing and stopped.

I didn't have an assignment because Clemons had cleared my schedule so I could get caught up on Mars. He'd assumed that I would say "yes." I mean, I could take the charitable view that he was trying to give me room to make a decision, but why argue with past experience?

Cradling the new punch card eagle in one hand, I headed to the astronaut wing to grab my purse. If I couldn't do any work, I may as well head out. Maybe I'd stop by a bookstore, go home, and sink my toes into our new rug.

As I headed into the office, Jacira and Parker were heading out with Betty, who had transitioned from being an astronaut over to public relations. As the astronaut corps had expanded, jobs wound up becoming more specialized, and Clemons had recognized that having Betty working in public relations made more sense than having her be a pilot. She seemed happier there, and did interviews on Earth and in space. I gave a cursory nod to Parker, but he smiled at me. I never trusted that smile. "York. We're heading out to the gate to do some autographs. Want to come?"

He knew I hated the autograph circuit. Betty brightened, rising a little onto her toes. Over their shoulders, Jacira made pleading hostage eyes and clasped her hands in supplication. It was hard to turn her down when she looked like a desperate puppy.

"Sure. Just give me a minute to get my bag." I brushed past them to my tiny office and grabbed my purse off my desk. Carefully, I tucked the eagle inside to carry home.

When I got back to them, Parker had his hands on his hips and his chin jutted out. "*No lo hiciste.*"

"*Mach quatro. Honesto.*" Jacira held her hands up. "*Você pode verificar os logs do computador da minha trajetória, mas isso vai mudar a maneira como viajamos.*"

He frowned, a line appearing between his brows as he mouthed a word. Then he nodded decisively and said, "*De que maneira?*"

I raised an eyebrow. "You speak Portuguese now?"

"Trying." He shrugged and spun us around toward the front of the building. "Figure it'll be useful with the Brazilian contingent on the Mars mission. But seriously. Mach four?"

"Yep." Jacira nodded.

"Is this the Tiberius-47?" I settled my bag in the corner of my elbow, more than a little jealous that Jacira had test-flown the thing.

"It's a beauty." She paused as Parker pulled the front door

open for us. "We're trying parabolic arcs as a way to skim across the planet with a lower fuel cost."

Parker followed us outside, letting the heavy glass-and-steel door swing shut behind us. "What kind of runway can you set down on at that speed?"

"I needed the full length at—oh, hell." Jacira sighed and shook her head. "The little girl from the Williams farm is here again."

It took me a moment before I realized what she meant by "the Williams farm." We'd dropped a rocket on the farm and killed most of the people there. Jacira was staring at a little girl with brown pigtails, dressed in ragged overalls standing amid a group of similar kids.

I'd seen her before, but in that way you see the same people every day without noticing them. Even then, with Jacira pointing to her, she didn't stand out from the crowd. Looking at her, there was nothing to indicate that she'd lived through a tragedy. Poor kid.

Betty turned to face us, smiling brightly as if nothing were wrong. "We'll have to handle her carefully. One of the reporters out there may have brought her as a plant, and—"

I stepped away from our little group and over to the fence. I couldn't stand to hear about how this child, whose family we'd killed, might be a tool. She was a kid. "Handle her carefully," my aunt Fanny. Slipping through the gate, I waded through a crowd of reporters and their entourage, all of them calling to me. "Dr. York! What did the protestors want?" "Elma! Were you scared?" "How bad are the space germs?"

I had a lot of practice at failing to hear questions by this point, and I kept going, leaving it to them to get out of my way. I walked right up to the Williams girl. She tilted her head back to look up at me.

Her voice piped up in that high treble of the very young. "You still going to Mars?"

I nodded, even though I hadn't ever been on that mission. "Maybe you can go someday too. What's your name?"

"Dorothy." She played with the end of a braid, while, around us, cameramen snapped photos. Someone was filming us, but they could go hang, for all I cared. Dorothy cocked her head to the side, as if she were considering. "You going to have kids on Mars?"

Out of the mouths of children. My chest seized, as if her words had evacuated an airlock. She could not have known about my conversation with Nathaniel. I say that as if it had been a single conversation. It had been a long discussion over the course of two years, and even if it seemed settled, it did not rest easy on me. But I put on the regulation smile, the one you learn to give while wearing seventy-three kilograms of space suit in Earth gravity while a photographer takes just one more shot.

I've learned to smile through pain, thank you. "Yes, honey. Every child born on Mars will be there because of me."

"What about the ones born here?"

What about the orphans like her, and all the people our government thought were unimportant? And, worse, if the space program was stripped down, what about all the kids like her who would grow up on a dying Earth? I knelt in front of Dorothy, my decision made for me, and pulled the eagle out of my bag. "Those most of all."

After talking to Dorothy and the other kids, I walked back inside, straight to Clemons's office. Mrs. Kare, his secretary, looked up from her typewriter, smiling. "Well, Dr. York. What a pleasure to have you back on Earth."

"Thanks." I nodded toward the inner office. "He in?"

"Yes, and it doesn't look like he's on the phone. Let me just check . . ." She pressed the intercom button. "Sir? Dr. York is here to see you."

"Which one?"

"The astronaut."

I could hear his grunt through the door as much as through the intercom. "Send her in."

Even after all these years, I still sometimes found my palms going clammy when I had to talk to Clemons. It wasn't reasonable, but the brain does funny things. In any event, I wiped my palms on my trousers before pushing open the door to the tobacco smoke-filled atmosphere of the inner office.

Clemons had a cigar in one hand. He leaned back in his chair, watching me as I entered. His paunch had expanded outward over the years, but his face had lost none of its sternness. "Have a seat."

"I won't take up much of your time . . ." I settled in the chair opposite him, annoyed that I was already apologizing for intruding. "I'll do it. I'll go to Mars."

He stubbed the cigar out and clapped his hands together with a delighted grin. "My dear girl, you have no idea how important this is."

I'd just met the kids that our success or failure would directly affect. I'm pretty sure that I had a better idea of what was at stake than Clemons, in his insulated office. "Anything I can do to help keep us moving forward."

"Excellent." He reached into the file drawer of his desk and drew out a folder. "I had Mrs. Kare make up a packet for you, hoping you'd say yes. This has the base timeline, and our plan to get you up to speed with the rest of the team."

We went through the packet as he gave me a brief overview. Looking at the parameters and seeing how much

I'd have to learn to catch up, I started to get excited. I hadn't been pushed in so long that my blood sang with anticipation.

Only after I left his office, packet tucked under my arm—only after I left the building and got on the streetcar for downtown—only after I had opened the packet and started to read again—did I realize that I'd never told Nathaniel my final decision.

Living in space on my own had made me forget how to be part of a couple.

FIVE

CLERGYMEN SEEK PEACE IN CHICAGO

City Calm as Ministers Move Through Negro District

Special to The National Times

CHICAGO, IL, Aug. 28, 1961—Chicago's riot-torn West Side neighborhood was quiet today, but National Guardsmen remained on call at five armories in the city. Reinforced police squads patrolled the area to prevent a recurrence of the violence that injured 60 persons Friday night. Taverns remain closed till further notice.

Civil rights leaders explained that most of the work in the region is for the space industry, but the average education level here stops at the eighth grade, because of the high number of refugees from the East Coast whose schooling was abruptly terminated by the Meteor. With many of these men unsuited for high-tech work, the unemployment rate is at 18 percent in the district. They said that community organizations lacked leadership, and militant fringe groups, such as Earth First, had sought to fill the vacuum with some success.

On the moon, I eat in the cafeteria with the rest of the colony, but at home, I cook. Sometimes, I stress cook. Sometimes, I stress cook an entire kosher dinner. After talking to Clemons, I also made pie. By the time Nathaniel got home, the apartment was muggy and smelled of chocolate, rosemary, beef, and red wine. I sat in front of the fan, leaning forward so that the air could go down my cleavage, and regretted my decision to cook dinner while also wondering if I should make another dish.

My regret faded when Nathaniel stopped in the doorway, head tilted up. He inhaled and smiled. "Is that your beef bourguignon?"

"And baked potatoes. And a salad." I stood up, flipping the fan back to oscillate. "And biscuits."

He set his briefcase down by the door, and put his hat on the rack. "Have I mentioned how much I've missed you?"

"I told Clemons I'd go." I bit my lips. Well, crap. I'd planned on talking to him over dinner. "Sorry."

Nathaniel crossed the room and took my hands in his. Gently, he squeezed each of them, looking down as if they were something rare. He sighed, but a smile softened his cheekbones. "Well . . . I knew you were going to go."

"I'm sorry. There's still time to back out."

"No. Elma . . ." He looked up and his eyes were wet. I went all over trembles. He brought my left hand up and kissed my ring finger. "I was pretty sure you wanted to go, but was waiting for you to come around to it on your own. In case I was wrong."

"But—"

My husband shook his head, still smiling at me, even though his eyes were reddened. "I don't want you stuck on Earth, wishing you were in the stars. That's no sort of marriage."

My time away from Nathaniel began almost immediately. The training that Helen had referred to was at the Adler

Planetarium. I keep waiting for them to come up with something better than a sextant for navigating through space, but without a magnetic field, we are reliant upon the stars. Granted, we have the IMU—inertial measuring unit—but we still needed the stars as a reference, and since the IMU was just a bunch of gyroscopes, that required a human to look at the stars first. With a sextant.

And . . . the IMU has to be reset periodically over the course of a long journey because gyroscopes wander off, so to restore it to precise stellar alignment, we again need to have an astronaut look at the stars. With a sextant.

I knew how to use one, of course, because I used it whenever I did the moon–*Lunetta* transit, but the stars we would need for the Mars trip were different. I'd joined the navigator-computers and pilots to learn to recognize the Mars transit stars. With a sextant.

The rest of the NavComps and pilots were already in Chicago at the Adler Planetarium, so I headed out to join them after a bare two weeks at home with Nathaniel. My preference would have been to fly a T-38 over, but taking a commercial flight meant that I could use the time studying the reams of documentation I needed to catch up on. While I was nowhere near up to speed, by the time I walked up the windswept stairs of Adler, I at least knew what questions to ask.

Don't let the dated Art Deco style of the Adler fool you. The marble might be thirty years out of style, but the planetarium itself is state of the art. Oh, but I do love a planetarium.

This is ridiculous on the face of it, since I live half my life in space these days, but . . . we rarely see the stars on the moon. We're buried in tubes, and even when we're not, we have to be in the Earth's shadow for the sky to be dark enough. Plus, planetariums can speed time up and rotate the sky to any orientation you want.

I pushed open the door to the planetarium proper with a smile and a giant binder. Betty hopped up from her chair with a grin. "Elma! I thought they were kidding when they said you'd be joining the team."

I gave her a quick hug. "Clemons has you out here, huh?"

Betty nodded and gestured to a photographer behind her. "Is Phil okay?"

"Sure." I nodded to the man and made an internal vow to ignore him, before turning to the rest of the team.

Or, teams, really. We had an unmanned cargo ship, the *Santa Maria,* but the two crewed vessels were duplicates of each other, lovingly dubbed the *Niña* and the *Pinta*. Each had two pilots and two NavComps, because the IAC did love redundancy. All of them had their noses buried in the thick binders that the IAC had loaded us down with. They barely glanced up as I walked over to say hello.

On the *Pinta* team, Derek Benkoski and Vanderbilt DeBeer were the pilots. The two men could have been twins, both coming out of the same military mold of square corners and chiseled jaws. The fact that one was Polish American and one was South African? It seemed trivial. Their NavComps were also white. Rumor had it that South Africa had threatened to withhold funding unless their people flew in an all-white crew.

Whatever the reason, the *Niña* had the only Black members of the Mars team, though neither of them were pilots. For a pilot, we had Stetson Parker, who leaned back in his seat with his legs stretched out in front of him. He had a sextant out and was trying to balance the brass device on his palm.

Our copilot, Estevan Terrazas, stood up, but his smile

seemed slow and stiff. We'd gone to the moon together and I recognized that look. He was trying to be cheerful, while being upset. "Hey, York."

I shook his hand, exchanging pleasantries, and couldn't ask him what was wrong because of Phil the photographer. All of us needed to be on best behavior when the press was around, even if it was in-house press.

Florence Grey was also on the team. We'd met at a company party last year and we were both friends with Helen. Florence was a petite Black woman who had been a wireless codebreaker in the war, and had a reputation for ferocious speed as a NavComp.

"Florence. How have you been?" I offered her my hand.

She looked at it for a moment before sighing and shaking it. "Fine." And then she turned back to her binder. That was . . . rude.

I glanced around the room. "Where's Helen?"

Florence slammed her binder shut. "Seriously?" She got up and stalked out of the room.

I stared after her, my mouth hanging slightly open, as Phil took photos. Trying not to grimace, I turned back to the rest of the team. For a brief moment, all of them were staring at me, then they snapped their gazes back down to their manuals.

Except Parker, who wore a twisted smirk as he balanced that damn sextant on his palm. He stared at me, drew breath to speak and—

Betty stepped between us. She gestured to Phil, who lowered his camera. Leaning in, she whispered, "Helen got bumped in order to make space for you."

The entire room went red and heat boiled off my skin. *What. The. Hell.*

Apparently I said that out loud, because Parker laughed.

"C'mon, York. You know the weight allowances . . . You think they could just *add* you?"

"You know . . . I really don't know why I thought that Clemons would be honest with me." That's what I got for believing him. "Well. I'll let y'all get back to work."

My face was still burning, but I couldn't tell you if it was anger or shame. I should have known. I should have *known* that they couldn't just add me. Each ship had only seven people on it. Of course they couldn't just add me and all the supplies for an additional mouth, not without taking something else off. And if they were adding a NavComp, of course they had to subtract one to keep the equations even.

I took a step back, shaking, before I started out of the room. Goddamned Clemons. He should have told me.

"Where you going, York?" A metal-on-metal squeak sounded from Parker's seat as he stood.

"I'm going to quit so Helen can have her spot back."

"Good. That's the right thing to do." His footsteps followed me up the carpeted aisle of the planetarium. "Want me to fly you back so our team can be restored faster?"

He was just doing that to annoy me, but I stopped in the aisle and spun to face him. "Yes. Yes, I would."

Parker and I . . . we still didn't really get along, but after four years of working together, we had managed to achieve a professional respect for one another. By the time we got through the preflight checklist and were in the air, I'd calmed down enough to remember to try to be civil.

Sitting in the backseat of the T-38, I had a view of Parker's helmet and the sound of wind around me for company. He'd taken us up above the clouds into glorious clear blue skies. I let out a sigh loud enough to activate the vox and carry my voice over the mic to him. "Sorry. I should have known."

"Yeah. You should have." Asshole. I mean, he was right,

but he didn't have to rub it in. His helmet turned as if he were going to look over his shoulder at me. "But Clemons should have said something. That was a shit move."

"I wouldn't have said yes if I'd known."

"I don't doubt that." Below us, the clouds rolled past in a sea of undulating white. "Honestly, I was surprised you would agree under any circumstances."

"Mars?"

"You turned it down before."

I had. Back when the program was first being considered, I'd decided that I would be content with the moon and hadn't wanted to be gone that long. "The funding cuts . . . Clemons wants to use me again."

Parker sighed and shook his head. "You know, it'd be nice if the space program were run by an actual scientist instead of PR flunkies and politicians."

"We are in agreement there." On the other hand, I wasn't sure what pulling out of the program would do. Nothing good, probably, but I wasn't going to take this opportunity away from someone who had worked so long and so hard. Reynard would probably curse me for it, because getting back on the team would send Helen away. "How's your wife taking the whole gone-for-three-years thing?"

Ahead of me, sunlight gleamed off of Parker's helmet. It didn't so much as move from side to side. The air hissed around us, carrying his silence.

Why did I think asking him a personal question was a good idea? We had professional respect for each other. That was it. "Never mind. Sorry. Shouldn't have asked."

Parker cleared his throat, his helmet moving so that reflected sun danced along its curve. "She's—" His voice broke. "She encouraged me to go."

There was clear love and pain in his voice. This baffled

me, because he'd been having an affair with Betty for the past four years.

I half expected Parker to follow me into Clemons's office to watch the show, but he peeled off and went up to the astronauts' wing of the IAC. Channeling my mother's poise and Southern cold fury, I walked into Clemons's outer office like I was balancing a book on my head.

Mrs. Kare looked up, smiling. "Dr. York! I thought you were in Chicago." Beyond her, the inner office door was open, and Clemons had his feet up on his desk, reading a magazine.

I spoke a little louder than strictly necessary, for his benefit. "I was, but something came up. Is the director available?"

He lowered the magazine and swung his feet off the desk. "Come on in."

When I did, I shut the door behind me, just in case I found it necessary to raise my voice. Clemons raised his eyebrows and picked his cigar up from the ashtray. "Is Parker giving you trouble?"

"No, sir." I tucked my hands behind my back instead of shoving them into my flight suit's pockets. "I'm here to offer my resignation."

Clemons fumbled his cigar and it plummeted to the ground, trailing smoke and ash like a dying rocket. "What the—" He snatched it off the floor. "What did Parker do?"

"He's not giving me trouble." Although the fact that Clemons's mind jumped there immediately did not bode well for the mission. "In fact, he offered to fly me back from Chicago, which I very much appreciated. My intention is to resign so that Helen Carmouche can be restored to the Mars Expedition."

If Clemons had ever paid any attention, he would know that the more formal and polite I became, the angrier I was.

"Don't be absurd." He clearly had not been paying attention.

"Absurd?" I strode forward and leaned my hands on his desk. The beautiful thing about planning to quit is that, for once, I didn't care what he thought of me. "Helen Carmouche has been in training for this mission for over a year. She's just as good of a computer as I am. What's absurd is pulling her off a mission and replacing her with someone who will be playing catch-up the entire time."

Clemons stubbed out his cigar and held up both hands in supplication. "I would like to ask you to reconsider."

"No. Absolutely not."

"Carmouche agreed to the switch." He stood, coming around the desk to where he could stare down at me. "Our agreement is that she *and* her husband will both be in the next colonist group, if she still wants to go. We need you on this mission."

"For publicity! In all other ways, I am a liability, because I am replacing a trained mission specialist."

"Yes." Clemons buttoned his jacket, and then unbuttoned it again, shrugging. "I am aware of the risks, and yes, it will make a difference. It has already made a difference in which senators are willing to back the mission. Do you realize how many of them have daughters who are in Lady Astronaut clubs? Because of you?"

That pit of dread opened up in the base of my stomach. "Is that really enough reason to jeopardize the expedition and all the people on it?"

"You already said yes. You were willing to do the catch-up work."

"Because you failed to inform me that I would be replacing someone." I shook my head, but it was impossible to get Helen's excitement about this mission out of it. "This is not what I agreed to do."

"If you back out, it will look very bad—very bad indeed. We've already made announcements." Clemons placed his hands on his hips, and even without the cloud of cigar smoke he loomed over me. "Think of what the press will say if the first woman astronaut quits the mission."

"Jacira was the first woman in space."

"You are the first *American* woman, and Jacira is leaving to get married." He shook his head. "It's the American Congress that we have to convince to stay with the program. If they pull their funding, the mission won't happen. Period."

I clenched my jaw, as if that would allow me to bite down on my heart and stop its galloping pace. "This is wrong."

"It is necessary."

I hated him in that moment, because he made sense. Maybe it would be different if I didn't have a brother who was a meteorologist, giving me all the latest information about Earth's runaway greenhouse effect. Maybe it would be different if I hadn't lived in space and seen the clouds and the great storms wreaking havoc on our coasts. "I am willing to do this much: I will delay my decision until I have spoken with Helen."

SIX

ITALY SUFFERS IN HEAT WAVE

ROME, Italy, Sept. 4, 1961—(AP)—Water is to be rationed in Rome, which is suffering through Italy's worst heat wave and drought in 70 years. At least 21 deaths have been attributed to the heat, the accompanying storms, and the drowning of persons seeking relief.

Scattered electrical storms yesterday brought respite from the heat to some areas, but not to Rome. Lightning killed several persons and dozens of farm animals and caused a number of fires. Rome's water company announced a rotation rationing program that will deprive every home of water for most of one day next week.

Clemons glared at the floor, the flesh of his neck turning a livid red where it rolled over his collar. He nodded decisively and turned to snatch his cigar and magazine off his desk. "Use my phone."

"I'll go to her house and—"

"Please." His plea shocked me into silence. Clemons turned the magazine to face me so I could see the cover. *Time* magazine had a huge artist's rendering of Mars, with a single word on it: *WHY?* "If you decide not to go, I need to know immediately because it's going to take everything this agency has to keep that from being meteoric."

I swallowed and nodded, but I wasn't going to back down. Once he was out of the room, I picked up his phone and called Helen at home. Curling the cord around my hand, I leaned against his desk, not quite able to sit in his chair. My sense of propriety is decidedly odd at times.

The phone rang three times before Helen picked up. "Carmouche residence. This is Helen Carmouche speaking."

"Hi . . . It's Elma." I cleared my throat into the silence on the line. That slight crackle of static answered a world of questions. "I just found out that they bumped you . . . but Clemons said that you agreed with it? Are you . . . is that really okay?"

"I get to spend more time with Reynard."

"But you've been working so hard." I waited to give her time to respond, with only the faint sounds of her breathing to let me know that the line was still open. "I told Clemons that I wouldn't go unless you were okay with being bumped."

"Yes. Of course, Elma. You have my permission to go." When Helen gets excited, her Taiwanese accent comes back. When she's angry, she sounds like mid-Atlantic aristocracy. Right now, I was talking to the Katherine Hepburn of anger.

"Look—if you're not okay, I'll back out. I mean, I already told him that."

"For God's sake! I told you I was okay with it. I give you permission to go. You want me to say I'm happy? I'm not. You're my friend, but you can't ask me to lie to make you feel better."

"I—I'm sorry. I didn't mean—I'll tell him I won't go."

"That would be sacrificing a piece for no good reason." Helen sighed and some of the fury went out of her voice. "You've been in all the papers already. If you pull out and make a stink, that would remove support for the program. I understand the situation, but I am not 'okay' with it."

"We can spin it, I'm sure—point to the time you've been training and how you're more qualified."

"Be realistic. This isn't about training." In her words, I heard the echo of Roy and the Earth Firsters. "I know where I stand in America, and in the space industry. If I acquiesce, then they will put me on the second wave of ships. If I had balked? He would have found an excuse to ground me permanently, and replaced me anyway. Of course I said yes, and smiled when doing so. It was the only intelligent move available."

"Then let's use the fact that I'm apparently invaluable . . . I'll tell Clemons that I won't go unless you do."

Even as the words left my mouth, I knew all the reasons that idea wouldn't fly—we both knew the allowances on the ships—but Helen voiced them for me. I could hear her disdain in her sniff. "They couldn't add another team member because of the additional resources and weight that would require."

"But—" I stopped, unsure how to answer that. There had to be a way.

"They would have to replace someone else and, thank you, but no. I do not want to be the person who got someone else kicked off the mission. That would leave the team with two people to hate."

The phone pulled my head down to my chest with the gravity of her words. "I'm sorry."

"I know." Helen packed so much into those two words. *I know you regret it. I know you don't want me to blame you. I know that nothing will change.* "I'll wait. It's not fair, but at least it's a familiar strategy."

And that . . . that just made me feel grosser.

As soon as I'd said "yes" again, it was as if the publicity department at the IAC went into overdrive. Maybe they had already planned these things, or maybe it was the magazine. Magazines. Because it wasn't as if the *Time* piece had been the only negative article. The resistance to the space program hadn't been that clear from the moon, where we didn't exactly get regular newspaper delivery.

Whatever the reason, two weeks later I found myself in Los Angeles standing backstage at *The Tonight Show* with Stetson Parker.

I had taken a Miltown in my hotel room. Now I faced the wall, running a Fibonacci sequence to try to calm down. At least I didn't throw up anymore. Usually.

1, 1, 2, 3, 5, 8, 13, 21, 34, 55, 89, 144 . . .

Behind me, Parker paced in tiny circles, shaking his hands as if he were trying to get blood back into them. An assistant with a clipboard waited by us, one ear covered with a giant earphone, as if he were at Mission Control.

. . . 233, 377, 610, 987, 1597, 2584, 4181, 6765 . . .

The man with the clipboard leaned next to me and whispered, "You're on."

Onstage, Jack Paar said, "Please welcome my next guests, Colonel Stetson Parker and Dr. Elma York."

I turned away from the wall in time to see Parker snap his genial smile into place. He gestured for me to lead the way. "Ladies first."

My smile felt brittle and plastered on. Crinoline shushing against my legs, I strode out into the lights and the wall of applause. Beyond the banks of lights and cameras, real people sat in the auditorium. Beyond them, millions of people sat on the other side of television sets.

. . . 10946, 17711, 28657 . . .

Mr. Paar shook my hand and then Parker's, and we went through the requisite smiling and waving to the audience before we were seated on matching leather chairs next to his. A silver microphone stood on the floor between Parker and me, and I had to cross my legs carefully to keep from hitting it with my pumps.

With a tug on one of his signature ties, Jack Paar leaned over to us as if we were the only people in the room. "Thank you both so much for joining us. I tell you, I don't think I've ever gotten over being five years old. I know it's obvious, but I just need to say it . . . You've both been to the moon?"

Parker laughed. He really does have a good laugh. "I can't believe it either. There are days when I have to pinch myself."

"And, Dr. York . . . You live on the moon, is that right?"

"Yes, I live in the lunar colony about six months out of the year."

"That must be fascinating." Jack Paar leaned closer, smiling with all the fidgety interest of a child. "What's it like?"

"More like Earth than you might think. I pilot one of the transport ships, ferrying geologists and miners out to various sites. I have a regular route, so it's not much different from being a bus driver, really."

Beside me, Parker chuckled. "Don't let Dr. York sell herself short. Piloting one of these ships requires a lot of skill because of mascons."

Jack Paar raised his eyebrows almost to his hairline. "Mass cons? Is that a convicted mascot?"

Bless him for making me laugh, even if it was a poor joke, or I would have gaped at Parker's compliment. "*Mascon* is short for mass concentration. There are local heavy spots on the moon where the rocks have more density, so it causes the ship to dip unexpectedly."

"Wait—there are really spots where there's more gravity on the moon?"

I nodded. "Here on Earth, too, but it's so slight that you wouldn't notice it. It's one of the reasons we can't automate a ship around the moon, because the math is too complicated for a mechanical computer that's small enough to fit on the spacecraft." Not that anyone wanted to hear about math. My job was to extoll the virtues of the Mars program. "But the lunar colony does give a taste of what our Mars colony will be like. It's much the way living on the frontier must have felt for early Americans."

"Is it true that there's an art museum on the lunar colony?"

"It is." I smiled even more brightly, until it felt like my skin was going to crack. "Although it's only about one and a half meters of closet, all told. We have a tiny rotating exhibit created by the colonists with sculpture, textiles, and drawings."

Parker gave his own shit-eating grin. "It's true. I enjoy stopping in every time I head to the moon. It helps me realize that humanity will thrive among the stars. Our drive to create art is one of the most defining features of mankind."

"I can't wait to see how Mars will inspire artists." Was it possible to be any perkier? But this is what they had asked me to do. My stomach twisted with each smile I gave, and for once in my life, it wasn't just anxiety. It was the way I was being used at the expense of others.

"Now, I want to ask a more serious question, if I may. Dr. York, on your return to Earth, your ship was hijacked by a group of terrorists. What was that like?"

"They weren't really terrorists—just a bunch of men out hunting who . . ." Who held me at gunpoint. "Who were worried about being left behind on Earth."

Parker jumped in, leaning forward with his elbows on his knees, fingers pressed together like a rabbi in thought. "That's something I love so much about our job at the IAC. We go out into space to prepare the way for others. Back in frontier days, you wouldn't have dreamed of taking Grandma across the country in a covered wagon, but now? She can go anywhere. It's the same for space."

"Right. We're making space safe for grandmas." When I'm spouting drivel like this, it's hard to tell that I have a PhD in physics and mathematics. But maybe this was a chance to talk directly to the people like Roy who were afraid they would get left behind. "It's such a team effort. We have people from all over the world working in the space program. For instance, Helen Carmouche is a NavComp—navigator-computer—who was originally from Taiwan. She's the one who came up with the idea that got everyone safely off the *Cygnus 14*."

"And you're the one who executed that idea." Parker's grin was blinding. "That's why we're so lucky to have you going to Mars with us."

Asshole.

"Oh, I'm just part of a larger team. We've got Kamilah Shamoun from Algeria and Estevan Terrazas from Spain and Rafael Avelino from Brazil . . . just to name a few." I wanted to turn to the cameras and appeal directly to Roy, who was probably in a prison somewhere, and just say flat out: *Look. It's not just white people. We're all working together.* Instead I said, "It's like a flying World's Fair up there."

That got a laugh from the audience. Yay. Bully for me and rah rah. Parker laughed with them and leaned over to Jack Paar. "And of course, everyone going has more than one expertise."

Jack Paar raised his eyebrows. "Oh? And what's yours?'

"Mission commander. But I'm also a pilot and linguist." Parker jerked a thumb over at me. "Dr. York is a physicist, computer, and pilot. She's a triple threat. If only she played chess, she'd be a complete package."

I kept a smile on my face and laughed right along with them. Because, of course, Helen played chess. I didn't.

After we finished with *The Tonight Show*, I should really have gone back to the hotel and studied, but how could I be so close to my brother and not visit? When the car service dropped Parker and me off at our hotel, Hershel was already waiting with Tommy on one of the plush velvet sofas gracing the lobby. My brother hadn't changed much since I'd seen him at Rosh Hashanah, but Tommy seemed to have grown a foot. I guess that's the difference between sixteen and seventeen. His face still had the baby softness of boyhood, but his jaw was firming into the same lines as my dad's.

My nephew jumped up, all puppy-eager smiles. He had already crossed the room to hug me while Hershel was still wrangling his crutches.

"Aunt Elma!" Tommy rocked me back a step with his enthusiasm. Please, God, never let this child of my heart lose his joy.

Child of my heart. For a moment, the reminder that I would have no child of my body nearly blinded me, and I clung to Tommy with an unnecessary fervor.

"Hey, Tiger." I released him and turned to Parker, who had stopped when I did. "May I introduce—"

"Gee! You're Stetson Parker!"

Parker gave that aw-shucks grin of his. "Yes, I am." He offered Tommy his hand, and they shook man-to-man. "You must be Tommy."

You could have knocked me over with a feather. To the best of my knowledge, I had never discussed my nephew with—No, I had. The death sim. All of the astronauts had workshopped what to do in case we died on the moon missions. We'd gone into great detail about who to contact and in what order, so Parker knew about Tommy the same way I knew his twin boys were Elmer and Watson.

"Yes sir, I am." Tommy was still shaking Parker's hand, but his chest was three sizes larger, thinking that I'd talked about him.

Hershel swung up to us with the slight click of his leg braces. "Tommy, I'm sure Colonel Parker has things he needs to do."

"Alas, I do." Parker retrieved his hand and very convincingly faked a rueful smile. "And I'm sure you want to spend time with your aunt."

There are things I notice, having a brother who survived polio. Parker didn't look at Hershel's crutches or glance down at his leg braces. Most people do, then make some pained expression. Parker, for all his flaws, gave my brother the gift of normal.

With a wink at Tommy, Parker strode away from us like the Great American Hero. Over his shoulder, he called back. "Don't keep her up too late—she has homework and it's a school night."

Jerk. True, but so unnecessary. I turned back to Tommy and Hershel. "Want to step into the restaurant? I'm famished." And I could use a drink. Thank goodness the restaurant kept Hollywood hours.

"Sounds great." Hershel swung along next to me toward the hostess stand at the side of the lobby. "Aunt Esther sends her love. Doris, too."

"Mom couldn't come because Rachel is grounded." Tommy shook his head, trying for the seriousness of an adult. "She was smoking."

"What?!" My thirteen-year old niece had been smoking?

"Tommy." Hershel frowned over the rim of his spectacles at his son. "That's not your story to tell."

"It's just Aunt Elma."

Hershel cleared his throat. "I'm not sure that your sister would agree."

The process of getting seated in the restaurant forestalled the laundry list of questions that I had. I just couldn't picture my niece with a cigarette. She was thirteen! No, fourteen. But still. Goodness . . . She'd be fifteen when we left for Mars and eighteen when I came home. Tommy would be in college.

"Elma—" Hershel put a hand on my wrist. "What's wrong?"

"Hm?" I blinked back to awareness, my eyes stinging. "Just a long day."

He glanced at my nephew. I'm not sure if I was relieved that Tommy was there, because Hershel couldn't ask probing questions, or disappointed that I couldn't tell my big brother everything. But, really, what was there to tell? Nathaniel and I weren't going to have children, and I don't think that decision would be a surprise to anyone. Least of all my brother.

Hershel fished in his pocket. "Looks like they have a jukebox. Tommy . . . why don't you pick out some music for us?"

Like a rabbit, my nephew had snatched up the dimes and was out of the booth. Hershel immediately turned back to me. "So?"

I sighed and shook my head. "You know me too well."

"And I know that you're stalling. He'll be back soon."

"I just realized how old they'll get while I'm gone." I shrugged and spun my water glass on the table. "I hadn't done the math."

"That is the first time I've ever heard you say you hadn't done math."

I stuck my tongue out at him. I'm a grown-up. Clearly. "I have enough trouble with how fast they're growing up without missing three years. And what's going on with Rachel?"

He glanced over his shoulder at Tommy, who was apparently reading the details of every song in the jukebox. "He doesn't know all of it. She was smoking pot."

"And you hadn't told me?"

"It was yesterday." He took his glasses off and rubbed the bridge of his nose. "There's a boy, who I did not kill."

"I can."

He chuckled. "You'd have to beat Doris to him. Anyway, he's a senior, and apparently very handsome, and he has a car. Offered her a ride home from band practice."

I went cold. "She didn't—I mean."

"No. That's why he's alive." The music started and Hershel glanced over his shoulder. "Time's up. Just bear in mind that Rachel will probably be grounded the entire time you're gone."

I nodded, swallowing my sickness as Tommy came bounding back over in time with the music. He'd picked "Sixty-Minute Man." I hate that song.

SEVEN

SPACE SPENDING CALLED AUSTERE

Clemons Opens Fight for Budget;
Reductions Suggested Priority for Tax Cut

By JOHN W. FINNEY
Special to The National Times

KANSAS CITY, KS, Dec. 4, 1961—The International Aerospace Coalition opened its fight to a skeptical Congress today asking for a $5.7 billion contribution to the United Nations space budget, warning that any substantial cuts would jeopardize the planned manned expedition to Mars.

There are widespread misgivings, bordering on resistance, about giving the agency another budget increase, with members of Congress saying that the United States has borne a disproportionate share of the costs of the space program. Behind this skepticism are a combination of factors ranging from such earthly concerns as tax cuts to concern about national objectives in space.

It would have, apparently, been too much to ask for me to be able to concentrate on training. Instead, for the past three months, I had to cram on a diet of IAC binders while flying between training and publicity opportunities.

I was in one of the classrooms with the rest of the team to learn about geology. A case of rocks sat in front of me, with numbers painted on them. It wasn't going to be enough to tell Mission Control that we'd found something red and crumbly on Mars. We needed to be able to say that it was hypidiomorphic granular, porphyritic, with medium-grained red phenocrysts.

Leonard was in his element. He picked over the case of minerals that the instructor had given him, grinning. He leaned over to me with a lump of red rock in his hand. "Doing okay?"

"Trying to be." I grimaced at the evaluation sheet I was supposed to be filling out. There was so much to memorize along every axis of the trip.

"Okay . . ." He pointed to a line of deeper red in the rock I was staring at. "This is pyroxene, which we think we might see—"

A quick knock at the door interrupted him, and Betty stuck her head in. "Hi! Sorry to interrupt, but I need to borrow Elma real quick."

"Well, I'm glad someone can use her," Florence muttered, glaring at her notebook.

I sighed and clenched the rock I was holding like it was a security blanket. "Can't it wait?"

"Sorry—it's just that the BBC wants you . . . It won't take long. I promise." She leaned farther into the room and caught Parker's eye with a wink. "You can catch her up, right?"

He shrugged in response. I wasn't sure if that meant yes or that he didn't care.

"Wouldn't they like someone else?" Why did it always have to be me? "Leonard . . . you already know this stuff."

"They want photos of you with Nathaniel." Betty

winced apologetically. "Sorry. But we're working the whole husband-and-wife angle."

Florence leaned over to Leonard. I don't think she meant to speak loud enough for me to hear, but I did. "At least she can't use us as shields this time . . ."

I set the rock down. "What's that supposed to mean?"

She pursed her lips and turned to stare at me with hazel eyes over a long patrician nose. She kept her dark hair straightened, and the neat bob framed her disapproval. "You really want to have this conversation now?"

"Now or in space. Better now." *2, 3, 5, 7, 11 . . .*

"All right . . . 'A World's Fair in space'? Please. There are six colored astronauts in the entire program."

"Yes. And I'm trying to celebrate you. The IAC was discriminatory in its early days, and I worked hard to—"

"You worked hard." She snorted and glanced at Leonard. "And I didn't? Leonard and Ida and Imogene and Eugene and Myrtle didn't? Helen didn't work hard?"

"Of course you did!" *. . . 13, 17, 23 . . .* I took a slow breath and tried to ignore the fact that everyone in the room was staring at us. "That's why I'm talking about how you're here, so that y'all don't get shoved into the background. I'm trying to help."

"Hm. You know what would help? If you'd learn to do your damn job." She turned back to the rocks on her desk. "Better run now. Don't want to keep the photographers waiting."

There were a half dozen things I could have said, but I just bit my tongue hard and pushed back my chair.

Here's the interesting thing: you don't have to like someone to work well with them. In fact, in some ways, it's more efficient when you aren't paired with someone whose company you enjoy, because both of you have a vested interest in finishing tasks as quickly as possible in order to minimize contact. When you're with a friend, there's likely to be joking or goofing around.

By this measure, I could be efficiently paired with half of the Mars team. Okay . . . that's an exaggeration, but it did feel like everyone was angry at me. And, honestly, I couldn't blame them. It was bad enough that I was a late addition and had to do a ton of catching up, but the way that I was being trotted around like a dog and pony show . . . that wasn't something an astronaut assigned to a mission was supposed to be doing. It meant that everyone else had to cover for me. Cover for me more.

As we walked down the hall, away from the classroom, Betty glanced over at me. "You okay?"

"Sure!" I chirped.

"I tried to put it off. Honest."

"I know. It's just . . . I'm already struggling to catch up."

Betty nodded with a grimace. "I'm refusing most interview requests, believe it or not. It's just . . ."

"I know. This is why I'm on the team."

She led me to the room that PR had co-opted as a makeup and prep room. With a sigh, I settled in front of the mirror and let other people worry about my makeup and hair while I concentrated on my binder of information, without the benefit of the rock samples.

On Mars, we'd need to know how to look for potential water flow. That could be identified by small laminations or cross-stratification that showed festoon geometry from transport in subaqueous ripples.

I rubbed my forehead, and the makeup lady gently pulled my hand away. "Mustn't smudge."

"Right." My priorities were a mess. In the mirror, it looked as though I were going to a holiday party wearing a flight suit. My hair fell in perfect soft curls that would never have survived if I'd actually been working. In sims and on the moon, I tended to keep it out of the way in a kerchief, but accuracy wasn't the image that publicity had wanted.

The makeup lady spun the chair around to release me, and, like a trained hound, I followed Betty down the hall to the engineering wing. Annoyed as I was, I still felt lighter when we rounded the corner into Nathaniel's office.

Someone had cleaned it. An orchid sat on his desk and a lamp warmed the corner by his drafting table. They hadn't made him change clothes, though. He wore his tweed jacket and a plain blue tie that—

On second thought . . . I didn't recognize the tie, but it brought out his eyes. They lit up when he saw me. "Hello, Dr. York."

"Good morning, Dr. York." I stifled the urge to kiss him on the cheek, less because of the photographer and the reporter, and more because I didn't want to leave a giant red stain on his face.

The reporter, a white man in his mid-fifties, rested a notepad on his paunch as he scribbled. "I'll try not to take up much of your time . . . Jerry. How do you want them?"

"Natural. How do you two usually work together?"

We didn't. Not these days, at any rate. I glanced at Nathaniel and shrugged. "What are you working on?"

"Um . . ." He went around to his desk and sat down. The desk drawer squeaked as he dragged it open. "I was reviewing the flight plans for the supply ships to Mars."

As he laid the folder on the desk, I went around to stand behind him. Leaning over his shoulder, I studied the equations and once again felt out of touch. I rested a hand on his back, frowning as I tried to figure out what "AMz squared" referred to.

A flash went off.

"Try to look happy." Jerry, the photographer, leaned in closer. Behind the camera, his lank black hair draped across his forehead.

I smiled. That damn regulation smile. Everything is wonderful and I just love outer space! Don't you?

Flash. I couldn't see the numbers on the page through the purple splotches floating in my vision. Flash. *2, 3, 5, 7 . . .*

"Dr. York—Elma. May I call you Elma?" The photographer didn't wait for a response, he just came forward and patted the edge of the desk. "Can I have you sit on the desk? I love the costume you have on, and I can't really see it behind your husband. Nathaniel, right? Great—right here. Good. Perfect."

I sat on the desk, which made it hard to look at the equations, but no more awkward than being in one of the early capsules.

"Is there something more sciencey you could do?" The reporter stepped forward, tapping his pencil on his notepad. "I mean . . . you could be looking at tax returns here."

Nathaniel looked down at the equations, which were really "sciencey," and rubbed the back of his neck. "Um . . . I just sent all of the models over for wind-tunnel tests. Blueprints?"

"What about one of these?" Betty lifted a punch card out of a box sitting on the edge of the desk.

"Don't— " Nathaniel pulled it out of her hand. "Don't get them out of sequence."

The reporter's eyes rounded at the sight of the card, as if Nathaniel had said nothing. "Oooo! That's perfect. Better than a model, which any kid could put together. But programming an electronic computer? That's Science with a capital S."

Jerry focused the camera on us. "Why don't you show it to your wife, Nate? Like you're explaining it to her."

Nathaniel shot me a look, brows raised, as if he were trying to figure out if that was a serious question. This really wasn't any worse than powdering my nose in a T-38.

I leaned closer to him, a laugh bubbling right at the back of my throat. "Yes, sweetie. Tell me what crucial piece of programming you have." I batted my eyes at him.

Nathaniel burst out laughing, holding the card up as if it were somehow meaningful by itself. It was a tiny part of a larger program, with as much relevance as an individual bolt. The spacecraft might fall apart without it, but it didn't define the thing.

The camera whirred and flashed and caught me with an unguarded, nonregulation smile. That's the photo they wound up using, billed as "The joy of space flight."

But we were laughing at the utter lack of science, while, back in the classroom, my teammates were learning actual science. If they really wanted something more "sciencey" they would have taken photos in that room. Instead, they had pulled me out of the pile and turned me into something as useful as an individual punch card.

The thing about wearing a space suit on Earth is that it's designed for lower gravity. Even being in the Neutral Buoyancy Lab's pool didn't change the fact that gravity pulled at me. Sure, it didn't pull at the suit, but inside it, I slid around every time I changed orientation. As a woman, I was smaller than the men the suits had been designed for, so I had to wear padding around my hips to sort of wedge me in. This kept the air bubble surrounding me inside the suit distributed evenly, allowing me to move from horizontal to vertical over the course of the NBL run without fighting gravity. Without the padding, the air bubble acted like a giant beach ball, strapped to my stomach, always wanting to be pointed up to the surface. It made it difficult to roll any other way.

In truth, having an air bubble inside the suit wouldn't be a problem in space, but the NBL was where people decided if you had what it took to do a spacewalk. So neither I nor any of the other women would complain. No, sir. Everything was splendid and we were happy to be in the pool.

I hung sideways in the water with the fiberglass shell digging into my armpit. My neck burned from holding my head up inside my helmet. My fingers ached from forcing my stiff gloves to close on the edge of the solar panel we were practicing "repairing." With the suits pressurized to 4.9 psi above ambient pressure, every movement felt like working against a heavy-duty spring. It wasn't exactly like working in a vacuum, but it gave us a sense of how exhausting it would be. A wrinkle in my glove felt like a metal wire across my knuckle as the pressure made it rigid. But if you asked me how I was doing, I would have been so very, very chipper.

On the other side of the panel, Rafael Avelino swore in Portuguese as his gloves slid off the wrench. Our support divers floated in a pod around us and let the wrench drift away. Their job was to keep us safe, and ours was to learn how to do repairs in zero-g. Tethered to the MWS or "mini-work station" on the chest of his spacesuit, the wrench didn't go far, but it was still a pain reeling it in.

As Rafael's curses buzzed over the comm, I grinned inside my helmet. "I'm beginning to understand why Parker is learning Portuguese."

On my left and slightly below me, Leonard helped me steady the panel as Rafael got the wrench back into place.

"We all need more languages to swear in. I've just got Latin and Greek, and there's only so far that can take you."

"Oh yeah? What's a Latin curse like?" Rafael placed the wrench again, and reseated his feet in the foot restraint secured in a WIF mechanical receptor on the mockup exterior of our craft. What does WIF stand for? No idea. At a certain point the acronyms just become the name. WIF was . . . Widget Interface Fuggedaboutit.

One of the many benefits to building the ships in space was that we didn't have to worry about aerodynamics. WIFs and grips covered the surface of the ship. Rafael's wrench slipped again, but he didn't lose his grasp. "Because I could use some more, now."

Leonard hesitated and then chuckled. "Actually . . . most of them aren't things I can say in mixed company."

"Please . . ." I braced against my foot restraint as Rafael finally got the wrench engaged. "Say the fucking Latin."

That got a huge laugh from both men, though my face flamed at having said it. Thank God the helmets meant they couldn't see me clearly. Even for a laugh, that kind of language was still not in my normal vocabulary.

And then, predictably, Jason Tsao, our Sim Sup du jour, crackled into our ears. "Language."

"*Vae me, puto, concacavi me,*" Leonard intoned with great solemnity.

Rafael's head came up in his helmet. "Huh. That is close enough to Portuguese that I actually understood it. Mostly."

"Gentlemen. Lady." For a guy from Chicago, Tsao could be so prim sometimes. "We have visitors and they are listening."

The three of us exchanged glances and Rafael rolled his eyes. "What language do they speak?"

"English." Through the microphone, we could just make

out someone talking in the background, but not the substance of the conversation. The Sim Sup's response was sharp and biting. "No. Bringing them up early is absolutely out of the—" and then his mic cut off.

What had that been? Through the water, I couldn't see what the guys thought, so I just stood there bracing the panel. It wasn't like the Sim Sup to leave his mic open, which raised the question of what sort of visitors would distract him that badly. To say nothing of who might be asking us to come out of the NBL run early.

Rafael got that bolt tightened down and we moved on as a unit to extend the next piece of the panel. This was the fourth time we'd done this particular NBL run, and each time we got a little faster. Of course, it wasn't likely that I would be the one doing the EVA, but the IAC believed in overpreparation, and after my late start, I supported them in that. Besides, it would make being the IV person—the intravehicular person—easier if I knew what they were facing. Given the communication lags we would have during the mission, we couldn't rely on ground control to coach the EV team in every scenario.

"Folks—we're going to stand down on extending the array." The Sim Sup's voice crackled, then the microphone rustled and shifted as though he were handing it off.

We floated underwater with the constant hum of fans and the sound of our own breath as company. Then Director Clemons came on the comm. "We have to pull Dr. Flannery out—but Dr. York and Captain Avelino will stay and work through the cleanup. Dr. Flannery, I need you out of the tank pronto."

Leonard drew a breath as if he were going to argue, then snapped his mouth shut so hard I heard his teeth click. "Yes, sir. See you topside."

I am ashamed to say that my primary emotion was not

curiosity or even annoyance that our training had been interrupted, but relief that, for once, it wasn't me. Leonard turned from us and let the divers drag him through the water to the platform that would carry him to the surface.

Rafael and I floated in the pool. I let my head slump against the side of my helmet, and closed my eyes for a moment, while our support divers reconfigured the ship mockup to the end state of the run. It took so long to get into the suits, that it made sense to let us practice the end of the run while we were already down there. I kept listening to the comm, waiting for Tsao to tell us something else about what was happening with Leonard.

When the divers were ready for us, we started the run again, but kept conversation to the bare minimum required for work. After I got over my relief, I had a huge case of What-the-devil-is-going-on. I'd been pulled out of training before, but not an actual NBL run. That required restarting the entire thing, which was expensive and an enormous loss of training time. Heck, the way the suits were configured, it took two days just to replace a crew member. Short of a medical emergency or an equipment malfunction, *nothing* interrupted an NBL run. So what would Clemons think was so important that it couldn't wait?

And why weren't they telling us?

The lift out of the NBL's pool took ages. As my helmet breached the surface of the water, the stand I was strapped to supported the 140 kilograms of my suit. Trying to walk in a full suit in Earth gravity is not possible. Even just the bottoms are like . . . it's like wearing diapers in a snow suit made of lead. The robot in *Lost in Space* had more grace than we did.

I hung in the donning stand as a swarm of suit techs helped us to disrobe. When you want answers, everything seems to take longer. I waited for my suit tech to remove the tools and tethers and leg weights. As much as I wanted to rush her, everything had to be done in sequence. On the other side of the donning stand, Rafael was going through the same slow, careful extraction from his space suit.

It was like my suit tech was moving underwater as she opened the valve on the side to depressurize the spacesuit down to below one. Sure, I could talk now and she could hear me, along with everyone else listening in on the comms.

My suit tech put her hands on the release of my glove. "Breathe out."

I exhaled as the remaining bit of delta pressure released when she popped the glove. It wasn't likely that I would blow out a lung, but over-precautions were IAC's stock in trade.

The suit settled around me as she pulled the glove away, then *finally* she reached for the helmet. The moment it was off, I asked her. "What's going on?"

"FBI." She glanced over her shoulder to the control room. "We were told to get you cleaned up fast."

I blinked like an idiot for a minute before my brain joined my body above water. If they wanted to talk to Leonard and me, then it must be related to the protesters, but . . . it had been nearly seven months since the hijacking. Why on earth would they want to talk to us now?

EIGHT

EXEMPLARS OF SOCIETY CHARGED WITH HOLDING UP RACIAL GAINS

By FRED POWLEDGE

KANSAS CITY, KS, Jan. 4, 1962—A leading civil rights lawyer has charged that the "exemplars of our society" are guilty of resisting the Federal Constitution. The lawyer, Jack Greenberg, director-counsel of the NAACP Legal Defense and Educational Fund, said in the fund's annual report: "Those who would maintain the racial caste system have resisted the Constitution and court rulings by force, by deceit, by tokenism, by stalling litigation, and by such legislative maneuvers as the filibuster. Sadly, those responsible for these evasions are exemplars of our society: school and university board members, superintendents of education, leaders of the bar, astronauts, and elected officials."

When I was *finally* escorted into the conference room, one of the FBI agents rose to greet me. He was a painfully slender man, with cheekbones that looked as if they would puncture his parchment skin. "Dr. York. I'm Agent Boone. This is my colleague Agent Whitaker."

Agent Whitaker stayed seated, scribbling in a notebook, and barely glanced up. He had generic white-bread good looks, marred by an ugly red scar across his forehead, just below his hairline.

Boone glanced at his colleague and gave a little shrug, as if he were used to the man's rudeness. "Thank you for making the time to meet with us."

"Did I have a choice?" I smiled to take the sting away, but I was more than a little annoyed. After rushing me out of the sim, they had kept me waiting for an hour and a half. "Honestly, it was a little bit of a relief to have some time to just sit and read."

"Well, we'll try to get you out of here as quickly as possible." He gestured across the conference table to a chair facing them. "Please. Coffee?"

"Thank you, that would be lovely." I did not comment on the fact that he was serving me coffee from the IAC's own stock. "Cream and sugar, if you don't mind?"

"I have a sweet tooth, so let me know if I go overboard." He snagged his mug off the table and walked to the back of the room. "We have some questions about the rocket crash and the men who held you."

"Of course . . . though I'm not certain there's anything I can tell you that I didn't already say in debriefing."

Whitaker drew a harsh line on his notebook, but still didn't look at me. "Oh, I think there is."

"I'll be interested to hear what you think that is." I kept my hands in my lap, resting gently together the way my mother had taught me. The fact that I was wearing trousers instead of a skirt would have appalled her, but the general appearance of ladylike refinement was still a good tool.

From the back of the room, Boone poured a generous amount of sugar into my coffee cup. "Well . . . Let's start with establishing some parameters."

"Now you sound like a rocket scientist."

He chuckled, and the parchment of his skin folded into deep creases around his mouth. "I wish I were that bright."

Whitaker shot a quick look toward his partner. "You and me both." He shoved his notebook away. "How long have you known Leonard Flannery?"

I opened and shut my mouth like a fish. That was not at all what I thought they'd ask. I'd been expecting to review conversations or go over some bit of minutia. "Um . . . two years? Ish?" I squinted, trying to remember which class he'd been in. "Yes . . . He was hired with the class of '59 recruits. I think. HR should be able to tell you."

"But you'd never met him before he joined the IAC?" Boone set my coffee cup down in front of me, steam curling off its surface.

"That's right." I kept my hands in my lap and didn't reach for the cup. Not that he would actually have laced it with anything, but the topic choice made me feel suddenly unsafe. "Why do you ask?"

"Can you talk to us about his temperament during the time you've known him?"

"I'm sorry. I thought we were here to talk about the rocket crash."

Whitaker tipped his chair back. "What's his temperament like?"

What. The. Hell. "You just spent an hour and a half with him . . . How did you find him?"

Whitaker dropped the chair forward, resting his elbows on the table. "Why are you refusing to answer questions, Dr. York?"

"John." Agent Boone pulled out the chair next to me and sat down. "Sorry. The investigation has been a long process. We know that you aren't required to answer any questions, but we'd greatly appreciate your cooperation. What's your experience with Dr. Flannery been like?"

The fact that he was polite didn't make me feel any better about his line of questioning. "Completely congenial. Prior to my assignment to the Mars mission, he and I didn't cross paths much, but I've never heard even a cross word from him. Nor have I heard of anyone else experiencing anything like that."

Boone sipped his coffee, seemingly at ease. "No signs of discontent?"

"No." I picked up my cup, more for the warmth of the mug than anything else. My hands had gone cold, and the slick porcelain seared my palms.

Nodding, Boone looked over at Whitaker and shrugged. Whatever that meant, it caused Whitaker to pick up his notepad and flip back a few pages. "Flannery spoke to the terrorists at length. What did he say?"

Boone leaned forward, resting a hand on the desk. "We want to confirm a witness statement without compromising your own testimony. So, just repeat whatever you recall to the best of your ability."

I blinked at him, uncertain what he wanted. "At length? I don't . . ." I shook my head, trying to rattle memories out of the corners. "I don't remember them talking much after they first came on the ship. He tried to talk them down, convince them not to go through with the plan."

"Why do you think he felt comfortable talking to them?"

I narrowly avoided saying *Because Roy was Black*, which was, I was certain, the answer they were looking for. Instead, I shrugged. "Because he was across the aisle from me and they had stopped there to talk to me? And I'm not sure I would characterize either of us as comfortable."

Boone took a sip of his coffee, which I half expected to stain his cadaverous cheeks from the inside. "Why don't you read that quote to Dr. York."

Nodding, Whitaker put a finger on his notepad to mark

his spot. "Did you hear him say, 'I agree with what you are doing and am trying to help?' "

"What? No." They were trying to paint him as a collaborator? "The closest he said to that was that . . ." But he had, in fact, said that he agreed with the why of what they were doing.

"Yes, Dr. York?"

"He was trying to keep them from using me as a hostage. He thought it would make things worse. That's all the help he was offering—the same sort of thing that I was doing. He wasn't—he wasn't collaborating with them."

Whitaker made a mark in his notebook. The silver barrel of his pen gleamed like a rocket as it scratched a trail of ink across the page. To my right, Boone sipped his coffee, watching me over the rim.

"You can't seriously think he was involved with the crash." They had no understanding of how rockets worked if they thought that he could affect the flight from the passenger compartment. "He's a geologist."

"How is that relevant?" Whitaker lifted his head.

"Because he's not a pilot." I looked from one man to the other, trying to get them to understand just how off-course their trajectory was. "He can talk about rocks, and find groundwater, and he's good at a half dozen other things, but he couldn't have done anything to affect where we came down."

"We never said he did." Whitaker looked back down at his paper. "Change of subject: Tell us about the copilot, Willhard Brumwell."

I nearly spilled my coffee as things clicked into place. Brumwell was Black too. "He's a good man."

"I'm sure he is." Boone's parchment cheeks creased with a smile. "How long have you known him?"

I carefully set my coffee cup on the table in the middle

of the condensation ring it had left. "You said I didn't have to answer any questions, so, if you'll excuse me, gentlemen, I've got work to finish up."

As I pushed my chair back, Boone set his own cup on the table and ran a finger around the rim. "Director Clemons wants you to cooperate with us fully." He looked up, smiling. "We're trying to find some answers. I'm sure you recognize how important it is for Congress to have a full understanding before they deliberate on budget issues."

Bastards. Why did it always come back to funding? As much as I wanted to drop out of their orbit, they were making it pretty clear that they'd try to ground all of us. I pulled my chair back to the table, feeling as queasy as an astronaut's first day on Earth. "All right. What can I tell you?"

I honestly don't know how Leonard kept working after the FBI incident. I had a hard time concentrating as I waited for the other shoe to drop, and yet . . . nothing. Weeks went past, and we just kept going with the routines of classes and sims.

In the mock cockpit of the simulated Mars Command Module, Parker sat in the captain's chair and scowled. "Right . . . we've just lost contact with Mission Control."

We all groaned at the latest "green card" that our simulation supervisor had just thrown our way—but not too loudly, because of course the Sim Sup was sitting just outside in the white-room control area, monitoring our test.

"We've got the transMars burn coming up," Terrazas said from the copilot seat.

Which meant that I was up—this was why they had a NavComp on board, in case we lost contact with Mission Control. "I'll calculate the burn."

"Roger." Parker nodded from his seat, continuing his job of keeping our craft "flying" on course.

I fumbled with the sextant, trying to sight it on the simulated stars outside our simulated window to calculate our simulated position. If only my uncertainty had been simulated as well. This procedure is supposed to be simple. I find the three stars that the IAC had been using for this flight, sight the sextant on them, and voilà—I know where "up" is, which then allows me to know how we're doing in relation to the original flight plan that the IAC had sent. If we were off, then I could calculate where our engine needed to point and for how long.

But.

But I had to find the "stars" that the IAC had chosen when they'd sent the last course adjustment in order to compare them with the tables that Mission Control had prepared for just such a contingency. So . . . which one was Alkaid?

Find the Little Dipper, then "arc to Arcturus, speed on to Spica," and . . . okay. Found that, which meant that Alkaid was . . . where? I ground my teeth and tried to pull the memory out of my brain. The thing is that star charts in a book are very different from the actual stars, which are different again from simulated ones. If I'd stayed at Adler during sextant training . . . but I hadn't.

"Clock's ticking, York."

I nodded and named the stars that I knew in that region, hoping that I'd be able to identify Alkaid in the process. Gienah, Acrux, Spica, Menkent . . . which meant *that* one was Alkaid. I sighted the sextant on it, and then began my calculations.

Five minutes in, I realized that the numbers were too far off for that to have been right. One of the stars I'd picked must be wrong. I was confident about Spica, but Alkaid . . . I could try again, but the clock was ticking, and if this happened for real, the best scenario is that it would be embarrassing. The more likely outcome was that I would send us out of the narrow flight path, we'd miss Mars, and we'd all die.

If I were uncertain in space, I'd ask for help. Sighing, I lifted my head from my calculations. "Can someone point out Alkaid for me?"

"On it." Florence slid over and laid her cheek next to mine so that our sightlines were as close as possible. Squinting, she pointed to a star three over from the one I'd picked. "That one. Forms the corner of a right angle. See?"

The image from the textbook suddenly snapped into focus. "Yes. Thank you."

"Anything I can do to keep you from killing us." She slid back to her seat and took up her position again.

I wish she had been joking.

The UN security team escorted me past the photographers outside our building and all the way up the stairs to our apartment door. Exhausted, I still remembered my mother's training. "Thanks. Can I get you something to drink?"

"No ma'am." He smiled and patted the back of the chair we'd put in the hall. "I've got a good book, and my relief comes soon enough."

"Well . . . holler if you need anything." My life was so odd. The itch of leaving someone to sit in our hallway didn't quite fade, even when I was in the apartment with the door closed behind me.

Nathaniel sat at the kitchen table, twirling a pencil in one hand while he hunched over a stack of papers. Our Murphy bed had already been pulled down, covers turned back, so it took up half of our studio. Still, the room looked so big after my quarters on the moon.

As I shut the door, Nathaniel looked up, smiling. "I was wondering if they'd let you go."

"Well . . . I killed us, so the sim stopped, otherwise we'd still be at it." That damn artificial star field kept tripping me up. "We're running it again tomorrow."

The smile on his face froze for a moment before he inhaled and laughed at the joke that was supposed to have been. Sliding his chair back, he stood. "Have you eaten?"

"Yes, but only rations as part of the sim." Coming all the way into the kitchen area, I set my binder down on the table. How do you define knowing that your husband is hiding something? A slight stiffness in his features? A delay in reactions, as if he's thinking about the correct thing to say or do? The way he moves with his back to you, with the pretense of opening the refrigerator? "Are you all right?"

He pulled the freezer door open. "I've got some soup, too, but I thought you might need one of these."

Nathaniel turned around holding two martinis, glass frosted from sitting in the freezer. He winked. "You'll be happy to know that rationing has been lifted enough so that gin is no longer worth its weight in gold."

"Forget the gin." I took the glass from his hand, sighing in relief at the slick, cold glass. "Where did you get olives?"

"Governor Wargin." He took a sip and some of the tension in his frame eased. "Won them on poker night."

I'd forgotten, somehow, that he and the other astronauts' husbands played poker while we were up. "How's Reynard? I mean, with . . ." I gestured at my binder, as if that explained the whole topic of Helen staying and me going.

Nathaniel shrugged, a line appearing and disappearing between his brows. "He's glad to have her home. It's . . . Right. Soup. I was going to feed you dinner."

I took a sip of the beautiful martini, watching him. He stood in front of the refrigerator, back to me, as he pulled out a pot. My sweet husband, pretending that nothing was wrong. I lowered my glass. "Do you remember . . . when I started seeing the therapist and didn't tell you?"

Nathaniel stopped moving, pot halfway to the counter. "Yes." He straightened and set it on the stove with a clatter of metal on metal.

"So will you tell me what's bothering you?"

He turned on the burner, striking a match to light the gas. With a soft *whoomp,* the blue flames caught and licked the bottom of the pot. Nathaniel reached for a wooden spoon from the pitcher of utensils by the stove. "Honestly . . . honestly, I would rather not."

"Okay." The agreement sprang automatically from my lips. He didn't want to talk about it? Fine. We wouldn't. I bent my head to the martini again, letting the briney scent give me a landing place. Taking a sip, I sat down at the kitchen table, trying to concentrate on the cool, herbal sting of the gin and the salt from the olive. But, goddamn it. What was bothering him?

He stood with his shoulders hunched a little over the stove as he stirred the soup. "What time do you have to be in tomorrow?"

"Seven a.m." I pulled the papers he'd been working on closer to distract myself with some math. *Contingency plans for mid-mission abort.* "Oh."

Contingency plans . . . That was the IAC's covert way of saying, "What do we do if someone dies?"

I set the martini down and stood. Walking over to the stove, I wrapped my arms around Nathaniel's waist and leaned into his warmth. "I'm just going to remind you that simulations are so that we make the mistakes here. The thing that killed us today is one less thing that will catch us in space."

"One less." He stopped stirring the soup and wisps of steam curled around the edges of the deep red liquid.

Through the back of his shirt, his breath hitched and caught. Nathaniel let go of the soup, and brought both hands down to rest on mine. "Sorry. I thought—"

Laying my cheek against his shoulder blade, I waited.

"I thought I'd gotten used to it. Watching you launch into space, knowing the giant list of things that could fail." One of his hands found my wedding ring and spun it. "But I know what can fail here. Out there? You might . . . you might just never come home."

"That is always true." I squeezed him tighter. "I mean, I could be hit by a streetcar."

"But I would know." In the circle of my arms, he straightened with a little chuckle. "Golly. That sounds great . . . 'Gee, honey, you might die, but could you make sure I know the details? Thanks!'"

I snorted and rose onto my toes so I could kiss the back of his neck. "You are a goof." I tugged at his waist. "Come here."

"Where?" Nathaniel wiped his face with one hand as he turned off the burner.

I led him around the table to the bed and gave him the courtesy of not noticing that his eyes were red. In truth, I had no idea how to comfort him. With so many flights, Nathaniel could no longer oversee them all, and Clemons, bless him, decreed that he wasn't allowed to work mine. Although maybe that was a cruelty, because it took away his sense of being able to affect the outcome. This thing he was afraid of? It was very real. Lebourgeois had died last year when a faulty switch caused his retro-rockets to misfire during a routine orbital adjustment. I pulled my husband down to sit on the bed, wrapped my arms around him, and just held him.

After a moment, he leaned back so that we both were lying on the bed, all tangled in each other. His face was close to mine, and those blue eyes, rimmed in red, searched me like a star chart. Nathaniel drew a line across my brows and down my cheek, leaving a trail of warmth behind. "I love you and—" He stopped and closed his eyes, swallowing. "And that's why I don't want to talk about this, because supporting you and being honest about . . . I don't know if I can."

My insides turned acrid with pain for him. I could only pull him closer and try not to cry, because the last thing I wanted was for him to be comforting me when I was trying to comfort him. Of all the things we'd talked about when considering if I should go to Mars or stay on Earth, Nathaniel's fear had not been in the equation. It was a hidden variable that kept the whole thing from balancing.

"What can I do?"

He laughed breathlessly. "Don't die?"

"I'll try not to." Raising a hand, I traced circles on his arm. "Anything else?"

Nathaniel sighed again. "The problem with being the lead engineer and married to an astronaut is that I know how you all lie on your reports about your health. You'll give us the brightest possible picture on anything you decide isn't mission critical."

I winced. He was not wrong. "What about—"

He opened his eyes and his pupils were as large and deep as space. "What about what?"

"Okay, this is stupid."

"I don't get to see you be stupid very often without thrust involved."

I slid my hand down to his trousers to see if launch conditions had been met. Not yet. Which meant that I needed to prime the fuel cells. "Well . . . You mentioned the reports. What if I could give you *private* reports?"

Nathaniel rolled up onto his elbow. "Private reports, you

say." And then he shook his head. "No good. At the bandwidth you'll be broadcasting, everyone on Earth will know your business."

"Not if it's a code."

"The moment people see a code, someone is going to try to crack it."

"Ah . . ." I pushed myself up on my elbow so I could kiss him. This is where my work as a computer came in handy, combined with learning how the teletype systems would work on this mission. "But if they don't see the code, they won't know there's anything to crack. For instance, say, it's in the garbage at the beginning and end of a teletype transmission."

Nathaniel stared at me for a moment—or, rather, he stared in my direction. But given the line between his brows, and the way his eyes darted back and forth like he was following a thought down a dark alley, I'm pretty sure he was programming a teletype. His focus snapped back, then he smiled and bent forward to kiss me. His mouth was warm and still tasted a little of gin.

Elsewhere, thrusters came online and we were go for launch.

NINE

RACIAL INCIDENTS AT ISSUE IN UN

KANSAS CITY, KS, March 24, 1962—With tact and assurances, United States officials have been striving to placate Asian and African diplomats aroused over a series of unpleasant racial incidents in the city. Episodes involving nonwhite diplomats have stirred resentment in the international community here. The latest was the attack two weeks ago on Youssouf Gueye, first secretary of the Mauritanian delegation.

The French-speaking diplomat, out for an evening stroll, was accosted by a group of white youths. The group yelled at him, he said, and then he was hit with a beer bottle. He suffered facial cuts requiring hospital treatment.

Helen met me at her front door wearing a mint-green day dress and a strained smile. "Thank you for coming over."

We did not hug. "It's good to see you." I'd seen her at work, of course, but we'd done nothing social since I'd replaced her. The invitation to come over for a bridge night had been a welcome surprise.

"May I offer you something to drink?" She led me back down a short hallway to the living room. Florence Grey sat on the sofa sipping a whiskey and soda.

Oddly, the card table and chairs hadn't been set up yet.

Helen walked over to the birch sideboard where a bucket of ice sat sweating on a silver tray. "Martini?"

"If it's not too much trouble, that would be lovely." I set my handbag on an end table. "Good evening, Florence."

"York." She picked up her soda and sipped it, watching me over the rim.

This was going to be a swell evening. The doorbell rang, which must be Ida. That offered me an excuse to flee for a moment. "I'll get it."

Helen nodded from the sidebar, where she was measuring out vermouth to add to the pitcher. I retreated down the hall and pulled the door open. Ida stood on the little stoop of the Carmouches' home with a big grin and a basket of strawberries. "Elma!" She gave me a quick hug. "When are we going to get you back out to the 99s airfield for some flying? We all miss you."

"You know how mission prep is." I gave a pained smile and glanced back toward the living room. Lowering my voice, I said, "I don't want to talk about the mission, though . . . Helen, you know?"

She grimaced. "Sorry. I forgot." Putting on a grin, she stepped past me and headed down the hall. "Ladies! I come bearing strawberries and shortcake!"

"You are a goddess among women." Florence stood up from the table and greeted Ida with a hug and a radiant smile.

"Strawberries!" Helen stirred the martini in its cut glass pitcher, but grinned at Ida over her shoulder. "Now I wish I had champagne to add to that."

"Honey, if you're making martinis, we don't need to look any further."

I drifted at the edge of the room, suddenly aware that I was the only white woman present. I tucked my hands behind my back, as if hiding the color of my skin would distract anyone. Moments later, Helen delivered the martini, and I had to untuck them. At least I had something to do with my hands now.

2, 3, 5, 7, 9 . . . Everything would be fine.

"Do you want me to set up the card table?" Once we started playing cards, the tension would drop away.

"Actually . . ." Helen poured another measure of gin into the pitcher. "I've invited you here under false pretenses."

Oh dear. I swallowed, then sipped my martini and swallowed that, too. The sense of unease in my gut didn't go away.

She poured in the vermouth, while I exchanged glances with Ida and Florence. At least they looked as confused as I felt. "Elma, you may already know about this," Helen continued.

"Not yet, but go on."

"At the last poker game that Reynard played with the boys, Governor Wargin mentioned the rocket crash." As we waited, she tossed in a couple of ice cubes and picked up a silver spoon to stir. "The FBI is investigating whether Leonard Flannery had anything to do with it."

I lowered my martini. "They asked me about that."

The clinking of the ice against the sides of the pitcher slowed as Helen stopped stirring and turned to stare at me. "They?"

"The FBI. A couple of weeks ago, they pulled Leonard and me out of a sim in the neutral buoyancy pool. They had a bunch of stupid questions about whether he could have brought the rocket down from inside. I told them that he wasn't and couldn't have been involved."

"Well, apparently they have a witness who says that he was." Helen tapped the spoon on the side of the glass and set it aside.

"The hell you say." Florence sat up on the sofa. "Who?"

Helen shrugged. "Reynard didn't think to ask."

And Nathaniel hadn't thought to tell me about the conversation at all. "When they asked me, they said that someone had reported on the conversation. A witness. So . . . someone on the ship. Right?"

Ida swore softly and strode over to the sidebar. "Better hurry up with that martini, because I can tell I'm not going to like the way this conversation is going to go."

I settled into one of the armchairs. "What else did Reynard say?"

Concentrating on pouring the martinis into the glasses, Helen grimaced. "Apparently Governor Wargin is concerned that if this business with the FBI gets out, the Congress might pull Leonard." She set the pitcher down and turned to face the room. "And Florence."

"What?!" We all said it at pretty much the same time, surrounded by varying amounts of cursing. Florence slopped some of her whiskey and soda over the edge of her glass.

As she mopped it up with a cocktail napkin, she said, "On what grounds?"

"You're both members of the NAACP, and so were all the men who boarded the ship." Helen shook her head and came to join us.

Ida trailed behind her. "So am I. So are most of the colored astronauts."

"They asked about the pilot, too." I set my martini on the side table next to my handbag. "Okay. So let's work the problem."

Ida took a healthy swig of her martini and responded with the question astronauts ask when things go wrong in space. "Right. What's going to kill us next?"

"I'm about to kill someone, that's for sure." Florence sat back on the couch. "But I'm guessing that my mouth is one of the problems."

"Public opinion." Helen sat down on the couch next to Florence. "That is what will kill us."

It had already killed Helen's shot at the Mars mission. I reached for my bag and dug out my notepad. "Okay. Public opinion. What else?"

"Lies." Florence shook her head. "We need to figure out who's lying about Leonard."

I scribbled that down as we began making a list of everything that could go wrong. And then Helen mixed more martinis, and we started finding solutions.

I didn't get home until after midnight, but Nathaniel was still up. Or rather, he was awake and reading. He sat propped against all the pillows on our Murphy bed with a sheet draped across his legs. The pale blond hair on his chest caught the amber lamplight like a cloud at sunset. He looked up and smiled.

"I am angry at you." That might have been my third martini speaking, but I set my handbag down on the kitchen table, kicked my shoes off, and went to stand on the new rug in my stocking feet. It really was gloriously soft. But the tufted oriental wonder did not diminish my irritation. "Or maybe irked."

He sat up, setting his book aside. "Why?"

"Because you didn't tell me about the FBI and Leonard and Florence."

"Oh." He threw the sheet off. He had no pajamas on beneath it. That was interesting, but would not distract me from the main issue. Nathaniel stood in his full nude glory. "Is that why Helen invited you over?"

"We are talking about why you didn't tell me."

Nathaniel sighed and gave a little shrug. "When?"

"When what?"

"When was I supposed to tell you?" He ran his hand through his hair so it stuck up, like gravity had stopped in his orbit. "You come home late. You leave before I wake up. At work?"

"I didn't leave before you woke up this morning. We went to synagogue together. And had lunch! We spent most of today together before I went to Helen's."

"Yes. Forgive me for wanting to spend a day with my wife instead of talking about work."

I rocked back a little. "We've always talked about work."

Nathaniel sighed again and covered his face with his hands. "I know." When he peeled his hands away, his shoulders had sagged. "The truth is, I forgot by the time we got to the weekend."

"You forgot. You forgot that the FBI is investigating two of my teammates?"

"Yes." He leaned over and snatched his dressing gown from the back of the living room chair. "Believe it or not, I have other things on my mind than a conversation over a game of poker."

"It's not just—"

"I know! I didn't ignore it. I told Clemons. All right?" He pulled the dressing gown on, tying the belt tight enough that it must have hurt. "You were already upset enough about Helen. I didn't think you needed more to feel guilty about."

My jaw dropped. "Guilty? Leonard and Florence aren't my fault. Why would I feel guilty?"

"You're Jewish. You're Southern. You feel guilty about being alive."

I snorted. "All right. All right. I'll grant you that point. That *one* point."

He dropped into the chair, leaning one elbow on the armrest. "Well, thank God for that." Looking up at me, Nathaniel tilted his head to the side. "Look. Elma. There's nothing you can do about it, so—"

"Ha!"

He sat up abruptly. "What are you planning?"

I drew a circle on the carpet with my toe. It really was a glorious carpet. And maybe I should've stopped after martini number two. "Maybe I should keep some secrets of my own."

"It wasn't a—you know what? Fine." He wiped the air with both hands. "Who won the bridge game?"

"We didn't play bridge."

Nathaniel stared at me. I'd seen him give this look to an engineer who failed to account for a drag coefficient in a design concept. The only time I could remember being on the receiving end of that flat, slightly aggrieved expression was the time I'd turned his tuxedo shirt pink in the wash. (Yes, I should have sent it to the cleaners, but I was trying to save money when we were newlyweds.) The stare wasn't quite as good as Mama's had been, but it was darn close.

I cleared my throat. "Do you really want to know, or are you just asking so you can shoot down the idea?"

He blinked, three or four times. "What—"

Nathaniel shook his head, shoving himself to his feet, then stalked around the room until he returned to stand behind the chair that he'd been sitting in. Pressing both hands on the chair's back, he leaned all his weight on it. "When have I ever—*ever*—stood in the way of what you wanted to do?"

Heat discharged through my face like a rocket venting at separation. He hadn't. Ever. Not even when I wanted to leave him for three years to go haring off to Mars. "I'm sorry."

"What are we fighting about?"

"I don't—" I sat down. On the coffee table, in front of the sofa, but I didn't really care at this point. "I don't know. I just wanted you to have told me."

Outside the window, one of the late-night streetcars clattered past over the tracks. I stared at my hands and knotted them together. My knuckles turned white from pressure. I shouldn't have had that third martini.

"I'm sorry I didn't."

It was not entirely clear if he was apologizing or just that he regretted doing something we were fighting over. Pushing that question seemed inadvisable.

I sighed, trying to vent some tension. "You're right. I'm not spending enough time with you."

"I know what the schedule is." Across the room, cloth rustled as he shifted behind the chair. "And how much catch-up you have to do on top of that."

"What did Clemons say?"

"That replacing Leonard wasn't an option. That he literally wrote the book on Martian geology and landing sites."

"But not Florence."

He shifted again. Not even a streetcar broke the silence in the room.

My toes dug into the intricate patterns on the rug. "She wasn't even on the rocket."

"She's been very outspoken about the inequalities at the IAC." Nathaniel cleared his throat. "And there have been complaints."

I lifted my head. She and I didn't get along, but I had never voiced that to anyone except Nathaniel. "You didn't—"

He scowled. "Who, exactly, do you think you're married to?"

"Sorry."

Tilting his head back, Nathaniel stared at the ceiling and took a markedly slow breath. He pursed his lips as he blew it out, like one of Clemons's smoke rings. "Elma. I do not share our private conversations."

"You did with the doctor."

"No." His gaze snapped down to me. "I fucking wanted to, but I. Did. Not. There are these vows that we made to each other? Remember those? I told the doctor about your physical symptoms, and that is all. The fact that you and Florence don't get along? Please."

"I'm sorry." The weight of it all grabbed me, and pulled my head down until it rested on my knees. I wrapped both arms around my head. "I'm sorry."

Outside the confines of my arms, Nathaniel's feet scuffed across the carpet. A moment later, his hand made a mascon of weight on my back. He kissed the crown of my head. "Why are you angry with me?"

Because I could be. I ground my teeth against the thought, but it had already happened. "Because . . . Because . . ." *You're here.* "Because I feel helpless."

His sigh stirred the hair at the nape of my neck. "Me too."

"I'm sorry."

"You've said that."

A chuckle escaped me, and I used it to help me sit up. My eyes needed wiping, but at least I didn't have snot running down my face. "Well, I am. I shouldn't have taken it out on you."

"And I should've found time to tell you." He grimaced and looked off to the side. "I forgot how much you feel these things, which is stupid—not you feeling them, but me forgetting."

I almost followed his train of thought. "What things?"

"Injustice." He sat down on the carpet with his legs crossed and looked up at me. "So what did you all figure out? What can we do about it?"

Have I mentioned how lucky I am to be married to this man? The dressing gown had fallen open to show most of his chest, and all of his calves. I reached out to run a hand down his cheek. "We have an idea. But—Oh." This was why I was really angry.

Nathaniel's raised eyebrows asked the question.

"I realized why I'm angry . . ." My therapist would be so proud: I'd figured it out, even with a third martini. "I feel angry because I feel guilty about what I'm about to ask for."

His gaze narrowed, but he held his tongue and gave me room to speak.

"The IAC is on American territory." I swallowed. "*Lunetta* isn't."

He stared at me for a moment, so I saw the point when his trajectory of thought caught up with my apparent nonsequitur, because the color drained out of his face. "Shit. All of you?"

I nodded. Helen had figured it out before we'd even arrived. The only way to be certain that Florence and Leonard weren't pulled into endless meetings with the FBI and Congress was to get them out of that jurisdiction. With launch only six months away, Clemons could make the budgetary case that we couldn't replace a team member without pushing the mission out by a year and a half and causing enormous cost overruns. But if Clemons sent just Leonard and Florence to *Lunetta,* we couldn't continue to train together as a team, and the motive would be blatantly transparent. The entire First Mars Expedition team would need to go.

"Helen thinks I have to be there, as the Lady Astronaut,

'to guide public opinion' about our reason for being on the station."

Nathaniel groaned and fell back to the carpet—except he forgot that the Murphy bed was down and cracked his head against its steel frame. "Gah!"

He curled over onto his side, grabbing the back of his head. "Shit."

I knelt by him with no memory of crossing the space between us. "Are you all right?"

"Yeah." He pulled a hand away and looked at it. No blood. "Just stupid."

"I'll get some ice."

"I'm fine."

"I'll get some ice." Standing, I kept my gaze on him as if his head might suddenly spew blood across the carpet. "You'll have a knot there."

He sighed and pushed himself up to sit, his legs spread so that his dressing gown hid nothing—yes, even in moments like this, I notice my husband's body. Nathaniel probed the back of his head with one hand. "I'm fine."

He is a brilliant rocket scientist, and yet completely stupid sometimes. The apartment is so small that it took only a moment to go to the freezer and pull the ice tray out. The cold metal burned against my skin as I grabbed the handle and yanked on it to crack the ice in the tray into cubes. Grabbing a clean kitchen towel, I dumped the ice cubes into it.

"Are you going to come home?"

"What?" I turned, with the towel wadded up in one hand.

"Nothing." He closed his eyes, still rubbing the spot on the back of his head. A breath. "After Mars. Will you come home?"

"Yes." What a question. Did he think I would stay on Mars forever?

His smile was pained. It might just have been the bump on his head. We both pretended it was. "Good."

I walked around the kitchen table and knelt to hand the ice to him. "Here."

"I'm fine." But he took it and set the wadded-up cloth against the base of his head.

"See?" I sat on the floor and leaned against him. "I have to come home, because someone has to stop you from being an idiot."

He chuckled, wrapping an arm around my shoulders to pull me closer. "Does Helen have a plan, or do you need me to make the *Lunetta* assignment happen?"

I nodded, my head sliding across the silk of his gown. "Sorry."

"Me too." He kissed the top of my head. "But I'll do it anyway."

TEN

CREW OF MARS EXPEDITION TRAINING IN SPACE

KANSAS CITY, KS, July 18, 1962—In three months, at 9:32 a.m. Central Daylight Time, the dreams of centuries and the technologies of the decade should converge in a fiery, thunderous instant to launch fourteen astronauts representing the United Nations toward man's first landing on another planet: Mars.

Preparations for the epic, three-year journey to Mars and back continue to run smoothly and on schedule. At Launching Pad 39-A Col. Stetson Parker, the Mars Expedition commander, and his crew are blasting off to continue their training on *Lunetta*, and in the Mars fleet itself, so that they will be free from worldly distractions as they complete preparations for the 34-million-mile mission.

Once we were on the station, I seriously wondered why this hadn't always been the plan. I mean, why stick us in the neutral buoyancy pool to simulate zero-g when we could practice in actual zero gravity? Well, I mean, besides the obvious fact that it was a lot easier to die in space. But other than that, everything got easier.

I aimed my sextant out the observation window at real stars. The tiny variations in color that might have been hidden by the atmosphere of Earth, even before the Meteor, blazed with crystalline wonder from the velvet blackness of the sky. There were thousands—hundreds of thousands—more stars visible in space than at even the best planetarium on Earth, and yet the job of picking out one star from a sea of them was easier.

I registered Alkaid and Spica, spun down to sight on Earth, and, presto chango, I had the coordinates I needed to confirm our state vector. I scribbled down the answer. *Plus 0771145, plus 2085346, minus 0116167, minus 15115, plus 04514, minus 19587.* "Finished!"

Behind me, Parker clicked a stopwatch. "Best time yet."

A snort came from one of the observers floating behind us. Even before his South African drawl began, I was pretty sure it would be Vanderbilt DeBeer. "She could write down any random memorized coordinates and still you would believe."

Heidi Voegeli, the *Pinta*'s NavComp, shut her notebook with a snap. "Please, DeBeer. You know better than that."

She took a linen handkerchief to her finely tooled Swiss sextant. I'll admit to some envy for the beautiful stainless-steel wonder. It had a built-in slot for a pen, a fold-out stopwatch that you could set to keep track of time elapsed, and really lovely, completely superfluous engraving on the supporting arms.

"Yes, but I am only saying that, since no one checks the work, either of you could cheat and we would not know."

I unhooked from my foot restraints to turn and give him one of my mother's patented cold, polite glares. "I thought I was practicing a skill that would keep my team alive. Cheating isn't something that even occurred to me. Why . . . I wonder what made *you* think of it?"

From the flush that rose to his cheeks, I may have put a tiny bit too much emphasis on the *you*.

Benkoski clapped a hand on his copilot's shoulder. "You haven't known York as long as I have. There's a damn good reason we don't bother to check her numbers."

"Ja, ja . . . The Lady Astronaut." DeBeer gave a smile and a little bow. "I know. I know . . . It is only my competitive nature. I meant nothing by it."

Heidi met my gaze with a little twitch of her eyebrows. DeBeer must be a joy to work with in sims if he questioned her all the time, and she'd be spending three years with the man? Suddenly I had a new appreciation for Parker, who never, ever questioned me in my area of expertise.

I pushed off from the wall to float over to the *Niña* group. "Who's up next?"

"Grey." Parker gave a little wave to Florence. "Have at it."

The theory was that we all needed to be versed in how to use the sextant, just in case something happened to me or Heidi.

But the practice meant that Parker was pulling Florence out into the focal range of DeBeer, a man who loathed her existence in general and her presence on the mission in specific. After three months in space with both teams mixing, I'd gotten to know the *Pinta* team better than we would have if we'd been running parallel training tracks on Earth.

DeBeer was a product of South Africa and a firm believer in the value of Apartheid. He'd also been on the rocket that had gone off course, and I would place solid bets that he'd been the one to lie to the FBI. So Parker suggesting that Florence have a go now was either cruel to her, or a dig at DeBeer. Actually . . . knowing him, it was probably both.

Florence drifted out from behind our group, where she and Leonard had been watching. Her jaw was set and she kept her gaze fixed on the rail where I'd been anchored. I held out my sextant. Florence took it with a nod.

Benkoski traded a look with Parker. I couldn't guess at what passed between them, but he turned to DeBeer. "Say . . . Why don't you go next."

DeBeer nodded, but also muttered something in Afrikaans. "*Teen die agterplaas aap?*"

Parker gave one push with his toes and bounded across the room to land with military accuracy in front of DeBeer. His voice was clipped with equal military precision. "*Ek vind dat offensief. Sê dit weer, en ek kry jy permanent gegrond.*"

Recoiling, DeBeer overcompensated and flailed comically backward. Benkoski stuck out a hand to right his copilot, shaking his head at Parker. "Jesus Christ. Afrikaans now, too?"

"I like languages. What can I say?" Parker shrugged, back to the charming, shit-eating, aw-shucks astronaut hero that he showed the American public.

Heidi laughed and handed her sextant to DeBeer. "*Wie viele macht das?*"

Parker cocked his head to the side, his fingers twitching as if he were counting on them. "*Elf? Nein—zwölf. Zwölf, aber ich bin wirklich nur Konversation in sechs oder sieben von ihnen.*"

Heidi laughed again, and it was easy to see why Switzerland had chosen Heidi as its poster child for the space program. Perfect teeth. A swan's neck. Capped by a braided coil of golden hair. "*Only* six or seven, he says."

As DeBeer hooked into the restraint next to Florence, he busied himself with Heidi's sextant. "How long have you had Afrikaans?"

"Started learning it the moment you were assigned to the Mars mission."

"I am flattered," DeBeer said.

"Eh. It was the only one I didn't have already." Parker shrugged. "'Course, I learned Taiwanese for no reason."

I winced at his not-so-subtle reminder of Helen. "But have you learned Yiddish?"

"Yiddish, not Judeo-Spanish? I thought your family was from Charleston."

I blinked at him while my brain struggled with which part of that was the most surprising. Was it the fact that Parker knew where my family was from? The fact that he knew that Charleston was mostly Sephardic Jews, not Ashkenazi? Or that he knew that not all Jews spoke the same language? "Um . . . yeah. Came over in the seventeen hundreds from Germany. How did you know . . . ?" I'm not sure which question I wanted answered.

"My mother-in-law is Jewish. Sephardic by way of Holland." He glanced past me, and a scowl surfaced for a moment before getting plastered over with a grin. "Incoming."

Parker pushed off and did a showy somersault over my head to land neatly by the door to the observation room, where Betty was shepherding in our reporting pool. Goddamn it. They were early. Hooking his feet under one of the guide rails, Parker did a nice imitation of someone standing at parade rest, even with the zero-g. Around me, twelve astronauts snapped on their regulation smiles.

You would think that being off the planet, I'd have escaped the orbit of the press. You would be wrong. Every country that had invested money in the Mars Expedition wanted news of it. The shenanigans that Nathaniel and Clemons had pulled to get us off-planet earlier had gotten us away from congressional hearings, but not the need to keep money flowing toward the IAC's coffers. I didn't even want to know what it took to get the press pool certified for space travel.

I pushed off to join Parker in greeting the press corps, hopefully giving the rest of our team breathing room to keep working with their sextants. After all, being a face for the public was why I was on the mission.

At the front of the group trailing Betty was—joy of joys—Jerry, the photographer from the *Times*. Maybe I could get him to take Parker's photo with a single punch card. Betty spun in place and smiled at her charges. We did so much smiling for the public. "Oh my! This is lucky. May I introduce the first man into space, Colonel Stetson Parker?" When she gestured to him, Parker grinned and waved. "And of course, Dr. Elma York—better known as the Lady Astronaut."

Smile and wave. Smiiiiile and wave.

My job was to make space look as glamorous and exciting as possible. It would be a chore, since at least two of the reporters looked green with the early signs of space sickness. With my luck, one of them would chalk any vomiting up to "space germs" instead of good old-fashioned vertigo. I patted a pocket on my flight suit for the reassuring crinkle of a vomit bag. "Welcome to *Lunetta*!"

"We're so pleased you could join us." Parker had the aw-shucks thing down pat. "Hope your flight up was uneventful."

"Betty, what do you have on the agenda for these fine folks?"

"I thought that they might want to take a look at the observation lounge while their luggage is being offloaded, but I didn't realize you all were in here." That was not true, since we'd discussed this trip at the Monday morning staff meeting. This little exercise was so they'd feel like there was some spontaneity to our dog and pony show. Funny what people respond to.

"We're practicing using sextants, but you're welcome to

watch." Parker turned to gesture to the window, where Florence was at work. "We're spicing things up a little by making it into a contest."

Here's a question: did Parker plan to have Florence be the subject of photographs, or was that an accident? It's hard to tell with him, but I was pleased she was getting the spotlight right now. Especially with the news from Earth about the sit-ins at the launch centers.

"Sounds fun, but it's not the view I promised you. Sorry, folks." Betty's curls bobbed freely, as if she were underwater. "If any of you want to head back to your quarters, one of the crew can escort you straight there."

If she'd said "cash bar," then we might have lost some of the reporters, but otherwise, none of them were going to risk being scooped. She knew that. Their cameras were already out and snapping away.

"Well, we'll get back to the contest, then." Parker pushed off, and I followed him back to the group of *Niña* astronauts. He stopped and hung upside down this time. You'd think that "up" and "down" shouldn't have any meaning here, but we tend to orient in the same direction because back on Earth, we train in gravity. The engineers install labels in gravity. The lights are "overhead" because of gravity. Also, there's the courtesy of making it easier to read facial expressions. We don't have gravity, but we do have "up" and "down."

I glanced at him. "You want to disorient them immediately?"

"I'm trying to provide a vivid photographic opportunity for the press corps."

Kamilah Shamoun, our medic, rolled her eyes. "If you fart, I swear to God I am going to light it."

"That's terrible for propulsion." Parker pulled out his stopwatch. "Okay. What's their goal? Benkoski?"

The pilot for the *Pinta* team shook his head. "York, you won the last round. You pick."

"Good call. Then she can go back and explain it to the peanut gallery." Parker nodded and stared at me expectantly, from upside down.

I considered for a moment. "Let's have the state vector for *Lunetta* using Deneb and Aldebaran for guidance."

While they worked, I kicked back to the press corps, who snapped photos. Or, rather, tried to snap photos. Most of them had forgotten to anchor, and one clearly hadn't yet learned to conserve movement, so not only was he floating free, he was also spinning. I snagged the lanky blond man and helped him settle.

Keeping a hand on the reporter, I smiled at the rest of the group. "Can I answer any questions for you?"

A reporter with a movie-star mane of dark hair raised his hand. "Justino Coronel, of *Folha de São Paulo*. What are we over now?"

"Good question." I gestured to the wall of windows to the right of the door. "Follow a guide rail over here and we'll take a look. We orbit the Earth about every ninety minutes, but since we're not oriented on the ecliptic, we see a slightly different part of the planet with each revolution."

I kicked off with my toes and flew down to the window, rebounding off of it to change orientation and face them.

"Is that safe?" The *Times* reporter hung back a little.

"Absolutely." Unless a meteor passed by, but there wasn't any point in alarming them. I snagged a handgrip to anchor myself. "Each window has four panes of glass that are each three centimeters thick. So there's twelve centimeters between you and outer space. A ninety-one-kilogram man could stand on this on Earth and even jump up and down without problems. In zero-g, I weigh significantly less than that."

The *Times* reporter raised his camera, as if he couldn't help himself. "Is that to protect against meteors?"

"An impact with someone's lunch box is more likely." I smiled. Again. And looked down to where the Earth spun past us in glorious blues and silver grays. Flashes of brown or green land peeked through the cloud cover like secret promises. "We're over Africa right now."

A lanky blond man pushed himself to the front of the pack. "Home!" His broad accent placed him at the bottom of the continent. He raised his camera and started snapping photos. "Do you think I could get Vanderbilt DeBeer in front of South Africa?"

"By the time he finishes, we'll have rotated off of it, I'm afraid." I glanced over to the cluster where Florence and DeBeer worked. "Our next orbit should still be over the landmass, though."

"Alas." The reporter straightened and it sent him careening up and away from the windows.

I snagged his foot and guided him to one of the rails. "Careful there. Make sure you always keep a hand on something until you get used to zero-g."

"How long did it take you?" The Brazilian reporter had one hand on a rail and used the other to steady his camera.

I shrugged. "By the second or third day, I was fairly comfortable, but it's different for everyone." I gestured to the group of astronauts. "For instance, Graeham Stewman, who is the geologist for the *Pinta*, was an Olympic diver before going into geology. He took to space as if it were water. Derek Benkoski, the *Pinta*'s pilot, had done skydiving with the air force, and that experience seemed to translate to weightlessness."

"What about the other geologist?" The South African reporter lifted his camera toward the group and adjusted the focus but didn't snap a picture.

"Dr. Flannery was about average. Though, in truth, one of the criteria that the IAC looked for in Mars Expedition candidates was our resilience to space sickness."

All of their heads snapped around toward me. One of the greenish men gurgled and swallowed with an audible gulp. "Space sickness? Like the disease that the astronauts had on the rocket that crashed?"

It is sometimes difficult not to laugh outright at people, but, honestly, weren't reporters supposed to know better? "If you are thinking of something microbial, there's no such thing. What astronauts are afflicted with is a disturbance of the vestibular system in the inner ear. It is annoying, but not dangerous. Think of it like seasickness."

In near unison, most of the reporters exchanged their cameras for pads of paper and dutifully wrote something down. That would probably translate to something like, "Elma York says that space sickness is like seasickness." It could be worse.

"Speaking of crashed rockets, are you comfortable with Leonard Flannery's continued involvement in the expedition, considering that he is under investigation for the crash of the *Cygnus 14* rocket?" This was the South African reporter again.

Years of anxiety gave me the ability to look calm and smile even when my heart started racing. Though, this time, it was from anger. "Leonard was inside the rocket, same as I was, and couldn't have had anything to do with the crash. So I'm absolutely fine with having him on the crew. Among other things, he literally wrote the book on the Martian landscape."

"What about his EVA?"

I blinked, which seems to be what I do when I'm surprised. I blinked again. "Excuse me?"

"According to sources, Leonard Flannery did an EVA

practice the morning before the *Cygnus 14* rocket returned to Earth. Couldn't he have damaged the ship then?"

"According to 'sources'?" The only good thing coming out of this circus was that it narrowed down our likely subjects for the person who was talking to the FBI. If they shared a source with the South African reporter, then it stood to reason that the South African astronaut was the link.

Vanderbilt DeBeer. He and I were going to have a very interesting talk.

ELEVEN

WHAT KIND OF MEN ARE THEY?

The Crew of the Mars Expedition

July 19, 1962—TIME Magazine—COLONEL STETSON PARKER walked into the room, a conservative plaid sports jacket draping his well-proportioned 5'11" frame, giving an immediate impression of suave urbanity. His disappearing blond hair, once thick, is closely cropped, accentuating his strong jaw. His lopsided grin suggested he was aware of his role as an historic figure and was trying hard to make people remember that he was just a man. It is easy to be blinded by his role as the first man into space and forget that beneath this charming exterior is a skilled fighter pilot who flew more than 80 missions in the Second World War.

After a day of trying to catch DeBeer without any of the others around, I had enough time to calm down and realize that I should talk to Florence and Leonard first. Leonard was in his lab, experimenting on . . . something. There were rocks. And a drill. Anyway, I went to track down Florence and found her in the gym, running on the treadmill under the gentle centrifugal gravity of *Lunetta*'s spinning donut.

I walked across the gently curving floor, past Terrazas at the weights and Rafael on the stationary bike. Some of the regular *Lunetta* crew were also there, wearing their UN-issued workout clothes. A reporter slouched in the corner, taking pictures of DeBeer while he did push-ups.

Florence had a towel draped over her shoulder and wiped her face as she ran. Even with the artificial gravity of the spinning section of *Lunetta,* sweat did not drip quite as quickly as it did on Earth.

She gave a little nod to acknowledge that she'd seen me, but kept running.

"Can I borrow you for a bit?" I glanced at the others, but no one seemed to care that we were talking. "There's a comm question I could use help with for the next sim."

Florence wiped her face. "Got another twenty minutes on the treadmill."

I nodded and shot a glance briefly at DeBeer to make sure he was still showing off for the reporter. "Okay. I'll be in the lab going over something with Leonard. When you get a chance."

She followed my gaze and raised her eyebrows. Pursing her lips, Florence nodded. "I'll come by."

Dr. Leonard Flannery looked every bit the mad scientist when I walked into the lab. He had on a white lab coat, safety goggles, and ear protection. Over the safety goggles, he had another pair of magnifying lenses, which made his eyes nearly vanish behind their curve. Whatever he was working on shrieked and threw sparks into the air. This, by the way, is one of the reasons we stopped using pure oxygen in space, well . . . that and the dangers of oxygen toxicity from long-term exposure.

Leonard looked up when I came into the lab and slapped

the off switch on his contraption, smiling. "York! What can I do for you?"

I waited until he had slipped the earmuffs back to rest around his neck like an odd tie. "There's some stuff I want to talk to you about, but I want to wait until Florence gets here."

"About . . . ?"

"The FBI."

His face went gray. He slipped the goggles up on top of his head and wiped his hands off on a rag on the lab table. "I'll shut things down."

Holding up my binder, I shrugged. "I brought something to work on until she gets here. She said it would be another twenty minutes or so."

"Well, I'm not going to get anything useful done in twenty minutes." He threw the rag back on the table. "This just isn't going to go away, is it?"

"I don't know."

Leonard pulled the earmuffs from around his neck and clipped them onto their spot on the rack of tools. Both sets of goggles followed before he turned his attention back to the contraption on the table.

"What are you working on?" I sat down on one of the lab stools next to the counter.

"Testing a new core sampler." He backed it out of the rock he'd been drilling into. "I'm not a fan. It has too much play and doesn't really cut a clean hole. But I guess some corporation wants us to use it and they're backing some aspect of the mission. You know how it goes. 'Our drill bits are used on Mars!'"

I snorted. "Yeah. I've got people wanting me to take their lipstick on the expedition."

"You're kidding." He stopped with the drill in one hand, then shook his head. "Don't bother. I know the answer."

Behind me, Florence asked, "The answer to what?"

I turned to her. "Have you been asked to take cosmetics to Mars?"

Florence had changed out of her tracksuit, but her hair was still pulled back into a tight bun. She rolled her eyes. "Hair straightener. As if I'm going to use lye in space. That stuff burns enough when you have gravity to keep it in place."

"Wait—you use lye to straighten your hair?"

Florence waved her hand, as if to wipe my question out of the air. "I stopped my run early. So tell me why I did?"

"Right." I set my binder on the counter and took a breath. Before becoming an astronaut, I probably would have beaten around the bush and taken my time, being careful to hedge my statements. Now? I wouldn't insult my teammates by wasting their time with anything but the information they needed to work the problem. "The South African reporter . . . He mentioned having a source. The FBI agents did, too. So . . . I wondered if it might be DeBeer."

"Of course it is." Florence sat down on one of the stools and set a squeeze pouch of water on the counter. "Is that all you wanted to talk about?"

"Well . . . What are we going to do about it?"

Leonard and Florence exchanged looks. He shook his head. "Exactly what I've been doing. Keeping my head down and trying not to cause trouble."

"But—but he's making things up, like . . . like the reporter said that you had gone on an EVA before the rocket left."

"And I did."

My jaw dropped.

Leonard rubbed his forehead. "Look, I talked to the FBI

about it, and they confirmed with Malouf, who was on the EVA with me, as well as with Mission Control, that we were nowhere near the rocket."

"Good." I tried again to make them understand what was happening. "But DeBeer is trying to get you kicked off the mission."

"We know." Florence sighed. "It's why we're careful not to spend too much time together—or with Kamilah and Terrazas, for that matter. Don't want him to think the 'darkies' are colluding."

"So let's talk to Mission Control and—"

"No!" Leonard straightened. "For the love of God Almighty, do not talk to Mission Control. I had a devil of a time convincing Clemons to keep me on after that mess with the FBI, and I am *not* going to rock the boat now."

I turned to Florence for support and she shook her head at me. "I know you mean well, but he's right. You know I'm outspoken as all get-out when I'm not happy, but there's no way I would go to Mission Control with this."

I slumped on my stool. There had to be something we could do. What they were saying sounded a lot like Helen's reasons for agreeing to bow out of the mission because the IAC wanted to send me instead. For that matter, it wasn't that far off from why Mama had always told me to be quiet and polite. As a young Jewish woman, I couldn't afford to give people any reason to notice me. I gnawed my lower lip. "What if . . . What if we spin it so it isn't about you? Is there a way I could use my whole Lady Astronaut thing to point out that DeBeer is a problem? I mean . . . I can rock the boat. They won't do anything to me."

Leonard tilted his head to the side and squinted, like he was Superman trying to see through lead. Then he shook his head, straightening. "Nope. It'll still blow back on me. You want to help, and I appreciate that, but I'm going to have to ask you to let it lie. Once we're under way, DeBeer will be on the other ship, and it won't matter."

Florence smiled bleakly. "This'll be the only time that Apartheid works in our favor." At my puzzled glance, she shrugged. "You didn't know? We're on the separate-but-equal ship."

One of the unexpected benefits of living in the Meteor Age was that telephone service had drastically improved with the advent of satellites. Telephone companies no longer had to string wires across the entirety of the United States or drag long transatlantic cables below the ocean. Instead, radio dishes bounced the signals up into space, where a satellite caught them and bounced them back down to a dish on another part of the planet.

The technology had been developed to allow us to communicate with Earth on the way to the moon, then refined for communication with *Lunetta*, and further refined for the Mars Expedition. All of which meant that once a week, despite being on an orbital platform, I got to talk to my husband.

I tethered myself at one of the cubbies in *Lunetta*'s comm module. The chamber hung off one of the weightless limbs of the station like a barnacle made of antennae. Pulling the headphones from their clip on the side of the cubby, I tried not to listen in on the other conversations happening in the little room. The other four "public" phones were in use by two crew members from *Lunetta*, one reporter, and a miner en route to the moon.

With the earphones settled on my head, the other conversations dulled behind a faint buzz of static. I toggled the line to let the operator know I was there and waited until her voice broke the static. British, this time. "What number, please?"

"Kansas West 6-5309." It was Nathaniel's desk phone, since it was still early afternoon in Kansas.

"One moment." The line clicked and buzzed as she made the connection, and a moment later it rang.

The phone didn't even get through the first ring. "Nathaniel York speaking."

"Hello, handsome."

"Hi." How can he put so much sweetness into a single syllable? How is it that I can melt and turn into jelly just at the sound of his voice? The difference between when he answers the phone professionally and when he answers me is like the difference between a practical slide rule and a kitten. Which is probably the strangest analogy I'll ever make, but it's true.

I pulled the microphone closer and leaned my head against the wall of the cubby, pretending that it was his shoulder. "I've missed you."

"Yeah . . . me too." The desk fan whirred behind his voice. "How's it going up there?"

This was where I wanted to tell him about DeBeer, and my conversation with Leonard and Florence, but I was in a room with other people, and he was on the company line. "Okay."

My husband heard the hesitation, I think. "Just okay?"

"Long days. Plus, there's a gaggle of reporters up here." There. I could talk about that. "You know how much I enjoy having reporters around."

He chuckled a little. "I know. But I've got to admit, I like the fact that I'm getting to see the occasional photo of you."

"At least none of them are asking me to pose with a punch card."

"The one of you 'flying' down a corridor was pretty sweet." The phone rustled as he shifted. "How are you holding up?"

"Ready to be finished with training, honestly. If it weren't for the orbital trajectories, I think DeBeer would take his team out now and try to beat us to Mars." I cleared my throat. "He's an . . . interesting man."

"Oh?" Listening to my husband, I could almost see the lift of his brows and the way he tapped a pencil on the desk when he thought. "Say, Elma . . . I hate to ask you about work on our personal call, but did you need to run a teletype test in the next day or so?"

Bless him. I'd been trying to figure out a way to do that on my own, and couldn't come up with anything. But being married to the lead engineer meant that he could, very occasionally, flex the schedule for me. And yet . . . if I told him what was going on with DeBeer, he would do something about it. I might as well just broadcast it to Mission Control and ignore Florence and Leonard. Exhaling, I bit the inside of my cheek before answering. "I think I'm okay."

"You sure?"

"Yeah." I wasn't, and he knew that, but he couldn't fix anything that was troubling me. "Promise, I'll let you know if I need to run a test."

"You do that." Oh God, there was so much reluctance in his voice, and I wanted to reassure him that everything was all right. And for me, it was. My teammates, not so much.

I tried to put a smile in my voice and change the subject. "How about you? Win any more olives at poker?"

"Alas, no. And I'm afraid that I had to relinquish a jar of pickled onions to Reynard last time. He and Helen say hello, by the way."

"Give my regards back. Everyone misses Helen up here." I had caught up a lot over the past year, but that didn't make up for how long she had been training with them. Or the injustice of the way she had been treated. The line hissed between us. Sometimes the weight of longing to be with him effectively silenced me. It wasn't the longing itself, but that everything I wanted to say got tangled up in one phrase. "I miss you."

"Me too." He sighed. "Oh—I'm getting an intern next summer."

"Really? I thought you hated interns. What prompted that?"

"He's smart and dedicated. And his aunt is my wife."

I lifted my head fast enough that the movement started me spinning in the cubby. Putting a hand out to stop myself, I laughed. "You stinker. You didn't open with that? When? How did that happen?"

He laughed, and warmth filled the space between us like the sun coming out. "Tommy wrote a very nice, extremely formal letter—addressed me as Dr. York, even."

"How do you know it wasn't addressed to me?"

"Ha! Point. The envelope said Dr. Nathaniel York, so I figured that narrowed it down. Anyway—he's putting together his university applications, and wants some practical experience on his application form. Astronomy, he says. So he's looking at Berkeley, Wyoming, and Hawaii."

"I'll visit him in Hawaii."

Nathaniel chuckled. "That's what I said! Anyway, he's going to come stay with me and sleep on the sofa."

I gave a little whistle, trying to imagine that. Tommy was sweet, but still a teenage boy, and our apartment was snug with just two of us. Of course, I wouldn't be there . . . "So it'll be a bachelor pad."

"Something like that."

"I'm picturing you fellows leaving your socks everywhere. TV dinners. Poker nights."

"I had dancing girls and cigars in mind."

"Don't you corrupt my nephew, Nathaniel Ezra York." I wound the cord of the headset around my hand. The rough cloth was a cold substitute for my husband. "They've got enough on their hands with Rachel."

"Yeah, I guess so. Any news there?"

"The last letter I had from Hershel said they were sending her to a boarding school." I didn't want to share the full contents of the letter with everyone floating in the other cubicles, although it wouldn't draw the same sort of attention that conversations about the Mars Expedition team might. "Apparently, she stole a ring from Aunt Esther and sold it at a pawn shop."

In my ear, Nathaniel whistled with astonishment.

"They got it back, thank God, and grounded her again, but she snuck out to be with that boy. I don't know what's going on with her . . . Hershel says that Doris is just beside herself, feeling like she's failed as a parent."

"She only has to look at Tommy to know that's not true." Nathaniel's breath in the headphones as he sighed reminded me how far away he was. "Sometimes people make inexplicable decisions, but Rachel is her own person, and those decisions are hers. Maybe boarding school will give her the space to start making better choices."

He would have made such a good father. I closed my eyes to keep the sudden surge of tears behind my lids. Crying in zero gravity was such a hassle—the tears couldn't fall, so they just built up in a salty hemisphere around your eyes that all but blinded you. "Well. Take good care of Tommy when he gets there."

"I will." He chuckled. "Although I've been instructed to call him Thomas when he's out here for the internship. He's worried that 'Tommy' seems too childish for a college-bound young man."

I lifted my arm to press the cuff of my shirt against my eyes, soaking away the tears that were collecting there. Three years. In three years, where would they all be?

TWELVE

WIDE RACIAL PLOT HINTED AT IN CYGNUS 14 CRASH

JOHANNESBURG, South Africa, Sept. 19, 1962—The belief is growing among moderate leaders in the United States that a National Association for the Advancement of Colored People group of at least 20 persons plotted the crash of the *Cygnus 14* rocket. According to sources within the International Aerospace Coalition, some of the conspirators are astronauts themselves. Speaking under the condition of anonymity, an IAC employee said that the Negro astronauts have been under close scrutiny by agents of the Federal Bureau of Investigation since the crash. "What bothers me most," he said, "is the unwillingness of so many people at the IAC to face the fact that this was premeditated. It wasn't an accident."

I slid down the ladder from the sleeping quarters in the weightless center of *Lunetta* and into the ring that circled the station. The transition from zero-g to gravity wasn't as rough as returning to Earth. You got heavier as you slid down the ladder, in sort of the same way as when you let all the water out of the tub while you're still in it. Or maybe I'm the only one who does that.

Anyway, I usually take a moment at the bottom of the

ladder to get my bearings before I walk away from it. But on my way to the Monday morning staff meeting, I could hear shouting even before I hit the bottom of the ladder. My feet slapped against the rubber floor, and I spun toward the conference room. The turn was too fast, and I had to throw out a hand to steady myself on the ladder as the Coriolis effect caught me. One of the many reasons we used the mantra "slow is fast" in space.

"—no proof that it was me!" DeBeer's voice belted out of the conference room and down the long curving halls.

Parker responded, loud enough that his voice carried, but not so loud that I could understand him.

What on earth? I sprinted toward the conference room. Behind me, I heard someone else land at the bottom of the ladder.

"It's a newspaper article. Am I to be blamed for everything coming out of South Africa?"

"Van, cool it." Benkoski's easy voice met me at the door. "That's not what he's saying."

Some of the astronauts were already in the room, along with cups of coffee and imported donuts. Parker stood at the head of the table with his hands resting on either side of the briefing reports.

His face was red, and a vein bulged on the side of his neck, but his voice was tightly controlled. "What I am saying is that this"—he slid a page forward—"and other news articles like it can cause the mission to be canceled or pushed back, which is the same thing, given the current economic climate."

"I had nothing to do with it." DeBeer had his arms crossed over his chest, and was trying to look down his nose at Parker.

"Then you have no reason to object when I say that, from here on, any contact with reporters will be in the company of an IAC representative." Parker scanned the room, his gaze resting briefly on me. "That applies to everyone. Including me."

"So I am not allowed to speak to a fellow countryman? Is this what you are telling me?"

"If that countryman is a reporter, yes."

DeBeer looked as if he wanted to spit on the floor. "I am going to object to the IAC."

"The order comes from Clemons." Parker shrugged. "So you can do that if you want to, but it's not going to go well for you."

"He will take the easy route, when his focus should be the charges brought up in the article." DeBeer flicked his fingers toward Leonard, who sat in the back of the room with his head down and his hands knotted together in his lap.

Terrazas and Heidi entered the room, both with the same "What the—" expression on their faces.

Whatever was going on, it had nothing to do with Nathaniel. Or me. Hopefully. "What charges?"

DeBeer spun toward me, with a sardonic smile. "The IAC is trying to cover up the involvement of a ni—Negro astronaut in the crash of the *Cygnus 14* rocket."

"They can't 'cover up' something that didn't happen." I crossed my arms over my chest to match him. "We were both there, so you should know it didn't."

His smile faltered, as if he suddenly remembered who he was talking to. "Yes. Yes, we were. But you were at the front of the rocket, so you may not also remember that Dr. Flannery spent much time in whispered conversation with the terrorists."

"No one remembers that, because it didn't happen." Although he was right: if Leonard had been talking with any of the protesters while I was at the door of the plane acting as their go-between, I wouldn't know. But I was confident that Leonard had not been involved. I turned my back on DeBeer. "Are there still donuts?"

Rafael leaned against the built-in plastic counter and gestured to the vacuum-packed pastries. "Straight off the last supply ship. They almost taste fresh."

Joining in the effort to change the subject, Terrazas gave a short laugh. "You've been up here too long if you think that's fresh."

Parker sat down, tapping his pages like he was Clemons. "Let's get down to business, people. We're a month out from launch and we need to be on task."

One month. And we had only a seven-day window for departure, or we'd have to put the mission off for another year and a half while the planets came back into alignment. DeBeer would have to be an idiot to keep trying to get Leonard kicked off the flight. I prayed that he wasn't an idiot.

I grabbed a packaged donut and a cup of coffee. One of the early problems with being in space was that the congestion and sip-packs meant you couldn't really smell the coffee, which took half of the joy out of it. It was just bitter water. Bitter water with caffeine, but still. The centrifugal ring made all the difference. If you think this isn't important, then you have no understanding of how much of the space industry is fueled by coffee. I inhaled the redolent steam as I headed to an empty seat between Rafael and Kamilah.

The *Niña* crew tended to sit together on the left side of the table, while the *Pinta* sat on the right. It wasn't really planned, but we also tended to sit more or less opposite our counterpart, so I nodded to Heidi Voegeli as I settled in my chair.

She nodded back and jerked her head toward DeBeer at

the front of the table. In the sigh that followed, I read a certain amount of commiseration.

At the front of the table, Parker gave everyone time to settle as he sipped his own coffee. Setting the cup down, he gave a brisk nod. "This week we're focused on inventorying supplies and making sure they are secured. The *Lunetta* crews have been ferrying them over and loading the ships for us, but we want to make sure it's all really there."

"Can't run out to the store for a gallon of milk on the way to Mars." Benkoski winked.

Parker ignored him and carried on. "The *Niña* team will be Terrazas, Avelino, and Flannery. Meanwhile, I want Shamoun to check the medical supplies. Grey and York, you're on the kitchen."

I was so terribly surprised that he had the women doing inventory on the kitchen. What could possibly have caused him to assign us there?

"*Pinta* team will be DeBeer, Schnöhaus, and Stewman. Donaldson is checking the medical bay and supplies. Kitchen duty is Sabados and Voegeli."

Donaldson, Voegeli, and Sabados were sitting next to each other on the *Pinta* side, as if they might get their girl cooties on the men of the mission. Voegeli leaned over and whispered something to Sabados, who pursed her lips to hide a smile.

"Benkoski. You and I will be on BusyBee duty to ferry people across to the ships, then to do a full checklist inspection of the Bees." Parker looked up from his papers. "Mission Control thinks this will take us six hours, and they want us back on *Lunetta* in time for a press conference this evening."

Down the table, Rafael snorted. I knew what he meant.

If everything were under gravity, then, sure, six hours might be adequate. But it would take a half hour on each end just to go from *Lunetta* to the ships in the BusyBees. To say nothing of suiting up. And a press conference after a full day doing inventory? Ugh.

I bit into the donut, and it was made of Styrofoam. The sugar on the outside had a slight plastic character from the packaging. They had better have snacks at the press conference.

Parker let us grumble for a moment before giving a lopsided smile. "I told them that was unreasonable, so we've got two days, but the press conference is still this evening."

Ruby Donaldson, the *Pinta*'s medic, lifted her coffee. "Bless you, Father."

Parker shook his head. "Just a reminder that no one is to speak to any of the reporters without an IAC representative present. Talk to Betty if you need assistance."

DeBeer muttered something in Afrikaans and drew a harsh line across a page in his binder.

Parker leaned forward. "Heard and understood. Why don't you say that in English for the rest of the group?"

DeBeer turned red and ground his teeth together, then he shrugged. "If we need Betty, will we find her in your bunk?"

The room went quiet, uncovering the constant hush of fans that was our backdrop on *Lunetta*. We all knew about the affair. We all knew that Betty and Parker had continued it on the station. But they were discreet. None of us said anything about it because, frankly, Parker was nicer when he was getting laid.

Parker kept his gaze set on DeBeer. "Thank you for sharing with the class. I'll note, for the record, that the Afrikaans word 'hoer' means just what it sounds like.

'Whore' is a harsh thing to call any journalist, no matter how annoying the press conferences are. These folks have jobs to do, same as we do, and cooperating with them gets it done faster."

"Is cooperating what they're—" Florence stopped and cleared her throat. "Is cooperating what the journalists are doing when they ask questions about the colored crew members?"

"That topic is closed." Parker pulled his attention back to his papers, ignoring Florence's scoffing huff. "As a heads up for next week, this is a reminder that Mission Control is sending a team up for last looks before departure. Slight change in staffing there, as they've added our lead engineer to that team."

Nathaniel.

The room went hot. Everyone turned to look at me and I wanted to melt under the table. No one else would get to see their family before we left. He shouldn't have made that change, and yet I was so very, very glad he did.

"York. You'll meet that rocket with Betty. Be aware that the press corps will be there, so I recommend talking with her ahead of time for any tactical advice." Parker grinned like a shark. "As a note, the BusyBees are soundproof."

I hate him so much. I grabbed the Fibonacci sequence and clung to it so I didn't lunge across the table and slap him. *1, 1, 2, 3, 5, 8, 13 . . .*

Across the table, Heidi glared at me with naked anger. Oh, Nathaniel . . . I had just gotten people to accept me as part of the team and not some interloper here for publicity reasons. Why had Clemons said yes? They had to know what this would do to morale.

While my face flamed out, DeBeer leaned toward Benkoski. "See. I told you they were the publicity ship."

Benkoski, who had known me for years, had a sour smile

on his face, like he was trying not to scowl at me. He laughed. "Yeah. Well. York's always been good at publicity."

"We all have our jobs to do." Parker's shark smile was still fixed, showing all his perfect teeth. "York. You'll have the morning off to make sure you can look real pretty to greet the old man. The press will love that."

I floated next to the airlock in one of the weightless sections of *Lunetta* as the latest rocket from Earth arrived. In training, on the station, I had fallen into the rhythms of my crewmates. When Parker had told me that Nathaniel was coming, the date hadn't occurred to me.

Nathaniel would be here for Rosh Hashanah.

Everyone was setting up for a dry run of the departure over on the ships. Well, everyone except for me, Betty, and the entire press corps. They all floated at my back, comfortable with zero-g after repeated trips up to the space station taking away seats from real astronauts.

One of the station crew kicked off with his toes and flew to the hatch, where he double-checked the pressure, then peered through the porthole for a visual confirmation. Just because the delta-pressure gauge was at 4.9 didn't mean that there was necessarily something on the other side of this door—it could be a short. After a moment, he pumped the rachet handle and hauled the airlock door back.

Inside, the hatch for the shuttle swung open and released a brief whiff of Earth. I'm sure this is my imagination, because my sense of smell is terrible in space, but it seems as if the air coming off of a flight from Earth smells different than the clinical recycled air we get up here. Passengers filed out and the crew greeted the ones they knew. Most of them were en route to the moon or coming up for rotation on *Lunetta*.

Once the astronauts were out, the team from Mission Control floated through the airlock. Bubbles, Michael Boundy, Ken Harrison, and Howard Teng. All white men, except for Teng.

And at the back, the very last person off the rocket, grinning like he was about to burst into tears, was my husband.

With the photographers at my back, I plastered my regulation smile on over every bit of joy and grief in my soul. "Welcome to *Lunetta*, gentlemen. The crew will stow your personal luggage while I zip you over to the *Niña* and *Pinta* in one of the BusyBees."

Behind me, the plummy British voice of the reporter from the *Times* called out, "Dr. York! How does it feel to see your wife?"

"Swell." Nathaniel kicked closer to the front of the group, moving awkwardly. He'd been in space before, but it had been a couple of years. It took him two tries to get his foot hooked under one of the guide rails.

Bubbles managed to bounce even while holding on to a rail. "Aw, go on and kiss her. You'll be useless until you do."

This was, I think, the only time in my life I have ever been reluctant to kiss my husband. The moment I did, all of the cameras would click and clatter and snap at once. I knew the system well enough by this point to know that every major paper on Earth would carry a photo of us kissing. But, as Parker so kindly pointed out, we all had a job to do, and mine was to make space and Mars look inviting to the women of Earth.

My paperwork might say computer, but I was a poster girl for the stars.

Still smiling, I pushed off with my toes and translated to the guide rail by my husband. Nathaniel's warmth radiated off of him. I inhaled, but the scent of him lay hidden behind the congestion of zero gravity. Shy as a new bride, I smiled up at my husband of twelve years. "Hello, Dr. York."

"Dr. York. It's very fine to see you." Nathaniel took my hand in his, and I found the callous on his index finger. He leaned in to whisper. "L'shanah tovah tikatevi v'taihatemi."

We wouldn't have a formal dinner or hear shofar blasts or even have candles to light, but we could at least greet each other for the New Year. I whispered back, "L'shanah tovah tikatev v'taihatem."

He smiled, and then nodded at the crowd behind us. "May I?"

I bit my lower lip and nodded. *3.141 . . .*

He bent, eclipsing the hangar and the reporters and the engineers and Betty and Earth and everything. My husband tasted of fresh mint and his own inscrutable self. His cheeks were baby-soft, except for that tiny patch of bristle right under his lip that he always missed.

Pulling back, my cheeks burned as the engineers broke into applause and cheers. Lights snapped and flashed around us. I clung to Nathaniel's hand for a moment longer, trying to draw in an even breath.

3.141592 . . .

As my therapist had taught me lo those many years ago, I forced a breath out until my lungs were empty and the inhalation followed almost naturally. Nathaniel rested his free hand on my lower back and cleared his throat. "Right. I think the IAC allotted 4.5 minutes for greetings, and we have a timetable to keep."

That got a laugh from the gallery, including some members of the *Lunetta* crew who were hanging around to see Nathaniel. I released my husband's hand and slipped back. "If you'll follow me, the BusyBee is right this way. The

Mars Expedition teams are looking forward to seeing all of you."

I shouldn't be working during Rosh Hashanah, but at least I wasn't alone.

Nathaniel split his team between the ships. I don't know who made the decision, but Nathaniel inspected the *Pinta,* rather than my ship, along with Bubbles, sending the rest to look at the *Niña*. Again, I don't know who made the decision, but I did notice that Teng was assigned to our "separate but equal" ship.

The day was long, and as boring as you could hope for from an inspection. I think the most exciting moment was when Teng found Rafael's chocolate stash and threatened to "inspect" it. Our team was solid, at least as far as the work was concerned.

I didn't get Nathaniel to myself until after the inspections, and a group dinner, and yet another press conference. When I did, I pulled him into the BusyBee. The tiny ship was little more than a shielded tube with an engine and seats. To be sure, it had life support, but it was designed for carrying people in airless space, and would never survive reentry.

I activated the fans that circulated air with the main station and shut the hatch, sealing us in. Nathaniel floated behind me and pulled me back into his chest. He wrapped his arms around me, burying his face against my neck. My whole body ached from missing him.

His breath warmed my cheek and stirred the fine hairs at the nape of my neck. "How bad is the DeBeer situation?"

I turned in his arms, which set us both to rotating slowly in the aisle of the BusyBee. "*That's* why you're here?"

Nathaniel gave a familiar smirk and found the zipper of my flight suit. "Well . . . there are other reasons, too."

I rolled my eyes at him, even while my engine was priming. "And here I thought you were up for Rosh Hashanah."

"That was a happy coincidence of timing." He ran his thumb along the edge of my collarbone. "As you know, I'm a terrible Jew."

"How are you going to survive three years?"

"Don't know." He sighed, then his foot caught one of the chairs, stopping his rotation. "Tell me about DeBeer."

Mine kept going for a moment, spinning me past him. With one hand, I gripped his upper arm and anchored myself. "I don't think he'll be a problem once we leave. I mean, he can still be an asshole, but there won't be the opportunities for mischief that he has currently."

"Yeah . . . I wish South Africa had sent us someone else." Nathaniel tugged at the zipper of my suit, letting in some welcome cool. "At least he's just the copilot of the *Pinta*."

"Benkoski will keep him in check." I hoped. Sliding my free hand across Nathaniel's shoulder, I sought the buttons of his shirt. "I told you that I was fine."

"And then the South African newspaper article came out, and everything surrounding the Black astronauts started up again. Clemons—"

"Tell me you didn't talk to him about this."

Nathaniel leaned in and nuzzled the bare skin below my collar bone. "How do you think I got rotated back onto the inspection team?"

"If I'd wanted you to—wait. What do you mean, 'back' on?"

He pushed the flight suit aside to bare my shoulder. Slipping a finger under my bra strap, he grimaced a little. "Ah. When you got assigned to the Mars mission, there was a general consensus that our relationship might cause me to have confused priorities relating to the mission."

"Clearly they don't know you."

"No, they do know me. I would sacrifice everyone on both ships to keep you safe." He pushed the bra strap to the side, followed it down to the cup, and then dipped inside it to cradle my breast.

"I need you to not make exceptions for me."

"I try not to, but it's not actually possible. It's why we pulled Carmouche from a lot of the work when Helen was tapped for the mission."

"Please." Pulling myself closer to Nathaniel, I kissed his neck. Here, with my face pressed against my husband, I could finally get a faint whiff of his familiar scent. "It makes things harder with the team if there's favoritism."

Nathaniel tugged the other sleeve of my flight suit down with no grace or finesse. We spun away from the seats, drifting down the center aisle of the BusyBee. "I was only allowed up because Clemons knows that, *after* you, there is nothing more important to me than seeing the crew to Mars and safely back."

I pulled my hands free of my sleeves, shivering a little in the cool air. Or maybe shivering because my husband was running his hands down my back, around my sides, up past my breasts, and then repeating the orbit. How can a person be cold and overheated at the same time?

"We have a conflict, then, because for me, seeing the crew to Mars and safely back is more important than just me."

Nathaniel lifted his head. "Is it more important than me?"

God help me, I hesitated.

His eyes widened, and he laughed. "Well. I guess I should have expected that."

"No—" I caught both of his hands and brought them to my lips. "It's not that. It's that I can't imagine a situation where I would have to make that choice, your life or theirs. You might."

"Yes." His blue eyes searched mine. I don't know what he was looking for. "I might. Forgive me."

Rosh Hashanah is a time of forgiveness and atonement. It is a time of joy and reflection. The rest of our conversation was all of those and conducted without spoken language, though it was not necessarily silent.

At least Parker was right: the BusyBee was soundproof.

THIRTEEN

14 ASTRONAUTS SPEED TOWARD MARS AT 36,000 MPH

By JOHN NOBLE WILFORD

Special to The National Times

KANSAS CITY, KS, Oct. 19, 1962—The fourteen astronauts of the First Mars Expedition soared through the black emptiness of space tonight on their way to man's first rendezvous with Mars. For those on Earth, when the three ships of the Mars fleet fired their mighty engines, they appeared to be bright stars circling the night sky in tight symmetry. Their ignition marks the beginning of man's most far-reaching journey yet. After they completed nearly two orbits to build up their speed to a blistering 36,000 mph, the fleet's booster rockets fired to send the crafts out of Earth orbit and toward Mars. It will take the astronauts 320 days to reach the red planet.

Do you remember where you were when the First Mars Expedition left Earth orbit? I have been told that a quarter of the people alive on Earth watched on televisions or through telescopes, or listened to us on the radio. One hundred percent of the people on the moon did. There were cameras in the command module to record our voyage for posterity. Farther out, they would not transmit a clear picture, but for the departure, the people of Earth got to watch us go about our business, intercut with commentary from Walter Cronkite.

I had been in the NavComp seat before. I sat at the window with my sextant and charts, my pencil and graph paper, and outside . . . darkness.

Darkness and the Earth. That spinning globe of luminescent blues and whites and the sparkle of cities, like stars scattered upon the ground. And somewhere below the clouds was my husband.

The comm crackled and Malouf came on the line as CAPCOM. "*Niña* 1, Kansas."

Parker toggled on the comm. "Go ahead, Kansas. *Niña* 1."

"Okay. Coming up on three hours and fifteen minutes as per flight plan; we have you Go."

"Roger. Go." Parker grinned and glanced around the cabin at us. Sure, we were professionals, but this was the call to launch us away from Earth.

"You can expect that the S-IVB will be ten degrees off in pitch at SEP attitude; however, that is Go. There is no problem involved."

"Roger." He toggled off the mic and glanced over at me. "You got that?"

"Confirmed." I updated my notations in the nav manual. A ten-degree pitch difference fell into the category of minor and expected things—heck, we'd run sims where it was further off than that—but if we didn't start taking it into account now, the error would muddy all the data downstream. I was the redundancy in case we lost touch with Earth and their computers.

Around me, the rest of the crew did their assigned tasks, while I busied myself with the mathematics of space. Numbers danced beneath my fingers like stars in the sky.

Malouf came on the line again. "*Niña* 1, Kansas. We

would like to ask whether you did a VERB 66 ENTER to transfer the state vector from MSM to MM slot. We didn't copy that down here."

Florence looked up from the mechanical computer, where she was mirroring my work. "I haven't done that yet."

Parker frowned. "We did not."

"Okay."

Okay? That was it? I held my pencil poised over the paper. "Does he want us to do that now? It's not on the schedule until—"

"Do you want us to do that now?"

"At your convenience."

"Roger." Parker toggled the mic off. "Got that, Grey?"

"Confirmed." She scribbled a number on a tablet to the side of the toggles for the mechanical computer.

The idea was that if we lost contact with Earth and something happened to me, the mechanical computer could function as a backup, but it could only hold about thirty operations in its memory. Why they wanted us to update it now, I couldn't tell you, but the ways of Mission Control were sometimes mysterious.

I leaned toward Florence. "Need any help?"

She shook her head. "I've got a breather on the radio until they want to test the VHF, and my memory of the sims is that you'll be pretty busy for the next—"

"*Niña* 1, Kansas. We would like to have an approximate GET of your SEP maneuver to use for our ephemeris tracking data."

I rolled my eyes. On the ground, they sometimes forgot how long it took to actually do things. If they'd been relying on the mechanical computer, Florence would still be keying in data. I tried not to sound smug as I beat her to the answer. "Three hours, forty minutes, zero seconds."

Parker raised an eyebrow. "You didn't even look that up."

"That's why I get paid the big bucks."

Parker repeated the GET to Malouf. Down on Earth, the folks in Mission Control would be conferring on the data we sent to make sure everything was calibrated and on track.

Toggling the occasional switch, Parker watched his gauges. "Got anything for Kansas, York?"

"I've got the exact callout here for you, and a burn status report." I nodded, without looking up from my paper. Poor Florence over at the mechanical contraption was still keying in the numbers. It might calculate faster, but that's only if you didn't count the time it took to program the damn thing. "DELTA-VX minus 00011, DELTA-VY plus 0002, DELTA-VZ minus 0002, roll 0, pitch 180, yaw 0."

Parker repeated all of that to the ground, while I went back to updating the nav plans. Granted, ground control should just send us the updated information, but I needed to have things already in place in case we lost communication.

"Goddamn it." Terrazas leaned toward the window and then sat back in his seat, shaking his head. "Inertia's got the S-IVB traveling right on our tail."

That was the rocket that had pushed us up to full velocity for the trip. I grimaced and met Terrazas's gaze. "This is going to be like the moon shot again. Parker, can you get us away from it? Otherwise, the star field will be obscured when it vents."

"Swell." Parker shook his head. "I'll have to do a couple small maneuvers to stay away from the S-IVB."

"Too late." Outside my window, the stars seemed to multiply into hundreds of thousands of little fireflies. Caught in the light, the frozen propellant sparkled like stars, and my job suddenly got hundreds of thousands of times harder, just like it had on the moon mission. Fortunately, I had a lot of practice at struggling to identify stars.

Parker sighed and toggled Mission Control. "Kansas, *Niña* 1. The S-IVB is venting, and it's right on our tail."

"Roger. Understand; that is supposedly a nonpropulsive vent. The big blowdown maneuver starts at 04:44:55, and the vent occurs at 05:07:55."

Terrazas snorted. "Nonpropulsive, maybe, but it's like a geyser."

Malouf asked, "How far away from the S-IVB you are now?"

"Between one hundred fifty and three hundred meters."

"Okay, Parker. On your additional separation maneuver, we recommend that you make a radial burn, point your plus x-axis toward Earth, and thrust minus X for .91 meters per second. Over."

"I don't want to do that; I'll lose sight of the S-IVB."

"Okay. The reason we want a radial burn is to increase your midcourse correction so we can use the SPS. Stand by on it."

I lifted my head. "We don't need to do that. Right now, our gimbal angles are about . . . roll's about 190, pitch about 320, and yaw is about 340. We could do it in this position."

"*Niña* 1, Kansas. Where are you relative to the booster?"

Parker studied me for a second before he responded. "We are directly above the S-IVB with the sun on the right side of the booster and visible in our left number one window." As soon as he toggled off the mic, he turned to me. "Get those numbers ready for me. They're going to ask."

"Copy." I nodded and set the numbers down on the page to describe the model of the ship I held in my head. I was fully an adult before I realized that other people did not relate to numbers the way I did. For them, they are abstract shapes on a page that, at best, relate to a physical number of objects. For me, they have form and definition and mass and texture and color. I could hold the ship and the S-IVB and Mars and Earth in my head until the impurities burnished away and only the pure, smooth calculus of space remained.

Back on Earth, Malouf said, "Okay. Understand; the sun is on the right side of the S-IVB and coming in your number one window. And are you—when you give us those angles, that means that your plus x-axis is pointed at it with those angles. Is that confirm?"

"Confirmed. But York thinks we can do the burn without changing our gimbal angles."

I flipped to a reference page in my binder, just to double-check my numbers. "You can do a P52 realign, and that should take care of it. The S-IVB pitches about . . . It'll pitch about ten degrees of its final attitude during the slingshot maneuver attitude."

From her station, Florence punched a button on the mechanical computer and it began to clunk away, with the snapping sound of vacuum tubes firing.

Parker pursed his lips and nodded to Terrazas. "Two point four meters a second sound right to you?"

"That'll get us away and keep us lined up." Terrazas leaned forward to look out his window. "It's still in the same position."

Nodding, Parker turned on the mic to Mission Control. "Kansas, we're going to have to hold up on the cisMars navigation until after this next little maneuver."

"Confirmed, Parker. We understand." Behind Malouf, I could just make out the muted hum of voices in Mission Control. Even straining, I couldn't pick out Nathaniel's among them. "Can you give us an updated readout of your gimbal angles when your plus x-axis is pointed toward the booster, please?"

"Stand by." Parker turned over his shoulder to me. "Clear enough for you to get COAS on it?"

"Confirmed." I couldn't sight back on Earth's horizon, but if I put the shade on my sextant, the Sun was an option.

"*Niña* 1, Kansas."

"Go ahead, Kansas."

"Could you give us those gimbal angles, Parker, when you have a chance?"

Parker rolled his eyes. I was right there with him. Everything took longer in space than Mission Control thought. His voice was very calm when he replied. "York is getting the COAS right on it now, so it will be accurate."

Still working, I murmured, "Thank you."

"Done right or done over, is what my old man always said."

I sighted the final angle and leaned back from the window. "Okay. With the COAS right on the S-IVB, the roll reads 105, the pitch is 275, and the yaw is about 325."

Parker repeated all of that to me, then turned back to the mic and repeated it to Malouf, who repeated it back to him in the endless call-and-response litany of astronauts. "I'm beginning the burn at 2.4 meters per second, radially upward."

The thrusters beneath us fired and my rump slapped against my seat as we suddenly had weight again. It was a fraction of G, but after being weightless for the past nine hours, it felt like being on Earth again. When Parker let up on the throttle, inertia lifted me up into my shoulder straps. This was why we stayed strapped in during maneuvers.

"Kansas, we made the burn at 7.7 plus X plus 00001 Y;

and Z's are all zeros. Gimbal angles, roll 180, pitch 310, and yaw 020."

"Confirmed. How is that booster looking now? Is it drifting away rapidly, or how does it look?"

Parker leaned forward to look out the window. "Terrazas, you see it?"

"Hang on." He also leaned forward. "Got it. We're ninety degrees from its x-axis, and we must be three hundred meters away and moving out."

Parker looked across Terrazas to me. "We get you far enough away to have a clear star field?"

I rested my head against the window and gazed out at the dark. The spray from the S-IVB's venting hung like artificial stars drifting in a clearly defined nimbus around the booster, but the rest of the night sky around us was dark and clear. "Confirmed."

"Kansas, this is *Niña* 1. I think we've got clearance; we got a little behind on our P23's, but I suggest we go ahead and start those now."

"Confirmed, Parker. Thank you. At your convenience, could you give us the PRD reading? And as far as the P23 goes, that's just fine to get started with it. It looks like your first star, which is number thirty-one, should be good until about 05:15 GET. Over."

Number 31. Arc to Arcturus, and straight on till morning.

FOURTEEN

ANNOUNCER: The American Broadcasting Company presents *Headline Edition* with Taylor Grant. November 2nd, 1962.

GRANT: General Bradley's speech in Kansas City today was one of several interesting news developments dealing with our military defenses. He addressed the Women's National Press Club, and told the assembled ladies that the United States must spend heavily on military readiness as far into the future as we can see at this time. Bringing order to the civil unrest at home and abroad is of paramount importance to provide a stable basis for economic growth.

We were only two weeks into the journey when we had our first equipment failure.

I floated into the zero-g toilet on my way to the command module and grabbed the door frame to brake hard. A spinning globe of urine floated in the middle of the tiny head, surrounded by accompanying satellites.

"Oh, for crying out loud." I pushed back to look up and down the spindle—the long hall that ran the length of the *Niña*—to see if the culprit was still in sight, but whoever had clogged the thing had just left it.

We had a gravity toilet in the centrifugal ring, but this one was used by whoever was on duty in the command module. Theoretically. In practice, it was usually faster to go down to the ring than mess with the zero-g rigging. But that didn't mean we could let it be out of order. Much as I wanted to ignore the problem, since I'd found it, and had time, it was on me to deal with it. The fact was that there were only seven of us on the ship. No one was going to want to fix the toilet any more than I did, and leaving it was a surefire way to make folks resent me. Again.

It really should have been on whoever fouled the thing in the first place, but my wrath could wait until after the urine had been contained.

The excrement satellites were gross, but not as problematic as the liquid waste. The last thing we wanted was for a ball of urine to go "whizzing" down the spindle. Partly because it was disgusting, but also because that much liquid could cause all manner of mischief in the electrical systems. And the air intake. And also, gross.

Trying to dodge the globules, I pulled off a length of toilet paper. The first order of business was to deal with the little spheres so I could get farther into the head without getting covered in pee. In a sort of weird dance, I swiped the toilet paper through the air, catching little droplets as I went. The paper soaked through almost immediately.

There's nothing quite as disgusting as someone else's effluence. I stuffed the paper into the disposal pouch and grabbed more tissue as my skin tightened with the sheer ick. Clearly, I couldn't just soak it all up with tissue, because that would throw our rations off. The toilet was designed to use a vacuum to pull the waste down into its tank so we only needed to use tissue for tidying at the end of operations.

I slid into the bathroom and pulled open the little cupboard for a clean disposal pouch. Opening it, I shoved tissue inside to create a little cushion. With both hands, I held it open and brought it down over the main globule.

It was sort of like snaring a butterfly in a net. But gross.

When the urine hit the tissue, its surface tension broke

and some of it wicked into the paper until it reached saturation point. The remaining dregs began spinning inside the bag. I pinched the opening shut and nested it into another bag. Then I used tissue as a sort of glove to snatch satellites out of the air and add them to the bag.

Really. Was it too much to ask that people clean up after themselves?

The job had been gross, but really hadn't taken me that long. I shoved the bag into the disposal slot. This was so coming up in the Monday meeting. Heck, I would probably bring it up at dinner. I grabbed an alcohol wipe and began scrubbing my hands. It felt like a film of grime coated them, particularly under my nails.

The toilet belched. An arc of urine floated up into the room like a long, yellow piece of rubber. It contracted, forming another globe.

"You have got to be kidding me." I grabbed another bag and shoved more toilet paper into it.

As I brought it over the urine sphere, the toilet belched again. I flinched, just a little, but enough that the edge of the bag clipped the sphere. Urine clung to my hand, wrapping around it in a warm, liquid glove. I swallowed hard and clenched my jaw. So. Gross. Moving carefully, I reached for the tissue with my clean hand and brought a wad up to the bag. One end went into the bag and the other into the stuff coating my hand. The surface tension wicked into the paper and drew a lot of the stuff into the bag.

At this point, I really didn't care about wasting paper. I just wanted my hands to be clean.

I also needed to get rid of the bag fast enough that I could pay attention to the toilet itself, because I was *not* doing this again. As soon as I had my hands mostly dry and the liquid contained, I tossed the bag into the disposal slot.

Pulling myself down toward the toilet, I let my legs drift out into the corridor.

Taking a breath, I forced myself to slow down. "Slow is fast, Elma." Rushing was just going to get my hands covered in muck again.

From this vantage, I was able to reach the toilet's maintenance hatch. Thank heavens it was a friction fit, so that I could pop it open. I pulled the lid off and laid it over the toilet. I was able to use the brace that held us on the seat to snug the lid down. It wasn't a perfect seal, but it would hold most of the mess inside the toilet. I hoped.

Once that was reasonably secure, I reached inside the maintenance hatch and slapped the cutoff switch. Nothing happened. I slapped it again.

It's a little embarrassing that it took me until that moment to realize the fan wasn't running. The reason the cutoff switch didn't work was because the vacuum flow was already off.

The good news is that this meant that the problem didn't arise from someone being a schlub. The bad news was that, without someone to blame for negligence, it really was my problem.

I sighed and kicked backward out of the head, spinning in midair to face the command module. Pushing off on the guide rails, I "supermanned" myself toward the CM. With a flutter of my left hand, I angled my body so I passed cleanly through the door and drew my knees up to transfer some momentum into the beginning of a somersault. Stretching out as I came upright, I hooked a foot under one of the rails on the floor of the CM.

Terrazas sat in the pilot chair, monitoring our distance from the *Pinta* and the *Santa Maria* supply ship. Unless something dramatic happened, our inertia should keep us all in an even progression through space. Later we'd be able to leave the bridge unmanned, but Mission Control was being properly cautious with the first part of the voyage.

Rafael was floating up, away from the pilot's seat. He looked over his shoulder and cleared his throat. "York. What's up?"

"The head is clogged." I pulled myself over to the supply chest. "Just grabbing the tool kit."

"Need any help?" He pulled the zipper of his flight suit higher and pressed a hand against Terrazas's shoulder to turn fully toward me. "I'm just finishing up here."

"I wish, but it's such a small space. I've got it."

"Great." He grinned and swiped a hand through his hair. "Holler if you need me."

I should have just said "yes." There are times when my Southern upbringing asserts itself in ways that are not actually helpful. Take, for instance, the fact that Rafael is our engineer and *would* be better suited to fixing the head than I was, and yet . . . And yet, I had demurred because I was trained not to make waves.

I had demurred because, in the South, he would have offered again, and then I could have accepted graciously. But Rafael was not Southern, this was not a social engagement, and he hadn't been offering me iced tea—it was a job. I swear, I can be so stupid sometimes.

But I grabbed the tool kit from its cupboard and kicked into the spindle, flying toward the head. Once there, I seated the kit in one of the sockets built into the walls of the ship. Popping the lid open, I slid out the compartment that held the gloves. Beautiful, glorious, latex gloves.

I have never been so happy to see latex. Well. I mean . . . not in a work setting, at any rate.

Ahem. With the gloves on, I pried a corner of the toilet lid up and peeked in. Yep. It had belched again.

While I'd been up in the CM, I'd had time to think through what was going on. Mind you, before training for this trip, I could repair an airplane or hotwire a car, but plumbing hadn't been in my skill set. The IAC believed in thorough training and redundancy, so all of us were pilots and plumbers and geologists now. At least at a basic level.

My bet was that a piece of waste was clogging the airflow and that the fan had shut down to keep from burning out. That meant that all I had to do was to clear the obstruction and restart the fan, and then it would all be fine. In theory.

I left my improvised lid in place and pulled myself down to the access hatch. Snaking my hand inside, I sealed the waste compartment shut. Thank goodness that the waste compartment was built in, so that we could empty the thing safely. With that sealed, I activated the dump function to send our waste matter down into the composter. That, at least, would keep the toilet from vomiting things back into the head.

Really, I should have done that earlier. As I said, there are times when I can be stupid.

"How's it going?"

Rafael's voice made me yelp in ways that are entirely embarrassing. See, this is the thing no one mentions about space. With fans running all the time to circulate air, it's noisy. When you float, there aren't footfalls. Sneaking up on people is stupidly easy, even when you don't mean to.

I caught myself with a hand on the wall. "Okay. I just dumped the waste so I could pull the suction pump out. I'm guessing it's clogged, and that's what's causing the backup."

"Sounds plausible." He reoriented so his head was in the room and both of us had our legs sticking out in the corridor. "You shut down the fan?"

"It was already off." I reached into the access space again

and loosened the pump, silently thanking the IAC for making things modular and easy to repair. We carried spares for every part of the ship, and had more on the *Santa Maria*. "Hand me a bag?"

If Rafael was here, he could darn well be useful. And if he offered further help, I would absolutely take him up on it. Plastic rustled, and he slid a bag into my field of vision, already open.

I grabbed it, wrapping as much of the open end around the pipe as I could, so that when I pulled the pump free, the mess was at least a little bit contained. The good part about zero-g is that you don't have to worry about drips. Floating around and bumping into things? Yes. But not drips.

I pulled the suction pump out into the light and there was, indeed, an obstruction across it. It wasn't feces, which is what I'd expected to find. Nothing except human waste was supposed to go in the toilets, yet this was pale and translucent, like a latex glove—a latex glove with one finger, designed for a very specific purpose.

With a gloved hand, I pulled the condom free.

Parker.

Sure, there were other men on the ship, but Parker had a history. I'd had to dry the tears of more than one young WASP who hadn't felt like she could turn him down . . . I sighed and turned to grab another bag. I'd have to discreetly check in with Florence and Kamilah to make sure they were okay.

Rafael already had a bag at the ready and let me plunk the condom in there. He twisted the top shut. "Hell. You shouldn't be seeing—I'll go ahead and finish up."

Almost—I almost declined again, and insisted that condoms weren't shocking. Heck, Nathaniel and I used them regularly now. Or did. Or would. Whatever. It didn't matter, because Rafael was the engineer on board, and it made more sense to let him do this. Drawing in a breath, I nodded. "Thanks. I appreciate it."

He tucked the bag into the disposal slot. "Sorry you had to . . ."

"I've seen condoms before." I pushed back to slip into the spindle, pulling my gloves off as I floated clear. "Don't suppose you'd be willing to mention it to the guys, though? It might be awkward coming from me."

Rafael snorted. "Yeah. I know whose it is. I'll talk to him."

"Thanks." But I was still going to talk to Kamilah and Florence, because proper disposal of waste was the smallest part of the problem.

FIFTEEN

ANNOUNCER: The American Broadcasting Company presents *Headline Edition* with Taylor Grant. November 9th, 1962.

GRANT: Thousands of members of the Earth First movement gathered outside the Kansas campus of International Aerospace Coalition to protest what they see as wasteful spending. They formed a human blockade across the entrances to the campus, preventing employees from entering or leaving. The United Nations was forced to deploy troops to get the protesters to disperse.

Kamilah walked into the kitchen with a handful of fresh radishes. My mouth watered at the thought of something that hadn't been freeze-dried or vacuum packed and irradiated. Holding the radishes in both hands, she struck a pose, lifting them over her head like the spoils of war. "I come bearing tribute."

"Your sacrifice is appreciated and accepted." In truth, I was a little jealous that she'd drawn gardening on this week's duty roster. The garden module was my favorite spot on the *Niña*. But this week, I was on kitchen duty. Originally, we'd rotated daily, but it turned out to be easier to plan if we stayed in the same area for a week. Selfishly, for me, it meant one week where I could keep more or less kosher. "Just set them on the counter."

"Need any help?" She plunked the little red spheres down on the counter. You don't really appreciate the merits of gravity, even centrifugally provided gravity, until you are trying to cook. Especially until you are trying to bake. You need gravity for bread to rise, and I was attempting challah tonight.

"I'm in pretty good shape—" Again with me being stupid. She and I were the only ones in the kitchen, and the guys wouldn't come in until the dinner break, so this offered an opportunity to talk to her about Parker. "Actually, yeah. Would you wash them while I work on the potatoes?"

"Already did it in the garden wing." She held one up for display. "Keeps the soil there. Want me to snap the leaves off?"

"Perfect. And then sliced thin?" Meanwhile, I was grating the potatoes into a bowl to make a kugel. "I am so glad things have changed since the early days of the program, because I don't know if I could handle three years of food from a tube."

Kamilah made a face, laughing. "I tried some of the 'meatloaf' on a dare. I never thought I'd taste something that made hospital food appealing."

"The applesauce wasn't so bad, because it was supposed to be mashed up." I ran the potato down the grater trying not to catch my fingers. "You never saw the kibble."

"You aren't serious." Kamilah looked up from the radish she was beheading with surgical precision. "Kibble?"

"A complete meal in a cup of kibble. Lightweight—which was a serious concern before they developed the U-MORS." That's an upper atmosphere molecular oxygen refueling station. "Some bright person on the UN Aerospace Committee had recommended a brother-in-law who was a military nutritionist. Only he was a veterinarian."

This got a barking laugh from Kamilah, making the tip of her nose curl down and her dark eyes crinkle nearly shut. She was easily the prettiest of us, with long, glossy dark hair that she wore pinned into a bun at the base of her neck. "What were they thinking?"

"Men. Bless their hearts."

"I dunno. Rafael is a pretty good cook."

"True." I grabbed another potato and contemplated my options for shifting the conversation. I couldn't quite bring myself to come right out and ask her about Parker, because I didn't want her to think that I thought she was that sort of woman. "Parker, though."

Kamilah wrinkled her nose, but didn't seem bothered by the mention of him. "Do you think we could ask Mission Control to arrange the duty roster so he's never in the kitchen again?"

"You don't like overcooked hotdogs and undercooked baked potatoes?"

"It's a good argument for rotating every day. Because, really . . . another week of that will kill me." She straightened up, waving her knife. "Actually. As flight medic, I could make a good argument that it's in the interests of the crew's health and safety."

Ah! A conversational opening. I lunged for it as I oh so casually set the grater on the counter. "Speaking of health and safety . . . I had to clear a blockage from the zero-g head at the aft end of the spindle."

"Ugh. You wore gloves? No open cuts?"

"Heh. Yes, Mother." I pulled open the cabinet to grab a baking dish and waited until I had turned around so I could watch her face. "It had been blocked by a condom."

Kamilah stopped chopping the radish and lifted her head, mouth open slightly in surprise. "No. Already?"

"What—What do you mean, 'already'?"

"We're only three weeks in, and—" She shook her head. "Sorry. Sexual activity was the subject of a fair bit of conversation among the flight surgeons. There was some argument for an all-male crew, but that was ix-nayed for publicity reasons. And thank you, Lady Astronaut, or I wouldn't get to be here."

My face was probably as red as the radishes. Yes, I was a married woman and yes, I am comfortable with "rocket launches" with my husband, but the idea of having a meeting about such things? As my mother would have said, perish the thought. "So, this was an IAC condom?" And then another thought occurred to me. "They aren't—I mean . . . They're not *expecting* us to . . . ?"

Kamilah laughed. "Oh, God no. Though, mind you, the general unofficial consensus was that some of the crew would probably pair off at some point, and that as long as no one talked about it and it didn't cause any problems, then there wasn't really any harm." She winked. "I have a massager in my medical kit. If you have any, um, sore muscles."

I had a sudden need to pay very close attention to greasing the pan for the kugel. It wasn't as if I didn't know what a vibrator was. Nicole had had one on the moon, and had laughed at me when I had been shocked by that. I'd just never used one, even when I missed Nathaniel painfully. I cleared my throat. "What's the solution for the men?"

Kamilah made a gesture with her left hand. It hadn't seemed possible that my face could feel hotter.

I am such a prude. "I keep forgetting that you were a military surgeon."

"Oh, I knew that gesture since I was little." She bent her head, sliding the radishes into a neat pile. "When you're the only girl, with two older brothers and three younger ones, you pick up some things that aren't so proper. We shared the same bedroom, so I heard all the conversations."

"Really? All six of you in one room?"

"My parents, too." She shrugged. "My family was not wealthy people."

Eight people in a single bedroom. It had been common after the Meteor, when housing had been in short supply—refugees had crowded in with relatives or strangers who were kind enough to open their homes. But Kamilah was my age. "What are your brothers doing now?"

"Moldering somewhere in Morocco." She wiped her knife off and laid it on the counter. "What do you want me to do with these radishes?"

"There's a bowl with lettuce . . . add them to that?" That's the funny thing about training for a mission like this. You can spend hours every day for a year with people and still learn only the narrowest swathe of who they are. I knew that Kamilah had an irreverent sense of humor. I knew she was Muslim and from Algiers. I knew that she had an aversion to cooked carrots as strong as my own. I hadn't known that all of her brothers had died in the Second World War.

As she slid the radishes into the bowl, I rehydrated some powdered eggs. "So . . . Do you think we should talk to Florence?"

"Why?" Kamilah's brows came together as she set the bowl on the counter near me.

"Well . . . I mean." I pressed my lips together, then shook my head at my foolishness. Whose sensibilities was I really protecting here? "Parker has a history, and I just want to make certain she's . . . I wouldn't want him to press her."

Kamilah leaned against the counter, her head cocked to

the side. "Huh. I'm not sure which question to ask first, so I will ask them both. Why do you think it was Parker and Florence? And what history?"

"If it wasn't you or me, that only leaves one other woman on the ship."

Kamilah stared at me and pursed her lips. She opened her mouth as if she were about to say something, then shook her head. "And the history?"

"In the war . . . I was a WASP and flew transport into his base. He was . . . There were young women who were afraid to tell him no." I opened the drawer of spices, all suspended in oil in little sealed jars and stuck to the bottom of the drawer with magnets. It was a holdover from the moon where we didn't have the luxury of artificial gravity to keep floating particulates out of the air. Drawing a breath, I pulled the jar of black pepper in oil out of the drawer. "My father was a general, and so I reported Parker. He faced a trial over it."

Kamilah took a long breath. "That's why he hates you."

A little stabbing pain went through my chest at how obvious it was, and I nodded. "Plus, he's never been a fan of women in the astronaut corps."

"Well, that's most of the IAC, isn't it?" She chuckled drily. "Yet another reason to wish I'd been born a man."

"Anyway, it's why I'm worried that he might have . . . put Florence in a compromising position."

"Do you honestly think she would be silent about such a thing? If it were against her wishes?"

I frowned, trying to imagine that, and kept bumping up against memories of women that I'd known who had, in fact, kept quiet about just such things. Forthright, brave women, who wouldn't discuss them out of misplaced shame. Or fear of not being believed. Then, too, there was the way Florence handled DeBeer, by keeping her head down and just smiling. "Maybe? I mean, if it was the commander of the mission, what recourse would she have? We're stuck together for three years."

Kamilah sighed and shook her head. "Well, I'll keep an eye out, but she might not have been involved."

What did she—"Oh. The men? Really?"

Again, her eloquent shrug. "It is not uncommon in all-male settings. Boarding schools. Submarines. Trenches. Unspoken and frowned upon, true, but quietly known."

"But . . . a condom? I mean—it's not as if men can get pregnant."

"Elma, Elma, Elma . . . Let me talk to you about the role of lubrication and—"

"My, it's warm in here." It was, but I overplayed my Southern accent and batted my eyelashes.

Kamilah burst out laughing. I joined her, thankful that I had escaped more education on that particular topic than I had really anticipated. Was I curious? Sure. But not enough to want any more details than I already had.

Rubbing her forehead, Kamilah's smile faded. "I'm more worried about this history of Parker's. That did not come up in any of the medical meetings."

"He was acquitted. None of the women would testify." I dumped some of the pepper into the egg mixture, watching the black specks swirl through the yellow like sunspots. "Except me."

She gave a low whistle. "Holy hell. Forgive me, but why the hell did they staff the two of you on the same ship?"

That, at least, I had an answer for. "We make good publicity together."

Even in space, there is something very satisfying about setting a table. This is one of the ways that you can tell that I am my mother's daughter. She had taken great pride in having an elegantly set table. Especially for Shabbat dinner.

In space, there was no day of rest. Letting a day go by without helping maintain the ship would put all of our lives in jeopardy, so the rabbis had ruled that Jewish astronauts were allowed to do necessary work on the Sabbath. Or at least my rabbi did. There were still debates, as I understood it.

But I did try to observe as much as I could. When my rotation came up for the kitchen, I made potato kugel. I baked challah—and let me tell you, getting the consistency right with dehydrated eggs was a challenge. I enjoyed the challenge of Shabbat in space.

Or maybe it was just that when I cooked a good meal, even Parker was nicer.

He was laughing at something that Leonard had just said in Latin. "That is my new favorite Latin sentence. '*Utinam barbari spatium proprium tuum invadant.*'"

Leonard grinned. "Mine, too!" He glanced at the rest of us. "English translation: May barbarians invade your personal space!"

Slapping his hand against the table, Parker sat forward over his plate. "Okay: this is mission critical. We need a broader range of swears for dealing with Mission Control. Help me out, here."

"Oh, beloved MC." Terrazas rolled his eyes and waved a forkful of radish salad. "Try this one: '*pollas en vinagre.*' Cocks in vinegar."

"Pickled dicks!" Parker clapped his hands, grinning. "That's perfect."

Across the table, Rafael leaned forward. "How about '*Vai pentear macacos.*' Go away and comb monkeys."

"No. No." Kamilah pointed a piece of challah at Rafael.

"That is too nice for MC. You have no idea how many blood draws I have saved you from. MC is *kos omak yom el khamees*."

I had no idea what she'd said, so I glanced at Parker, who mouthed the words, and then burst out laughing.

Kamilah wrinkled her nose and translated for the rest of us. "Your mother's vagina on Thursday."

"You have a wicked mouth."

"Said the girl to the soldier." Kamilah winked, and the room filled with laughter, like life-giving oxygen.

Wiping his eyes with his napkin, Parker turned to me. "How about it, York? Got something Yiddish for me?"

"For you? Or for Mission Control?"

"Whichever is more blistering." He grinned, and I think it was even sincere. "So, something for me."

I laughed and tapped my finger against my lips to think for a second. Truly, I didn't really speak Yiddish—or, at least, I only had a child's grasp of it from talking to my grandmother. "How about this . . . 'Ale tseyn zoln dir aroysfaln, nor eyner zol dir blaybn af tsonveytik.'"

Parker's eyes widened. "Say that again? Slower?"

"Ale tseyn zoln dir aroysfaln . . ." I waited until he nodded, eyes intent like he was docking at *Lunetta*. "Nor eyner zol dir blaybn af tsonveytik."

"I . . . I don't know any of those words." He pushed his chair back. "Terrazas. Change seats with me."

Laughing, Terrazas pushed his chair back and grabbed his plate as he stood. "What happened to mission critical?"

"There is a language I don't know, man. Must conquer." Parker raised his hands, fingers curled together like a wizard summoning a demon. "Must! Conquer!"

Sweat started crawling down the back of my neck. Parker

had done this before, where he'd seemed nice only to smack me down later. I mean, not about language, but other moments where he seemed like he was over his hatred for me, only to have the bitterness jump back up.

I wiped my hands on my napkin as Parker rounded the table and plopped into the chair that Terrazas had vacated. He was smiling like a kid with a new toy. "What does it mean?"

"May all your teeth fall out, except one to give you a toothache."

"Oh, that's good . . . Give it to me again? Slow as you can."

I enunciated each word, pausing between them. "Ale tseyn zoln dir aroysfaln, nor eyner zol dir blaybn af tsonveytik."

Parker mouthed the words along with me almost as if he were tasting them. "Tseyn . . . Tsonveytik. Tooth and toothache?"

I shouldn't have been surprised. "Exactly so."

"Show-off!" Leonard wadded up his napkin and tossed it at Parker. It bounced off his head and landed on the table.

"I got two words! That's it." Parker snatched up the napkin and threw it back. "*Supprime tuum stultiloquium!*"

The main speakers crackled and all movement in the room stopped. "*Niña* 1, Kansas."

Parker jumped out of his chair and ran to the microphone built into the wall. "Kansas, *Niña* 1. Go ahead."

Mission Control could always use the systemwide ship speakers, but to date they had only done it for tests of the system. In sims, it meant something had gone wrong. I pushed my chair back and started grabbing dishes from the table. If we had to do any hard maneuvering, everything needed to be secured.

Five seconds later, Mission Control's response made it to us from Earth. Malouf's voice was as calm as if he were discussing what a pleasant day it was for a picnic. "*Niña* 1, there's a report of a fire on the *Pinta*."

SIXTEEN

ANNOUNCER: The American Broadcasting Company presents *Headline Edition* with Taylor Grant. November 9th, 1962.

GRANT: Today marks the fifth anniversary of the founding of the United Nations lunar colony. From a temporary outpost with six inhabitants to a thriving small town of three hundred people, the *Artemis Base* represents a combined global effort. To commemorate the occasion, the inhabitants have created a memorial rock garden, the centerpiece of which is a glass obelisk inscribed with the date and time of the Meteor's strike nearly ten years ago.

Before Mission Control got to the second part of the sentence, the entire crew was already in motion. To look at us, it would seem to be nothing more than an orderly cleanup of dinner, as we slid into the roles we had rehearsed in various sims before departure. Fire was a constant concern in space. To keep costs down and to make EVAs easier, the ships ran at 4.9 psi with a 70 percent oxygen atmosphere to deliver the necessary partial pressure of O2 to the lungs. But it meant that fires burned hotter and faster than if we had an Earth normal atmosphere with 21 percent O2.

So those simple words, "report of a fire" meant a disaster.

"Prepare for possible rendezvous. Crew report to these stations: Terrazas and Avelino to BusyBee to prep for evac procedures. Shamoun to medical bay in case of incoming wounded. York and Parker to the CM."

"Kansas, confirmed. All crew is going to positions now." We were already in motion by the time Parker turned from the wall. I had my foot on the bottom of the ladder leading up to the spindle.

The weird thing is that my heart rate had dropped from when Parker was quizzing me about Yiddish. A fire was bad, but it was a problem I could work. He wasn't.

Leonard said, "You want us in medical or the hangar?"

Below me, Parker shook his head, even as he grabbed the ladder up to the spindle. "You and Grey secure the kitchen. I don't want anything floating around if we have to maneuver. York, don't make me push you up this ladder."

I scrambled away from the centrifugal force until I could start to fly. As my weight dropped away, I kicked upward, stretching out my arms to slap against a rung above me and push even higher. Emerging in the spindle, I grabbed a guide rail to change my vector. Behind me, Parker popped out of the ladder tube, and the two of us flew up the spindle to the CM like superheroes in one of Hershel's comic books.

As soon as we swung in, Parker slapped the switch so we could listen to the *Pinta*'s comm. Benkoski's voice was steady across the void between us. ". . . in sleeping quarters. We've sealed bulkheads four and five."

"*Pinta* 1, Kansas: Confirmed that bulkheads four and five are sealed. You are Go to purge oxygen." Malouf's tone could have belonged to an accountant discussing an audit.

I slid into my seat and leaned toward the window to spot the *Pinta*. The lights on her outside and the glow from her windows popped her out of the ever-present night sky. "Visual range looks about 1.5 kilometers off."

Over the speakers, Benkoski said, "Confirmed. Beginning purge sequence. Attention, all crew, secure yourself for oxygen purge."

With the sextant, I sighted on the line of positioning indicator lights that circled the *Pinta*'s girth. That angle, calculated with her known size, gave me a precise distance. "1.37 kilometers."

"Copy. 1.37 kilometers." Parker had strapped into the pilot's seat and was checking his gauges. "If we have to get closer, I'm going to want to approach from ahead of them in case of any debris fields."

"Confirmed. Plotting course, unless you want to fly seat of the pa—Whoa!" Outside my window, the *Pinta* vented oxygen, which crystalized into a spray of stars.

Over the speakers, DeBeer reported. "Kansas, *Pinta* 1. Venting completed. Indicators are reading a vacuum in the gymnasium."

Five seconds later, Mission Control said, "Confirmed, *Pinta* 1. Indicators here read the same."

Behind Malouf, very faint amid the murmur of Mission Control, I heard my husband's voice say, "Tell them to wait for half an hour before repressurizing to make sure everything is cold. Don't want atmosphere in there if something can reignite."

It was like an ion particle had shot through my heart and left a blazing line between me and the Earth. The longing pressed a breath out of me.

Parker reached over and put a hand on my shoulder. He gave it a single squeeze and then returned his hand to the instrument panel. "Get those coordinates for me, okay?"

I've seen him do this with other people under his command, that touch, and the moment of sensitive understanding. It's part of what makes him so frustrating, because he can clearly read people well enough to know exactly which buttons to push to get what he wants. And sometimes what he wants is to be cruel.

But right now, that touch, and the understanding that it was hard to hear Nathaniel and be unable to respond to him, was exactly what I needed to steady me. I pulled my NavComp pad out of its slot on my chair and flipped to a clean worksheet. "On it. Do you want to keep the option of docking the ships together, or just for evac purposes?"

"Evac only. We'll—"

"*Niña* 1, Kansas. The emergency is contained, so you can all stand down." Malouf sighed into his microphone. "But expect a new protocol next week about cleaning the dryer lint."

I lifted my head from my worksheet. "You are kidding me."

Parker laughed, shaking his head. "Who was on laundry duty this week?"

"Graeham Stewman," Malouf said. "And he left the machine while it was running. Expect that protocol to change too. I'm surprised you couldn't hear Ruby giving him what-for even through the vacuum."

I grinned at the image. Ruby Donaldson, the *Pinta*'s medic, was at the very bottom limit of astronaut height and wore her blond hair in pigtails. It would be like having Dorothy from *The Wizard of Oz* tear into you. "I do not envy him."

"Hell, no." Parker chuckled, which marked one of the few times I'd ever made him laugh. "Tell Clemons that this is exactly why we should have put the laundry on the women's duty roster. If you're going to send them into space, at least take advantage of their areas of expertise."

Right. He was an asshole. I closed my NavComp book and slid it back into the slot. "I assume that means I am Go to head back to the kitchen? Where I belong."

Parker rolled his eyes and toggled off the mic to Mission Control. "It was a joke, York. Lighten up."

I saluted. "Confirmed lightening up."

As I turned to leave the CM, Parker sighed behind me. "Someday, I hope you get that stick out of your ass long enough to stop being such a bitch."

I caught myself on the door to the CM before I could float out of it. "Me? You're the one who keeps making belittling comments."

"It was a joke."

"Do you see me laughing?"

"That would require a sense of humor." Parker unbuckled his harness. "Try it sometime, laughter. It makes everything go a lot smoother."

"It's easier to laugh when one isn't the butt of the joke."

"'When one isn't . . .' Do you ever listen to yourself?" He shoved himself out of his seat and used the momentum to swing toward the door. "You are such a princess."

"Lovely. Now you're adding anti-Semitism to your repertoire."

He caught himself on the door and turned to face me, so there was barely an armsbreadth between us. "My wife is Jewish."

"That would carry more weight if you weren't so clearly ashamed of her."

His fist raised and for a moment I thought he was going to punch me. Parker was many things, but he was not violent. He set his jaw, and veins bulged at the side of his neck. "My wife is the bravest and best woman I know."

I should have apologized, or at least backed down. I didn't. I could blame the adrenaline still racing through my body from the emergency on *Pinta*—all that energy summoned up with nowhere to go. I tilted my head and met Parker's gaze. "And yet, you keep her hidden away like something that is unclean."

"She's in a fucking iron lung!" Parker caught himself and then leaned in, closing the space between us. His voice was low, pitched to a razor edge of control. "I told you once that she was off-limits. Needle me on anything else your petty, little vindictive heart desires, but not her, or so help me, I will end you."

He grabbed the sides of the doorframe and hurled himself down the length of the spindle. I floated, adrift, in the CM, staring after him as dozens of little pieces clicked into place from the years that I had known him. His ease with Hershel's leg braces. His pain when saying that his wife had encouraged him to go. God. As difficult as the conversation that Nathaniel and I had had about the mission, what must it have been like for her? Miriam. I knew her name from the death sim.

The apology I should have offered before was right there, making me queasy with the words jammed in my throat.

An iron lung. My brother's polio was normal for me. It had happened before I was born. Hershel wasn't brave or inspiring because he wore braces. He was just Hershel. But . . . but the disease remained a specter that had haunted my childhood with an awareness that it could have been so much worse.

I followed Parker down the spindle, slower, hoping he'd have time to cool down a little before I caught up with him. Hoping I'd have time to calm down myself. Rafael and Terrazas floated up the length of it, bantering in Spanish about something.

Terrazas saw me and grinned. "I'm going to ask Parker to redistribute the duty roster to take men off laundry. For the good of the mission."

Giving Terrazas a shove, Rafael floated in the equal and

opposite direction. "I am quite capable of doing my own laundry."

"Thank you, Rafael. I'm glad someone recognizes that anyone can do laundry, with proper training." I twisted in the air to aim my feet toward the ladder. Grabbing the side rails, I pulled myself down until the artificial gravity caught me like water getting sucked down a bathtub.

Kamilah stood not far from the bottom of the ladder, doubled over with laughter.

Parker had his hand over his face. "Why? Why do I have this crew?"

"Why, massa. I'se done wha yew sed!" Across the spotless kitchen, Florence had folded a coffee filter and stuck it in her hair as an improvised maid's cap. "Ain't we done good, massa?"

Behind me, Terrazas and Rafael landed with a thump. Rafael laughed. "What?"

Leonard sat at the table, shaking his head. "I had nothing to do with this."

"All right, Grey. What's with the maid act?" Parker lowered his hand. "Did I insult you by having a woman do the cleanup or something? Flannery was here too."

She dropped the mincing routine and put her hands on her hips. "And what do we have in common?"

Parker looked from Florence's pale brown skin to Leonard's deeper tan. "Oh, for crying out loud. You know that's not it. You know this room had to be secured. You know the other stations were covered."

"Yes. And I also know that Flannery is better at EVAs than Avelino or Terrazas, so ask yourself why Mission Control left both of us off the assignment list." She snatched the coffee filter out of her hair. "Sir."

They glared at each other for a moment longer before Parker turned to me. "York. Did you make a dessert?"

"Chocolate chess pie." My apology would have to wait until we weren't in a room full of people. But whatever else was going on, I was reasonably certain that we'd have heard about it if Parker had forced himself on Florence.

The code that Nathaniel and I had come up with for the teletype was fairly simple. Before and after each transmission through space, there was some garbage generated while the machines were connecting. If you wrote something that looked like garbage, then anyone on the receiving end would assume that the message simply hadn't started yet, unless they knew what to look for.

We used a keyed Caesar, but shifted the key with each transmission, just in case. I'd played with encryption in college, but Nathaniel had gotten very interested in it during the war. As I understood it, he was a coin toss away from winding up in the intelligence department, doing encryption work during the war.

I typed in "78, 14, 3," which represented the page, line, and word in a copy of Rudyard Kipling's *Just So Stories*. When Nathaniel got the transcription, he'd look up the word in the book, which would then be the "key" for the Caesar. Today's was "elephant," which meant that I'd reordered the alphabet to read "ELPHANTBCDFGIJKMOQRSUVWX YZ." So "Dear Nathaniel" became "Haeq Jesbejcag."

I tended to compose the letters before I went up to the comm module, because some parts of them were fine for Mission Control to read. I'd leave all the safe babble in plain text, and go back to add the rest to the beginning and end of the letter before I keyed them in.

Today's coded part read:

C pkimgecjah elkus cs. Huqcjt sba nctbs—ejh C'i jks axepsgy ruqa bkw wa tks sbaqa—ba skgh ia sbes bcr wcna ber mkgck ejh wer cj ej cqkj gujt. C naag durs bkqqclga elkus egg sba sciar sbes C'va sbkutbs rba wer elurah kq sbes ba durs hchj's peqa ajkutb elkus baq sk lqcjt baq qkujh sk ejy kn sba geujpbar. C'i e gcssga rsettaqah, jkw sbes C'va beh scia sk sbcjf elkus cs, sbes baq pkjhcsckj werj's sba rkuqpa kn knncpa tkrrcm. Mgaera sagg ia yku hchj's fjkw.

Which translated to:

Parker and I had a knock down drag out fight today. He made a crack about how laundry should be women's work, and I complained about it. During the fight—and I'm not exactly sure how we got there—he told me that his wife has polio and was in an iron lung. I feel just horrible about all the times that I've thought she was abused or that he just didn't care enough about her to bring her round to any of the launches. I'm a little staggered, now that I've had time to think about it, that her condition wasn't the source of office gossip. Please tell me you didn't know.

Dear Nathaniel,

The voyage continues apace. As you must know, we had quite a bit of excitement here earlier when the *Pinta* had their little trouble. There was a moment during Mission Control's transmission when I heard your voice as clear as anything. I hadn't thought I could miss you any more, but that little bit made the pining start all over again. Still, I don't want you to worry about me. I soothed myself with a slice of chocolate chess pie.

It's not quite the same as a real one, but I've learned that I can get fairly tolerable results from dehydrated eggs by whipping them a bit after I reconstitute them. Plus, the chocolate helps cover the slight chalky character.

You'll be pleased to know that the positioning lights on the *Pinta* worked exactly as planned, and I was able to give Parker the distance to their ship without any trouble at all. In fact, the whole mission is going so smoothly that we're almost bored. Now that Ruby tells us that everyone is okay on the *Pinta* (aside from the blister on Stewman's hand from trying to slap the fire out) I can admit that having a bit of excitement relieved some of the tedium.

Terrazas has suggested doing a radio play for the folks on the other ship, just to have something to break the monotony. Oh dear. I sound like a socialite afflicted with ennui, but, really, darling, it's just that all your efforts to make sure everything runs smoothly have paid off.

I love you dearly.
Elma

Cj qarmkjra sk ykuq gers gassaq, C ei waeqcjt iy ngctbs rucs lus hk jks beva e lqe kj. Cn yku waqa baqa, C wkugh sefa yku cjsk sba teqhaj ikhuga ejh gaej kvaq sba skiesk lahr rk sbes er yku skkf ia nqki labcjh, iy nepa wkugh la mqarrah cjsk sba nqetqejs tqaaj gaevar wcsb aepb sbqurs.

(Translated: In response to your last letter, I am wearing my flight suit, but do not have a bra on. If you were here . . .

(On second thought, I probably shouldn't translate this one. Nathaniel knows what I said, and that's enough.)

Parker avoided me. You would think it would be hard to avoid someone when there are only six other people in your world, but you would be wrong. The *Pinta* and the *Niña* were built to hold fourteen crew members, in case we had to evacuate one of the ships, so there were times when you could go from room to room and not find anyone.

I walked the full circuit of the ring, partly because I needed the exercise, but also hoping I'd catch him alone. I crossed from the long curved hallway into the garden module and just the smell of damp soil and greenery made my shoulders drop. I took in a deep breath, letting the knot in the pit of my stomach unclench a little.

Terrazas looked up from the tomato plants and held up one of the red orbs. He, at least, was always happy to see me. "I can't stop thinking about how different this is from our moon trip."

I snorted and made my way through the shelves and racks of plants. "I think you could fit two of our tin cans in the BusyBee."

"Oh, hey. I have an idea I want to run past you." He placed the tomato in the basket with some others. "What do you think about a *Flash Gordon* for our radio play?"

"*Flash Gordon*?" I'd been expecting something about using the BusyBee for some auxiliary purpose, or something at least related to work. "Isn't that a little . . . on the nose?"

"Maybe." He set the basket down and leaned against the hydroponic bed. "But here we are in actual outer space, the way I dreamed when I was a little kid listening to *Flash Gordon* with the radio."

"They had *Flash Gordon* in Spain?"

His teeth flashed in a blinding smile. "It's how I first learned English. Anyway. I was thinking that we could use the intership broadcast system to do a radio show for the *Pinta*. A soap opera, since they have to do their laundry by hand. It would be fun."

"York." Parker's voice made me jump. "I didn't think distracting people was on your duty roster."

"I'm on my exercise break." Please note that I was very good, and did not rise to the bait. "And I was hoping to run into you."

Behind me, Terrazas picked up the basket of tomatoes. "I'm going to take these up to the kitchen."

"York can do that for you. She's got free time." Parker stepped around me and took the basket of tomatoes from Terrazas. He thrust it at me. "Hop to it."

"If I can just talk to you for a moment?" My hands closed on the basket, and I clutched it to my chest as if it were a form of armor.

"Wish I had time. Sorry." He turned his back on me and used his shoulders to block my view of Terrazas. Just in case that signal wasn't clear enough, he switched to Spanish and rattled off something too fast to hear even the separation between words.

I stood there for a moment, feeling uncannily like I was back in college at the age of fourteen. I felt simultaneously outside events and ignored, but also at the center of attention because Parker was pretending so hard that I wasn't there. Nice leadership style he had. The longer I stayed, the more awkward it got, but I kept hoping he'd relent.

He produced some papers from an interior pocket on his jumpsuit and spread them out on the hydroponic table. Past him, Terrazas shot me a pained look and shrugged, as if to say that there wasn't anything he could do.

I hugged the basket of tomatoes and walked off to complete my circuit of the ring. Parker was the commander of the mission, after all.

SEVENTEEN

ANNOUNCER: The American Broadcasting Company presents *Headline Edition* with Taylor Grant. November 23rd, 1962.

GRANT: A massive hurricane has swept across Haiti without losing any of its force and continues across the ocean toward Florida. Thanks to early warning from the *Lunetta* orbiting station, the island nation was able to prepare for the devastating storm and evacuated the coasts before the storm struck. The government reports that while the property damage is severe, the loss of life is not as great as it might have been. Still, this is the earliest hurricane on record, and marks a continuing change in weather patterns in the region.

Florence snapped a pillowcase like a whip. "This is not why I got two doctorates."

"If the IAC had sent us with starch, I'd starch Parker's underwear." I pulled a load out from the strange front-loading washing machine, which had been invented for the moon colony—although, if the magazines were to be believed, a number of housewives on Earth were installing the Space-O-Matic cleaner in their own homes. "I can't believe that Mission Control fell for the whole 'women's work' argument."

"Cultivated incompetence." Florence snorted and grabbed another pillowcase. "Men are good at it."

"I'll admit to doing that sometimes myself." I put my

hand to my chest and fluttered my eyelids. "Oh, could you help little ol' me? You're so big and strong."

She rewarded me with a laugh. "Well, if men are going to be all up in my face about how they're 'protecting' me, then there's not a thing wrong with taking advantage of them. It's not my fault they're too stupid to live."

"Not all of them are *so* bad." I dumped a stack of wet laundry into the dryer—after cleaning the lint trap, thank you very much. "Rafael's pretty good with the laundry."

"That's a pretty small sample size."

"Nathaniel makes a mean cocktail. And he does dishes."

She just gave me this vaguely disappointed look, as if she had glasses to peer over. Shaking her head, Florence grabbed a shirt to fold and gave an expressive sigh. "How's he coping with you being gone?"

Now it was my turn to sigh. I shut the dryer with my knee and slapped the button to turn it on. "Okay." The dryer started to rattle and thump as the clothes spun in their own tiny orbit, and I wandered over to help her fold. "My nephew is going to come stay with him and intern at IAC. Nathaniel's got a regular card game he goes to. And work. He works all the time, even when I'm home."

"How long you two been married?"

"Thirteen years." I smoothed one of Terrazas's T-shirts on the table. The soft cotton bunched under my hand. "How about you? Anyone special?"

"Nope. Had a fellow who proposed, but he wanted me to stop working. 'It's the job or me.' Well . . . that was an easy choice. Since then . . ." Florence has this little shrug where she cocks her head to the side. She gave one of those and set the shirt she was folding on the stack of clothes. "You know how it is. Men get intimidated when you're smart."

This was the most intimate conversation we'd had. I'm

not sure what changed to get her to open up, even that much. Maybe it was just the shared task and indignity of folding laundry together. Whatever it was, I wasn't going to question it. "Yeah, well, the guys we're working with don't seem particularly intimidated."

"Please." She snorted and rolled her eyes. "Why do you think they have us doing laundry? It ain't because they're incompetent or lazy."

The shipwide speaker crackled and Parker's voice intruded into the laundry room. "Grey. Parker. I need you in comms."

"Well, well . . . I actually get to do my job." She stood up and walked over to the speaker to press the reply button. "Parker. Grey. Copy. On my way to comms."

I saluted her with a shirt. "Enjoy using your doctorate."

I didn't find out what Parker had needed Florence for until I got to dinner that night. I walked around the ring to the kitchen module, following the scent of something made with all the garlic in the universe. Even if I hadn't seen the duty roster, it would have been clear that Terrazas was cooking.

When I walked in, he was stirring something on the stove. ". . . have to do something."

From where she sat at the table, Florence spread her hands. "Mission Control says no."

"Well, there's not really anything we can do that they can't do for themselves." Kamilah was slicing fresh tomatoes at the counter. "And the chances of bringing the infection back here is pretty high."

"Infection?" The old specter of space germs came and danced in front of me like a latex-rubber monster suit in a drive-in movie. As far out as we were from Earth, who knew what could happen? "What's going on?"

Kamilah slid the tomatoes onto a plate. "There's an *E. coli* infection on the *Pinta,* which Ruby thinks started with a *Bacillus cereus* infection from the rice."

Florence looked up at me. "See? I told you they were too stupid to live."

"Wait—what rice? Is that something we have to worry about on the *Niña*? And how sick? And—I should stop asking questions and let you answer them." I knit my hands in front of me and tried to wait.

"I'll back up and start at the beginning. Parker called me up to comms because the *Pinta*'s antenna was out of alignment, so I had to massage the receiver to get a clear-enough signal. According to Ruby, when they had the fire, they left the dinner out and afterward went back to it. She thinks the rice got infected with . . . what was it, Kam?"

"*Bacillus cereus.* It's a very common agent and shows up frequently in rice. That struck Stewman and Sabados, and unfortunately the symptoms hit while they were in zero-g. At which point, one of them became a vector to infect everyone else with *E. coli.* It is not pretty over there."

I winced. Diarrhea in zero-g gets in everything. Urine is unpleasant, but diarrhea was a million times worse—and that's a hard statistic. "Are we going to do something?"

Terrazas pointed his spoon at me. "That's what I asked."

"No." Parker landed at the bottom of the ladder. "Mission Control and all of the flight surgeons there have confirmed that we are not to do anything. Ruby, who is actually there to assess the situation, has also said that we are not to come over."

"But—" I'm not sure what I was even objecting to. It was a sound decision, and not far off from some of the sims we'd done. This was the reason we had two ships, so each one was redundant. But it was hard not to want to help, which I guess was the difference between the anonymity of the suffering masses and the immediacy of people you know. "There are things we could do that don't involve coming into contact with them."

Parker raised his eyebrows, but that was all the response I got from him. He walked across the kitchen. "Smells good, Terrazas."

Terrazas smacked his spoon against the side of the pot, shaking off whatever delicious thing he was making. "York is right. We could leave something in the airlock. Or go into the ship in our spacesuits to help with cleanup. Or put the crew in a BusyBee and use it as—"

"That." Parker pointed a finger at him. "That right there is why we aren't. Because, in just three sentences you edged them closer to us. Now, *E. coli* is highly contagious, is that right, Shamoun?"

"Yes."

"Mission Control has more brains focused on the problem than we could muster up even if both ships were healthy. We are holding course." Parker clapped his hands together. "What's for dinner?"

Terrazas wiped his hands on his apron. "Mock paella. It's . . . it's a rice dish."

Two things to know about Terrazas: He is a ham with a deep and abiding love for theater. And, of course, he's an astronaut, which means that once he sees a problem, he needs to work it until he has a solution. Those two things combined with his desire to help the *Pinta,* and somehow I found myself holding a pair of shoes and crowded into comms with Leonard, Terrazas, Florence, and Rafael.

We were far enough out that radio shows from Earth were getting fuzzy and hard to make out without nursing the radio equipment a lot. Florence had explained it, but while I understood waves and the theories of bandwidth, she eventually lapsed into jargon that left me smiling and nodding.

The short form was the crew of the *Pinta* was too ill to play nursemaid to the radio.

The slightly longer form was that we were doing a radio serial to entertain them while they were ill. Apparently having a microphone is the space version of "My uncle has a barn."

Terrazas leaned into the microphone and, with appropriate dash and vigor, narrated the thrilling scene: "Racing high above the Earth, comfortably seated in a giant airliner, Flash Gordon, internationally famous athlete, looks admiringly across the aisle at Dale Arden, the lovely young companion of his air voyage. Suddenly, there's a violent jar."

As he paused, Florence shook a balloon—I say balloon, but it was a condom, blown up and filled with grains of dry rice. When she shook it next to the microphone, it sounded for all the world like an explosion.

Terrazas's voice grew more intense. "The plane lurches into a spinning nosedive. Flash Gordon's trained muscles carry him across the aisle to the frightened girl, to gather her in his arms and then leap free of the falling plane. And pulling the ripcord of his parachute, glides to Earth."

Leonard took his place at the mic, floating upside down over it. Terrazas was not our only ham. "Don't be frightened, Dale. The plane has crashed, we're safe."

That was my cue. I tried to simper accordingly. "Yes, thanks to you. Oh, look, Flash! There's a large steel door. It's closing!"

"Why, that's the laboratory of the great scientist Dr. Hans Zarkov. He's coming this way! I hope you'll pardon us for breaking in on you so unceremoniously, Doctor, but you see, we had to bail out."

I covered my mouth, because I knew what was coming next: Rafael. Rafael, who was 5'9" and loved to dance, could do the most ridiculous German accent I have ever heard. If you've seen Charlie Chaplin's *The Great Dictator,* Rafael would have made a great Adenoid Hynkel.

Rafael waggled his finger at the ceiling, even though no one on the *Pinta* could see him. "I see you for vhat you are—SPIES! Come to steal my SECRRRRRETS! But I haf zhe answer for dat. Come vit me!"

I bit my tongue and tried to hold my breath. He was just so funny.

How Leonard managed to get his next line out, I don't know. "Put that gun away, Professor Zarkov." Leonard got closer to the microphone and whispered. "The man is mad, Dale. We'll have to humor him."

"All right, Professor, all right." Hopefully I sounded breathless, rather than like I was fighting laughter. "We'll come with you."

"Get down dis ladder, into dis tower. Down, I tell you!" As Rafael pointed at the ceiling, Florence and I each clapped pairs of shoes together to make a sort of walking sound. Sort of. I am many things, but a sound effects artist is not one of them. Rafael shook his finger. "There now. Ve are in my rocket ship, and in ten seconds ve vill be on our vay to the new planet. Ve will all DIE—die for SCIENCE!"

And then he laughed maniacally. "Bwahahahaaha! Ha haaaaa! Ha!"

While I doubled over, trying to keep my laughter inaudible, Terrazas floated smoothly to the microphone. "Tune in next time for more thrilling adventures of *Flash Gordon*!"

Florence reached up and switched off the mic. "We're out."

My laughter bounced around the comm module, carrying

me with it like the "Laughing Gas" chapter in *Mary Poppins*. Wiping my eyes, I drifted over to kiss Rafael on top of his head. "You are going to be the death of me."

His ears went red. "I wasn't menacing?" But he grinned and winked.

"I was terrified for my life." I wiped my tears away on my sleeve before they could spin out into the room. "See, I'm weeping."

The intership radio crackled. "Thanks, gang. That was swell." It took me a moment to recognize the rasping voice as Ruby. "We all loved it."

Florence picked up the mic. "How are you all doing over there?"

"Oh, we're fine. Don't you worry about us." Somewhere behind her, someone was making a retching sound. "Gotta run. Thanks, though. Means a lot that you're thinking of us."

The line went quiet.

Florence sighed and restowed the mic in its usual spot. "I've never heard such a bald-faced lie."

"Never?" Leonard raised an eyebrow. "Not even the time I complimented that pie-thing you made?"

"You hush." She gave him a shove that sent him spinning up to the roof of the comm module. "It was a Japanese fruit pie. My mama's recipe."

"Is your mama Japanese?"

"You hush." She looked back at the speaker as if she could see through it to the *Pinta*. "I don't mind saying that I'm worried about them."

"Kamilah says that they should be just about over the worst of it." I mean, I was worried too, but there really wasn't anything we could do. Medicating *E. coli* made it worse, apparently, so it had to run its course.

Drumming her fingers on her console, Florence gnawed her lower lip. "It just seems as if—"

The ship intercom came on and Parker drawled, "If the band of Merry Players have finished with their derring-do, perhaps they would deign to return to duties."

Florence picked up the mic. "I don't know what you're talking about. I'm right at my station."

The rest of us floated out the door, heading up the spindle. Ahead of me, Terrazas asked Rafael, "Do you think Parker listened?"

"Of course." He nudged Terrazas gently with his shoulder. "You did good."

At dinner that night, Parker walked in holding a piece of teletype paper in his hand. We were all still laughing and a little giddy from the show. Like a switch, the laughter stopped.

There is a face that accompanies news of death. As astronauts—as survivors of the Meteor—as veterans of World War II—all of us had seen it too often not to know what was coming.

What we didn't know was who.

I set down the stack of plates I was holding. The air in the room seemed to stop circulating, even though the only sound was the high whir of the fan.

Parker looked down at the page. "Ruby Donaldson is dead. She had a seizure. Mission Control believes that it was hemolytic uremic syndrome caused by the *E. coli*."

"Damn it." Kamilah sat down and rested her forehead on her fists. "We should have gone over there."

"There's nothing—"

"That is a fucking lie." She slapped her hands on the table. "Ruby was dosing herself with anti-diarrhea meds so she could keep helping the rest of the crew. You do that and the Shiga toxins don't get flushed. Don't flush the toxins, and they start causing clotting. That seizure wasn't a byproduct of *E. coli,* it was a byproduct of our decision. We chose this."

The silence in the room echoed with that truth. It raised a cold shiver down the length of my spine, along with memories of all the contingency scenarios where an astronaut might have to choose to let a colleague die, because to try to save them would doom both people. Had that really been the case here? Would we have been so at risk if we had gone over to help?

Parker broke the silence with an audible inhalation. He crossed the room and crouched in front of Kamilah. "I'm sorry. And you're right." He rested a hand on her shoulder. "It was still the correct call when Mission Control made it."

"I'm going over there."

Still clutching that paper in his hand, Parker drew a long, slow breath. "I'll back you on that." He wet his lips and looked at me. "York. You've had nursing training, right?"

"Just field medicine in the war. And what I picked up from my mother." Which made her sound like a hedge witch or something. "She was a doctor."

Parker nodded and shifted his weight, looking at the floor. "Are you willing to pilot the BusyBee over?"

Terrazas stepped forward. "I can do that."

"I know you can." Parker looked up and pursed his lips. He sighed again, squeezing Kamilah's shoulder as he stood. "But the fact of the matter is that York and I can get away with bucking Mission Control's orders in ways that none of you can. If the Lady Astronaut takes Shamoun on a mission of mercy, they won't ground her when we get back."

"Well . . . there's got to be something I'm good for." I shrugged. "It'll make good publicity. They'll love that."

Parker gave a twisted smile. "And stay suited. I don't want any of that coming back here or infecting either of you."

EIGHTEEN

ANNOUNCER: The American Broadcasting Company presents *Headline Edition* with Taylor Grant. November 28th, 1962.

GRANT: Aboard the First Mars Expedition, tragedy has struck with the death of Lt. Ruby Donaldson of Grand Haven, Michigan. Lt. Donaldson was a medic aboard the *Pinta* and succumbed to an infection introduced from a contaminated food supply. Flags around the world are being flown at half staff in recognition of her sacrifice.

My breath hissed in my ears, surrounded by the hard shell of my Mars suit's helmet. This was not a full EVA suit, just a pressure suit like the one I wore on my first launch. My hands in the stiff gloves were clumsy on the controls of the BusyBee. At my side, Kamilah sat encased in her own suit. We occupied the same space, by some definitions, and yet we did not breathe the same air.

The docking hatch on the side of the *Pinta* stayed centered in the BusyBee's viewfinder as I eased it in to dock. Even in the midst of all of this, a part of me was still thrilled that I was being allowed to dock solo. Absurd. And yet, when the nose of the BusyBee bumped against the hull of the *Pinta* and our automatic clamps grabbed hold, I looked at Kamilah as if she should be proud of me.

She had already begun unbuckling her belt.

I activated our between-suit comms. "Let me secure the BusyBee first."

"Do you need me for that?"

"No, but—"

"Then I'll get going. We only have seven hours of air." She pushed out of her seat, floating up over the back of it.

"At least let me make sure that we're docked securely." My checklist still had half a dozen retro-thrusters to secure.

"The delta-pressure gauge is at 4.9." She had drifted back to the door.

"Kamilah." She knew better than this. Rushing was a sure way to get killed in space. "Let's go through the checklist. Slow is fast."

"By all that's holy, you sound like Parker." But she slowed down and checked the indicators, and got visual confirmation through the windows.

"Well, he and I did start going into space in the days where the rockets were held together with aluminum foil." I switched bands to broadcast back to our ship. "*Niña*, BusyBee 1. We've docked and all systems are optimal."

"Make sure you get visual confirmation before you open that hatch." Parker's command caused Kamilah to look at me and smirk. "Slow is fast."

Trust him to recite that particular mantra now. "Yes, sir. Kamilah is doing that right now."

"I'm glad one of you has sense."

I ground my teeth and hoped that the microphone picked it up. "Once I've finished securing the BusyBee, we'll board."

"Don't forget that you only have seven hours of oxygen."

Why do people like to say the obvious? "Yes, sir. We'll keep an eye on the time and our indicators."

"You'll need to allow enough time to get back here and be hosed down."

I am fairly certain that my sigh was audible. "Yes, sir. I'll remind Kamilah of the time constraints. BusyBee 1 out."

By the time I had the BusyBee secured, Kamilah had unpacked her med kit and opened the port. On the other side, the *Pinta*'s airlock awaited us, a single light shining to indicate which way was "up" in the metal cube. The round window in the interior door showed a glow from the spindle beyond.

In the early days, the hatches could only be opened from the inside, but they changed that after a sim in which EVA walkers had died because the crew inside was incapacitated. It's funny how things can seem so obvious in hindsight. This was one of the positives about the IAC and all of their simulations: we can also gain hindsight from things that aren't actually lethal.

I picked up the second med kit that Kamilah had packed, and floated after her into the airlock. We had to wait while the pumps circulated, verifying that the pressure in the two spaces matched before we could open the door.

It didn't seem like the occasion for one of the airlock games, even if they usually made the time pass faster. What else was there to say? We'd worked the problem back on the *Niña,* and I knew what our game plan was. Reviewing it would just make me more like Parker, apparently.

On the other hand, he wasn't wrong. I cleared my throat. "Gym first?"

"That's where Ruby said they were bunking." Kamilah glanced over at the indicator. "I swear this gets slower every time."

So maybe it *was* time for an airlock game. "We could try some mime?"

Kamilah snorted. "Did you just make a rhyme?"

"I don't think it's a crime."

"That's a question of paradigm."

I gnawed my lower lip. "Paradigm" was a good one . . . "Well, some people think that a rhyme is sublime."

Inside her helmet, Kamilah nodded. "And some people think it's—finally!" The delta-pressure gauge rose into the safe zone and she reached for the door. "About time!"

That merited a laugh. Kamilah anchored herself with one of the rails and pushed the door open. We floated through, med kits in tow, into the spindle of the *Pinta,* about a quarter of the way up from the rear of the craft.

The lights shone on the long white tunnel at full brilliance. Somehow, I'd expected everything to be gray and dim over here, but the electrical system worked perfectly. I looked up the length of the spindle toward the intersection where the ring supports met and gasped. A brown, lumpy, watery globe as large as my head spun slowly in an air current.

Another smaller one hovered farther up the spindle. Now that I was looking for them, there were dozens of small globules littering the air. "My God. They need a Hoover, not a doctor."

"They need both." Kamilah pushed the med kit in front of her and floated up the spindle. "I'll head to the gym. You want to see if you can get this cleaned up?"

And I thought the stopped-up toilet had been bad.

Even swathed in a suit designed to protect me from the harsh environment of Mars, I still had the urge to scrub my hands with lye. In truth, I did wash the gloves of the suit after I finished cleaning up the spindle. It took over half of my allotted five hours, and I hadn't even gotten to the crew quarters yet. We slept in zero-g, and I was willing to bet that area was a nightmare. Ruby had been smart to move them all down to the gym, where the gravity would keep the diarrhea more contained.

I slid down the ladder to the ring and clumped over to the gym module. The Mars suit wasn't as heavy as a full EVA suit, but was still ungainly. I stopped in the bathroom to wash my hands again and recoiled at the sight of a brown streak down one wall. Someone had made an attempt to clean it up, but had really just smeared it further.

What I wanted to do was to go back to the *Niña,* get all the bleach, and soak in it. Instead, I washed my gloves, then opened the supply cabinet to get out the Lysol, "Proud Sponsor of the Space Program" emblazoned on the side of the bottle. It took thirty seconds, maybe a minute to clean up that smear.

Weird that the spinning globes of excrement didn't say "illness" as much as this imperfectly cleaned smear did. Those might have just escaped from containment through a malfunction. This . . . this was an astronaut who had known that they needed to clean and who had been too sick to finish the job.

I washed my gloves again and spritzed Lysol on them for good measure.

Then I headed into the gym.

Kamilah knelt by Benkoski, wiping his forehead with a damp cloth. I'd honestly half expected her to have taken off her suit in some sort of heroic measure of helping the sick, but she hadn't. The tableau reminded me of exactly how far we had come since the Meteor struck. I know—you'd think that being in outer space would be enough, but it had become routine. In this context, the Mars suit stood out, and I saw it anew, all silver Mylar and white tubes and chrome and steel and plastic. We might have been something out of *Flash Gordon* or *Buck Rogers.*

"What can I do?"

"Give DeBeer an IV. He won't let me touch him." She looked at me, face framed by her helmet and—much like seeing the Mars suit out of context—I was reminded of how brown her skin was. It was not that I had forgotten that Kamilah was an Arab, but I had forgotten that DeBeer could see only that aspect of her. She indicated the med kit with a toss of her head. "You know how to administer an IV?"

"I understand the principles, but I've never done it." I walked over to the med kit, which sat on the weight bench, and knelt next to it. "He won't let you touch him? Really?"

"He's delirious." She stood and clomped over to join me. "I'm choosing to believe that."

"He's slime. Of course, that's just a rhyme."

"If I had a dime . . ." She opened the kit and pulled out one of the bags of saline she'd packed. "You'll have to set him up with a subcutaneous drip, unless you feel like you can find a vein in these blasted gloves."

"I've never even done it without gloves." What I find fascinating is that, while my heart rate had ticked up a notch, the idea of administering an IV was significantly less nerve-wracking than having Parker grill me about Yiddish. The brain makes absolutely no sense sometimes. My hands were steady as I took the IV from her. "Can you talk me through it?"

She shrugged and grinned. "Since we aren't going into a vein, you can basically stab him anywhere. It hurts more if you go into the hand, because there are more nerves there, and failing to let the alcohol swab dry is definitely painful because some of the alcohol enters the bloodstream with the needle. It produces a burning sensation—just as a point of information, as Parker says."

But despite her implied threats, she still bled the air from the line and followed me over to where DeBeer lay curled up on one of the wrestling mats. He was wrapped in a stained blanket. What skin I could see had taken on a yellowed papery texture and cracked at his lips.

When I knelt by DeBeer, his eyes opened. Red veins spiderwebbed around the blue of his irises, and mucus clung to the corners of his lids. His tongue flicked out to wet his lips. "York."

He coughed once, then closed his eyes again. I watched his chest with an intentness usually reserved for a launch to make certain he was still breathing.

How is it that I can simultaneously loathe someone and also not want them to die? Taking in a breath of recycled air, I slid the blanket down to expose his arms. His eyes snapped open again and he grabbed the blanket.

I nearly fumbled the needle and dropped it. Or stabbed myself.

His breath hissed as he said something in Afrikaans.

I'm not actually sure what he said, but from the way his gaze darted to Kamilah, I could make a fair guess. He wasn't delirious, just a racist asshole. "What if I sit on him?"

"I don't want to risk him cracking your faceplate. Although . . ." Kamilah turned away from me. "Huh."

"What?" I shifted to follow her gaze, which was taking in the rest of the gym. With the exception of DeBeer, the rest of the crew had clean blankets and had been given at least a sponge bath. All of them had IVs going.

"Well. It's just that there are all of these weights." She picked up a pair of ten kilogram dumbbells. "And he really is weak as a kitten. And he needs fluids."

"And a bath."

"Or face my wrath."

I stood, laughing as I understood her intention. We could

put these on the blanket and pin him down that way. "I like this path."

The dumbbells seemed like they might roll, so I grabbed a flat weight for the barbells. Getting a good grip with the gloves meant I could only carry one, but Kamilah saw what I was doing and put the dumbbells down. She grabbed the matching weight and, like some sort of space Valkyries, we approached DeBeer from either side.

His eyes were closed again, and he had the blanket conveniently pulled up to his neck with both arms inside, as if he were trying to cocoon himself. I plunked my weight down next to his right shoulder, capturing the blanket underneath it. Kamilah did the same thing on the other side, effectively pinning his chest. If he'd been at full strength, this would only have slowed him down, but, as it was, by the time he opened his eyes, I'd already straddled his legs, and had them held down beneath my full body weight.

He thrashed and grunted, then abruptly stopped with a moan. One side of the blanket had been rucked up at his waist, and a pool of watery brown discharge crept across the wrestling mat.

Across the room, Heidi and Dawn leaned against each other, propped up by the wall. Dawn had her arm around Heidi, who was clapping. "No one likes him."

The thing about emergencies is that people don't waste energy on white lies. After the Meteor, some things the refugees said were . . . "blunt" would be generous.

I patted his knee. "DeBeer. You have to let Kamilah give you fluids."

"You."

"I don't know how. The best I can do is subcutaneous, and it's not as effective."

He shook his head, ending with it pressed to the mat on the side away from Kamilah. This was stupid. We had him pinned, so I looked up at Kamilah and gave the best shrug I could in the suit.

She grimaced and came down to me. "I'll go into a vein in the legs, if you can hold him."

Benkoski pushed himself up on an elbow. "Oh, for fuck's sake, DeBeer. Take the goddamned IV like a man. That is a direct order."

"I'm in a Mars suit, so my 'taint' won't touch you." Kamilah scowled at the puddle on the mat. "You can let me do my job, or you can lie here in your own shit."

DeBeer kept his face pressed against the mat, but he didn't struggle. If anything, he went limp. Kamilah gestured for me to get off his legs, then she slid the weights to the side. Standing, she ripped the blanket off of him. "We'll get him cleaned up first."

"Hopefully there won't be another outburst." I stood and headed to the bathroom to grab the Lysol.

Behind me, Kamilah said, "Eh. He won't be the first asshole I've nursed."

NINETEEN

ANNOUNCER: This is the BBC World News for Wednesday, 28th November 1962.

Reports from the First Mars Expedition have raised concerns in the international community after the death of Lt. Ruby Donaldson. Some of the vigils following her death have been marred by Earth First protesters who claim that the stated cause of death is part of a government cover-up to hide so-called space germs. These germs, they say, are a threat to life on Earth, and raise questions about what other contaminants will come back from the surface of Mars.

When we finally finished getting DeBeer cleaned up and put an IV line in him, Benkoski struggled to his feet. He leaned on the chair that held his IV bag.

"Hey!" Kamilah sprinted to him, which I didn't know you could do in these suits. "What are you doing?"

"Ruby." He shrugged and looked at the floor. "I got her in the bag."

The bag. That was one of the scenarios covered in that report on mid-mission contingencies that Nathaniel had been reading back on Earth, "contingency" meaning that an astronaut dies in space. So far, none of the deaths in space have left a body to bury. The rest of them had received the astronaut's version of a Viking funeral, but without warning, or even the opportunity to die first. Morbid, but sometimes we make these jokes just to survive.

So what happens when an astronaut dies in the middle of a three-year mission? You can't send the body into the Earth's atmosphere to burn up, because you are millions of kilometers away. Do you store it until you reach Mars? Or get back to Earth? What does that do to the crew, knowing that their colleague's body is along for the ride?

Or, being the IAC, do you create a new system that allows the remains to be returned home in a compact and sanitary way? "The bag" was a heavy plastic body bag that contained the astronaut's remains so they could be placed in an airlock and exposed to the vacuum of space until the body within froze solid.

When an organic form has been exposed to the vacuum of space for about an hour, it fractures easily. Shake a bag containing frozen organic material, and it becomes dust, even the bones and teeth. Dust can easily be compacted into a neat cube for transportation home and interment in the ceremony of choice.

The bag had not been used on a human yet.

I took a slow breath, wishing that my air supply had a little more oxygen in the mix. "Is she in an airlock?"

He nodded. "The number three forward. I just couldn't . . . do the rest. I tried, but I'm so goddamned weak right now."

Kamilah rested a hand on his shoulder. "We'll take care of her."

"I'll come with you." He picked up his IV bag and rested it on his shoulder. "And before you tell me no, I promise not to exert myself, and to come straight back here, after."

Putting her hands on her hips, Kamilah glared at him. "There won't be anything you can do."

"I can say goodbye." Benkoski drew himself erect. Seeing him with something that passed for military bearing made the amount of weight he'd lost during the past week painfully clear.

The three of us trooped out of the gym—or rather, Kamilah and I clomped out, and Benkoski trailed after us, resting one hand against the wall. I stopped and waited until he caught up. "Lean on me."

The corner of his mouth turned up in a wry smile. "Thanks. I feel useless."

"You aren't." I tucked an arm around his waist. "You got DeBeer to behave."

His arm settled across my shoulders, pressing the O-ring of my helmet down into the muscle at the base of my neck. "If you can call it that. I should have reined him in early, but I figured ordering him to behave would just make him dig in on the racism."

I looked up at him as best I could in my helmet. With his weight on its O-ring, all I could really see was his chin. "I'm surprised that he was included in the crew."

"Parker tried to get him kicked off." Benkoski sighed and then coughed.

I stopped to let him catch his breath. "I didn't know that."

"Clemons said no. Budget. South Africa was kicking in a huge amount of money." Benkoski straightened and kept going. "But my job is to try to keep the ship running, and he's my copilot. Good times."

"Does the IAC know he's still giving you trouble?"

"Nah. Nothing they could do, and they'd probably try counseling or some shit like that. With a time delay." He let go of me when we reached the foot of the ladder up to the spindle. "I should be good from here."

"I can always give you a push if you have trouble climbing."

Benkoski laughed and patted his own rump. "Yeah. Diaper's not full yet, so have at it."

Kamilah looked down from above us. "I am not washing your ass again."

"I can do it myself." Benkoski started hauling himself up the ladder.

I followed, just in case he slipped, though what I would have done if that happened, I don't know—wedged my suit into place in the ladder shaft? As I came out into the spindle, Benkoski had anchored himself to the wall with one hand and Kamilah was at his side, looking at the IV bag.

"Goddamn it. Sorry. I should have thought of this. I was just distracted . . ." Kamilah shook her head. "You have to go back down to gravity."

"What? Why?"

"The saline dip is gravity fed. It's doing no good right now." She took him by the shoulders and turned him back toward the ladder. "Sorry, but that is fact."

"I'll be fine." He looked to me for support. "Elma. Tell her I'll be fine."

"No." I shook my head. There are many things I will argue with, but not a doctor who is making a declaration. "And don't make me get Parker on the line to give you a direct order."

He opened his mouth like he was going to argue, then clapped it shut. "All right. I will be sensible and go back down."

Kamilah waited until he started down the ladder before she turned toward the forward airlocks, up near crew quarters. As we floated up the length of the ship side by side, I kept looking for something to say. The weight of what we were heading toward almost provided its own gravity.

Even if Benkoski hadn't told us which airlock, it would have been obvious, since the delta-pressure gauge showed a vacuum on the other side. Kamilah pressed the button to close the exterior door and once it was shut, I opened the valve to let atmosphere roar into the airlock. I could think of no rhymes or even a sentence to start the game.

Kamilah cleared her throat beside me. "Ruby Donaldson was a fine medic and a wicked hand at bridge. She could dance the lindy hop and make it look like she was in zero gravity, even on Earth. We were in the same class of astronauts, and I will never forget the first day we met. She had those pigtails that make her look like she's twelve years old, and when some guy asked if she'd gotten lost from a school tour, she looked up at him and said, 'Yeah. I'm from the fucking school of hard knocks and I'm here to teach you not to make assumptions.' I'll miss her."

I hadn't needed to cry up until right that moment. The tears threatened to form pools in front of my eyes and I blinked hard and fast to clear them. "Ruby Donaldson was a dedicated astronaut and a compassionate doctor. She took every part of her job seriously, even when it wasn't glamorous. I never heard her complain about long hours, and she even offered to stay later if a teammate needed help. The first time I met Ruby, she was on the moon to learn how to drive a Rover. I will never forget her yelling 'Yee-haw.' I wanted to buy her a lasso."

The hiss of my breath filled the world around me as I stared through my helmet at the indicator. We waited for another two minutes before the pressure rose high enough to open the hatch. I looked through the window into the dimly lit cube to confirm that the outer hatch really was shut. A translucent plastic bag floated in the middle, with thick handles on both ends. It had settled against Ruby's neck so you could just make out her shoulder and the side of her head.

Swallowing, I undogged the hatch and pulled the door

open, bracing against one of the guide rails. Kamilah followed me into the airlock. She rested a hand on the body and squeezed. "Solid."

I glanced at my oxygen indicator. I think I was hoping that it would be too low to stay here and that we'd have to leave, but the gauge showed that I had plenty of air to do this and still get back to the *Niña*. Setting my jaw, I grabbed one of the handles and wrapped my other hand around one of the guide rails. In my mind, I began reciting the Mourner's Kaddish. *Yitgadal v'yitkadash sh'mei raba. B'alma di v'ra . . .* "On three?"

Kamilah nodded, taking the other handle. "One. Two. Three."

. . . chirutei, v'yamlich malchutei, b'chayeichon . . .

The bag lofted toward the ceiling, as easily as if we were shaking out a sheet. At the top of the arc, we snapped it back down. For a moment, the plastic outlined Ruby's face and chest and even her pigtails. Then she began to shatter. At the bottom of the swing, the bag shook with three distinct thumps.

. . . uv'yomeichon, uv'chayei d'chol beit Yisrael, baagala . . .

Up. The bag trembled as myriad rigid sharp angles struck it.

. . . uviz'man kariv. V'im'ru. Amen.

Down. The bag shuddered in my grip with the fall of dozens of rocks.

Y'hei sh'mei raba m'varach, l'alam ul'almei almaya.

Up. Something round pressed against the bag, like a child's head devoid of features.

Yitbarach v'yishtabach v'yitpaar, v'yitromam . . .

Down. The airlock had full atmosphere, rather than the blessed silence of vacuum. The pebbles in the bag drummed and rattled.

. . . v'yitnasei, v'yit'hadar v'yitaleh v'yit'halal . . .
Up and down and up and down and goddamn it—

After we finished. After we got back to the BusyBee. After I had to take my helmet off because I couldn't see to fly. Even after we got back to the *Niña*, I could still feel Ruby's body shattering through the lingering vibration in my hands.

The only thing—the only thing for which I could be grateful—was that Benkoski hadn't been able to come with us.

TWENTY

DISASTER EFFECTS FOUND TO PERSIST

Report on Meteor Survivors Given by Psychiatrists

By EMMA HARRISON

Special to The National Times

TORONTO, Canada, Nov. 29, 1962—Ten years after the Meteor slammed into the Chesapeake Bay, wiping out Washington, D.C., and much of the Eastern Seaboard, the Meteor's survivors showed marked psychological deterioration, two psychiatrists said yesterday. The survivors also reported a variety of physical complaints that physicians believed were psychologically induced.

Psychiatrists have tended to believe that a victim's previous personality is a major factor in the degree of mental disturbance after the accident, but Dr. Robert L. Leopold and Dr. Harold Dillon posited that the similar reactions of a large group of men over a long period open the pre-accident personality theory to question. The two psychiatrists first examined the men right after the disaster and found typical post-accident behavior. Many were bewildered, anxious, could not sleep, and had digestive disturbances. A few seemed overwhelmed.

Upon reexamination, most of the survivors were

> found to be more disturbed than they had been ten years earlier. They had developed many new complaints, feelings of isolation, of being watched, and hostility and distrust toward others.

I needed Nathaniel. Ruby's . . . whatever the hell that was . . . had left me with nightmares. I had not needed to ask Kamilah for a Miltown. She offered it as soon as we got back. Of course she'd read my file. Of course it would be on the ship for when I needed it. But I didn't want it to be so obvious that I needed one.

I didn't want to need one.

And I don't know what Kamilah took herself.

We did not talk about Ruby, although in my incident report I said that "the bag" should never, ever be used for a person.

But I needed Nathaniel. So I took myself up to the comm module along with a binder covering the various burns we would need to do on the journey. The transmission delay was long enough now that I would need something to keep me occupied while I waited. Plus, it would cover me working out the code from Nathaniel's response.

Florence looked up from a novel when I swung into the module. "Need anything?"

"I was hoping the teletype was free." It sat idle, bolted to its spot on the side of the comm module. "Got a message from Nathaniel to answer."

She waved a hand toward the machine. "Be my guest, but hope you don't mind if I ignore you—Valentine Michael Smith just laughed." She buried her nose back in her book.

That was fine by me, because it would reduce the likelihood that she'd notice me writing garbage. Today's word for the keyed Caesar was on page 30, line 7, word 4—"rhinoceros." So the alphabet was RHINOCESABDFGJKLMPQTUVWXYZ.

30 7 4—Wo srn tk uqo tso hre tsaje tk hpord ul Puhy'q hkny. Lforqo toff go tsrt yku wopo jkt aj tso gootajeq tsrt rllpkvon tsrt skppahfo tsaje. A irj't eot at kut kc gy sorn. Wsrt tso soff wrq lfogkjq tsajdaje tk ikggaqqakj tsrt? Rjn wsk toqton at tsrt ikufnj't aggonartofy qoo tso lpkhfogq? Jk kjo qskufn ovop, ovop srvo tk uqo at. A wkujn ul trdaje r Gaftkwj tk eot tk qfool..

(Translated: We had to use the bag thing to break up Ruby's body. Please tell me that you were not in the meetings that approved that horrible thing. I can't get it out of my head. What the hell was Clemons thinking to commission that? And who tested it that couldn't immediately see the problems? No one should ever, ever have to use it. I wound up taking a Miltown to get to sleep.)

Dear Nathaniel,

I'm not sure what they're saying on Earth about Ruby's death, but I'll tell you that she was working right up until the end. I wish we'd gone over sooner, but I understand why Mission Control made the decision they did. Hindsight is always 20/20, and all that. Still. I can't help but wonder if we could have saved her.

Everyone on the *Pinta* is doing much better. But I guess you know that, since they're back in communication. Benkoski says they're all still reeling a little, but everyone feels better to be working.

Speaking of working, I was glad to hear that Tommy came out for fall break. I think that's a good way for him to start getting used to life in Kansas City before he starts his internship. Thank you for taking him bowling and introducing him to the folks from Adler. He's been talking about wanting to be an astronomer for ages now. I think this will be a great opportunity for him. Please take pictures so I can see them when I get home.

All my love,
Elma

Wsoj A qran tsrt A ujnopqtkkn wsy Gaqqakj lkjtpkf grno tso noiaqakj tsoy nan, A faon. A nkj't. A gorj, A nan rt tso tago, hut rq qkkj rq wo sornon kvop aj tso Grpq quatq at buqt qoogon qk khvakuq tsrt wo ikufn srvo nkjo tsrt qkkjop. Rff ikjvopqrtakj rhkut ekaje kvop wrq qsut nkwj hockpo wo ovoj srn r isrjio tk wkpd tso lpkhfog. Skjoqtfy, A tsajd at'q ipagajrf tsrt Puhy'q norn

(Translated: When I said that I understood why Mission Control made the decision they did, I lied. I don't. I mean, I did at the time, but as soon as we headed over in the Mars suits it just seemed so obvious that we could have done that sooner. All conversation about going over was shut down before we even had a chance to work the problem. Honestly, I think it's criminal that Ruby's dead.)

I could have kept going, but I sat back and waited for him to respond. Or, rather, I waited for the signals from the teletype to travel millions of kilometers to Earth. In five minutes, someone would get the message and give it to Nathaniel. He would be at the office now, so unless he was in a meeting, he'd come to the machine right away.

Especially since I had mentioned Miltown.

He was going to tell me to be careful and ask if I'd talked to anyone about how upsetting dealing with the bag had been. As if there were anyone I could talk with on the ship.

The only person who made sense was Kamilah, and she had gone through the very same thing. I couldn't exactly complain to her.

I grabbed my binder and flipped it open to the first page. Launch. That wasn't a page we needed anymore. I popped the binder open and pulled the launch pages out, tucking them between my legs to keep them from floating away.

Had anyone asked an actual astronaut about the bag? I would ask Nathaniel when he responded, because if they had, then I wanted to talk to the S.O.B. who said that it would work. And if they hadn't, that was a whole 'nother angry conversation.

The next pages in my binder covered Earth orbit and transition out of orbit. Those could go too.

The force of pulling them out caused me to drift a little toward Florence, so I put a hand on the ceiling to stop myself. Pushing gently, I eased back over toward the teletype machine. Nathaniel should have my message by now. Unless he was in a meeting. He might be in a meeting . . .

I used to know his schedule down to the second. Now, all I knew for certain was that he was at work, and even that might not be true. He might be out of town—no. He would have told me that he had a trip planned. Wouldn't he? Besides, he wouldn't go anywhere with Tommy in town for the week.

I gnawed on the inside of my lip and turned back to my binder. TransMars injection burn—those I still needed. In another six months, we'd be crossing out of Earth's sphere of gravitational influence and into the bare edges of Mars's pull. I closed the metal rings of the binder and flipped to the back so I could insert my loose pages there. Granted,

I didn't need them anymore, but the IAC always wanted them back, complete with my handwritten notes all over them. For posterity.

The teletype rattled to life next to me.

Florence flinched at the sudden noise, spinning upward before she grabbed the desk to steady herself. "Lord. That thing gives me a fright every. Single. Time."

"I know what you mean." I wedged my binder between the teletype and the wall.

As the paper scrolled over the carriage, it began to lift up toward the ceiling like a paper beanstalk. Nearly half a page of random characters went past before I saw 30 7 4, which meant that everything after that would be Nathaniel, using the same keyword. Now the machine began to slow because it was responding to human touch.

In films, they sometimes show teletypes as these fast, automated things, but that's not what they are. Not even at this distance. They instantly transmit the typist's touch, so each stroke, each pause, each hesitation as you think of what to say next are sent to your correspondent. I put my hand on the side of the machine, which hummed under my touch.

As Nathaniel typed, I relished those tiny impacts against the carriage as echoes of his fingers against mine.

30 7 4—A'g qkppy yku'po srvaje quis r pkues tago kc at. A porn ykup ckpgrf polkpt rjn at qkujnon fado tso hre cujita-kjon rq ajtojnon. A joon qkgo sofl ujnopqtrjnaje wsrt nanj't wkpd rhkut at. Srvo yku joonon tk trdo rjy ktsop Gaftkwj rctop tsrt capqt jaest?

There was a long pause there, long enough that part of me was wondering if the transmission had been interrupted.

The rest of me could imagine Nathaniel leaning over the keyboard with his lower lip caught between his teeth and a line drawn between his brows.

Yku djkw A wkppy rhkut yku, hut A'g efrn yku toff go tsajeq fado tsaq.

(Translated: I'm sorry you're having such a rough time of it. I read your formal report and it sounded like the bag functioned as intended. I need some help understanding what didn't work about it. Have you needed to take any other Miltown after that first night? [That—that is where he paused.] You know I worry about you, but I'm glad you tell me things like this.)

My dearest Elma,

You and the rest of the crew have my sincere condolences. Everyone here is gutted about Ruby, particularly her colleagues in the flight surgeon's department, who feel like it is a personal failing of theirs. And of course, they all knew Ruby better than I did and speak of her in the highest possible terms.

It has been a blessing having Tommy here this week. His presence has been a good distraction and is encouraging me to eat meals on a regular basis. I wonder if I consumed the sheer amount of food that he seems to need at each meal when I was his age. Actually, I know I did, because I remember our housekeeper complaining about it. She said she couldn't keep a gallon of milk in the house, and I know now how she felt. On the plus side, our refrigerator is spotlessly clean.

He's a good worker. I'm looking forward to having him here for the summer, although I might move into one of the one-bedroom apartments, just for a little privacy. You wouldn't mind having more room when you come back, would you? We can always move again if you don't like it.

As always, I adore you.
Nathaniel

Sq jiitmp qj fo qurq yjt fseuq qrdb qj Brfsdru rhjtq wurqovom sp qmjthdsge yjt. S bgjw qurq Krmbom sp gjq r pjtmio jc ijfcjmq, htq Brfsdru rq dorpq jteuq qj ho, qumjteu uom fonsird hribemjtgn. S atpq wjmmy rhjtq yjt doqqsge quo rgxsoqy jvomwuodf yjt rersg.

(Translated: It occurs to me that you might talk to Kamilah about whatever is troubling you. I know that Parker is not a source of comfort, but Kamilah at least ought to be, through her medical background. I just worry about you letting the anxiety overwhelm you again.)

There is a substantial difference between being upset about having to pulverize a colleague and anxiety. I put my fingers on the keyboard to tell him so, then jerked them away again. I couldn't write that in plain text—I'd have to put it into our code first.

I took a slow breath and rearranged the letters of the alphabet in my mind. To be on the safe side, I wrote it out on the back of the old launch worksheet, driving my pencil into the paper so hard that it left an indentation. Then I propped it open and let it float next to the teletype as I copied out the text.

Jrtsrjaof. Tsaq aq jkt rjxaoty. A rg jkt rjxakuq rhkut rjytsaje. A rg, skwovop, vaqioprffy naqtuphon hy tso lpkioqq kc lufvopazaje Puhy Nkjrfnqkj. Yku rqdon wsrt "nanj't wkpd rhkut at." Tso hre cujitakjq rq noqaejon rjn rffkwq tso lufvopazrtakj kc rjytsaje cpoozo npaon. Hut nupaje tso lpkioqq, at aq lkqqahfo tk qoo poikejazrhfo laoioq kc tso noiorqon qtpadaje tso hre. Yku irj rfqk coof oris qtpado tspkues tso srjnfoq.

(Translated: Nathaniel. This is not anxiety. I am not anxious about anything. I am, however, viscerally disturbed by the process of pulverizing Ruby Donaldson. You asked what "didn't work about it." The bag functions as designed and allows the pulverization of anything freeze dried. But during the process, it is possible to see recognizable pieces of the deceased striking the bag. You can also feel each strike through the handles.)

Belatedly, I realized that I couldn't just send the coded message or it would look like garbage going through without anything attached to it. What had we been talking about "in the clear," as it were? Oh. A new apartment.

Dear Nathaniel,

I think you should make yourself as comfortable as you can while I'm gone. It's a little ironic that you need more space without me than with me, but it makes sense to want a place to retreat from Tommy. Besides, then you won't have to deal with the Murphy bed every day, which will be nice, I think. I know I don't miss putting it up and down.

It'll be another two and a half years before I can see the place. All I ask is that there is at least a view of some trees. I find that the garden module is one of my favorite spots on the ship. I think the aroma of earth and vegetation gives me comfort. I loved our tiny little "Central Park" on the moon for much the same reason. You don't realize how amazing the color green is until you live without it for so long.

Love,
Elma

Poerpnaje tso hre: Lforqo agreajo ac at wopo go, rjn yku qrw gy crio lpoqqon rerajqt tso ajtopakp kc tso hre. Lforqo agreajo coofaje laoioq kc gy hkny sattaje tso hre rjn tso qtpadoq vahprtaje tspkues tso qtprl aj ykup srjnq, ovoj wats efkvoq kj. Lforqo agreajo coofaje tskqo laoioq eot qgrffop rjn qgrffop ujtaf yku coft kjfy tso saqqaje kc qrjn rerajqt tso ajqano rjn yku djow tsrt at srn kjio hooj go.

(Translated: Regarding the bag: Please imagine if it were me, and you saw my face pressed against the interior of the bag. Please imagine feeling pieces of my body hitting the bag and the strikes vibrating through the strap in your hands, even with gloves on. Please imagine feeling those pieces get smaller and smaller until you felt only the hissing of sand against the inside and you knew that it had once been me.)

I took my hands off the keyboard and floated back, fingers still vibrating from the machine, as if I had shaken Ruby's remains all over again.

"You going to keep fighting with him?" Florence had looked up from her book with her head cocked to the side.

"Why—why do you think we're fighting?" I plucked my notebook out of the air and shut it.

"As hard as you were hitting those keys?" She snorted and closed her book. "What'd he do?"

"Weren't you reading?"

Florence wedged her book into a small net bag on the wall next to the radio. She crossed her arms, lips pursed. "If you stop fighting, maybe I will, but the racket you were making? Uh-uh. What's wrong?"

If I hadn't been trying so hard to build some sort of rapport with Florence, I might have continued to dodge this question. As it was, I felt like I needed to respond to any interest in my personal life. I sighed, and spun in the air to face her fully. "The bags. I want the IAC to scrap them and come up with a different plan."

She shuddered. "Yeah. Kamilah told me about that. Jesus."

A bitter volt of jealousy coursed through my body. But why? What right did I have to be jealous that Kamilah confided in Florence? They'd worked together longer than with me, and had a right to a friendship outside of work. But—

It's funny, what can snap something into focus for you. I had colleagues on the ship, but I had not become friends with anyone. Kamilah and Florence spent leisure time together. So did Rafael and Terrazas. Parker and Terrazas. Leonard and Florence. Kamilah and Rafael . . . There were pair bonds and friendships stretching throughout the crew, but I didn't have any of my own. Not truly. I'm not sure if it was because they still resented me for taking Helen's place, or because I was married to the lead engineer, or just because . . .

I swallowed the bitterness. "Nathaniel thinks it sounds like the bag worked within expected parameters and doesn't see what the problem is."

"Why are men such idiots?"

"It boggles the mind. It really does." I rattled the page he'd sent. "And Nathaniel is one of the good ones. I mean, he cooks, he's hosting my nephew, he's . . . he's amazing in all other ways. It's only when he gets his engineer hat on that he sometimes can't see past the design parameters to the people. 'The bag functioned as intended.' Ugh."

"Well, you tell him where he can store that bag. And if I pass, you can just jettison me. I'd rather spend eternity floating in space than as a bunch of sand."

Not that I'd be aware either way, but the thought made me shudder. "Same. Though . . ." I scanned the module looking for something wood and settled for knocking on the paper in my binder. "Let's hope there's no need to worry about that for anyone."

"Oh, I dunno. There's some folks . . ." She shrugged, cocking her head to the side. "I'd be tempted to just shove 'em out an airlock at the first opportunity."

"Maybe I should just 'accidentally' lose our store of the bag."

"Yeah. Be a damn shame if anything happened to those." She grinned slowly. "Kam and Terrazas would help."

That would be a pleasant letter to type and send home. *Dear Nathaniel: I'm ever so sorry, but we somehow accidentally jettisoned all the bags on both ships. I don't know how we managed to get rid of such a barbaric piece of equipment. I do hope—*

The teletype rattled to life. Both of us jumped at the abrupt noise, and then laughed.

"Every. Single. Time." Florence had a hand on her chest, still laughing. "Every time."

The laughter helped propel me over to the machine. As the actual garbage rolled into the "garbage," I leaned over the machine, decrypting in my head.

> (Translated: I'm sorry. You are absolutely right that none of us thought about the effect on the crew. I am so sorry. May I please ask you to send a follow-up report with the details so that I can share it in the next meeting? We will find another solution, although I hope to God there will never be a need for it.)

I had been so prepared to have to fight to get him to understand that I was left with a ball of anger that had no target. It was mingled with relief and gratitude that I was lucky enough to be married to a man who understood—and also shame, because I should have known he would understand. Nathaniel was the best of men.

Dear Elma,

I will absolutely look for an apartment with a view of trees. And thank you for reminding me that I take the greenery on Earth for granted. I think we all do, when surrounded by so much life all the time. It's hard to remember what an exception our planet is in the solar system, without a reminder of how fragile life is.

You have all my love,
Nathaniel

And then there was a single string of "garbage":

Every day I think of you and all the ways in which you might die in space. Please don't.

This time, I didn't wait, and I didn't bother encoding anything, because my response to both parts was the same.

Thank you. I love you.

I pushed back from the teletype to find Florence looking at me over her book. She cocked her head to the side. "And?"

"He just apologized and asked me to do an update to my report, with details about the effect on the crew." I folded the pages he'd sent, running my fingers over the crease as if it were the back of his hand. "He'll present it in the next meeting."

"Huh." Shaking her head, Florence opened her novel again. "Wonders never cease. A man with some sense."

And it would be two years, five months, three weeks, and four days before I saw him again. Not that I was counting.

TWENTY-ONE

CYGNUS SIX TRIAL CONTINUES

By ROBERT ALDEN

Special to The National Times

KANSAS CITY, KS, Dec. 14, 1962—The trial of six men accused of hijacking an International Aerospace Coalition rocket last year continued today. The United States government asked that the trial be moved to Kansas City due to security concerns.

Thirty-two armed guards, including six soldiers armed with submachine guns, crowded into the small courtroom. Heavy cordons of United Nations troops ringed the courthouse, and persons entering were searched before they were admitted.

The man accused of being the leader of the group is a handsome 34-year-old Negro insurance agent. He is considered by the police a key man in the plot and a key man in many terrorist activities.

In a corner of the observation dome—which, despite the name, is not actually a dome—Rafael played his guitar. The facets of the dodecahedron shaped the sound and bounced it around us. Aside from Parker and Kamilah, we had all gravitated toward the dome for our off-duty time. I was drifting near the apex with a copy of *The Gods of Mars* from the ship library. For reasons that remain unclear to me, we did not have the first book in the series, but the *Pinta* did.

Sometimes, the decisions that Mission Control made were opaque. Fortunately, you didn't really need to have read *A Princess of Mars* to follow what was going on in the sequel. It was harder, however, to ignore the weird popping sound that Terrazas kept making with his lips.

Somehow, I hadn't noticed it on our trip to the moon, but—dear God—it was constant when he was thinking.

I glanced over the edge of my book, where he floated with a clipboard—making notes, no doubt, on his next radio script. "You aren't even eating anything."

"What?" He lifted his head.

"That noise is just . . . Could you stop? Please?"

"What noise?" Terrazas scratched his nose with his pencil.

Rafael saved me by popping his lips like a slow-motion fart. "Love ya, but it's obnoxious."

Terrazas laughed, shaking his head. "I do not—do I?"

"Oh, hell. Elma—" Leonard snapped his mouth shut so hard his teeth clacked audibly. He held the "newspaper" so tightly that the teletype pages crinkled beneath his fists.

I lowered my book. "What's wrong?"

"Nothing." He gave a smile that I didn't believe for a second and straightened the sheet. The movement set him drifting in a loose circle.

Florence glanced over from the needlepoint she was working on. "The article about the march, or the one about the trial?"

"It's nothing. I—I, um, I just remembered that I needed to ask Elma to help me in the lab, but it can wait."

Well, that was obviously bullshit. I shut my book, and

Rafael stopped playing the guitar. Pushing off, I floated a little closer to Leonard. "What trial?"

"For the Cygnus Six. Old news." He grimaced and turned the page. "Hey, Florence. Looks like you've got a fan on Earth. Gene Roddenberry is saying you inspired a character on his new TV show."

"What are you leaving out?" I tucked my book into one of the pockets on my flight suit.

Leonard leaned his head back to stare at the stars. Florence stopped with her needle poised over the fabric. "May as well tell her. You know she's not one to leave well enough alone."

He sighed and lowered his head, turning back to the page that evidently held the story about the trial. "'. . . Among the questions raised was the possible involvement of IAC employees in the crash of the *Cygnus 14* rocket. While the so-called Lady Astronaut has been acclaimed as a heroine for her efforts, recent investigations by this paper have uncovered that she has a history of mental illness.'"

A wave of cold revulsion swept through me. I wanted to have misheard him, but I knew Earth well enough to know that I'd heard him with perfect, dreadful clarity. I did what I always do when I'm trying to mask my anxiety. I made a joke. "Given our choice of careers . . . they could say that about all of us."

"So it's true." Florence stabbed the cloth with a vengeance.

"Hey." Terrazas let go of his clipboard and set it spinning in front of him.

"That's—" I swallowed and crossed my arms across my torso. God. I wanted to lie to them, and I'm so proud of myself that I didn't. "I had problems with anxiety."

"Had." Florence snorted.

She wasn't wrong, but I still bristled. "It's not a problem."

"And Mission Control knew. Didn't they?"

"Well. I mean, I'm married to the lead engineer." Although I'd hidden the worst of it from Nathaniel for years. "So, yes. Parker and Kamilah knew too."

Florence stared at me, then bent her head back to her sewing. Other than that, the only reply was the whirring of the fans.

I cleared my throat. "Well." I had to stop saying that, but my Southern roots were strong sometimes. "The good thing is that it's pulling attention away from Leonard."

"Who should never have been under scrutiny in the first place." Florence's needle darted in and out of the cloth, silver catching the light with each stab. "Must be nice, not having to be perfect all the time."

That shocked a laugh or a sob out of me. "You have to be kidding. What do you think the anxiety was about? I'm Jewish. And I'm a woman in science. There's never a moment where I don't get to be perfect."

"Taking Miltown is a mark of perfection?"

"How did you—" I closed my eyes, as if that would hide me from scrutiny. "It's in the paper."

"Florence—" Leonard's voice was low and urgent.

"No. She just got to waltz in and take the spot of someone else. You think there's no link—"

1, 1, 2, 3, 5, 8, 13 . . . I didn't have to worry about what people would think. I knew. My breath came in shallow pants, and I forced my lungs to shudder into a longer breath as I opened my eyes. "Oh, for God's sake! What the hell do I have to do to prove to you that I'm pulling my weight?"

Florence whipped around in the air to face me, thread

trailing behind her in an arc. "You still don't get it. Was I angry that Helen was bumped? Yes. But ask yourself why Mission Control chose to bump the Taiwanese computer and not the white computer."

I opened my mouth to retort, but had nothing, so I just floated there, mouth gaping. "I—I know. But there were reasons beyond the fact that Helen wasn't white. Publicity wanted Parker and me on the same ship."

"Sure. Let's go with that theory." Florence gave a single nod.

"Look—if it were just that, they would have pulled Leonard at the first hint of trouble."

"Trouble." Florence glanced over at Leonard. "You hear her?"

"I do."

Maybe I was just trying to get attention away from me. I don't know. "You know it's true. I mean, DeBeer did his darnedest to make that happen."

"And why not you? Hm?" Leonard folded the newspaper into quarters, then folded it again, and again, driving his thumbnail along the edge of the paper. "Why was I 'part of the conspiracy' and not you?"

I knew the answer, of course: He was Black.

"Okay. I see your point." My hands were sweating. I jammed them farther into my armpits. "But the fact is that you still got to come on the mission. You're here. Right? So neither of us has to be perfect."

"But your imperfection is in your brain." Leonard held up his hand. "Mine is *here*."

"I'm not—" *. . . 21, 34, 55, 89 . . .* This wasn't about me. Florence had just told me that. "That is not an imperfection. You are a brilliant astronaut and damn well deserve to be on this mission."

"And what do they have us doing here?" Florence tilted

her head. "Scrubbing walls. Cleaning toilets. Cooking. Laundry."

"Well, we all do that. I did a toilet repair two weeks out, and—"

"Stop talking, Elma." Leonard crumpled the teletype paper. "For the love of God, stop talking."

My heart rate began to achieve escape velocity, and sweat clung to the back of my neck in warm droplets. Leonard had never so much as raised his voice. "I just—"

"I am trying to remember that you mean well. But at the moment, I cannot take the protestations of a well-meaning white woman. I do not have the energy to reassure you or to pretend I am happy and content with my lot in life."

"I'm sorry." I dug my fingers into my sides. "I'm sorry. I was only trying to help."

"Help?" Florence folded up her sewing. "You can help by shutting up instead of being openly clueless."

Terrazas snorted. "You're acting like she's DeBeer. In case you haven't noticed, cleaning the ship is part of all of our jobs."

"Not you, too. Pay attention to the duty roster next Monday. Tell me that it isn't uneven." She shoved her sewing into a bag that had been floating tethered to her waist. "Now, if you'll excuse me, I should check the laundry."

She was being ridiculous. There were only seven of us on the ship, so it wasn't like there was a staff that came in to tidy up after us. "But we all clean; that's part of basic maintenance."

"Yes." Leonard slapped the folded newspaper against his palm. "Yes. We all clean. But the rest of you are assigned to do other tasks relating to the maintenance of the ship. Florence and I aren't."

Rafael said, "It's true. Leonard was trained to assist me

in engineering, but Mission Control's roster keeps giving me Estevan, who only shadowed him."

Terrazas turned his head, brows raised. "I thought you liked having me help."

"I do." Red flushed Rafael's ears. "But you're missing the point. It should be Leonard."

"Thank you." Leonard scowled down at the pages.

I turned to Rafael and Terrazas, although I'm not sure exactly what I wanted. Reassurance that I wasn't a terrible person? Confirmation that I was? The lines of Rafael's face looked as dragged out as if he'd spent the day in the Neutral Buoyancy Lab. Compressing his lips, he turned back to Terrazas and smiled. Sort of. His lips curved up, at any rate. "What was that song you wanted me to learn?"

Breathing hurt. I bit down on the inside of my cheek. Rotating, I pushed off and flew through the door into the spindle.

And because I'm a professional, I actually made it to the gravity toilet in the centrifugal ring before I threw up.

From the toilet, I made my way up the spindle to the comm module. I figured that chances of Parker or Kamilah being there were slim, and I was rewarded by finding the module empty and dark. Chewing the inside of my lip, I hung in the doorway for a minute. The teletype sat there, a link to Nathaniel. I wanted to tell him everything, and also didn't want to worry him. But . . . I'd promised I would be honest with him, and being 97 million kilometers away didn't change that vow.

I pushed through the door and floated to the machine, rotating to a good working position. Stretching out, I hooked my feet under one of the guide rails to anchor myself as I wrote.

I didn't have Kipling's book with me, so I picked a word we'd already used, RHINOCEROS.

A buqt tspow ul. At'q tso capqt tago kj tsaq gaqqakj. A qullkqo yku'vo qooj tso rptaifo rhkut tso lyejuq Qax tsrt trfdq rhkut gy rjxaoty lpkhfog. Fokjrpn hpkuest at ul. A tskuest rff kc tsaq wrq hosajn go rjn wrq hfajnqanon. Tsoj qkgoskw tso ikjvopqrtakj buqt noeojoprton ajtk rjeop rff rpkujn. A'g cajo jkw. A djkw yku wkj't hofaovo go, hut tso crit tsrt A'g toffaje yku tsrt A wrq ulqot kuest tk porqqupo yku. Rt forqt r fattfo? A sklo at wkj't srlloj reraj. Ekn. At'q hooj qk fkje qajio A tspow ul fado tsrt. A irj't hofaovo tsrt at uqon tk ho poeufrp. Hut, porffy, A'g cajo. A'g kjfy toffaje yku hoiruqo A lpkgaqon A wkufn.

(Translated: I just threw up. It's the first time on this mission. I suppose you've seen the article about the Cygnus Six that talks about my anxiety problem. Leonard brought it up. I thought all of this was behind me and was blindsided. Then somehow the conversation just degenerated into anger all around. I'm fine now. I know you won't believe me, but the fact that I'm telling you that I was upset ought to reassure you. At least a little? I hope it won't happen again. God. It's been so long since I threw up like that. I can't believe that it used to be regular. But, really, I'm fine. I'm only telling you because I promised I would.)

Dear Nathaniel,

The news from Earth seems fairly bleak sometimes. I feel awful for those who were hit by the typhoons in the Indian Ocean. I have to remind myself that our mission exists to provide some hope for those trapped in untenable situations on Earth. As the weather worsens, we hope to establish a new beachhead for humanity in the stars.

I've been reading *The Gods of Mars* and am quite enjoying the absurdity of it. The first book in the series is on the *Pinta,* so I've asked Kamilah to pick it up the next time she goes over on a medical visit. Everyone's health continues to be good, thank heavens.

How goes the apartment search?

All my love,
Elma

Ovopykjo'q lsyqairf sorfts aq ekkn, rq aq gajo, hut toglopq rpo qtpotison tk tso hpordaje lkajt. Tsopo rpo tagoq tsrt A waqs wo wopoj't eottaje jowq cpkg skgo hoykjn fottopq cpkg crgafy rjn cpaojnq. Lforqo nk dool tskqo ikgaje. A gaqq yku toppahfy.

(Translated: Everyone's physical health is good, as is mine, but tempers are stretched to the breaking point. Thoro aro timos that I wish wo woron't gotting nows from home beyond letters from family and friends. Please do keep those coming. I miss you terribly.)

It was late in Kansas, and a weekend. As much as I wanted to hear from Nathaniel, I hoped that he wasn't still at work, though, knowing my husband, he very well might be. On second thought, he should be at his poker game tonight. I sighed, trying to release some of the ache in my chest, and went to find Leonard.

I found Leonard in the garden module. He sat on the bench in the middle of the hydroponic rows of tomatoes. I guess the original design hadn't included seating, but it didn't take long to understand how much humans craved the sight of greenery in space. As I walked in, I scuffed my feet against the metal grates in the floor to catch his attention.

Leonard looked up, hands knit together, and sighed. "Elma . . . I'm sorry I yelled at you."

That stopped me in my tracks. "You don't—I was coming to apologize to *you*. I was wrong."

He snorted. "My mother once told me that an apology wasn't about being right or wrong, but showing that the relationship was more important than the problem. And you aren't actually the problem."

"I contributed, though. And I was wrong. And you're important to me."

"I appreciate that." He stretched his hands out, flexing the fingers wide. "But I was explaining why I apologized to you."

"Oh." I stood on one foot, feeling like my dad was disappointed in me. The leaves of the tomato plants stirred in the breeze from the fans and spread their earthy scent in the air. With a finger, I reached out and traced the veins on a leaf. "Do you . . . Back on *Lunetta,* you and Florence asked me not to get involved, but if you want, I can nudge Nathaniel to nudge someone else about the duty rosters. But only if you want."

Leonard shook his head, standing with a groan. "Thank you. I appreciate the offer in the spirit in which it was made. But, no. I think Rafael might request me now, and that will do more good than anything else. Probably should have talked to him sooner."

"Is there anything I *can* do?"

Leonard shrugged. "No. Thank you." He started to walk out of the module, but stopped at the end of the row, framed by the verdant plants. Turning, he held up a finger. "One thing: Don't explain my experience to me. It's annoying as hell."

I winced, because that's exactly what I had done, multiple times—everything from explaining that we all cleaned to telling him that he wasn't being singled out. And I knew how annoying it was, because Parker did it to me all the time. "Copy. No explanations."

"Roger." He winked. "See you at dinner."

After Leonard left, I settled on the bench he had vacated. It was only after I had relaxed into the green that I realized that I had effectively chased him out of the module.

TWENTY-TWO

ADVERTISING MAGAZINES SHOW AN UPTURN IN BUSINESS

By PETER BART

Dec. 27, 1962—Magazine advertising salesmen, who have been wearing baleful expressions for months now, are beginning to look a little more cheerful. Business, they report, is picking up. The pattern is far from uniform, to be sure. But many magazines predict that the advertising they will carry for the first half of 1962 may be well above the levels of the 1961 period and that the ten-year decline, begun when the Meteor struck, is at an end.

A couple of weeks after my . . . discussion with Leonard and Florence, I slid down the ladder into the kitchen module to set up the kitchen for the Monday morning meeting.

And yes, since they'd pointed it out, I had paid attention to the duty rosters. Leonard wound up on cleaning or kitchen duty only. Florence had cleaning, laundry, kitchen, and comms, so at least she got to work in her area of specialty. And, amazingly, the men never had to make coffee for the meeting.

The Christmas decorations that Mission Control had packed were still up, with the silver garland taped in loops to the top of the wall. In the corner, seven bulbs glowed from an electric menorah. It wasn't the same as candles, but I was glad to have it.

Parker was already in the kitchen, writing the agenda on one of the whiteboards with his usual crisp, angular strokes. He gave me a guarded nod, then moved on to another perfectly spaced line. I've written on more than a few chalkboards during my career, and his handwriting was shockingly precise.

"Why is your handwriting so good?" I opened the cabinet to pull out the pack of ground coffee.

"Test pilot." He glanced down at the next item on his agenda.

"I'm not following."

"After writing reports on a clipboard strapped to my leg, while pulling a plane out of a spin . . ." He thumped the board with his marker. "This doesn't move."

"Huh." I dumped the dregs of yesterday's coffee into the reclaimer. "Gotta admit, I never thought about that."

"Well, you don't think—"

"I don't think about most things." I finished with him.

Parker looked up from his clipboard with a snort. His dimpled grin flashed for a minute and—I'm almost ashamed of this—I wanted to make him smile again. If I could just figure out how to keep happy Parker around, the whole trip would be so much easier.

Staring at the glow of the menorah candles, I wiped out the inside of the coffee pot. "Say . . . Parker. I've been wanting to apologize."

My back was toward him as I slid the coffee pot back into place. Behind me, the marker squeaked on the board. Of course. Of course he wasn't even going to respond to that. Sighing, I shook my head and pulled the filter out of the coffee maker.

I'm not sure why I tried to make peace with the man.

"About . . . ?"

I turned around fast enough that the Coriolis effect threw my balance off, and I had to grab for the counter. Old grounds scattered across the stainless steel and spilled onto the floor. "Damn it."

"Not an apology." He glanced up from the clipboard. "Need help?"

"No. Thanks. I'm just an idiot." I tossed the filter in the composting and grabbed one of the rags. "But you knew that already."

"York." He sighed and lowered his clipboard. "I think you are many unflattering things, but not an idiot."

"'Least you're honest." I swiped at the grounds on the floor, folding the cloth over to gather them inside. Belatedly, I realized that, for Parker, that was a compliment. Almost. He didn't think I was an idiot. With another sigh, I sat back on my heels. "I'm sorry about your wife. I mean, about the assumptions I made, and needling you and everything."

"I asked you not to talk about her."

"I—" My mouth hung open at the chill in his voice. "I know. I'm sorry. I just wanted to apologize. I won't bring her up again."

Why did I try? Wadding the cloth up, I scrambled, carefully, back to my feet. Once the coffee was set up, I would clear out until the meeting started. With a clean corner, I wiped up the grounds on the counter.

Behind me, Parker pulled out the bench, its metal feet scraping on the floor of the kitchen. He sighed as he sat down, and the clipboard rattled against the table. "Thank you."

This time, I did not turn quickly. I did not turn at all, in fact. I kept my focus on the rag, and shook the used grounds into the compost bin. Only after biting the inside of my lip was I able to not cry. God. I hated the fact that I wanted to cry. This man gave me such grief that a little bit of kindness made me tear up. "What can I do to make you stop hating me?"

"I don't—I mean, I did. For a long time. But I don't hate you. Honest to God, York. I don't hate you."

Folding the dishrag into quarters required my full attention. The rough cotton bumped under my thumbs as I smoothed the corners. "You don't like me, either."

"The feeling is mutual, I'm sure." Parker cleared his throat. "So what can I do to make you stop hating *me*?"

"Stop being an asshole?"

He barked a laugh. "Sorry, sweetheart. It's baked in. But I'll try to remember that you're a delicate flower."

"That." I slapped the cloth down on the counter and turned. "That is the kind of thing that I'm talking about."

Parker's mouth hung open. He blinked twice, before snapping his jaw shut and trying again. "I'm joking."

"It doesn't feel like a joke."

He threw his hands into the air. "For the love of God. Your feelings are not my responsibility. I *meant* it as a joke."

"There's nothing funny about telling a woman that she's too delicate to handle something. We get told that all the time by people—by men—who are trying to keep us in our place. It's offensive."

"And calling me an asshole isn't?"

"It is." By this point, my hands had started to shake with anger. "But I wasn't joking."

"That would require a sense of humor." Parker grabbed his clipboard and slid off the bench. "Thanks for the apology. I'll treasure it always."

As he stalked back to the whiteboard, I squeezed my eyes shut. God. I really was an idiot.

By the time Florence slid down into the kitchen, I had the coffee going and a reasonable facsimile of a calm demeanor. My teammate, on the other hand, was grinning. She whipped her hand away from the ladder and waved a sheaf of papers over her head. "Got the morning paper here!"

"I can't remember the last time I was happy to see the paper."

"Oh, you'll like this one." She held up her free hand as if framing an imaginary headline. "Front page: DR. MARTIN LUTHER KING AWARDED NOBEL PEACE PRIZE."

"Mazel tov!" I clapped my hands together. "I'm so glad they recognized his work."

"That's great." Parker left his seat by the whiteboard and came to stand behind Florence so he could read over her shoulder. "Was he the first?"

Florence shook her head, not asking what he meant by "first." Heck, even I knew what he meant, and was glad he'd asked. I'd wondered, but didn't want to reduce Dr. King to his race. I was curious, though.

"Nah. That was Ralph Johnson Bunche." She handed Parker half the papers. "Elma, you got mail. I swear I didn't read it, but you tell your husband that if he keeps writing notes like this, the steam is going to damage my machine."

"And you say you didn't read it." A blush heated my cheeks, but it faded as I took the page from her. She had neatly trimmed the paper so that the "garbage" was removed.

It made sense, but the garbage always contained the best parts of letters from my husband. Still. It was a letter from

Nathaniel. I took it to the table and sat down, waiting for the rest of the team.

Dear Elma,

I cannot wait to show you our new apartment. As requested, it has green—in fact, it faces onto a courtyard that has apple trees, azaleas, and a privet hedge. Our bedroom is on the first floor, tucked behind the trees, so that we can have the curtains open and still have privacy. I am looking forward to showing you the morning light here.

Florence thought this was steamy? She should see the garbage.

Kamilah slid down the ladder and into the kitchen as Terrazas and Rafael jogged in from the tube leading to the gym.

With grabby hands, like a small child, Kamilah staggered toward the counter. "Coffee."

"Weren't you the one talking about its toxicity?" Florence peered over the rim of her own cup.

"Nothing is as toxic as me without coffee." She poured a steaming cup with a little moan.

Parker snorted. "Where's Flannery?"

"Here." He dropped down the tube into the kitchen. "Sorry. I was sciencing."

"I will admit that English is not my first language, but is that a word?" Terrazas swung a leg over the bench opposite me, folding his long frame to hunch over his cup.

"Absolutely." Leonard made a beeline for the coffee. "I can conjugate it for you."

Parker swung back to the whiteboard and wrote a hasty list next to his agenda. "I science. You science. He/She/It sciences . . ."

The juxtaposition of words on the board made an

accidental sentence, and a laugh escaped me. Pointing at the board, I read aloud. "I science duty rotation. You science Mars. He/She/It sciences waste disposal."

"Incorrect, York." Parker pointed at himself. "*I* science duty rotation. According to which . . . you science kitchen."

Florence clapped. "I love it when Elma sciences the kitchen. Will you science your chess pie?"

"I will science the heck out of that." I saluted, and a little frisson of pleasure ran up my spine. Am I Southern? Yes, I am. And if someone compliments my chess pie, I will bake them pies until the end of the universe.

"Good." Parker grinned. "You are also sciencing the calculations for our midpoint course correction."

"Terrazas and Avelino are sciencing the oxygen units and system checks on the BusyBees. Shamoun, you are sciencing the water reclamation here and over on the *Pinta*." Parker was grinning as he went down the checklist. "Flannery, you science the waste disposal. Grey sciences laundry and comms."

Funny how a simple word can change your perspective. Sure, Leonard and Florence had mentioned that they got only cleaning duty, but throwing the word "science" into the mix made it clear that Leonard wasn't doing anything but cleaning. All of his lab work happened on his leisure time.

I opened my mouth to point that out, but I could preemptively hear Parker tell me that it was a joke. Coward that I am, I just didn't have the energy to be the focus of his scorn at that moment. Besides, Leonard and Florence had asked me not to try to fix this.

But, really, it was just cowardice and exhaustion.

I closed my mouth and sank a little onto the bench. Across the table, Rafael nudged Terrazas, who straightened and cleared his throat.

"Can I swap with Leonard on the oxygen units?" He tapped his nose. "Got a sinus thing. Don't want to put a mask on."

Parker lowered his clipboard. "And that won't be a problem with the BusyBee? You'll be in zero-g."

"Um." Terrazas darted a look at Kamilah, who was still hunched over her coffee. "Well. It's just that Leonard trained on the oxygen units and not on the BusyBee, so . . . swapping that would be easier? I mean. If Leonard doesn't mind."

"Fine by me." Leonard gave a restrained nod that only barely hid his grin.

Parker looked between the three men and then back down at his clipboard. He cleared his throat. "No." He set the clipboard aside and leaned forward to rest his weight on the table. "Because I want them to forget that Flannery is on the ship until we get to Mars, because I need him there. Anything goes wrong and his fingerprints are on it? What do you think Mission Control will do with that?"

"Come on." Terrazas shook his head. "We all make mistakes."

The grin had drained out of Leonard's face, along with, seemingly, all the joy in the room. "I don't get to make any." He sighed. "I'll stick with waste disposal."

Parker pushed back up and shook his head. "You've got better chops with the oxygen systems than Terrazas, and I know it." He sighed and shoved his hand over his close-cropped hair, coming to a rest with his palm covering the bald spot in back. "But I'm sorry. Mission Control's duty roster stands."

TWENTY-THREE

HALFWAY TO MARS

Special to The National Times

March 28, 1963—Even in an era when technical and scientific wonders crowd close on one another, there was a special quality to yesterday's teletype from the First Mars Expedition as it sped through the void roughly halfway to our sister planet. These astronauts are pioneers voyaging in a realm where, so far as men know, there has never been life of any kind. The human organism is an evolutionary product that has been molded over millions of years by the special conditions of this planet—the force of gravity, the constitution of the atmosphere, the nature of the Earth's seas and lands. But in space, gravity is neutralized to produce what is called weightlessness, and there is no oxygen to breathe, no land to walk on, no water to swim in. Yet in this bizarre environment astronauts can live and function because their spaceship is a cocoon that reproduces the essential elements of this planet's ambiance. The day will come—and many younger people now alive may well live to see it—when space liners will take off daily for Mars as routinely as airplanes now depart for Chicago or London or Tokyo. When that time comes, no doubt human beings will be as blasé about that miracle as they are now about crossing the Atlantic overnight. But for the moment,

> while the first transMars crossing is still in progress, and courageous men are doing and seeing things no humans have done or seen before, one must be dull indeed not to be overcome by a sense of wonder.

Strapped into my seat on the bridge, I stared out at space as if the marker for the halfway point would be visible. It seemed as if being one hundred and sixty days away from both Earth and Mars ought to come with a golden gateway or some other extravagant signal. Instead, what I had was a sheet of printouts from Earth and a sextant.

Parker appeared to be calibrating his right-hand controller, methodically moving it through its range of motion, his strong jaw clenching as he worked. "I need those set points to update our navigation state."

"Give me a second to make a trunnion bias determination." Over the past three months, the tension between us had faded to low-level background radiation, which somehow vanished when we were working. I'll take the small blessings. I sighted my sextant on the stars that Mission Control had specified. The individual lights in the sky had become familiar over the course of the trip. I no longer needed to "Arc to Arcturus" or "Speed on to Spica." The blue-white of Spica shone with an unblinking gaze at me.

Noting the angle, I moved the trunnion off a couple of degrees and came back to take a second reading—I needed two consecutive measurements that were within 0.003 degrees. Then I referred to the printout that Mission Control had sent up.

Their predicted numbers matched mine. "By the numbers we're looking for, roll 8.37, pitch 61.33, and yaw 339.87."

"Confirmed. Roll 8.37, pitch 61.33, and yaw 339.87." He paused for a moment in the ritual call and response.

A moment later, Florence's voice crackled over the intercom from the comm module. "Confirmed. Roll 8.37, pitch 61.33, and yaw 339.87."

She was copying everything down on the teletype and sending the numbers back to Earth. The delay meant we were running more or less on our own, but Mission Control still wanted to double-check everything.

Parker continued setting up the ship for the burn. "Go ahead and give me the full correction, York."

"Okay . . . SPS/G&N; 63059; plus 0.97, minus 0.20." Even as I was rattling off a string of numbers and phrases, a part of my brain was laughing at what gobbledygook it sounded like. "GET ignition 026:44:57.92; plus 0011.8, minus 0000.3, plus 0017.7; roll, 277, 355, 015; Delta-VT 0021.3, 00:3, 0016.8."

My job was to figure out the *Niña*'s velocities as well as its local vertical and horizontal position with respect to Earth. Later in the voyage, I would start using Mars as our reference point.

Parker and Terrazas alternated between jotting down numbers on their own sheets and flipping switches on the control panel. Florence repeated that long string back. I paused to let them all catch up with me.

As I did, the line from the *Pinta* lit up with a question from their NavComp desk. Heidi's Swiss-German accent crackled across space. "*Niña,* what stars did you use?"

"For the GDC align, Vega and Deneb. You?"

"That's what Mission Control recommended, but I'm having trouble getting a clean reading."

I nodded, suddenly grateful that I had struggled so much and so recently with sighting on star fields so I could help her out. "What's your shaft and trunnion reading?"

"Shaft, 331.2, and trunnion, 35.85. I see Vega, but Deneb is not showing up in my sights."

I leaned forward and looked out the window toward the *Pinta*. The other ship caught the thin light of the sun and shimmered against a backdrop of stars. Like us, their command module faced inward, toward us, and with a view of the *Santa Maria,* where she sailed between and behind us. Their problem was immediately obvious, but it was also clear why it wouldn't be to them. "Looks like y'all need to roll, or sight on different stars. I think the *Santa Maria* is in your way."

A moment later, Heidi came back on the comm with the sort of steady calm that betrays an astronaut who has just been cursing off-mike. "Thank you, *Niña*. I did not see her."

"From your angle, you've only got the shade side of her. Practically invisible."

To my side, I could feel Parker and Terrazas watching me. Neither of them interrupted as I talked with Heidi, but Parker's fingers flexed as if he were itching to do the next thing. And I owed him more numbers. Turning off my mic, I turned back to them. "Roll align 007, 144, 068."

As he worked, Parker glanced out the window. "Looks like our heads will be pointed roughly toward Earth on this burn."

Now that Parker had everything ready, we had to wait. Despite the time delay, Mission Control had to confirm my numbers, and only then could Parker fire the engines. Over on the *Pinta,* they'd be waiting for the same thing, but with a different CAPCOM and a different set of computers.

Who would be on duty in Mission Control now? There had to be a team of computers going over the calculations. Maybe Katherine Johnson, and perhaps my old deskmate, Basira. Helen was still in the astronaut corps, so she wouldn't be doing the math for this, though she might be in Mission Control watching. Or maybe she was avoiding news of us.

Nathaniel would be there. I tilted my head toward the window as if that would allow me to see him somehow. The austere sky with its unblinking stars stared back.

Florence's voice floated into the command module. "Mission Control says, '*Niña*, you are go for mid-course correction burn. Confirmed Go and Godspeed.'"

Parker nodded, settling his hands on the controls. He blew out a quick breath, almost as if he were nervous, and my breath caught in anticipation as he did. "Terrazas, let the crew know that we've got a twenty-one-second burn coming up."

"Roger." Terrazas picked up the mic, and his voice suddenly went all *Buck Rogers*. "Ladies and gentlemen, in this thrilling installment, Captain Stetson Parker and his intrepid crew brace themselves for a twenty-one-second burn. The 'burning' question is, did the whole crew secure themselves when ordered, or were some of them scrambling even as his finger inched closer to the ignition? Closer. Cloooooser."

"*Payaso.*" Shaking his head but grinning, Parker said, "On my mark, in five, four, three, two, one—mark."

The *Niña* shuddered. *1, 2, 3, 4, 5, 6* . . . The low roar of the engines vibrated through the metal and plastic and fiberglass of the ship . . . *10, 11, 12, 13* . . . The stars wheeled to the side in time with our prescribed roll and I clenched my pencil until its hexagonal edges bit into my knuckles . . . *16, 17* . . . My seat slapped against my rump as the main engines pushed us forward . . . *18, 19, 20, 21.*

The silence hit as the engines cut off, and I was flung against my shoulder straps. Parker pulled his hands away from the controls. "Report?"

Terrazas looked at the velocity and relative position gauges amid a great wall of instrumentation. "Right on target."

With a sigh, Parker tilted his head back and smiled. "Look up."

Above our heads, a tiny blue pea floated in a sea of ink. And somewhere on that little ball, my husband would have to wait another fifteen minutes to know that everything was okay.

You'd think that passing the halfway point would bring about some change on the ship, but we just went about our work. Duty rotations shifted us to different responsibilities, but the sky outside continued to be the same inky black. I had pulled my favorite duty rotation, the garden module, this week. Oh, I liked kitchen duty, but being in the green and humid air of the garden module made tension bleed out of my veins.

Leaning over one of the radish beds, I pulled a small red globe from the dirt. Soil granules clung to the thready white roots and raised a scent of earth. I tapped the radish to release the dirt back into the bed. Once I would have objected to the bits that got caught under my fingernails and turned the tips of my fingers dark.

Kamilah had her feet up on the bench in the middle of the module with a book in her lap. "Can I borrow you after this?"

"Sure. For what?"

"I think it's time to press the raisins, and I want a second opinion." She stretched, lifting her arms over her head. "You've actually made this stuff before."

I shook a finger, coated with dirt. "Uh-uh. Myrtle made the raisin wine. I just sampled her wares."

"Still. You've got the closest thing to direct experience."

"I should never have told you that story." I wrinkled my nose against the memory of the tart, harsh liquor.

"Myrtle's raisin wine wasn't good. It was just alcohol. And you don't drink."

"This is medicinal. And . . . I have a secret weapon that she did not."

I laid another radish in the basket and paused to look at Kamilah. Her face had a smug beatific expression, her lips pressed together and her brows raised. "Oh?"

"I have a lab. And, specifically, I have a still."

"So . . . you're going to make it worse by concentrating it?" The brandy that they'd made from the raisin wine on the moon had been . . . challenging.

Kamilah shook her head, shutting her book and setting her feet on the ground. "I can make vodka. And there are juniper berries in the spice drawer. And citrus."

I stared at her, still not seeing what she was getting at.

"I can make gin."

Laughter bubbled out of me. Gin. Did we have any olives on the ship? "You are a genius, and—"

"What the hell, York." Florence stalked into the garden module with a wad of papers in her grip. "I had started to like you. I almost felt sorry for you. You piece of shit."

I dropped the radish, which bounced off the edge of the raised bed and rolled down the aisle. My heart tightened. "What?"

"This." She slapped the paper down on the radish bed, crushing some of the leafy greens.

Kamilah jumped to her feet. "Hey. Watch it."

Of course. She was worried about the radishes, but didn't defend me at all. I swallowed, trying to clear my throat so I could breathe. Florence stood too close, jaw clenched so hard that it looked like it hurt. Her gaze had the narrow focus of a laser.

3.14159 . . .

I dragged my gaze down to the papers that she'd carried

in so I didn't have to look that hatred in the face. It was a letter from Nathaniel. My rib cage locked around my lungs. Pencil marks marched above the lines of garbage. She'd decoded it.

... 26535897 ...

"I—" I coughed, trying to break the cage that held my breath. It only drove the air out, and I wheezed as I inhaled.

Kamilah stepped past Florence and grabbed my arm. "Elma. Breathe. Slow breath. Count it: 1, 2, 3, and hold ..."

"Oh, don't baby her." Florence jabbed the paper. "She's been spying on us. Sending coded messages."

Kamilah snorted. "Please. She's telling them that Parker can't be trusted in the kitchen?"

Snatching the paper up, Florence read: "I understand your concerns about the duty rosters, but Mission Control has reasons for making the assignments that they do. You don't realize how bad it is here. I'm glad of that, but we're sending the rosiest possible news to keep morale up. Trust me when I say—"

I snatched the papers out of her hands. They rattled as I hugged them to my chest. "That's private."

"What the hell are you actually doing on this mission?" Florence took a step toward me, forcing me back.

Kamilah let go of my arm, but her hand was still outstretched as if she were holding a ghost. Through the papers, my heart stuttered and thumped against my chest. I shook my head. "It's just ... It's just so we can ... He's my husband. I miss him. That's all."

"He's the lead engineer!" Florence buried her fingers in the dirt. "You think you can just tell him about our fights and the way we chafe at orders and that's not going to get back to someone?"

"It's not—" For the first time in my life, I was relieved that someone knew about the anxiety. It gave me an angle from which to explain. "It's the anxiety. He's—he's a safety valve. Nothing else."

"Thought you said that wasn't a problem anymore. Which is it, York? Either you are perfectly healthy and sending coded messages for no reason at all, or you are a neurotic mess clinging to a safety blanket."

My knees shook hard enough that I had to grab the edge of a bed to steady myself. I looked to Kamilah, hoping she could help explain, but her brows were drawn down and together. She stared at me as if we'd never met before. I shook my head. "Mission Control didn't send me—I mean, they did, but I'm not spying. Nathaniel isn't breaking any confidences."

"Oh yeah?" Florence pulled her hand out of the dirt and folded her arms over her chest, leaving a smear of earth against the blue of her flight suit. "Then why are they censoring our news now?"

"What are you talking about?"

"'Rosiest possible news'? You haven't noticed that all the news we're getting is sunshine and light? You think that's a coincidence?"

"I don't . . ." I looked down at the papers clutched against my chest. "I don't know."

But I did. Because of course Nathaniel would try to change things. Hadn't he told me before we left that he would sacrifice everyone on this ship to keep me safe? And hadn't I said that tempers were high? Hadn't I said that I almost wished they wouldn't send us letters from home? He wouldn't share things told in confidence.

But he would still try to "help." The same way I had, and made everything worse.

TWENTY-FOUR

April 9, 1963

Dear Elma,

I'm sorry that all of this is going to be "in the clear," as they say. I've just had a very interesting meeting with Director Clemons, in which he gently suggested that this would be for the best. There's not much to say about that, I suppose.

The apartment is pleasant enough, when I'm there. Nicole is back from the moon for a couple of months, and has come by to help with furnishing it. She and Myrtle seem determined to make certain that it will be cozy for you when you get home. I think they are worried that I will become too set in my bachelor ways. Myrtle chided me—you can imagine this—for the state of the pantry. Honestly, though, you know that dry toast is usually all I eat in the morning.

Everyone seems very determined to take care of me while you are away. Hershel tried to get me to come out for Passover, but I couldn't manage it, so he's coming here, ostensibly to help me prepare for Tommy—Thomas's visit. I told him that wasn't necessary, but—family will be family, eh?

I trust all is going well.

With all my love,
Nathaniel

I had not realized how vital the private messages were until we could no longer send them. Something was not right, and Nathaniel wasn't saying what it was. He and Hershel got along well, but there was no reason my brother would be coming out now, especially not if it meant being away from his family during Passover.

Parker cleared his throat. "Do you have a reply you want to send?"

I did not throw the paper at him. I did not roll my eyes. I did not huff. I set the paper down on the table in the kitchen and tried to deliver one of my mom's death stares. "Is this really necessary? Mission Control will look over everything I send. If there's a code, they'll spot it first."

"Following orders." Parker held up his hands. "Promise. I can have Grey send it, if you'd prefer."

"She hates me."

He shrugged. Of course it was no skin off his back. People hating me probably seemed natural to Parker. "Right now, she and I are the only ones authorized to use the teletype. Which of us is going to bug you less?"

Beneath the table, I had my hands wadded into balls in my lap. My nails bit into my palms. The injustice of this situation left me shaking with the suppressed urge to scream. Being able to express myself freely made me a healthier and more productive team member. That would go for any of us. And they were mad because I was talking with my husband about . . . what? Sex? Anxiety?

But none of that would be seen as sufficient justification. I tried to take a deep breath, but my rib cage caught and left me short. Prying my hands open, I pressed them flat on my lap. "I would prefer it if you sent the message." Parker grunted, brows going up in surprise. That was fair—I was surprised myself. "I trust you not to repeat anything." That realization made me shift on my seat. Anything that was public knowledge Parker would use against me, but he had never told anyone about my anxiety issues even when he was trying to keep women out of the space program.

With a nod, he slid his clipboard over to me. "I'll shred it after I send it. Won't help with Mission Control knowing, but at least you'll have some privacy on the ship."

"Thank you." I took the clipboard and picked up the mechanical pencil tethered to it. Rolling the smooth barrel under my fingers, I bent my head to the page.

Dear Nathaniel,

I'm sorry to have caused you trouble. I'm glad, though, that Myrtle and Nicole are helping with the apartment, particularly with the pantry. And it's good that you won't be alone for Passover. I know you don't have much of an appetite in the morning, but, to quote every doctor including my mother, it's the most important meal of the day. I don't expect I'll be able to change your habits from here, but it's still worth a try.

I hope you didn't expect me to defend the habit. Mama always said—

I broke off, pencil stuck on the page. Mama had always said he'd make himself sick that way. And the way he overworked meant he sometimes forgot to eat unless he was reminded. Who would stop him and make him go home? Or eat? Well . . . I guess Myrtle and Nicole were trying. The fact that Hershel was coming out to visit struck me with a more sinister force, though. I bit my lower lip, trying to figure out how to ask.

—Mama always said that you would end up with an ulcer if you didn't take better care of yourself. It would be a shame if Hershel came out to find you suffering from that. I remember how she would make you drink a glass of milk with your toast in the morning. Raise a glass for me? The powdered milk we have on the ship is nothing like fresh. Mr. Yoder, at the Amish Market, has farm-fresh milk that I dream about sometimes.

Lately, most of my dreams seem to be vivid memories of Earth, but nothing dramatic. Simple things like drinking a glass of milk, or standing on the street corner as the trolley comes down the lane, or the scent of your aftershave.

I stopped again. If I continued to talk about his aftershave, it would lead me to writing about how his skin was smooth and soft after he shaved and the warm line of his jaw when I nuzzled his neck. None of that was something that I could put into a letter that anyone might read. I dreamt about him in more . . . carnal ways sometimes. But this recitation of banal dreams was as close as I could come to reassuring him that I was all right.

Not perfect. Angry. Frustrated. Embarrassed. Yes, all of that, but I was weathering it better than I thought I would. On the other hand, anger had always given me a route out of the anxiety.

I've discovered that I can make a fairly decent chocolate chess pie, even without real eggs. Lemon meringue is out of the question, though. Maybe on the next mission, they can send along some chickens.

With love,
Elma

I must have sighed when I finished, because Parker looked up from the book he was reading—something in French—and raised an eyebrow. "You all right?"

I nearly snapped at him. I even inhaled, about to say something about how I was surprised he cared, but I stopped. He hadn't, in fact, rubbed my nose in this. "Frustrated."

"I can imagine." He closed the book and sat forward, resting his elbows on the table. "For what it's worth, I think anyone who thought of it would have tried to set up something similar."

The topic froze my tongue. Was it all right for me to respond to that? I wet my lips and picked the safest part of it to answer. "Maybe we should suggest that Mission Control give married couples a sanctioned encryption system on long trips."

Parker pursed his lips and nodded. "I'll suggest that in my next report."

"Then why won't you let me write to Nathaniel directly? Mission Control will still get to read it before he does."

"Because, believe it or not, I follow orders. Even when I don't agree with them. It's my job."

"You broke the rules to let Kamilah and me go over to the *Pinta*."

"That was—" Parker ran his hands through his thinning hair. "Look . . . chances are this is going to blow over pretty fast. Just keep your head down for a couple of weeks and I bet they'll relax the teletype rules."

"The same way they relaxed the laundry rules?" I slid the clipboard over to him.

"What do you mean?"

"Just that they're still only assigning laundry to the women."

He rolled his eyes. "York, that's just about utilizing an area of expertise. Most men haven't done laundry at all, much less as often as women."

"Are you saying that people who can operate a state-of-the-art aircraft can't be trained to empty a dryer filter?" I rubbed my face. It seemed like I managed to wind up in a fight with Parker no matter what the topic was. "Sorry. I'm just a little wrung out."

He studied me for a moment, blue eyes moving as if he were doing a preflight check. Finally, he leaned forward and took the clipboard back. "I'll make a note about laundry rotation in my report."

The bitterness in my voice was practically a real taste. "Thanks."

"Well, on that topic, at least, you aren't the only one complaining." Parker pushed back his chair and stood. "I'll get this sent. You can use the time to catch up on your duties."

"Yessir." What I really wanted to do was to crawl into my sleeping bag in crew quarters and not climb out again until we reached Mars.

But besides that, I was fine.

"York . . ." Parker stood at the bottom of the ladder, staring at the letter I had written. I wanted to rip it out of his hands. "I'm going to rotate you onto kitchen duty tonight. For next week, too."

"Pardon?" It was a Tuesday. Duty rosters changed on Mondays, and I had been on cleaning and sanitation this week.

"Areas of expertise." He tapped the clipboard. "Who else on the crew can prepare a Seder?"

I was so shocked that I couldn't form a sentence before Parker vanished up the ladder. The man baffled me.

Why is this night different from all other nights? Just this once, I wouldn't question.

About two weeks after Passover, I secured the hatch to the BusyBee for Kamilah's biweekly trip over to the *Pinta,* the door cutting off the constant hum of the *Niña*. I kicked off and floated up to the pilot's chair. The raw metal of the

Niña's sides filled the viewport. The angle of the ship since our last burn let sunlight sneak around the edges of the BusyBee to polish the raw metal into sterling.

"Buckled in?" I swung into the pilot's seat and grabbed my straps.

"Ready." Kamilah nodded and then cleared her throat. "So . . . How are you?"

"Fine, thanks. And you?" Her inflection had meant it to be a larger question, but I kept it to the safest corridor. "*Niña*, BusyBee. Am I clear for release?"

Terrazas answered me. "Confirmed, BusyBee. Nothing is blocking your path."

"Releasing grapple." I flipped the switch that withdrew the grapple from the airlock of the *Niña*. With a low *chunk*, we drifted away from the larger ship. I let us get about two meters out before I fired the retro-rockets to push farther back. As soon as I had enough distance, I'd turn the Busy-Bee and fly her over to the *Pinta*.

"Safe travels, BusyBee. *Niña* out." With a click, the buzz of Terrazas's mic went quiet.

Kamilah cleared her throat again. "Since you won't come visit me in the medical module, I have to ask here. And *don't* give me more social noise. How are you?"

With the early moon missions, we'd had flight surgeons on Earth who we talked to about health matters. They were a lot easier to dodge than a doctor who was on the ship with us.

"How am I? I'm flying a ship in outer space." I tapped the retro-rockets, and the tiny amount of thrust shoved us into our shoulder harnesses. This was not a conversation I wanted to have at any time, but while in flight was perhaps the least desirable. No. That wasn't true. At dinner would be the worst. But Kamilah was just trying to do her job. "I'm upset and frustrated, but not fragile."

"That's good." Kamilah shifted in her seat to face me. "What does it look like when you're . . . fragile?"

My teeth ground together, almost of their own will. "Difficulty sleeping. Nausea. Sweats."

The gap between the BusyBee and the *Niña* grew until long shadows and harsh white light bathed the side of the larger ship. The trip over to the *Pinta* took about twenty minutes when all was said and done. It was going to be a long twenty minutes.

"When was the last time you had those symptoms?"

If I were being completely honest, I was having trouble sleeping now, but only on some nights. And I wasn't having nightmares, just trouble securing the engine of my brain. It rattled around in my head with random thoughts pulling it one way and then another. "It's been a while."

"Does that mean before or after we left Earth?"

"After. But only once." I considered the fact that I was answering her questions to be a victory of sorts. Did I resent them? Yes, very much, but I wasn't foolish enough to think that she would believe me if I lied. Once, I would have, but we lived in quarters too close for little changes of behavior to be ignored. Heck, even my dense, old-fashioned self was pretty sure that Terrazas and Rafael were . . . involved. "Honestly, Kamilah. I'm all right. Not wonderful, but it's manageable."

"Tell you what. I'll believe you, if you promise to come by the MedMod so I can do some simple stress tests." She cocked her head to the side. "Parker is worried about you."

My laugh bounced off the viewport like a rock. "Oh. Well. If *Parker* is worried." On the other hand, he'd arranged it so I could host a Seder, so maybe he was. "The Seder helped."

"Good. Good . . . I'm glad to hear it."

Belatedly, I realized that I had no idea what holy days

Kamilah was missing up here. "What about you? What would help you? Any . . . observances?"

She shook her head. "Wait. Actually, yes. Would you call me Kam, instead of Kamilah?"

"Kam. Confirmed. Is there anything—"

"Don't think I haven't noticed that you changed the topic."

I sat forward, my attention caught by a spray of white down near the fuel cells. "What is that?"

"Elma—" Kam followed my gaze and gave a sharp intake of breath. Something was venting from the side of the *Niña* in a wide cone of mist. It froze in the vacuum of space and drifted back toward us like snowfall.

I slapped the mic on the BusyBee's comm. "*Niña,* BusyBee. Something is venting from the port side by the fuel cells. I'm swinging over for a closer look."

"BusyBee, *Niña*. What sort of venting?" I guarantee that Terrazas had just swung into high alert, but his voice remained steady.

"A white plume, from what looks like a single source. Give me a second to get closer." I nudged the BusyBee forward with a gentle tap of the thrusters. When I got to the fuel cells, I kept well back from the mist as I swung the ship so the viewport pointed straight at the venting column.

Kam leaned against her shoulder straps, trying to see better, as did I. It took a little attention to hold us steady in relation to the *Niña,* but not so much that I couldn't report. "*Niña,* BusyBee. Looks like it's originating from a small puncture. Small enough that I can't actually see the hole from here."

"Copy that, BusyBee," Parker answered. Terrazas must have called him the moment we registered the problem. "I've got Avelino headed down to look at the gauges and see what we're losing."

I shifted our orientation to the ship so that I was looking transversely across it from the front, hoping that it would give me a view of what was venting. We could be looking at water from the fuel cells, oxygen from that module, or coolant. None of those were good options. A crosshatch of tubes wrapped the fuel cells to keep them cool when they were being hit by direct sunlight. The venting plume began as a whisker of white in the joint of one of the tubes, which I followed back to its source system. Oh, hell and damnation.

"It's the coolant system. We've got an ammonia leak."

TWENTY-FIVE

HURRICANE TIME STIRS FLORIDIANS

***Weather Bureau Preparing with Help of* Lunetta**

By R. HART PHILLIPS
Special to The National Times

MIAMI, FL, May 7, 1963—A strong weather disturbance last week near the French Antilles, 1,500 miles from Miami, brought the attention of the people of Florida once again to the operations of the United States Weather Bureau in watching for hurricanes. In conjunction with the observatory on the space station *Lunetta,* the forecasters are able to accurately predict and monitor the behavior of this unusually early hurricane.

No one panicked. That was the beautiful thing about working with astronauts, and for the IAC. We had spent so much time in simulations learning to work the problem that the moment one appeared, all the interpersonal stuff just dropped away.

I sat at the kitchen table, paper and pencils ready, with a stack of reference books piled in front of me. Rafael, Leonard, and Parker stood at the whiteboard with a diagram of the coolant system taped to the board and notes scrawled alongside it. In the comm module, Florence listened to us over the intercom, transcribing the conversations for Mission Control and reporting back on what they said. She also kept the lines open to the *Pinta,* where our counterparts listened in.

Terrazas sat in the command module in case we needed to roll the ship in or out of sunlight. And Kam prepped a set of EVA suits. Fortunately, we kept the Mars Expedition ships at 4.9 psi, just like the moon colony and our EVA suits, so our spacewalkers wouldn't have to spend hours decompressing.

"I think we'll need to replace that section of pipe." Rafael pointed at the spot where I'd seen the leak. "Patching it is going to be unreliable at these temperatures."

Leonard nodded, then tapped the same section of the diagram. "But as a stopgap measure, that might be preferable until we know specifically what the problem is. If it's a puncture from a micrometeorite, that's a different issue than a material failure."

"Different how?" Parker hadn't spoken in a while, letting the two scientists hash things out.

"A micrometeorite is a one-shot deal. Sure, we might get hit again, but it's random chance. A material failure is likely to occur again in the same way, and points to a larger systemic problem."

The words "larger systemic problem" sent a chill down my neck. If we had a failure point in the coolant system, we would probably have to scrap the mission and limp home. Only . . . from where we were, we might have to keep going to Mars to slingshot home anyway. I hissed and started scribbling down notes to work those calculations, in case they asked.

"What is it, York?" Parker's ears were annoyingly

astute for a man who'd spent his life around airplanes and rockets.

"Just working the worst-case scenario of needing to scrub." I looked up from my paper, even though my equations were still half formed. "Slingshot."

He gave one quick nod to indicate that he understood. We'd worked that scenario in more than one simulation. "*Pinta, Niña.* Your systems all still look good?"

"Affirmative." Benkoski's voice crackled over the ship-to-ship line. "My vote is for the micrometeorite scenario."

The *Pinta* had rotated to aim its telescope at us, but really they couldn't see any more than I had. It was all guesswork until we got someone out there for an in-person look.

"Prep for both." Parker studied the board with his hands on his hips. "Avelino, you get the material together that you need to replace the pipe. Flannery, I want you to prep a patch in case you get out there and find something unexpected. Grey? Tell Mission Control that we're planning an emergency EVA."

"Been typing as you talk." Her snort popped in the microphone. "Can't believe I got a PhD to do transcription."

"And laundry." Parker grinned at the speaker. "Let me know as soon as they reply."

"Do you think everyone but you is an idiot?"

"Yep." Parker turned to face me. "York, prep a flight plan in case of worst-case scenario."

I could have made a joke here, but we were on the clock, so I just nodded and kept working. It was fine that I could feel my way through calculations, but for this, I wanted the comfort of warm, solid numbers on the page.

On Earth, they would be about fifteen minutes behind us. By now, Nathaniel would be on the floor of Mission Control, working with his team on solutions. He'd have his pencil gripped tight in one hand, shirt sleeves rolled up to his elbow. The cloud of Clemons's cigar smoke would billow around my husband as he paced, working the problem at their end.

I kept my pencil moving across the page, working course corrections, and could almost imagine that he was pacing behind me. The places our minds go for comfort are odd sometimes.

"Got an answer." Behind Florence's voice, the teletype rattled with commands. "Ready?"

I looked up from the page as if I could see her. At some point while I had been working, Leonard and Rafael had left the room, leaving just me and Parker. He stood at parade rest, watching the speaker. "Go ahead."

"Bobienski suggests an EVA with two primary goals: to diagnose the cause of the rupture, and, if possible, to patch it. If that isn't possible, then the spacewalkers should attempt to replace the failed section. We want to limit the EVA span, hence attempting to patch first."

I frowned, listening to her. Clarence "Bubbles" Bobienski was Nathaniel's assistant. Why wasn't Nathaniel the one answering? I mean, I know that Clemons didn't want him to work my flights, but this was different. This was his design, and he was still the lead engineer.

"Well, that's what we'd settled on, so that's reassuring." Parker wheeled around to grab his clipboard. "I'll tell Avelino and Flannery to suit up."

"Better hold on that. I'm not finished reading."

Parker cocked an eyebrow at that, as if Florence could see him. "Go on."

"Mission Control says that Rafael and Terrazas should do the EVA. They want Kam standing by in the MedMod, you on flight, with Leonard and Elma to help them suit up."

"What does Nathaniel say?" The question was out of

my mouth before I had a chance to register that it wasn't a good idea. Mission Control sent up the orders through the CAPCOM, and second-guessing them was just going to annoy everyone. "Sorry. Never mind."

"No . . ." Parker turned and looked at me, his free hand resting on one hip. The other drummed the clipboard against his thigh in an uneven tattoo. "Flannery should be going out, not Terrazas. Ask them for clarification on that staffing choice, and tell them I want Dr. York's opinion specifically. Also tell them that Flannery has more experience with EVAs and adhesives than Terrazas, and my opinion is that he should be the one to go."

That was the thing about communicating with a time lag: You had to include everything you could think of, because the delay meant that any sort of back and forth was useless.

"Oh, hell." Parker shook his head. "I'll come up and send it myself. It'll be faster."

"Glad you realized that. Come on up."

He headed out of the kitchen and left me alone with my numbers.

Kam walked into the kitchen with her hands shoved in her doctor's coat. "How are the numbers going?

"Just about finished double-checking them . . ." I ran my pencil down the long equations that described the path to Mars and back to Earth. Buck Rogers would have been able to just reverse course, but real gravity meant that the fastest return would be a slingshot around the planet. The problem was with how long it would take.

"Coffee?" she asked.

"Thanks." Even at best rate of return, we were still close to a year from home. Scrubbing was a worst-case scenario, but if the cooling system failed, we'd have to move over to the *Pinta* and abandon the *Niña*. And if anything went wrong with the *Pinta*, we wouldn't have any redundancy to save us. The *Santa Maria* was filled with things for the surface of Mars and had no living quarters. Maybe Rafael and Mission Control could figure out a way to keep *Niña* limping along so we could at least use her for storage.

Kam set the steaming cup of coffee in front of me with a clatter of plastic on metal. It smelled deceptively good, with all the rich bitterness you could want. I pulled the cup closer to myself, enjoying the aroma.

"Elma . . . Parker asked me to come talk to you." Kam turned her own mug in her hands.

I lifted my gaze from the equations to her face. She had a line between her brows, and her eyes were tight with concern. I set my pencil down. "About?"

"First, I want you to know that everything is all right." Her lips pressed together. "But Mission Control says that Nathaniel is in the hospital. He had an ulcer and ignored it, and they had to do surgery. He's fine—he's just taking some time off from work, as he should. But he's fine."

2, 3, 5, 7, 11, 13, 17, 23 . . .

"Elma? Do you hear me? He's fine."

"He is such a . . . a *man*." His last letters suddenly made sense. I now understood why Hershel had come out. Why Nicole and Myrtle had been restocking his pantry. Why he hadn't been home. "Why do you know?"

"Because Parker asked Mission Control about Nathaniel and they sent this answer back with, I should add, instructions not to tell you." Kam kept her hands loosely folded around her mug.

"Of course they did." Beneath my flight suit, my arms were tight with the effort of not slapping the table *. . . 29, 31, 37, 41, 43 . . .* I swallowed hard, trying to keep my voice calm and level. "I'm surprised Parker did it anyway."

Kam lifted one hand and waggled a finger. "Mm-mm . . . Parker did not disobey an order. *He* most definitely did not tell you."

I snorted, which my mother would have been mortified by. "Well, I won't thank him, then." Sliding my hands off the table, I tried to keep my spine straight, when what I wanted to do was lean forward and hide my head in my arms. "He should have told me. Nathaniel, I mean."

"Why? What could you have done from here?"

"I—I'm his wife." Under the table, I pressed my hands flat against my knees. If I had been home, I would have noticed that he wasn't eating. In fact, he would have been eating regular meals. And I certainly wouldn't have let it get so bad that he needed surgery. "I can nag him from anywhere in the galaxy."

"Well, he's fine. He's supposed to be back at work in another week or so. On half days for a bit." She reached across the table for me, one strand of her dark hair falling forward over her brow. "Do you need anything?"

From Kam—or rather, from Kam to me—that meant a Miltown. And, oh God, yes, I wanted that comforting cotton batting to muffle the anxiety that was swarming under my skin. Wetting my lips, I let out a breath as slowly as I could. "No. It slows down the numbers." I put a hand on the equations I'd been working on. "I can't be slow right now. And I'm fine. Thank you. But I'm fine."

Sometime during hour two of the EVA, after Terrazas and Rafael had gotten the lights set up so they could see the breach, but before they'd begun replacing the broken piece of tubing, Parker cleared his throat.

"Terrazas is doing okay out there." He nodded toward the viewport—not that we could see either man. "I don't . . . It's why I don't second-guess Mission Control often."

"Oh." Brilliant response, I know, but I was so surprised by Parker opening up what sounded like an actual conversation that I was afraid to, I dunno, spook him. Or something.

"Sometimes you get so close to a problem that you can't see all the pieces." He fiddled with the volume knob on the speaker, even though the sounds of Terrazas's and Rafael's breathing were coming in perfectly. "Did Shamoun talk to you?"

I nodded, then realized he wasn't looking at me. "She did." Saying something more felt like a risk, but it also felt necessary. "Thank you."

"I would have killed Clemons if he'd tried a stunt like that about Mimi."

"How is—" I caught myself before I could say more than that. Just because he was talking about his wife didn't mean he had given me permission to do the same. "Well. I appreciate it."

"Good. She's good . . . Out of the lung for about an hour a day now."

"That's great." What strange reality had I wandered into? Parker was voluntarily talking to me. About his wife. I presume because Nathaniel was in the hospital. "It's hard . . . knowing he's sick and there's nothing I can do."

"Yeah." Parker compressed his lips and gave this weird stiff twitch of his neck. "Yeah. But the IAC has access to world-class medical treatment. They'll take good care of him."

So, here's a question . . . Was Parker on the mission because he wanted to make sure his wife had the best possible care? Or was that the story he told himself to feel good about being out here and leaving her behind?

For that matter, was the story that I told myself any more

believable? Or true? "My brother is visiting to take care of him."

That caused Parker to turn and look at me. "The one from California?"

See, these moments of kindness leave me so confused. Though I guess someone with a wife in an iron lung wouldn't identify Hershel as "the one with polio." I nodded, trying to keep the conversation going, as if it could somehow spread out into the rest of the trip. "Yeah . . . Nathaniel mentioned that Hershel was coming out. I just didn't understand why."

Parker snorted. "Sounds about right. Mimi once mentioned that she was 'sleeping better.' Only after I asked did it turn out that there'd been a squeaky bolt on the lung that had been keeping her awake. Did she mention it while it was actually a problem? Not a chance."

I laughed and his eyes widened. That might have been the first time I'd laughed in front of Parker. It was so tempting to say, *See, I* do *have a sense of humor*, but I'm a grown-up and didn't. Also, a chicken, because I was afraid that I'd lose what little rapport we had. "I wonder what they say to complain about us."

"Well." Parker leaned over the armrest of his seat. "One thing I can tell you is that your husband hates—"

"*Niña*. EV1. We have a problem." Rafael's voice cut in, tight and professional.

Like a machine, Parker snapped back to attention, slapping the control to pipe Rafael through to the whole ship, even as he answered him. "Go ahead, EV1."

"Estevan's suit is caught on the ammonia lines. As far as I can tell, the sizing ring bracket between the lower right leg and boot has gotten snagged by the 4F.37 ammonia line bracket. I'm taking a look at it and I can't for the life of me figure out how it's connected. It's solid. So, I'd love to hear the ideas you have."

I grabbed the reference book on the ammonia lines that we'd brought up from the engineering library with us. The large-format schematics were still in engineering and I was willing to bet that Leonard already had it open.

"Copy that, Avelino. We'll start looking for solutions from in here." Parker glanced at me, giving a nod as he saw me leafing through the book for the right page. "Can you confirm for me what your current consummables are?"

"With CO2 scrubbers, O2, and batteries . . . I have about three hours left."

"Terrazas?"

There was a staticky pause. I looked up to the viewport, but all it showed were the hard light of stars and the distant blue dot of Earth.

Terrazas cleared his throat. "Closer to two hours for me."

"Understood." Though Parker didn't say it, I'll bet the same thought went through his head as went through mine: The accelerated consumption was a sign of an inexperienced spacewalker. They exerted more effort just staying still. Parker, though, just kept his calm captain's voice on. "What have you tried so far?"

"Rotating. Shaking. Pulling. Twisting. Cursing."

"Excellent technique. How many languages?" He toggled off his mic and switched over to talk to the lab. "Flannery, give me some options."

On one channel, we had Leonard saying, "Can he get in to cut the t-clamp?"

On the other channel, Terrazas was saying, "English, Spanish, and Portuguese. Any further recommendations?"

Parker switched back to Terrazas while Leonard was still talking. "Latin is always good for science cursing. You have your emergency shears . . . Flannery is asking if you can cut the t-clamp."

Rafael said, "To be utterly honest, I cannot even get a good sense of how the hardware is connected. I'm concerned about putting a hole in Estevan's suit. Can we disconnect the line?"

"Understood. Stand by." Parker flipped back to Leonard. "Flannery. You heard that?"

"Yeah . . . That section is permanently attached. Unfortunately, the best bet is to cut the line. It's depressurized right now, so we wouldn't have to worry about losing more ammonia."

"Tell me how hard the repair will be."

"Not . . . great. But doable." Leonard sighed. "Rafael will have a better idea."

Which made sense. Rafael was our engineer so knew the *Niña* better than anyone. I kept looking through the man ual, but everything I saw confirmed Leonard's assessment that they'd probably have to cut the line.

"Copy." Parker rubbed his hand across his face once and turned to me. "You said we'll have to abandon the *Niña* if the ammonia system doesn't come back online? No way around that?"

"If we lose cooling, the ship will overheat before we reach Mars on even our best-case trajectory." I shifted inside my shoulder straps, drifting in a tiny circuit within those restraints. "But I don't know all the contingencies for getting the ammonia system back online."

He leaned back over to the mic. "Flannery, if they have to cut the line to get Terrazas free, what does that do to our options for cooling?"

"We've got the ammonia shut down, so we won't vent anything. There should . . . Yeah, there should be enough to replace what we've already lost between us, the *Pinta*, and the *Santa Maria*. Give me a minute to run some stuff past Wilburt Schnöhaus over on the *Pinta*."

"Roger. We should work this to the bingo time of thirty minutes before we call it." Parker leaned back in the command seat and rubbed his forehead again. "Hell. York, start working course corrections for if we're all on the *Pinta*."

I nodded, understanding the decisions he was balancing. Under the circumstances, since we could retreat to the *Pinta*, Terrazas's life took priority over the ammonia system. Thank God for Mission Control and their flight rules. With flight rules, all the decisions about contingencies had been made ahead of time. It took emotion and quick reactions out of the equation. It gave us the redundancies we needed because we'd thought about how things could go wrong before we got there. And yet . . .

It was bad enough having to simulate leaving someone to die.

I shuffled the reference books I'd brought to grab volume 44B. "Mission Control already came up with the single vessel contingency, so—right. I'll refine it."

He nodded tersely and toggled the mic back on. "Avelino and Terrazas? We have to preserve thirty minutes of oxygen so you have an hour to try to work this before we go with cutting the line."

"Roger. We'll keep working the problem out here."

Terrazas answered, "Confirmed. In this thrilling installment, our intrepid band of space adventurers face THE WRATH OF THE SPACE TUBES. As we listen, our brave hero, Rafael Avelino, prepares to free his hapless sidekick from the wily space tubes."

After that, Rafael muttered something else in Portuguese that made Parker laugh, but his laughter died as soon as he turned his mic off. Parker reached for the switch again, as if he were going to call another station, but then pulled his hand back and set it in his lap. Jaw tight, he stared out the viewport and waited, the murmur of Rafael's commentary in the background.

Me? I did math, although there wasn't really that much to do, so I reviewed equations to make sure that I was ready when I needed to plug in the specifics.

Leonard's voice buzzed into the room. "All right. I want to go over it again when Rafael and Terrazas are back on the ship, but we're pretty sure that if we lose too much ammonia, then I can make more. Probably. But that's a worst-case scenario, and everyone would be happier if I didn't have to."

"Good work. And why do we not want you to make it?"

"Toxic. The chances of poisoning the air supply are not insignificant." Listening to him work out a problem was almost as much fun as listening to Nathaniel. "Figure I do it in the BusyBee, wearing a Mars suit. Should be fine that way. But we probably won't need it."

"Understood." Parker shut the mic down and sat, staring out at the void as the minutes ticked past. He sighed and reached for the mic again, switching it to the MedMod. "Shamoun, keep me posted on their telemetry, would you? If Terazzas's lithium hydroxide canister gets low, we'll call it sooner."

"I have my eyes on it. Everything is within acceptable parameters."

You would think oxygen would be the big worry on a spacewalk, but that's the consumable we can pack most efficiently. Carbon dioxide scrubbing, battery life—these are the things you worry about on an EVA. The oxygen is the least of the worries. You'll overheat before you run out of air.

At a certain point, I ran out of equations and joined Parker in staring into space as we listened to Rafael and

Terrazas work. It was an endless cycle of trying to pry the sizing ring bracket free, punctuated by random Portuguese curses.

Finally, Parker sat forward. "Thirty minutes. We have to call it." His jaw clenched. "You are Go to cut the line."

"Are we sure these lines are depressurized? It's like a steel rod."

Even as Parker was flipping to engineering, Leonard was back on the comm. "The gauge down here is flatlined on zero. That line is part of the permanent installation—I think that's why it's rigid."

"Understood." Parker glanced at me and we had a moment of rare rapport. The staffing on this spacewalk was all wrong. Leonard should be out there, not in engineering which wasn't his area of specialty. Sure he'd trained to back Rafael up, but most of his training had been on actually performing the EVAs. I could see Parker regretting his decision to use Mission Control's duty roster. "Avelino. Leonard says the gauge is at zero. He thinks the rigidity is caused because it's a permanent part of the cooling system."

"Copy." Rafael gave a small laugh. "I am only nervous about cutting my baby."

"I told you not to call me that. Oh—you mean the ship." Terrazas was such a ham.

"We can make the repair." Parker sighed, bending his head as if it were a prayer more than a command. "You are Go to cut the line. Repeat. You are Go to cut the line."

"Confirmed. Cutting the line and—" Rafael suddenly cursed in Portuguese.

Slapping the mic on, Parker leaned toward the speaker, as if that would get him closer. "Avelino. Report."

A spray of white fluttered around the viewport, twinkling in the sunlight the way the stars used to on Earth.

So beautiful, but my heart froze with it as I pointed. "Parker! Ammonia is venting."

Those lines should have been clear.

Some larger clumps drifted past, spinning and turning almost red in the sunlight. The sun wouldn't do that out here—that took the diffraction of an atmosphere.

We were looking at frozen blood.

TWENTY-SIX

ESTEVAN TERRAZAS 1924–1963

Kansas City, KS, May 7, 1963—The second casualty on the Mars mission comes a little over a month after the crew passed the midway point. Critics are pointing to the death of Estevan Terrazas as a sign of incompetence on the part of the IAC. An anonymous source high within the organization says that Captain Stetson Parker had objected to sending Terrazas out, saying that he lacked the experience, but was overruled by Director Clemons.

The director of the IAC characterized the death as a freak accident. According to reports, Terrazas became mired in the ammonia cooling system while doing repairs. In an attempt to free him, the crew cut an ammonia line. Tragically, a faulty gauge indicated that the lines were empty, and when cut, the pressure caused the sharp end of the metal line to whip past his suit and breach it. The suit lost integrity, subjecting Terrazas to the vacuum of space.

Kam and I floated outside the airlock. Again.

I couldn't summon a single rhyme. My head was filled with the sound that Florence was piping through the ship. Sounds, really: Leonard's voice narrating as he guided Rafael back to the airlock.

"Okay, reach forward with your right hand and you'll feel the guide rail at the door."

The other sound was Rafael's ragged breathing, the sound of someone trying not to sob. It hitched and tore, hissing through his teeth, then there was heart-stopping silence as he held his breath, until it escaped again to catch on the edge of his voice. But when he spoke? God . . . he was professional and dead calm. "Confirmed. I have the guide rail."

"Good. You're going to feel my hand at your waist as I secure you."

"Copy." Then the cycle of Rafael's breath began again.

I rested a hand on the cold metal of the inner airlock door and leaned toward the port, looking for the men. Leonard's suit was just a dark silhouette against the darker sky. His face was lost in shadows.

"Rafael's local tether is bail closed. Slide lock. Black on black. I'm picking up our safety tethers and heading through the hatch."

In my head, I went through the motions with him of clipping the tether hook and sliding the lock closed so that the indicator showed a solid black line.

"I'm cleaning up my safety tether so we can take everything up back inside."

Beside me, Kam shifted the towel in her hands. We had practiced having an incapacitated crew member in sims, but there is a large emotional difference between a sim and the reality.

I twisted my own towel into a rope and the soft white terry cloth added its own hush to the ship sounds. To fill the void, I said the obvious. "Once Rafael's eyes are clear, I'll help Leonard get him out of his suit."

"Good." She drifted by the med kit she'd strapped to a socket on the side of the spindle. "If he becomes combative, I have a sedative."

Leonard's voice continued his quiet commentary. "We're both secured so I'm going to guide you in."

"Copy."

Nothing in his voice said that Rafael was combative. It was just a contingency, like all the other things you prepared for. Through the port window, you could see their silhouettes come into the dim light of the airlock. Were it not for the stripes on their suits, you could not have told which man was which, except that Rafael groped for the walls and Leonard guided him with precise movement.

"We're in the airlock. I'm letting go for a moment to dog the hatch shut, but you're tethered to the interior rails."

"Copy." The suits were so bulky that you couldn't see the movement of Rafael's chest. As he drifted closer to our side of the airlock, the light slid over the curve of his helmet and lit the haze that coated the glass. His face was just a dim shape inside.

I pulled myself to the side of the door to give them some room to come through. As Kam waited by the IV pressure gauge, I folded and refolded my towel, as if there were some optimal way to hold it. Surely the IAC had done some sort of study on this, or some graduate student somewhere had made "maximizing terry cloth" their thesis.

Above my head, the delta-pressure gauge rose as Kam opened the IV hatch valve to let atmosphere flood into the airlock. The air roared through the valve as if a freight train were passing the spindle.

It nearly drowned out Leonard's voice. "Pressure confirmed. Nearly there, Rafael."

"Confi—" His voice broke on a cough.

My heart leapt through my chest, as if it could get the airlock open. My training moved faster than that. I shoved the towel between my knees, gripping it with my legs, while I grabbed the ratchet handle and pumped it. Five pumps to release each of the fifteen latches that held the door sealed.

Leonard saw me through the port.

He grabbed Rafael's helmet and undogged the latches holding it on.

All that redundancy fought us as the same safeguards that kept the helmet secure slowed him down.

Over the loudspeakers, we listened to Rafael aspirating his own tears.

I jackknifed, still holding that damn towel between my legs, and kicked hard against the wall to haul the inner hatch open. As soon as I had a gap, I let inertia carry it the rest of the way and swam forward, grabbing the towel.

Rafael, bless him, held still, even though his hands jerked and twitched in distress. He didn't fight Leonard as he yanked Rafael's helmet free. Training might say that it wasn't possible to drown in your own tears, but globules of salt water and snot floated into the airlock. His eyes and nose and mouth were coated with silvery balls.

I slapped him in the face with the towel. The recoil pushed him back from the water, just a little, and the towel started absorbing stuff. Now, he moved, and lifted a hand to guide the towel into his mouth.

Coughing and spitting, he cleared the salt water, while Leonard braced him. Outside the airlock, Kam glanced up at the speaker. "Parker. We have him. Rafael is secured."

"Confirmed." I have never heard so much relief in a single word. "Good work."

At that, Rafael's flagging control cracked. "Good work?" He flung the towel away. "I fucking killed him."

I caught his gloved hands and pressed them tight together between mine. The cold of space's shadow still permeated the material and bled into my bones. "Sweetie . . . I know it's hard. I know. But it isn't your fault."

"Yeah? Whose is it?"

Over the speaker, Parker said, "Mission Control's." His breath sighed into the mic. "And mine. And God's. And, yes, yours. And you'll carry that guilt, I won't pretend that you won't, but it is not yours alone. You did the best you could to keep Estevan safe."

At the sound of Terrazas's first name, coming from Parker, Rafael crumpled. Fresh tears crowded around his eyes, building into mounds. Leonard snagged the towel from where it was floating and pressed it against Rafael's face. I let go of his hands, and he clutched the towel, weeping into it.

I twisted, slipping out of the airlock so Kam could fit in. Her voice was cool and dispassionate. If you just listened, you couldn't tell that her eyes were red and swollen. "Just hold steady and we'll get you out of the suit."

If Rafael responded, it was lost behind the towel. As we worked to get him out of the suit, he slowly went limp and nonresponsive. Kam kept up a steady meaningless murmur as if her voice was a tether to keep him with us. At some point in there, Parker arrived and helped Kam get Rafael down to the MedMod. That left me and Leonard to stow the suits.

His jaw was tight as I helped him shuck out of his EVA suit. Our only conversation followed the checklist that the IAC had set up for post–extra-vehicular activity. When the last boot was secured in its bin, Leonard floated, staring at the empty spot where Terrazas's gear should go.

"Elma? May I . . ." He brought his hands up to cover his face. "Could you—?"

All the tears I'd been fighting off burned at the back of

my throat. I pushed over to wrap my arms around Leonard, and we both floated, spinning slightly, as our grief formed constellations around us.

Rafael slept in the MedMod.

Four of us sat in the kitchen drinking the hot cocoa Florence had made for all of us. Leonard huddled under a gray wool blanket next to Kam, who stared into her cup as if it would speak to her.

I clutched my own cup. It should have warmed my hands, but they still ached. Hours later, and my hands still ached from touching Rafael's suit. At least, that's what I told myself it was. In truth, every part of me ached, as if the grief had frozen all my joints the way that—

I swallowed, and picked up the mug.

Parker slid down the ladder. His eyes were red around the edges and he carried a bottle under one arm. Head down, he walked to the table and set brandy in the middle.

Florence straightened and reached for it. "How'd you get this on board?"

"Get what on board?" Parker settled on the end of the bench, next to me. "Mission Control strictly forbids alcohol on IAC ships to avoid cultural misunderstandings."

Kam snorted and slid Leonard's mug toward Florence. "I hate being used as an excuse. This is medicinal."

I slid my mug forward too. "Doctor's orders."

Parker rested his head on both hands. He addressed the table. "I want to go over what we're doing with the body."

"Not the bag." Cocoa sloshed over Kam's mug.

"That's what Mission Control wants us to use, because Terrazas is already frozen."

"No." I shook my head, fury rising up my spine, and I reached for that heat, gratefully. Goddamn it, Nathaniel had said that we wouldn't—but he wasn't in the office, was he? I clenched my jaw and swallowed so I could speak. "I recommend against that."

"I agree." Parker still kept his gaze fixed on the table. "Based on your report, it would traumatize an already traumatized crew."

"Parker . . ." Kam reached across the table and touched his elbow where it rested on the hard surface. "We're all exhausted and in shock. It might be best to wait for a bit."

"I know." He straightened, and his face was military calm. "But I want this resolved before Avelino wakes up. I don't want him to have to hear us discussing it, so let's do our goddamned job and work the problem."

Leonard pulled the blanket a little tighter around his shoulders. "Estevan is still attached to the ammonia line, so we're going to have to finish cutting it to free him. That section should be completely clear of ammonia." He swallowed. "Now."

"It should have been clear before." My voice was sharper than I intended.

Leonard held up his hands. "The gauge read empty."

"Stop." Parker laid his hand flat on the table. "We are not looking to assign blame. We are working the problem of what to do with Estevan. At the current juncture, the line has been cut and is clear of ammonia."

"And we have to do that EVA regardless, to repair the cooling system." I nodded, trying to match the calm that we were all pretending to possess, as if this were just another sim. "I can go out with Leonard to . . . to clear the lines."

"Then what?" Florence stood and walked over to the stove. "Do we bring him inside?"

Leonard looked over his shoulder at her as she retrieved a mug. "He's got one arm stretched out. We wouldn't be able to bring him in through the airlock. And it would take some work, still, to get the lines off . . . There's a block of ammonia around his foot. It would . . . it would take some work."

Except for Rafael, Leonard was the only one who had seen the . . . the problem. We could probably take the Busy-Bee out for reconnaissance. "What about the BusyBee? Could we load him in that?"

"To what purpose?" Parker's face was a blank mask.

"Well . . . then we could work under atmosphere."

Leonard nodded. "Yes, I think he'd fit through the larger hatch. Only—" He winced, tilting his head to the side. "That ammonia is going to thaw."

Florence set a mug of cocoa in front of Parker. "So wear a Mars suit, like you were telling Parker you'd do if you had to make replacement ammonia."

"You heard that?"

"Baby, I hear all." Florence rested a hand on Parker's shoulder until he reached forward and picked up the mug. "I've got one job on this ship, and don't you dare say that laundry is that job. It's just because some folks are too foolish to do their own."

Parker stared into the mug. "We should decide what the end goal is." He set it down again, without drinking, and stood. Grabbing a marker, he uncapped it and faced the whiteboard. "I figure we're looking at these options."

On the board, he wrote:

Burial in space
Storage for burial on Mars
Storage for burial on Earth
The bag

That last, he drew a line through. "We've eliminated one." Parker looked over his shoulder at us. "What other options are there?"

We all stared at the board. I half raised my hand and then put it down again. Because, truly, the idea in my head wasn't a real option. Half a dozen things could go wrong with it.

"York."

"It's not—" Someone else might get an idea from it. That was the point of this exercise. "Incineration."

Parker's lips pursed for a second before he nodded and wrote that on the board too. "Any others?"

Leonard raised his hand. I don't know why we'd started doing that, like we were children in a school. "Instead of ground burial on Mars, how about a reentry burial at Mars?"

Parker nodded, wrote that, and also: *Reentry burial at Earth.* "Anyone else?"

The fans hummed in concert with the refrigerator and the quiet pings of the ship as the ring segment rotated through space. I took a sip of my cocoa, which was too sweet, and coated the insides of my mouth like glue. Setting the mug down, I reached for the brandy.

Still staring at the board, Parker asked, "Any guesses on which he would have wanted?"

"You should ask Ra—" Kam stopped herself and stared down at her mug.

"I don't want to bother him more than I have to. Bad enough that he feels responsible for this without putting that burden on him."

"No—it's just that they were . . . close." Kam looked down, lower lip tucked between her teeth.

I suppose it's a sign of how much the world had changed since the Meteor that I had already known this: The way they spent all their off-duty time together. All the times I'd seen them touching. Rafael saying that he knew who the condom belonged to . . .

Glancing around the table, I saw that same awareness sitting in the others, but the world hadn't changed enough that any of us would say it aloud. Even with Kam's assurance that Mission Control had known this kind of thing was "not uncommon," they were both military men.

Parker sighed and rubbed the back of his neck. "All right. Let's work the problem on each scenario. Shamoun . . . may I ask you to present the options to Avelino for his opinion? It might be better coming from—"

"Yes." She nodded, fingers tight around her mug. "Times like this, I wish I drank."

With the exception of DeBeer, the entire crew of the *Pinta* came over to the *Niña* for Terrazas's service. It wasn't safe to leave both ships entirely uncrewed, and I was grateful to Benkoski for making the staffing choice he did. We sat in two uncomfortable rows in the garden area, listening to Wilburt and Graeham play a haunting duet on flute and violin.

Florence and I had dragged in the benches from the kitchen and the chairs from the MedMod. I'd picked a spot in the back row between Benkoski and Florence. Directly in front of me, Rafael sat between Kam and Leonard. His posture was so rigidly correct that it hurt to look at.

In front of him, across the radish bed, we'd made a sort of byre. Not that we were going to burn anything. Anyone. But we'd used small packing boxes and a locker door to create a raised surface above the gently waving green leaves.

Kam had wrapped Terrazas in a winding sheet. His body lay, almost like a mummy, upon the plank. On the corner that lay over his face, Florence had stitched a simple Roman cross using blue thread that she had unraveled from his uniform. I'd taken some old punch cards and reports and cut them up, curling the edges and twisting them into a spray of flowers that rested in an ecru bundle on his chest.

I think, being so far from home, we were clinging to every ritual or comfort we could. Even though Terrazas was Catholic, I had recited the Mourner's Kaddish for him. Others were marking his passing as we had not been able to do for Ruby. Or had been directed not to, I suppose. Either way, I think we all needed this, and I was genuinely grateful to Parker for ignoring Mission Control.

Graeham and Wilburt brought their song to a close and left us with the quiet susurration of the leaves and our own uneven breath. Parker stood from the front row and walked to stand next to Terrazas's body. "There is no good way to mourn the passing of a person. But we can remember him, and remember him well. Estevan Terrazas and I met for the first time during the war. We were on a base in Normandy, refueling. I flirted with a young woman, who turned out to be his sister. Despite the fact that I outranked him, and that they were in France as refugees, he . . . suggested that this was not a good choice." Parker gave a sideways smile and briefly met my eyes. "I will always remember that he has a solid right hook. And that he was fearless, loyal, and a complete *payaso* with his friends. I was proud to have him as a copilot and even prouder that he granted me his friendship."

In front of me, Rafael's back was rigid. His shoulders had stopped moving, and I think he was holding his breath. I reached forward and rested a hand on his upper back. For a moment, Rafael leaned into my touch, and then the shell surrounding him cracked. Folding forward, he clapped both hands over his mouth, and even that didn't quite muffle the sound.

Kam turned in her seat, but before she got there, Benkoski already had Rafael wrapped in his long arms. She pulled them both into her embrace, and they sandwiched Rafael. Leonard slipped forward and joined that huddle, which propelled me forward as well. All ten of us wound up wrapping ourselves around him in awkward postures hunched over benches, chairs, and each other. It was as if we were trying to make an ablative grief shield of our bodies.

Times like this, you don't count in minutes or breath or anything except the waves of pain that ebbed and flowed through us. Rafael was not the only one weeping.

I was empirical evidence of that.

A pallbearer has a different role in zero-g. Rafael and Leonard guided Terrazas's shrouded body down through the spindle and into the airlock. Except for that breach in the garden module, Rafael's hull of control had remained stable. Internal flaws are not obvious, though, and his apparent calm fooled no one.

I think that's why Parker sent all of us to the observation dome before they opened the outer airlock. He probably would have sent Rafael, too, if it hadn't been obvious that he would refuse to obey that order.

We clustered next to the windows on the port side—not that port and starboard have much relevance in space, but old nomenclature dies hard. Heidi drifted over to me and floated with her arms wrapped around herself.

At a funeral on Earth, there would have been small talk as we caught up and reminisced about the deceased. My urge to bake pies and casseroles had been clawing at the underside of my skin for the past two days, but I couldn't for the life of me remember how to start a normal conversation.

Though perhaps "for the life of me" is not the most appropriate phrase under the circumstances.

The observation dome stuck out just far enough that we could look back along the length of the ship. We were sunside, so the ship gleamed against the ink of space. You never really get used to how deep that black is. The word "deep"? That is appropriate, because it feels like something you could fall forever into.

Which is, I guess, what we were about to do with Terrazas.

The loudspeaker crackled on and Rafael's voice joined us. "Ladies and gentlemen." His voice roughened and he cleared his throat before starting again. "Ladies and gentlemen, in this thrilling installment, our intrepid adventurer Estevan Terrazas embarks upon an exploration of deep space."

Aft of us, a spray of paper flowers blew out from the side of the ship, followed by Terrazas's wrapped body. The winding cloth bound his body into a torpedo that followed the laws of inertia and floated alongside us. Slowly, our speeds diverged, and he drifted back, almost as if he were conducting an inspection of our hull. O, brave, intrepid adventurer.

I had to turn away from the window and close my eyes. Lord . . . we'd gone to the moon together. My first time in space had been with this man. So many years ago, and I still remembered that as if it were in present tense.

"Wait—" Terrazas puts a hand on my arm and then gestures to the windows. "Look."

There is nothing to see but that vast blackness. Intellectually, I know that we've passed into the dark side of the Earth. We slide into her shadow and then magic fills the sky. The stars come out. Millions of them in crisp, vivid splendor.

Look. I opened my eyes again, to bear witness. Facing sunward, there were no visible stars in the sky, but my paper flowers caught the sunlight and seemed impossibly bright against the black of space. Terrazas spun as if he were taking in the glory of everything around us.

"Oh no . . ." Florence floated to the window and pressed her hand against it. "No. No . . . Shit."

She saw the impact coming before it happened. Which gave the rest of us time to see Terrazas's body hit the antenna that pointed toward Earth.

TWENTY-SEVEN

CHILE TAKES OVER RAILS AS STRIKES AND RIOTS SPREAD

SANTIAGO, Chile, May 20, 1963—A growing wave of demonstrations by thousands of citizens over food shortages prompted the government to place the railroads under army rule today. The government also reinforced guards at strategic points and increased the number of police patrolling the city streets with water-spray cannons.

Mission Control moved us all over to the *Pinta* because of the damage to the *Niña*. After seven months of living with only six other people, the past ten days had felt strange and claustrophobic.

I pressed against the wall of the Monday morning staff meeting as the crews of both ships crowded into the kitchen on the *Pinta*. Parker and Benkoski stood at what felt like the back of the strangely disorienting room.

The two ships were identical, or had been built that way, but seven months of habitation by two very different crews had changed them. Some of the differences were blatant, such as the Alpine border that Heidi had painted along the wall where wainscoting would go. That was easier than the small changes. For instance, the coffee cups were on the third shelf in the right-hand cabinet, not the first shelf on the left. In the silverware drawer, the spoons lay between the knives and forks, rather than to the right—which is where they should be. Why wouldn't you put them in the drawer in the same order they go on a table?

Perhaps oddest was that they had put the whiteboard on the opposite side of the room from where we had it. Not that it made a difference, but I kept feeling like I was facing the wrong direction. Parker kept turning the wrong way when he reached for a marker.

"All right. It's mission critical to get the *Niña*'s cooling system back online, along with our antenna. I know the *Pinta* team wants us out of their hair as fast as possible, but we're going to do this nice and slow and right. We'll take advantage of having both teams on one ship and combine forces. Now, Mission Control has put together a plan that they think will work. We're going to start with the cooling system." Turning to the board, Parker wrote two names. "York. You and I will be on the bridge of the *Niña*. I want you doubling as my copilot for this, so start your prep now."

The entire room went hot as all my blood rushed to my face. It was like being in high school, younger than everyone else by four years, and getting picked for the kickball team. And not as a grudging last choice, but first.

On the other hand—who was I kidding? All the blood drained down, leaving me cold. Parker followed the rules. I was Mission Control's choice, and he was accepting me because he obeyed orders.

"Schönhaus and Flannery, you're on the EVA. Avelino and Grey will help you prep. DeBeer, you and Stewman are—Yes, Sabados?"

Dawn's sharp cheekbones seemed poised to punch through her skin with disapproval. "Mission Control said that Wilburt and DeBeer should do the EVA."

"Thank you. I am aware of that."

While Parker turned back to the board, Benkoski folded his arms over his chest and met Dawn's eyes. He gave a little headshake, which stopped her in the process of opening her mouth.

At the side of the room, leaning against the kitchen counter, DeBeer had his jaw set and his chin lowered as he looked out from under his brows. Leonard's mouth had rounded into an "O" of astonishment, and his color had deepened with a blush.

"DeBeer, you're going to be in the BusyBee, so if there are any eventualities, you can pull our people in faster and get them immediate medical attention. Your first task is working with Shamoun to make any modifications you need to turn it into a floating sickbay."

That pairing worried me. On our trips over to do regular checkups of the crew, his racism had never been as blatant as it had been while he was sick, but little things always slipped through. None of them would have made it into a report to Mission Control, except as a line like "suboptimal communication between copilot and medical specialist."

"Avelino, you, Schönhaus, and Flannery are in charge of going over Mission Control's EVA plans with a fine-toothed comb. We've been out here for seven months and they don't know what our actual conditions are. Look for any hole. Any flaw. Any potential failure point. You have any doubts at all, I trust you over them. Clear?"

"Not sure anyone should trust my judgment." Rafael gave a little shrug, staring at the floor.

"Are you questioning an order?"

Rafael jerked his gaze up. "No, sir."

"Then sit up straight and pay attention." Parker jabbed

his marker toward Rafael. "You have a job to do, and I damn well expect you to do it."

That was hardly fair. The man was still in shock and grieving. I mean, I know it wasn't his fault, but he was allowed to feel all the pain and self-doubt that came with—Oh. Parker was giving him a purpose. Goddamn it. I was happier being angry at him, but had to admit it was a good strategy.

Parker tapped his pen against his palm and glared at all of us. "We are millions of kilometers from home. We haven't all been in the same room since we left Earth orbit seven months ago, so let me remind you of a few things. One. I am mission commander. Two. Benkoski is second-in-command. Something happens to me, you obey him. And you obey him over what Mission Control says, because for all the brain power they've got banked down there, they can't see what we can. They can't know the nuances of our situation, which means they make mistakes. *I* made a mistake on the last EVA, because I knew that Leonard was better qualified, and I didn't push. So. You see a failure point, I expect you to bring it up. I expect you to work the problem. But I also know that none of you are failure points. The twelve of us? In this room? We are our entire world. So do your goddamned jobs and let me do mine."

It was such a strange feeling to want to applaud Parker.

May 22, 1963

Dear Nathaniel,

I feel like a bad wife because I've been updated about your health, but it's still taken me several days to write to you. I'm sorry it's been so long, although I'm sure you understand why. The hours have been long and I haven't wanted to ask Florence or Dawn to spend extra time at the teletype. Florence chivvied me into it, FOR WHICH I AM GRATEFUL.

I guess you already know that Wilburt and Leonard managed a partial repair on the ammonia system. All of us are looking forward to having it at full capacity again, partially so we can bring all the systems back online, but mostly so we can go home. The *Pinta* crew has been gracious, but having us all crammed into one ship means we're constantly tripping over each other. You would think it would reduce the workload, since we could split it among more people, but we just seem to be creating more work for each other.

I imagine that's what it'll be like for you when Thomas arrives. Please tell me that he's still coming out to intern with you. Mostly because that will mean you are well and hopefully he'll make sure you eat on a regular basis.

I see the face you just made. Yes, even from millions of kilometers away. Remember that I can nag from any distance.

Other aspects of marriage require proximity, so I look forward to when we are in the same gravitational field again.

All my love,
Elma

There is something strangely satisfying about making a piecrust. You take three ingredients and they turn into magic. While I would have preferred to do a true butter crust, the butter-flavored oleo that they'd sent with us was shelf stable and not bad. On the other hand, I'd been eating in space for so long that my bar for "not bad" had lowered significantly.

Fortunately, so had everyone else's, so my chocolate

chess pie still worked as a bribe. With any luck, it would put everyone in a better mood. We'd been on the *Pinta* for two weeks now and the cramped quarters made everyone tense.

I gripped the bowl against my hip to steady it as I cut the oleo into the flour with a fork. I'd already made the filling, which sat on the counter in a chocolatish soup. Through trial and error, I'd learned that when using powdered milk, I got a better consistency if I let it sit before baking—one of the many adaptations to space that the IAC didn't anticipate.

Much like what it would really be like to put both crews on a single ship. Behind me, some of the crew of the *Pinta* were using the kitchen as a recreation space. I guess they'd picked this room over the observation dome, which worked out well for sharing. Last I'd seen, Florence and Kam were up in the dome.

Dawn and Heidi had added a makeshift table, made from a crate lid and a box, and had a jigsaw puzzle going, which showed a partial view of a Venetian canal. DeBeer sipped a cup of coffee while poring over an old newspaper from home.

Funny, the things we do for comfort. After a while, the parts of the paper that you never normally read become sources of comfort. I'd found myself engrossed in the baseball pages, just because they contained words like "Chicago" and "San Francisco."

With the flour and butter cut into fine breadcrumbs, I set the bowl back on the counter. Next up were four tablespoons of water. At home, I only needed three, but the humidity was so low on the ships that it took a little more to get a good consistency.

Rafael slid down the ladder into the kitchen. He had

barely hit the floor when he pushed off again and used the rebound to land near DeBeer. He slapped a hand-lettered sign against the taller man's chest. "This was you?"

"Could have been anyone." DeBeer pushed Rafael's hand away, exposing the full sign.

Colored Restroom.

I slammed the measuring spoons on the counter. "You asshole."

"It was over the zero-g toilet." Rafael ripped the newspaper out of DeBeer's hands. "*Vai pentear macacos.*"

DeBeer surged up out of his seat, shoving the chair back. He had a good seven centimeters on Rafael, and used all of them to loom over him. "Don't you dare touch me."

"Why? Am I too dark for you?" Rafael put both hands on DeBeer's chest and shoved. "Are you dirty now?"

DeBeer pushed back. And then they both just snapped, fists and words flinging around the room.

I ran forward. "Guys! Stop. Stop! This isn't—"

I had to dodge backward as they tumbled toward me. Dawn chose a more useful course, and ran to the wall intercom. She slapped the button. "Parker. Benkoski. Fight in the kitchen. Request aid, ASAP."

Heidi and I both circled around the men. DeBeer had blood streaming out of his nose. Rafael nailed him with another punch to the gut, but came in too close, and DeBeer grabbed him. They tussled, spinning around like a pair of angry cats.

I reached back for the bowl of chocolate filling and flung it at their heads. The syrupy mess smacked into both of them, coating their eyes and cheeks with mud. Sputtering, they broke apart just enough that Heidi and I could push between them.

I got my hands on Rafael's chest and tried to stay between him and DeBeer. Beneath my hands, Rafael's heart beat against his chest like a series of sonic booms. This close, I could see he wasn't just angry, but had tears streaking his cheeks and mixing with the chocolate.

"Please." I dug my fingers into his flight suit, trying to keep a grip on him. "Please, don't."

"DeBeer!" Heidi grunted and staggered into my field of vision.

A moment later, he barreled into Rafael from the side. My hands were tangled in his flight suit so I staggered along with them.

"What the hell is going on?" Parker grabbed DeBeer, throwing an arm around his neck and hauling backward.

Benkoski pulled Rafael back, too. I let go. Sticky chocolate coated my hands.

Now all the adrenaline made itself known. My hands shook and my pulse pounded in the backs of my knees and heated my neck.

"I repeat: what the hell is going on?" Parker had somehow gotten DeBeer's arm twisted up behind him and had forced the man to his knees. Chocolate coated the front of his flight suit.

Both men glowered at the floor, but their damned military "honor" kept them quiet. They'd throw a punch, but God forbid they snitch. The evidence of their fight was all too clear, though, even if I hadn't thrown chocolate on them.

"York. Status." Parker turned his glare on me.

I suppose I have just as much pilot's honor as they did, because I did not want to get Rafael in trouble. If DeBeer had instigated it, I wouldn't have hesitated, but the military would turn a blind eye to the sign. All that would matter was that Rafael began the physical conflict.

"York, you were in the thick of it when I came in, and I'm covered in chocolate. Status. Now."

Sighing, I bent and picked the sign up off the floor. "DeBeer put this on the zero-g toilet."

DeBeer winced. At first I thought it was because he had been confronted with his sign, but his breath hissed in slowly. Parker had cranked his arm higher up his back. "That your work?"

Behind Rafael, Benkoski rolled his eyes. "Jesus Christ, Van."

How the hell had DeBeer gotten cleared for this mission? He didn't back down, even a little. He jutted his chin toward Rafael. "No one else saw this except him. Maybe he put it there."

Parker switched to Afrikaans and bent his head to DeBeer's ear. "*Begin met 'n verskoning en laat my glo dit, of jy sal nie aan Mars raak nie.*"

Whatever Parker said to DeBeer caused him to pale a little. He wet his lips and had a moment of blinking in bewilderment at the taste of chocolate. "Am I to get an apology from him as well?"

I could have slapped him, but that would have been useless. Still tempting, though. What surprised me was that Rafael had succumbed to the temptation. He was probably the least volatile of all of us. On the other hand, he had reason to be unsteady now. Poor guy.

In Benkoski's grip, Rafael had sagged, so it looked more like he was being supported than restrained. He lifted his head. "I am sorry that I struck you. It would have been more appropriate for me to take my concerns to my S.O. I apologize for the problems I have caused. And for wasting Elma's pie."

You could almost feel the gravity in the room shift to DeBeer. I wouldn't have been able to stand being under the weight of all of those gazes. Parker had not relaxed his grip at all, and the pressure caused DeBeer to bend forward.

Maybe Parker tweaked DeBeer's arm further, or maybe he finally realized that he wasn't going to convince anyone that he hadn't made the sign. Whatever the cause, he let his breath out in one explosive rush, free shoulder sagging. "It was a joke."

"Funny thing." Parker bent over DeBeer's shoulder, but he was staring at me. "Turns out that doesn't stop it from being offensive. Also. Not an apology."

My breath caught in my throat. DeBeer hadn't apologized, but had Parker just apologized to me?

"You're both confined until you've had a chance to cool down." Parker released DeBeer's arm. "Benkoski, you got them?"

"Confirmed." He released Rafael and stepped back, hands on his hips to look at both of them.

Heidi, Dawn, and I stood awkwardly for a moment as Benkoski led Rafael and DeBeer away. I walked over to the counter to grab a towel. Behind me, Parker said, "Next time, York, don't throw the batter on them."

"It was the first thing I could grab."

"Sure. But it's a waste of a damn fine pie." Parker cleared his throat. "Sabados . . . Don't send that to Mission Control. I don't want it to get into the news back home. We'll deal with it internally."

I stared at the letter I'd written to Nathaniel, chewing my lower lip. Much as I wanted to tell him about yesterday's fight, I agreed with Parker about keeping it out of reports.

The corner of the paper stirred in the breeze from the fan circulating air in the observation dome. Leonard floated in the dome too, reading the latest data from the Mars orbiter that had been circling the planet since dropping the Friendship probe. With DeBeer released from confinement,

I didn't like leaving him alone, but I wanted to go to comms when Florence was on shift. And Leonard was an adult.

Clearing my throat, I pushed off to float a little closer to him. "I'm heading down to comms. Holler if you need anything."

"I'll be fine, Elma." He lifted his head, countering the movement with a twist of a hand to keep himself from spinning.

"I know. I just . . ." The fact that both of us had had the thought that it might not be fine was a giant glaring red alert. I hadn't managed to work that problem, though. Not yet.

I twisted in the air and pushed toward the hatch. One of the ways in which our crews had handled the merger was that Florence was sending the letters for the *Niña* crew, and Dawn handled them for the *Pinta*. It had the effect of making me reluctant to write, and knowing that Florence had to key in the letters made me keep them short. I didn't want to give her additional reasons to resent me by making more work for her. I assumed Nathaniel was keeping them short for similar reasons. Our rapid back-and-forth exchanges had been cut out with the garbage.

I kicked down the spindle toward comms with a letter folded in my flight suit pocket. Ahead of me, Parker hung in the spindle just outside the ComMod. As I closed the distance between us, I flipped to orient myself with him. He barely glanced away from the door.

The tension on his face . . . I did not like it. Grabbing a guide rail, I pulled myself to a stop next to Parker. Inside, Dawn and Florence bent over the comms unit, while Rafael and Wilburt floated below them, looking at the innards of the teletype.

"What's . . . ?"

"We've lost contact with Earth."

TWENTY-EIGHT

First Mars Expedition Mission Log, Cmdr. Stetson Parker:
May 29, 1963, 11:47 a.m.—Contact protocols completed. After two days, communication with IAC not reestablished.

"York." Parker's voice made me jump, spraying dirt around the garden room, where I had retreated to try to stay out of the way. "Sorry. Didn't mean to . . . Got a minute?"

With my hand to my bosom like some bimbo out of the old *Flash Gordon* serials, I turned to face Parker. I was pretty sure he could see my heart pounding through my hand, but my voice was calm, at least. "Sure."

"I need your opinion on a staffing question."

I walked over to the tool rack, ostensibly to get the broom so I could salvage the dirt before it got tracked everywhere, but really so that I could let my jaw drop open in peace. Parker wanted my opinion. Mine. Wind whistled through my open mouth before I swallowed. "Go on?"

When I turned back, he looked relieved. Who was this man? With a nod, he got down to business, and the confident pilot came back to the surface. "They can't find anything wrong with the *Pinta*'s comms system. We can still get the remote guidance signals the *Santa Maria* is bouncing at us, but nothing from Earth."

In that hesitation, I saw why Parker was so troubled, even if he was masking it beautifully. We'd been out of contact with Earth for two days now. "The problem might be on the IAC's end."

"They have five radio dishes pointed at us, and auxiliary systems for the auxiliary systems."

"Right." It's strange to hope that something is wrong with your ship while you're millions of kilometers from home, because the alternative is that something terrible has happened on Earth. They would have spotted another meteor, wouldn't they? With all the satellites we had now, and *Lunetta*? Surely everyone on Earth was fine and it was just an electrical thing here.

"So it's still likely that it's us, and the best way to eliminate that possibility is to get the *Niña* fully back online and check our radio as well. Do you think Avelino can handle an EVA?"

Gripping the broom, I swept the dirt I'd scattered into a little pile. He hadn't fought anyone else, but the grieving was deep. On the other hand, he was a professional, and knew the *Niña* better than anyone. "Yes . . . But maybe do a three-person team, the way we did for the solar panel deployment. That way if he runs into problems, there are two people who can guide him back in."

Parker nodded. "That's similar to what I was thinking. So, you and Flannery."

That time I made an actual sound, somewhere between a laugh and a gasp, as if I'd been punched. Crouching, I scraped the little pile of dirt into the dustpan. "Where does this sudden faith in me come from?"

"Sorry." That was another apology. I clutched the broom just in case he turned out to be a space alien who had taken over Parker's body. "I . . . I'm aware that we're—that we haven't exactly been compatible in the past, but with Terrazas gone, you're the senior astronaut. I function better with a copilot."

He was staring at the floor, leaning against one of the raised beds. It suddenly and belatedly occurred to me that he had known Terrazas longer than any of us had. Parker was so good at that military mask of calm that I hadn't actually considered that he might be in mourning. He just got on with business.

Straightening, I dumped the dirt back into the radish bed and then set down the broom and dustpan. "I miss him too."

The muscles in Parker's jaw stood out in hard contrast to his relaxed body posture. His gaze stayed cast down to the floor, but he gave one of his signature sharp nods.

"Good. I'll speak to Flannery and Avelino, and then we can all start working the EVA plans." Parker straightened, turning toward the door without meeting my eyes. "Carry on."

Inside my helmet, my breath competed with the hiss of my EVA suit's fans. I kept my eyes on the delta-pressure gauge so we could open the airlock into space. The airlock closest to the antenna wasn't big enough for all three of us to exit at once. Even if we hadn't each had gear for the repair, we couldn't have all fit in our stiff, pressurized EVA suits, so we were using one of the larger forward airlocks, which was designed for loading cargo into a BusyBee.

Outside the suit, our gear drifted from tethers, clanging metal against metal. The delta-pressure gauge eased down as the air evacuated and left us drifting in an eerie silence. I floated forward, pushing against the suit's pressurized rigid joints, and undogged the hatch. Pulling it open, I reached through to clip the tether hook for my safety cable to one of the handrails that covered the surface of the *Niña*. *Bail closed. Slide lock. Black on black.* Next I guided my bag of gear through and secured it as well. A tug of my fingers sent me floating through the broad hatch. Using one of the handholds, I translated down to the far end of the handrail to make room for Rafael and anchored myself with a local tether.

Both tethers tugged me gently toward the ship. It doesn't happen in the NBL pool, because of the water resistance, but in space they exert a steady pull. As if I needed a reminder that this was not a sim. My nails scraped the inside of my gloves as I tethered the bag of gear to my suit so I could haul it with me down the outside of the spindle. Only when everything was secure and double-checked did I stop to look out.

All the tight grief and anger in my chest unpacked a little as I floated in space. There is a part of me that expects it to be blue, because of the hours spent in the NBL pool, with the mock-ups of the *Niña*. But space was a rich black. If the lights were off inside the ship, and we were pointed nightward, you could see the stars, but there was always a barrier. On an EVA, I was still looking at space through glass, but with no limit to my field of vision.

It doesn't matter how many spacewalks I do, the stars will never lose their wonder. Against that limitless black, they blazed. Our ship defined the only edge, etched in gold and silver by the sun.

As Rafael reached out, I didn't start breathing again until he'd clipped on. He faced away from me, looking out over that expanse in one of the few leisure moments we would have during the spacewalk.

While we waited for Leonard, I stared into the infinite. I don't think it will ever matter how many times I see the stars like this, it will always seem holy. Under my breath, I murmured, "*Baruch ata Adonai, Eloheinu, melekh ha'olam, she'hekheyanu v'kiy'manu v'higi'anu la'z'man ha'ze . . .*"

Parker crackled in my radio. "Come again, York?"

"I was . . ." *Praying.* "Talking to myself."

"In Yiddish?"

"Hebrew, actually." Of all the times to trigger his love of languages, this was not one I wanted to explain. "We'll do a lesson when we get back."

"Try to keep the channels clear until then." As if he weren't the one who was asking me about language.

But we were doing an EVA without being able to consult with Mission Control, and even after taking three days to plan it, Parker had to be feeling the pressure. I wasn't going to give him any grief for this. "Yes, sir."

Leonard clipped on and spun to pull the thermal shield into place over the airlock hatch. The hatch would stay open in case there was an emergency and we needed to get back in quickly. I prayed to God that we wouldn't need that contingency.

As he turned from the airlock, Leonard said, "*Niña*, EV1. All three spacewalkers are in position and ready to begin."

"Confirmed, EV1. We have you in our sights."

"Let's get this done." Rafael's urgency fairly pushed me away from the hatch.

I propelled myself after Leonard with carefully placed grips on the handrails. As we worked our way down the spindle, my legs trailed after me like Superwoman. Of course, she didn't have a tether to keep her from drifting off into space. Coming untethered . . . that's my fear. As much as I love this view, it is impossible to forget that if you fall, you fall forever. But, being afraid of that means that I'm very, very careful about clipping the tether hook and following proper tether protocol at all times. *Bail closed. Slide lock. Black on black.*

"My nephew thinks I'm Superman, because of this." Leonard did not get chastised by Parker for chattering.

I resecured my tether at the next handrail and kept

translating down the ship. If Tommy could see me he would be whooping with excitement. A lump filled my throat. "Same with mine."

Ahead of me, Leonard reached the stump where the antenna used to be. He hooked his feet into a foot restraint and reeled his bag of gear in. The Mylar container had a slender profile, nearly as long as Leonard himself. He had the spare pole for the antenna, in order to give it some distance from the ship.

Rafael and I stopped next to Leonard. I unspooled my foot restraint's tether and inserted the plug into one of the WIF mechanical receivers that peppered the *Niña*'s surface.

The collar on the foot restraint's bayonet dropped down to lock it into place, revealing the black line for visual confirmation. I still did the twist and pull check to make sure that was mechanically stable. Bracing myself, I slid my toes under the foot restraint's loop and rotated my heel inward so that I could slide the heel ridge into its restraining slot. Once both feet were restrained, I secured my bag to a handrail on the hull.

Rafael floated by me. His bag idled in the vacuum, turning a little. It was hard to see through his helmet, but I think he was looking at where Terrazas's body had hit.

"You okay?"

"Absolutely." Rafael began moving like an automaton brought to life. "Just reviewing the order of operations. Nothing I see here makes me think we need to change procedure. We'll start by removing and securing the damaged section."

I extracted the "garbage" bag from my gear. It was a clever design, with layers of bristle that met in the middle. The bristles were easy to push through, but would hold a drifting piece of debris inside. Useful for zero-g, when you needed to keep your hands clear. Snapping its retractable equipment tether to a handrail, I secured the garbage bag to a WIF where Rafael and Leonard could get to it easily.

Leonard had oriented his foot restraint so that he was facing the broken shaft the antenna had been bolted on. Rafael, meanwhile, had begun tracing cables from the antenna. Some of them had snapped off cleanly, while others floated several meters out.

Leonard unspooled a socket wrench from the MWS strapped to his chest and fit it on the bolt. As his stiff gloves slid off the wrench, he swore in a random language. Tethered to the MWS, the wrench didn't go far, but there's still that heart-stopping moment when you think you're about to lose a tool to space.

I grinned through my helmet at him. "Was that Latin or Greek?"

"Greek."

I helped him steady the antenna stump as he got the wrench back into place. "You're not going to translate it for me, are you?"

"'Go to the crows.'" Leonard placed the wrench again, and resecured his feet. His wrench slipped, but he didn't lose the tool. "There are a couple of reasons I like this one. First, it's ironic coming from the mouth of a Black man."

I stared at him, trying to put that together. "Because . . . it's Greek?"

He laughed. "You're adorable sometimes. No. Because of Jim Crow. So 'Go to the crows' takes on this modern connotation that it didn't have in ancient Greece. It sort of becomes a 'Don't throw me in the briar patch' kind of thing." He lifted the bolt from the base and handed it to me. "Please tell me you get that reference."

"Yes, Brer Astronaut."

Leonard gave a belly laugh that made his mic distort.

My skin flushed with relief, because honestly, that joke was probably crossing a line. It's the sort of thing I could have said to Eugene, but I wasn't sure that Leonard and I had that sort of trust built up. I slipped the bolt into our garbage bag. "So what was the connotation in ancient Greece?"

"Burial was very important." He placed the wrench on the next bolt and took a moment to make sure it was seated. "So saying 'Go to the crows' meant that someone was hoping your body would just rot and get picked over by crows."

Beside us, Rafael had stopped moving again, a cable partially coiled in his hands.

"Being unburied messed with their ability to participate in the afterlife and—"

I put my hand on Leonard's arm to stop him. Although, in the pressure suit, he saw the movement more than felt it. "Want to hear my favorite Yiddish curse?"

"Sure."

And here, suddenly, I was stumped. There were a lot of wonderful options, all of which revolved around death or burial. Or were too close in other ways, like, *Trouble is to man what rust is to iron.* Others were concepts that Mama wouldn't have approved of me knowing. I shifted the garbage bag closer on its tether to mask my dilemma. What was something Aunt Esther would say? And that unlocked a raft of them. "A yid hot akht un tsvantsik protsent pakhed, tsvey protsent tsuker, un zibetsik protsent khutspe."

Parker's voice came into our helmet. "I've been trying to keep out of this, but what does that mean?"

"I thought you wanted me to keep the airwaves clear."

Across from us, Rafael's eyes opened, and he resumed wrapping cable as if he had never stopped.

Parker snorted. "You are tempting me with language."

"It's something my aunt Ester always said: 'A Jew is twenty-eight percent fear, two percent sugar, and seventy percent chutzpah.'"

"This explains everything."

"Bless your heart. Bear in mind that I'm a Southern Jew, so the sugar percentage is higher."

Leonard handed the next bolt to me for disposal. "You mean the sugar is all on the outside. Ain't no one going to believe you're sweetness all the way through."

As Leonard's language dropped into the informal rhythms I heard from Eugene and Myrtle, I grinned with something like triumph. It was the closest I had come to feeling like part of a team in too long. Speaking of team . . . "Rafael. What's a good Portuguese curse?"

He tied off the cable he was handling and moved on to free the next. "In Brazil, we don't do things 'to show off,' we '*para inglês ver*.'"

Parker whistled. "Ouch."

"Which means?"

"We do it 'so the English can see.'"

Technically speaking, we did not all need to be in or near the *Niña*'s ComMod when Florence powered up the system two days after we finished the repairs. In fact, everyone except Florence and Rafael could have remained on the *Pinta*. Instead, the entire crew came over. Ostensibly, this was so we could save on fuel for the BusyBee by making only one trip across.

The garden module needed tending. Kam wanted to make certain everything in the MedMod was secured. Leonard needed the paper he'd been reading. I had reference books I needed for computation.

Parker put up with all of those fictions.

In the spindle, it felt like twilight, with only every third light powered. The original plan had been to finish the ammonia system repair before the radio, but Parker and Benkoski had wanted to confirm that the communication blackout wasn't just a *Pinta* problem. And for that, we needed a second working long-range radio system.

When all the panels were lit with green, Florence spoke into the mic. "Okay, *Pinta*. Go ahead with the test signal."

In the Pinta's ComMod, Dawn said, "*Niña,* confirmed. Commencing test signal."

I floated just above Leonard's head so I had a clear line of vision to the dials and gauges jumping in response to invisible waveforms.

It's funny how you can have two simultaneous responses to the same stimulus.

On the one hand, I was relieved, because this meant that our repair had worked.

On the other, my entire body sank as if despair had become a gravitational force. If the *Niña*'s signals were good, then that meant the problem was on Earth.

It had now been a week without contact. An hour, two, maybe even a half day, could have been chalked up to a malfunction. But with all of the IAC's resources—heck, with the resources of an entire planet—the fact that they were still out of contact left me cold.

Nathaniel . . . what is happening at home?

TWENTY-NINE

First Mars Expedition Mission Log, Cmdr. Stetson Parker:
June 10, 1963, 11:13 p.m.—Ammonia system repairs completed on *Niña*. Communication with IAC still not reestablished after fourteen days.

One of the ways you can tell that I'm Southern and Jewish is by the strength of my drive to feed people. The Monday morning meetings on the *Pinta* did not take place over breakfast the way they had back home—back on the *Niña*, I mean. I'm not sure why they didn't set out refreshments beyond coffee. Maybe Dawn and Heidi were trying to assert their roles as scientists and avoided homemaking. Maybe no one on their crew liked to cook.

But it had been two weeks since we had heard from Earth, and I needed to cook.

There are few things more satisfying than the smell of fresh-baked biscuits. Given the powdered milk, dehydrated eggs, and artificial butter, these were not bad. Mama would have been appalled at their lack of layers and faintly chalky taste, but at a certain point that become normal.

Parker and Benkoski slid down the ladder and into the kitchen, one after the other, like a carnival ride. Benkoski lifted his head and sniffed. "I dunno, Stetson . . . I might change my mind about the split."

"You can't have her." Parker walked over to the whiteboard. "But we'll send care packages."

"Split?" I wiped the mixing bowl out in the recycle sink.

"We'll go over it at the meeting." Parker picked up a rag and tossed it to me. "Wet this for me?"

It smacked onto my clean counter, leaving a grayish smear on the stainless steel. "Of course."

I set aside my mixing bowl and devoted my full attention to the needs of our mission commander, bless his heart. Wringing the water out from the rag, I managed to not say any of that out loud. Though I may have wrung it a little too hard. "Here you go."

Secretly, I will admit to hoping it would hit Parker when I tossed it back, but he snatched the cloth out of the air like an intercept missile. He turned to the board and wiped away the notes scrawled across it. "Benkoski, set up a pilot/NavComp breakout after the all-hands meeting."

"I'm your secretary now?"

"You're my wingman."

"I could make the argument that since you're on my ship, you're *my* wingman."

"Second in command? Copilot? Right-hand man? Whatever." Parker tossed him a pen. "It means you do the paperwork."

So *that's* why Parker needed a copilot. Shaking my head, I turned back to clearing the dishes. The swish of my rag competed with the squeak of marker on plastic. After setting the bowl in the UV sterilizing rack, I wiped down the counter. Really, it is amazing how much better I feel when the kitchen is clean.

Opening the oven door, I checked on the biscuits. Despite theoretically being identical, in practice, at home the *Niña*'s oven tended to run a little hotter, and I was still getting the hang of cooking with this one. A waft of steam rolled out into the room, carrying the scent of browning dough and buttery deliciousness. The tops were beautifully golden brown. So noted. A slower, cooler oven seemed to do nice things for my biscuit concoction.

I grabbed a pot holder and pulled the baking tray out of the oven. Whether out of generosity or the desire for praise, I turned with the biscuits to offer one to Parker and Benkoski.

On the board, Parker had written a staffing list. In the way that happens, I spotted my name first. Next to it were the words "NavComp/Copilot."

Somehow, I did not drop the biscuits. I did squeak, though.

Benkoski looked around. "Oh, man . . . you are an angel."

"Um. Thank you." I carried the biscuits closer, still staring at the board. They'd split the crews again, and it looked like we were going back to our own ship. "Careful. The pan is hot."

Parker tucked his clipboard under one arm and grabbed a biscuit. "Thank you, ma'am."

"Ma'am? Since when do I rate a ma'am?"

"Only when you're baking." He waggled the biscuit at me, and then passed it under his nose, inhaling with gusto. "Woman's place, and all that."

I rolled my eyes. "Of course. I walked right into that one."

"Well, the rest of the time, you're a computer."

I gestured to the board with my chin. "Or a copilot . . . ?"

Benkoski clapped me on the shoulder with one hand and grabbed a biscuit with the other. "Congratulations on your promotion."

"Wait . . . that's permanent?"

Parker shrugged as if this was no big deal. "You want the duty roster where we shift crews around and put DeBeer on the same ship as Flannery and Grey?"

He couldn't be serious about wanting me as his copilot. Women still weren't getting staffed on piloting the big rockets down from *Lunetta,* not even as copilots. "What about Avelino?"

Watching me, Parker took a bite of the biscuit and chewed slowly. Swallowing, he wiped a lingering crumb away from his lips with a thumb. "I am writing nothing in the log but praise for him. Do you think that's accurate at this time?"

When we'd finished the antenna repair and gotten out of the suits, one of Rafael's eyes had been obscured by tears. He hadn't mentioned it. Aside from his quiet, and the occasional freeze, you wouldn't have known that anything was bothering him. But a copilot couldn't afford to freeze, not even for a moment.

And what about my anxiety? I walked over to the counter to set the biscuits down. The other crew members would be arriving any minute now. "May I speak with you for a moment?"

Parker sighed and handed the clipboard to Benkoski. "Write up the rest of this."

"Not a secretary."

"Don't make me pull rank, wingman." He walked over to me and leaned against the counter, taking another bite of biscuit. Around the mouthful, Parker said, "Well?"

"I understand your concerns about Rafael, but . . . you know my history."

"You think there's anyone on either ship who isn't feeling anxious right now? It's been two weeks since we've had contact with Earth."

I squared the baking sheet with the edge of the counter so I wouldn't have to watch him. "I only mean that if you can trust me, surely you can trust him."

"What's this? What happened to 'women are just as

capable as men' and 'my anxiety isn't a problem' and 'rockets are safe enough, even for ladies'? Are you telling me you were wrong? Are you saying you aren't capable of more than baking and laundry?"

"No." God, he was such an asshole, throwing my words back at me like this. "I'm just questioning why you're picking me over Rafael."

"So you're questioning my judgment. That shouldn't surprise me."

"See!" I pivoted on my heel to face him. "We fight all the time. Why do you want me as your copilot?"

He leaned forward. "Because you don't take my shit. Because I've seen you in a crisis, and you are disciplined as hell. Because you are a damn good pilot. Because I'm the mission commander, and I said so. Now, do you have any more goddamn questions?"

My entire body thrummed as if my pulse were an unbalanced engine. I don't know how, but I managed to lift my chin. "Yes. Were those compliments?"

Parker laughed, and, damn it, he had a good laugh, with his head thrown back and dimples. It cut off abruptly and he straightened. "No. Those were critical assessments." He held up the remnant of the biscuit. "This is a compliment: damn good biscuits."

Tossing the last piece into his mouth, he walked back to the whiteboard as if he'd said nothing at all.

Before I had a chance for the shock to run through my system, DeBeer and Heidi walked into the kitchen from the garden module. I shook my head to clear it and opened a drawer to grab a spatula—except it was the towel drawer. Why would anyone keep their kitchen towels next to the stove? Since I had it open, I grabbed one to toss into a bowl for serving the biscuits. Behind me, other crew members entered the room for the meeting. Snippets of conversation floated through the room. ". . . Rossini's best opera . . ." ". . . and then halfway through the book, the main character dies . . ." ". . . I think the gin might be ready . . ."

"Gin? I volunteer as t—" I looked over my shoulder and spotted Kam talking with Leonard. "You cut your hair."

Stupid, I know. But she had cropped the long dark hair that had waved down to the middle of her back into a military buzz cut, and at first, all I could see was that.

She blushed and ran a hand over the dark velvet at the side of her head. Without the abundance of hair, her eyes seemed huge. "I just got tired of fighting with it in zero-g."

"Maybe I should think about it." Although I didn't think Nathaniel would like it much. My gut twisted a little at that. Everything, even small things, reminded me that we had no idea what was happening on Earth. There weren't enough biscuits in the universe. Opening the random drawer where they kept cooking utensils, I pulled out a spatula and began transferring the biscuits to the bowl.

By the time I finished, everyone had arrived and was in various stages of settling for the Monday meeting. Scents of coffee and biscuits made the room seem almost like home. I settled next to Leonard, who grinned as he reached for a biscuit.

DeBeer had been moving toward the bowl, but stopped, the corners of his mouth turned down. He sat next to Heidi with only a cup of coffee. His loss.

"All right, people." Parker tapped the board. "You'll notice that we're splitting the crews back to their original formation, with a couple of adjustments. York is going to pick up copilot duties on the *Niña,* and over here, Voegeli will train with Shamoun to brush up on medical skills. Shamoun will still make house calls if there's anything serious, but hopefully this will cut down on the number of BusyBee trips."

Graeham raised his hand.

Parker gestured with his chin. "Go ahead."

"I am only wondering, if the goal is to reduce the number of BusyBee trips, why we are splitting the crews again? Would it not make more sense for you to all stay here? Especially given the circumstances."

"The goal is to get us all safely to Mars and back to Earth." Parker tapped the board. "Before we lost contact, Mission Control wanted the *Niña* operational and staffed again, so that's what we're going to do."

DeBeer shifted in his seat, but Dawn touched his knee before raising her hand. She didn't wait for Parker to call on her, though. "That's not the way Mission Control was going to staff us. DeBeer was supposed to move over to the *Nina* and join the Mars landing party."

Ah. That was what this was about, then. A cold tremor seized the back of my neck. Once again, I was taking someone else's spot, and DeBeer didn't have any reason to back down.

Benkoski stepped forward with a downward slash of his palm. "At this point, Mission Control is not in full possession of the facts, so this is the staffing."

"Right." Parker's shark smile came out and he turned it on DeBeer. "We're doing a pilot/NavComp breakout after this to talk about the course correction that's coming up. DeBeer—I want you taking notes on that. Now that I know how good your lettering is."

I kicked up the spindle toward the bridge of the *Niña,* hauling a baggie with a piece of chess pie. As the ComMod came up, I grabbed the rail and used the momentum to swing through the door. Florence floated in her sleeping bag, which she'd moved into the mod just in case there was a peep from Earth. Which there hadn't been for three weeks and one day.

She had her needlepoint out, and it was far enough along now that you could recognize Orion in the star field. Florence tucked the needle into a corner. "To what do I owe the pleasure?"

"I brought you some pie." I sent the baggie spinning across the mod to her.

Florence snatched it out of the air with a grin. "You are my favorite person."

I snorted.

"Right now." She winked. "Keep plying me with your pie . . ."

"Ply pie."

"I sigh . . ." She opened the baggie and inhaled deeply. "Seriously, though. Consider me bribed. What do you need?"

"Nothing." I stopped as she gave me The Look. "Caught me. Did you run my burn plan through the mechanical computer?"

"Every time, as per protocol. You know it's never caught you out even once." She narrowed her gaze at me. "Why?"

"I just . . . Reassurance? I'm working without all the numbers that I'd have if Earth were . . ."

"It's fine, Elma. No errors."

I swallowed. "Thanks. Anything I can do for you? I mean, you're sort of trapped in here."

She shrugged, as if the schedule adjustment to keep the ComMods on both ships staffed at all times were no big deal. "Eh. At least it means I don't have to do laundry anymore. And Parker has me rotating with Rafael and Leonard."

"All the same . . . need anything?"

Florence patted the intercom next to her. "I'll call if I do. And I'll call the moment we hear from them."

The longer the silence went, the more worried we all got. But while the undercurrent of fear grew, so did our kindness, in much the same way people rallied together after the Meteor.

Please, God. Please let it not be another meteor.

"Well. I'd better get up to the bridge. Just wanted to drop that off on my way."

"Much appreciated." She clipped the baggie to the wall. "It'll be my treat after I finish this bit."

With a wave, I kicked out of the ComMod and grabbed a handrail to propel myself up to the bridge. I wanted to be there before Parker, so he couldn't complain about me being late.

As I passed through the hatch of the CM I hesitated, gnawing on the inside of my lip. Sitting in the copilot's chair on the bridge shouldn't be a big deal—it was only one seat over from the NavComp station—and yet it made me keenly aware of Terrazas's absence. I gripped the back of his chair. What would he say about all this? "In this installment, our intrepid adventurers . . ."

Behind me, Parker sighed. I froze, blushing because he'd caught me being silly. He cleared his throat. "Our intrepid adventurers begin their approach to Mars . . . He was a good man."

"Yeah."

Parker put a hand on my shoulder. "You'll do fine, York."

Goddamn it if my eyes didn't fill with tears. I wiped them off on the back of my sleeve before they could blind me. "Well, I don't have his radio voice." Pulling myself around the seat, I settled into it. One meter to the left of where I usually sat, and it was an entirely different world. "You look over the burn plan?"

Of course he had. It was insulting to ask, but I had to fill the silence with something. Parker slid into his own chair, buckling in. "Looks good. It's just a little off the original flight plan."

Which was to be expected, and yet . . . I wasn't used to being worried about my math.

Rafael had reconfigured the CM a little to put my Nav-Comp tools within reach of the copilot chair, including plugging a gimbal arm for my sextant into a WIF socket so I could keep it out, but not have to hold it. It was more for comfort than anything else, because Heidi and I had calculated the burn already, and Florence and Dawn had fed that information into the mechanical computers on the *Santa Maria,* which would do an automatic burn.

But what if I was starting from an erroneous data point? It could be like the time that I'd misidentified Alkaid in the sim and sent us all to our deaths. Yes. Yes, I know that there were safeguards, but I hate computing without the benefit of all the information I'm used to. "Okay . . . Set to roll 198.6, pitch 130.7, and yaw 340."

Parker began flipping switches on the control panel, calling out his settings as he did. "198.6, 130.7, 340."

As copilot, my job was simply to make certain that everything was set correctly. Nothing more, right now, but I watched him set up for the burn like a hawk.

The timer ticked us closer to the mark for the burn. Wetting my lips, I pulled the mic to me. "Prepare for burn. Ten, nine, eight . . ." Everyone would already be in lockdown. "Seven, six, five . . ." Next to me, Parker held the ship's joystick lightly in his hand. ". . . four, three, two, one—"

He fired the engines. The seat slammed forward to meet

us, and outside the viewport, flame blossomed from the back of the *Pinta* as they started their burn.

I dragged in air past the weight sitting on my chest. If I needed reminding that the spinning section of the *Niña* only had Mars gravity, this was it. Ten seconds. An eternity. They are much the same thing sometimes.

Ten seconds and everything had changed. We had begun the slowdown for Mars.

THIRTY

First Mars Expedition Mission Log, Cmdr. Stetson Parker:

July 19, 1963, 1:05 a.m.—*Niña* and *Pinta* teams have completed preparations for insertion into Mars orbit. Day 53 of communication blackout with IAC.

I thought it was a dream, at first. I was floating in the dark of crew quarters when Florence very calmly said, "Parker, come to the ComMod. Repeat. Parker to ComMod."

She was so calm that I almost drifted back to sleep. There were no alarm bells. No Klaxons. It wasn't an emergency, and she had sounded so gentle. Kam whispered, "Is it Mission Control?"

That ratcheted me to full alertness. I twisted in my sleeping bag to peer out of my cubby.

Parker floated in the middle of crew quarters, pulling a flight suit on over his underwear. "Don't know yet. Stay here."

I had been undoing the straps that kept my sleeping bag closed, but stopped as I woke up a little more. Right. They didn't need everyone crowding in there. Not that I'd be able to sleep, wondering what was going on. It could simply be a call from the *Pinta*, though few calls in the middle of the night were innocuous.

Still zipping up, Parker kicked off and drifted over to me. "York," he whispered. "With me."

And that woke me the rest of the way up. As his copilot, he'd need me, in case whatever this was required moving the ship or God knows what.

I pushed the neck of the bag the rest of the way open and slipped out. Grabbing my flight suit, I nodded. "Right behind you."

He didn't wait, and spun in the air to aim toward the hatch into the spindle. As I wriggled into my suit, the rest of the crew poked their heads out of their cubbies like gophers.

Leonard's teeth flashed in the dim light. "Do you know what's going on?"

"I know as much as you." I zipped my suit shut, twisting to head to the hatch. "Parker will give a SitRep as soon as he has it."

SitRep—situation report. So much tension packed into those syllables. I flew down the spindle to the ComMod as Parker hooked around the corner and vanished into its hatch. As I got closer, the constant hum of the *Niña*'s fans seemed to part and let the clatter of the teletype through like angels singing hosannas.

"*Baruch ata Adonai, Eloheinu, melekh ha'olam, hagomel lahayavim tovot, sheg'molani kol tov.*" The prayer of thanks slipped out, even though I still had a list of worries as long as my arm.

As I caught the edge of the hatch and swung into the ComMod, Florence's face gave me a lot of the answers I needed. Or raised more questions. Or both. She was smiling, but her eyes were red, as if she'd been crying. "Yes, it's Mission Control. Yes, Nathaniel is on the team sending the message."

"Thank God." I clutched my chest as if I were a damsel in a melodrama. But, honestly, I felt as if someone had just untied me from the railroad tracks. I still didn't know why the Earth had been out of contact for almost two months, but my husband was alive and well. I swallowed the tears of relief and tried to focus on my job. "What happened?"

"Protesters." Parker hunched over the teletype, reading the pages as they fed out of it. "The Earth Firsters knocked out the satellites."

"My God."

Florence pushed off the desk to get closer to the teletype. "How the hell?"

"Apparently that conspiracy theory about someone in the IAC being a member of Earth First . . . not so crackpot. Someone in the computer department sent up bad code that deorbited both satellites. Jesus." He ran a hand over his hair, resting it on the bald spot. "They took out the power grid in Kansas, too."

"Wait—who was it?" I also pulled myself closer to the teletype, which continued to rattle as if it were a small child that had been waiting all day for Daddy to get home.

"Um . . ." He scrolled down the page. "Curtis Frye, Jennifer Lynn, and Tyler Richter."

"I don't know them."

"New hires, apparently—" Parker stopped moving. The pages scrolled up through his limp fingers. He took a breath and turned an utterly impersonal mask to Florence. "Let the crew know that we've reestablished contact with Earth. I doubt any of them went back to sleep. York, help facilitate the distribution of personal mail and prepare updated duty rosters. I'll review those before we hand them out. Now, if you'll excuse me."

Parker turned a somersault and kicked off to swim smoothly out the hatch of the ComMod.

Here's the thing: I know what it looks like when Parker gets bad news. I remember, from the days when he had trouble with his leg going numb, how he goes cold and concentrates on business. I know the faint green tinge that colors his cheeks.

As Florence grabbed the edge of the desk and pulled herself closer to the teletype, my mind unfolded the facts into a rigid equation. Personal mail was coming through. The Kansas power grid went down. His wife was in an iron lung.

I was halfway to the hatch before I'd thought about it. It would kill him to have anyone offer sympathy. So why did I follow him? I don't know. Or, no . . . I do. There are some things you don't let anyone, not even your worst enemy, go through alone. And I was his copilot.

The spindle was empty. He had tucked into some nook while I was still sorting things out.

Some nook—I stopped outside the hatch to the BusyBee. Soundproof.

Through the porthole, the interior was lit only by sunlight reflected from the *Pinta*. Parker floated in the middle in a silent ball.

I tried to undog the hatch as noisily as possible, so he'd have plenty of warning. But when I pulled it open, the sound came out. He couldn't have heard anything.

I said that I knew what it looked like when Parker received bad news. No. I knew what his public face looked like. This . . . Each sob shook his entire body and bounced off the walls of the BusyBee in ragged waves. He floated in the middle of the aisle, wrapped into a tiny ball, as if he could contain his own grief.

For a moment I hesitated, because he didn't know I was there and would not thank me. But who else was I supposed to get? Kam, maybe. Benkoski, if we were still on the *Pinta*. It didn't matter. I was here, and I had made the choice to follow.

"Parker?"

He jerked, lifting his head. Even with his back to me, I could see his effort to pull the mask into place. His breath tore into coughs and ragged pants. Parker swiped his arm across his eyes, spinning globules of water across the cabin. "Does Mission Control need me?"

I shook my head, then realized he still couldn't see. "No." Biting my lip, I pushed closer until I floated just behind him. I almost asked him directly, but I still didn't have permission to talk about his wife. "The power grid . . . I'm so sorry."

He broke.

That thin hull of control shattered on reentry and he disintegrated into racking sobs. I wrapped my arms around him, as if I could help him stay together, or maybe just find the pieces afterward. Parker hung in my embrace. One hand latched onto my forearm and dug in as if he were trying to pull himself back.

We rotated in that dark space as his grief spun out around us.

"I'm sorry." Parker's voice was rough and thick. He rubbed his sleeve across his eyes. "Jesus Christ, I'm—" His voice broke again, and, for a moment, his chest jerked with silent weeping.

He coughed and cleared his throat. "Shit. Sorry."

"What can I do?"

"Cover for me?" He stretched out a little from the tight ball he'd been in, and I let him go. "I'm going to be a mess for a while."

"Sure." I let momentum create some space between us. "Do you want me to get anyone else?"

"Fuck, no. Don't tell a goddamned soul."

"Okay." I bit my lip, aware that I'd left Florence with

all the papers pouring out of the teletype. "Florence might have told people."

Parker drifted slowly through the BusyBee, his face as red and swollen as if he'd been stung by wasps. He shook his head. "There's no way she could know. There's a message 'from' Mimi with all the other personal messages. But . . . heh . . . you weren't the only one with a private cipher. Just the one who got caught."

"Oh."

"Bet you got a lot to say about that."

"Teach me how to not get caught?"

He laughed until it turned into weeping again. He wiped his face. "I knew they'd pull something like this, that they wouldn't want me to be upset if she died, and they'd fake letters from her. So there was a code. It went into everything. Even the shortest of messages. Wasn't there."

"Maybe they edited—"

"Don't." He straightened and jabbed a finger at me. "Don't you fucking dare give me false hope, York. She couldn't survive outside the iron lung for more than an hour. Two, at the most. Our backup generator would last for twenty-four hours. A week and a half without power? She would have made damn sure her code was in the message after that. Mimi is—"

His face crumpled as his mouth snapped shut to keep back a moan.

I pulled closer, but he shook his head, so I stopped. "I'll . . . I'll go cover."

He nodded. "Be there as soon as I can."

"Take your time."

He gave a half laugh and waved me away. It felt wrong to leave him alone, which was a new sensation—usually I wanted to get away from him as fast as I could. Putting a hand on one of the chairs in the BusyBee, I reoriented myself to face the hatch. With a push of my fingertips, I floated up to that end of the cabin.

"York?" The humming fans almost masked his voice.

"Yeah?" I used the hatch edge to turn and face him.

"Tonight, will you . . . will you help me recite the Kaddish for her? I don't . . . I don't know it, and—" Parker pressed the heels of both hands against his eyes and ground his teeth together.

"Yes. Of course."

He nodded, jaw still tight. I slipped out and let the door of the BusyBee mask the rest.

THIRTY-ONE

TWO SATELLITES REVIVE IN SPACE

KANSAS CITY, KS, July 19, 1963—Two United Nations communication satellites which had been presumed dead following terrorist acts by Earth First in May were restored through a herculean effort by the International Aerospace Coalition. These satellites, which have provided easy telephonic communication on Earth, were also part of the network that allowed communication with the First Mars Expedition. The astronauts and astronettes have been isolated from the rest of humankind as their ships hurtled through fathomless space. The entire world is thrilled to learn that their mission has continued and that they were preparing to enter Mars orbit. In a teletype interview, Mission Commander Stetson Parker said, "We were entrusted by the people of Earth to carry out this mission and I look forward to showing them the grand sight of our sister planet."

The letter from Nathaniel burned a hole in the pocket of my flight suit, but I was resolutely not reading it. Parker hadn't emerged yet from the BusyBee, and we had work to do.

I stood at the front of the kitchen next to the whiteboard. Where Parker should be. Thank God for his clipboard, which hid how badly my hands were shaking. I have to say, my anxiety is incredibly stupid. It chose now, when I was faced with a room of four whole people—people I knew—to decide that my throat should close.

1, 1, 2, 3, 5, 8, 13 . . .

I cleared my throat. Or tried to. Good thing I had experience talking around a lump. "This is the duty roster that Mission Control sent up, but Parker is reviewing it before we lock anything in." Not that I really thought his "review" time would set him to rights. "Until we're ready to send the lander down, there are no changes from what we rehearsed back on *Lunetta,* so our plans this week will start with reviewing material."

Parker slid down the ladder into the kitchen. "Thanks for getting us started, York." He had bathed, and carried the scent of aftershave into the room. "Just got off the line with Benkoski, and I have some updates."

I held out his clipboard. He took it with a nod, but didn't meet my gaze. He held the board in one hand, letting it hang at his side in a seemingly casual pose, but his knuckles stood out white against his skin.

I took a step to retreat to the safety of the kitchen table, but Parker stopped me. "Stay put." Then he did that thing, where he rolls his neck to crack it before starting work. "All right, people. You have a lot of questions, and I told Grey and York to hold off until I could talk to Mission Control directly. There's information they couldn't say in the clear, and, truly, they would probably rather that I not tell you either, but fuck 'em. Here's the SitRep."

My teammates came to full attention. Leonard had his elbows on the table with his hands steepled in front of his face. Rafael lifted his head. Florence cocked hers to the side, eyes narrowing. And Kam sat forward, uncrossing her legs.

"The Earth Firsters weren't working alone. They had a collaborator inside the IAC computer department. They also made a strike at the Kansas spaceport, and knocked out the power grid, using arms from the former Soviet Union—we're still not sure if Russia was an active participant, but it seems possible."

Kam raised her hand. "What about the Artemis base and *Lunetta*? Are they okay?"

Parker nodded. "The Brazilian and European spaceports could handle the traffic, but all the communications were running through Kansas and up to the satellites. The long and short of it is that Mission Control can talk to us, but they can't see us. When we do the Mars orbit insertion, we're going to be relying entirely on our NavComps."

On me. On Heidi. Were they getting the same lecture over on the *Pinta*?

"The same might be true for the trip home, because building new satellites is not fast and—to be blunt—we aren't a funding priority to Earth right now." Parker turned the clipboard over in his hands. "This means that our NavComps have just become our most important crew members."

Hello, anxiety. My mouth flooded with saliva in the old, familiar precursor to vomiting. *3.14159 . . .* I swallowed hard and breathed in slowly through my nose.

"Benkoski and I have decided that the next decision is one that you should all share in, so this is the rare time where I will ask for a vote. Getting home safely is significantly more probable if we slingshot around Mars and don't land."

"Hell, no." Rafael slashed the air with his hand. "Not after everything. You can throw me out the airlock, but I'm going down."

"Yeah." Leonard nodded. "You think they'd let me come back and try again? No way."

"That's two." Parker turned to the board and made two tick marks, as if we had so many people that they needed to be counted. Or maybe he just needed to turn his back to the room for a minute. "What do our ladies say?"

"I'm with Leonard, for the same reasons." Florence shrugged. "Didn't come all this way just to turn around and go home."

"Same." Kam laughed. "I can't believe you guys thought that anyone would want to go home."

"York?" He held up a finger. "Wait—before you answer, you should know that, given the new constraints, you and Voegeli won't get to land."

Florence snorted. "Hold on—what was the point of me learning how to use that damn mechanical contraption if it wasn't to be a backup for York?"

"That aspect is not up for a vote."

"It's okay . . . It's the way I went to the moon the first time. Just circled the darn thing." I'd promised Nathaniel that I would come home, and if this is what it took to get us back, then so be it. "Mars or bust."

Parker appeared to stare at the five tick marks on the board for a moment. Because I was standing next to the board, I had a view of his face that none of the rest were privy to, and his eyes were clamped shut. He did not draw a sixth mark for himself, but let out a very slow breath. "Well, that was simple."

If you couldn't see his face, he would have sounded breezy and confident.

When Parker opened his eyes, he swiped away some of the roster I'd written on the board. "So, looking at the duty roster, some things are going to change. York is going to need time to make sure our flight plan is one hundred percent accurate, so I'll be shifting her other duties to the rest of us."

Terrific. I studied the scuff marks on the kitchen floor so I wouldn't have to see the resentment creep back into their eyes. Rafael shifted in his chair. "I can . . . you want me to move over to copilot?"

Parker turned, lips pursed, and studied Rafael. "Let's talk about that after the meeting. For the moment, I need you and Stewman to concentrate on making sure the landers are in order."

I tucked my hands behind my back so no one would see them shaking. "I don't mind doing other work. I'll need a break from calculations."

"Then take a goddamned break. Or do you not know how to do that?"

He was mourning. Or, at least, I could pretend that the sharp bite in his voice was part of an effort to mask grief. It wasn't about me.

That thought made me lift my head and turn to face Parker: it had never been about me.

It was like the ball of anxiety in my stomach sublimated into space, going from a solid knot to vapor. It escaped in a sort of laugh. I think the laugh startled him as much as it did me. Let him think it was me discovering a sense of humor. I lifted my chin. "I take a break by cooking. So keep me on the goddamned kitchen roster, or, so help me, I will bake pies and give you none."

Florence laughed. "She's got you, Parker. She's got you good."

"Well." He cracked his neck and faced the board again, this time with a grin. "So long as you're admitting that your place is in the kitchen."

"Yep." I slapped the whiteboard. "Standing right next to you."

Dear Elma,

I love you. Thank God you're safe. No, I haven't been sleeping enough—none of us have—but Thomas has been a trooper. (And, yes, he's kept me fed.) I don't know what I would have done without him. More later when the official communications are caught up. For now, know that I'm well; I love you; I'm proud of you.

I'll say it again: I love you.

Nathaniel

Parker was already sitting on the weight bench when I got to the gym. It wasn't used much late at night, and while the BusyBee was soundproof, gravity seemed important for this.

He looked up when I came in and gave a little wave. "Thanks. For covering."

"My job." I sat down on the floor in front of him. "What'd you and Rafael decide?"

"He'll take the lander down to Mars with Flannery. I should *not* be flying, and getting the *Niña* into orbit just involves following your directions."

"No pressure or anything."

"Please." He snorted, picking at a loose thread on his flight suit. "I kept trying to get you to crack back at the beginning. You're unflappable. No sense of humor, but you're iron."

I gaped a little at him. Me? Unflappable. "You know I was throwing up almost every day."

Parker's head came up sharply. "You're shitting me."

"Why the hell did you think I was on Miltown?"

"I don't—I figured it was some woman thing." Parker shrugged and rubbed the back of his neck. "Look. I'm sorry."

Please notice my restraint; I didn't ask him if he was

sorry because of the "woman thing" or because he had made me throw up. At the moment, it really didn't matter. "Apology confirmed."

Parker's face twisted and he bent at the waist, covering his mouth with his hands. I scooted forward as a series of sobs shook him. Even with his hands pressed over his mouth, you could hear the sides of his throat ripping open. Rising onto my knees, I pulled him into my arms. Parker let his head rest on my shoulder.

It didn't last long. He shook his head, pulling back. "Sorry. Shit." Parker pulled a handkerchief out of his pocket and blew his nose with wet, gross vigor. "I can't tell what's going to set me off."

Nodding, I settled back on my heels. "It's awful. It'll catch you by surprise. The worst are the happy moments."

He swallowed, clenching his jaw, and stared over to his left as if the weight rack were the most important thing on the ship. After the Meteor, when my parents—most of my family—died, I kept doing exactly that, forgetting they were dead. I still do, sometimes. Then the memory smacks me in the face, that I can't share something with Mama, or that Daddy will never know that I was an astronaut. That I *am* an astronaut.

"How old are your sons now?"

"Sixteen. In her last letter, Mimi said that they were already arguing about who was going to pick me up when we got home." His face spasmed again and he shut his eyes, grimacing like he could squeeze all that pain back inside.

Sixteen . . . He was going to miss their graduation. They'd be off at college by the time we got back, but reminding him of that seemed cruel.

A couple of short breaths later, his eyes opened again. "Even in the lung, you know, she was such a good mom."

That seemed like my best opening to actually talk about her. "Besides the Kaddish, we do something called sitting shiva. It's . . . it's a mourning period, and it starts with telling stories about the one we lost."

"Kind of like a wake."

"I guess."

Parker straightened a little, running a hand over his hair. "Mimi was a really private person."

"Is that why you never talk about her?"

"Pretty much." He stretched his hands out and his wedding ring caught the light. I'd never seen him wear it before. The way we deal with grief is weird. "After the polio . . . she hated feeling like a burden. Hated it. Hated having people stare at her. But she was trapped. And wicked smart. I wouldn't have gotten into the space program if she hadn't been there helping me study. But then I was the first man in space, and suddenly we had reporters everywhere."

I winced, remembering my transition to being the Lady Astronaut. "They're like leeches."

"And she would have been the human interest story of the century." He held up his hand. "I stopped wearing my ring. I bribed people. Took every high-paying job so I could set her up with private care. Moved her out of the house. Everything I could do to keep her out of the spotlight."

The ship's fans whispered around us as we sat opposite each other. "What kind of music did she like?"

"Ragtime." The corner of his mouth turned up in a half smile. "She had a player piano and collected rolls of music. Had one that was signed by Scott Joplin, even."

"Golly."

"She composed for them too. Couldn't play anymore, on account of the polio, but she figured out how I could rig it so she could punch sheets of music. Told you she was wicked smart."

"She sounds spectacular." I was curious, so curious, to know how he rationalized his affairs when he clearly loved her. None of my business, but, oh, I wanted to know. "I'd love to hear some of her music."

"When we get back to Earth." He almost lost it again.

I used the only line I could think of to reel him back in. Language. "Ready to learn some Aramaic?"

"Not Hebrew?"

"Not for this." He should be standing to do this, but I wasn't going to force my entire culture on him. "*Yitgadal v'yitkadash sh'mei raba. B'alma di v'ra . . .*"

Parker cocked his head. "*Yigtadel yigkadesh*—that's not right, is it?"

It wasn't, but it was closer than most Jews on their first attempt. I slowed down. "*Yit-ga-dal v'yit-ka-dash.*"

"*Yitgadal v'yitkadash.*" That attempt was green-lit, and I hated him a little for picking it up so quickly.

"Glorified and sanctified be God's great name."

He nodded as if he already knew the meaning. Being Parker, he probably did. "She said it every year on the anniversary of the Meteor."

"A lot of us do." I did. Every year. For my mother and my father, and my aunts and cousins and the hundreds of thousands of people who died. "*Yitgadal v'yitkadash sh'mei raba. B'alma di v'ra . . .*"

He rubbed his eyes with the back of his hand. "Don't think this gets you out of teaching me Yiddish."

"We'll do that while everyone else is on Mars."

He nodded, and then Stetson Parker, widower of Miriam Parker née Kaplan, began the Kaddish again. It took us a long while to get through it.

I think it helped.

September 3, 1963

Dear Nathaniel,

Unless I really botch things, by this time tomorrow we'll be in orbit around Mars. I'm not actually worried about the calculations because Heidi and I have triple-checked each other and Florence and Dawn have run everything through the mechanical computers—well, Dawn did. Florence's jammed twice when she was feeding the punch cards in, and Rafael is still trying to get the feeder clear.

But I guess that's why I'm here, and why Mission Control won't let me go to the surface. Or Heidi. Neither of us take it personally, although I'll admit that it is hard to be this close. The logic of it makes sense, though.

I wish you could see Mars. Leonard has had the big telescope aimed at it for the past month. He's got his eye on a couple of potential landing spots, but won't make that determination until we've been in orbit for a while. You know that. I don't know why I keep telling you things that you know, except maybe that I miss you.

Mars is beautiful. In very different ways from Earth. We always call it the Red Planet, but it's more of a soft salmon, with smoky grays and the occasional patch of umber. I am fairly certain that when we send pictures back it will become the new spring fashion palette.

Please tell Thomas that I send my love and that I'm very proud of the help he's giving you.

All my love,
Elma

Mars filled the viewport. Reds and ochers and umbers and a patch of white ice at the pole, and I could pay attention to none of it. Not until we were in orbit.

Sitting in the pilot's seat, Parker's hands were steady on the controls. Thank God. I think he still crumbled, but he was keeping it together in public. Quieter than usual for the past month. Less likely to make verbal jabs. But he was steady at the helm.

Parker flipped the shipwide mic on. “Stand by for the burn.”

From the engineering mod, Rafael said, “Your intrepid adventurers await.”

“Confirmed intrepid.” Parker switched off the mic and his voice was hoarse. “Will you do the count?”

“Roger.” Maybe he wasn’t as steady as I thought. I turned on my mic, keeping my eye on the clock and our altitude. “On my mark. Ten, nine, eight, seven . . .” These numbers only made my tension grow. “Six, five, four . . .”

“Starting engines.”

“Three, two, one . . . mark.”

The great engines of the *Niña* fired, slamming me into my harness. The side of the viewport lit up as the *Pinta* and the *Santa Maria* mirrored us. As suddenly as it came, the thrust vanished.

Parker took his hands off the controls and let out a long breath. That was it for a display of nerves. “Burn status report. DELTA-TIG zero, burn time 557, shaft value on the angles, VGX minus 0.1, VGY minus 0.1, VGZ plus 0.1, no trim, minus 6.8 on DELTA-VC, LOX 39.0, plus 50 on balance.”

“Confirmed.” I flipped off my mic and pulled my papers closer. “For the record, that was a perfect burn.”

“And you turned your mic off for that?” Parker leaned forward in his seat and pointed out the viewport. “That’s the likely landing approach, isn’t it?”

Below us, the red hills rolled underneath the window. We had a “down” again. Leonard had brought pictures of it to the meeting, but it was like the difference between a radio program and a live performance. The textures and sharp definition of the setting sun made the edges pop with ruddy gold.

Parker sat back in his seat, grinning for the first time in days. "Altitude . . . 204 kilometers. I am *good.*"

"I thought you were just following my numbers."

"With precision."

I snorted and kept working with the data coming in. We were using the early lander and the orbital satellites that IAC had sent ahead of us to get positional readings. Parker's burn might have been perfect, but until we had confirmed orbit, my numbers were still suspect. My pencil flew over the paper, sketching out our orbit as Mars turned below us.

It looked good. I bit my lip and did it again.

Same result. I circled it. "The preliminary tracking data for the first few minutes shows us in a 61.6 by 169.5 orbit. We're stable."

Parker pulled the microphone closer and, from somewhere, pulled out an announcer voice that would have made Terrazas proud. "Bold adventurers, the Lady Astronaut has just pronounced a stable orbit. Welcome to Mars."

THIRTY-TWO

SURVEY FINDS PUBLIC BACKS MARS LANDING

With the First Mars Expedition scheduled to land tomorrow, the American people now favor landing a man on Mars by 51 to 41 percent, according to a new poll by Louis Harris published yesterday in the *Kansas City Post*. That opinion has changed dramatically in the past year, largely as a backlash against the Earth First movement.

Maybe we'd picked up the habit from the *Pinta* crew, or maybe it was just because the best table was in the kitchen, but for whatever reason, Rafael, Leonard, and I had started doing our work there. It was probably the table, because Leonard had a series of photos spread out at one end of the table and was working on a map of the landing site. Rafael squinted at the Mars lander's manual with his fingers pressed to one temple.

My eyes were starting to cross from staring at numbers all day. Shutting my binder, I stretched. "Cake or pie?"

"Pie." Leonard raised his hand.

Thwacking him with his pencil, Rafael said, "Cake."

"So I get to make whatever I want. Noted." I slid my legs around the end of the bench and stood. Truly, cakes were harder with the materials on hand, but I had a hankering for Mama's pound cake. Although I wasn't sure how I was going to fake sour cream . . .

Rafael rested his head on the binder with a thump. "I should take a break too."

"That looks like a nap." Leonard pretended to consult an imaginary clipboard. "Hm . . . that doesn't appear to be on today's agenda."

"Leave him alone. Those landers have a console that is stubbornly counterintuitive at first." It had been a pain learning to use the console for the moon, but after that, the thing was dead simple. Leaving my binder of calculations, I wandered over to the kitchen. Could you sour powdered milk with lemon juice? Maybe I should do pie after all.

Rafael grunted behind me. "You're not kidding."

"You should ask Parker if you can go over to the *Santa Maria* and pull the lander out of mothballs." On the other hand, a simple chocolate cake might be nice. I could add some cinnamon to it. "It's easier to remember the shutdown sequence when you're looking at it."

"You say that as if you have personal experience."

Grabbing a bowl out of the cabinet, I glanced over my shoulder at Rafael. "It's the same console as what I was flying on the moon."

His jaw dropped. "*Puta que pariu.* I knew that. I had just . . . Why the hell am I taking it down?"

I set the bowl on the counter and turned to face him fully. "It's not the same. I wasn't flying in atmosphere."

"Yeah, but—you still have more flight time on it than I had on the simulator."

Being a pilot, the urge to agree was very strong. I did have more flight time. I wanted to go down to Mars so badly I could taste it. But I also knew why I wasn't. I gestured at my binder on the table. "Open it."

Rafael rolled his eyes. "Come on, Elma . . ."

"I'm serious. Can you do any of those equations?" This, right here . . . this was what Helen had done when she gave up her spot to me. Not that the causes were the same, but the fact of bowing to a world that you couldn't change. She wasn't happy about it, and I won't pretend that I was, either, but these are the realities. "I'm staying here and doing math. But, first, pie."

Leonard smiled. "I do like pie."

"Me too. 3.14159265 . . ." I winked at him, but I was going to make a pie. "Meanwhile . . . O Pilot, have you thought about what you're going to call the lander?"

Rafael looked down, smoothing the pages with one hand. "The *Terrazas*."

Do you remember where you were when mankind landed on Mars? I was on the bridge of the *Niña*, sitting in the copilot's seat with my pencil and paper, ready to plot. Parker sat in the seat next to me with nothing to do. We stared out the viewport and listened to the radio channels as the *Terrazas* entered the atmosphere of Mars.

The rest of our crew was aboard. They would go first, and then, assuming all went well, the crew of the *Pinta* would descend in two weeks.

Leonard's voice came through clear and steady. "Our radar checks indicate 15.24 kilometers periMars. Our visual altitude checks are steadying out at about 16.15 kilometers."

I added that to the worksheet for the *Terrazas*'s descent. "Confirmed. I recommend you yaw 10 right. Then you're Go for powered descent. Over."

"Confirmed Go for powered descent."

They had five minutes before they initiated the descent. Until that point, they were just in a lower orbit than we were. Beside me, Parker flexed his hands on his knees, as if he wanted to reach for the controls himself.

Rafael's voice came faintly through Leonard's microphone. "Stabilization and Control circuit breakers. DECA Gimbal AC, closed. Command Override, off. Gimbal enable. Rate Scale, 25."

Aside from the Red Planet filling the viewport, it was almost like being in a sim. "On my mark, 3:30 till ignition."

"Confirmed."

I watched the clock, and their position. "Mark. 3:30 till ignition."

"Confirmed. Thrust translation, four jets. Balance couple, on. TCA throttle, minimum. Throttle, Auto CDR. Propellant button, reset. Prop button." Leonard's voice was cool as he read off the checklist for Rafael. "All right. Abort/Abort Stage, reset. Att. Control, three of them to Mode Control. AGS is reading four hundred plus one."

In my head, I could see the cockpit of the *Terrazas*. They were flying with their engine forward so they could use it to slow down and had their windows pointing planetward in order to confirm their trajectory. They'd do a 180-degree yaw so they could point their radar at the surface. From there on, it would be all up to Rafael's flying.

I kept my pencil out anyway.

When Rafael said, "Ignition," Parker lifted both hands, fingers crossed.

I watched them on our radar. "Their rate of descent looks good."

Parker muttered, "God. I don't know how Mimi stood it . . ."

My gaze stayed fixed on the radar, but with my free hand, I reached over and gave his arm a quick squeeze. "She knew who she was marrying."

"Heh."

Like a radio play without narration, Leonard said, "Throttle down . . . six plus twenty-five, throttle down."

I bit my lip. They were going to reduce thrust six minutes twenty-five seconds into the burn, which made sense. I just wanted something to do. It was the longest six minutes and twenty-five seconds of my life.

"Throttling down. Fifteen-hundred-meter altitude. Thirty point five meters per second. Attitude control is good."

Finally, numbers I could do something with again. It was simple enough that I could do it in my head, but I plugged them into the worksheet for safety. "You're Go for landing. Over."

"Confirmed. Nine hundred fourteen at 21.3."

I nodded, even though he couldn't see me. "Confirmed. Go for landing. Nine hundred fourteen meters."

"Six hundred and ten meters. Six hundred and ten meters."

Parker leaned forward, as if he could see them outside the viewport. The reds and ochers scrolled underneath us. Theoretically, the *Terrazas* was directly below. As thin as Mars's atmosphere was, the streak of their entry didn't light up as much as it would have on Earth.

"Thirty-five degrees. Thirty-five degrees. Two hundred twenty-nine meters. Coming down at seven meters per second." Leonard could be announcing stocks rather than landing on a planet. "One hundred eighty-three meters, down at 5.8."

I tracked them on my sheet, not because there was anything I could do, but just so I had something to do with my hands. I traced the arc of their descent the way I used to track Parker going into orbit.

"One hundred and seven meters, down at 1.2. We've got a shadow."

It would be different landing in an atmosphere, even a thin one, but I knew that shadow. They were nearly down.

"Thirty point five meters, 1.1 down, 2.7 forward."

Kam and Florence must be staring out the windows from the back of the lander.

"Twelve point two meters, down .76. Picking up some dust."

I held my breath, and I'm pretty sure Parker did too. In fact, the entire ship seemed to go silent, as if the fans had stopped blowing while we waited.

"Contact light."

For the first time in the last ten minutes, we heard Rafael speak, as calm as anything. "Shutdown."

"Engine stop."

Parker let out a whoop as if he'd been holding it in since Earth. I threw my papers into the air and they floated around us in a snow globe of calculations.

Through the speakers, I could just barely hear Florence in the background laughing with glee. Rafael's calm must have been masking an ear-splitting grin. "*Niña,* this is Bradbury Base. The *Terrazas* has landed."

At the sound of their new call sign, my eyes pricked with tears. God. They had really made it.

Parker grabbed the mic. "Glad to hear it, Bradbury. Congratulations on a beautiful landing."

"Bradbury, *Pinta.*" Behind Benkoski's voice, I could hear the crew of the *Pinta* cheering. "We're all—congratulations. Can't wait to join you."

"Thanks. The view is something. It looks all red from up in the air, but some of the rocks outside look bluish." Rafael laughed. "Leonard just rolled his eyes at my science. We'd better get busy, or he'll start the EVA without us."

"Get to it. And take pictures." Parker turned the mic off and looked over at me, grinning. Papers spun between us still. He snatched one out of the air, looking at the calculations that covered it. "You done good, York."

"It's my job."

Parker's grin softened into something, I don't know . . . something almost fond. "I'm sorry you don't get to go down."

I shrugged, looking out the window as Mars turned below me. I wanted Nathaniel to see it, and Rachel, and Thomas, and Hershel, and Helen, and everyone . . . "Not this time. But it won't be my only chance."

When I got back to Earth, I was going to use everything in my power to get the colony ships here, full of people from every walk of life. I'd been the Lady Astronaut long enough to know how the game worked. From here on, I would be the Lady Astronaut of Mars.

EPILOGUE

FIRST MAN ON MARS ADDRESSES UNITED NATIONS

Today, Dr. Leonard Flannery addressed the United Nations on the forthcoming Second Mars Expedition. Dr. Flannery will be heading the expedition to establish a colony on Mars. In his address, he urged all nations to work together peacefully to create a new home for humanity on our sister planet. This was not intended, he said, as a way to replace Earth, but rather to offer humanity new frontiers and opportunities. As a Negro, he was living proof that in space, all men were created equal, and he hoped to serve as an inspiration to future generations.

He was joined by his copilot, Dr. Elma York, who rose to fame in the early days of the space program as the "Lady Astronaut." She wore a smart blue ensemble, with a string of pearls at the neck.

I am landing on Mars today. The *Esther* shudders around me as atmosphere brushes over the skin of our lander. In the NavComp seat behind me, Helen calls out our approach to Mars's surface. "On my mark, 3:30 until ignition."

"Confirmed 3:30." My mouth is dry, but my hands are steady on the stick. The rest of the crew in the lander holds their tongues, but they have the same view I do, of the red surface spreading out to meet us. I pull my gaze away and watch the mission clock instead, so I'll be ready when Helen calls it.

"Mark. 3:30."

"Confirmed." The digital numbers flick over in the countdown.

To my left, in the copilot seat, Leonard reads out the checklist the way he had for Rafael on his first trip. "Thrust translation, four jets. Balance couple, on. TCA throttle, minimum. Throttle, Auto CDR. Propellant button, reset. Prop button . . . okay."

In response, I flick the appropriate switches. It's like landing on the moon, and it is nothing like that, all at the same time. I am landing on Mars. The sequence of actions is familiar, but Mars's atmosphere changes everything. It is too thin to sustain life, but it could break us up in a second.

"All right. Abort/Abort Stage, Reset. Att. Control, three of them to Mode Control. AGS is reading four hundred plus one."

The remaining numbers bleed away from the countdown clock. "Ignition." I squeeze the control, firing four of our jets.

They kick, roaring, into life. One of the colonists behind us yelps, I presume at the sound, since we've experienced the seats slamming into our backsides before. Gravity grinds me into my seat and I tighten the muscles in my abdomen to keep blood in my head. Carefully, I yaw the ship over so the engines point down to the planet, and we begin our descent in earnest.

Mars is hidden beneath us. Outside the viewport, plasma flicks past the glass. I keep my gaze split between the horizon and the altimeter. "Throttling down."

Leonard nods at my side. "Fifteen-hundred-meter altitude. Thirty point five meters per second."

I start to do the math in my head, and then jerk my attention back to the controls. I have one job on this ship, and it isn't to do math. I am landing on Mars today.

"Nine hundred fourteen at 21.3."

Behind us, Helen says, "Confirmed. You are Go for landing."

Which is good, because an abort would be hell on everyone at this stage—if I could even do it. I ease off the throttle more, dropping us lower toward the surface. At 305 meters, the glint of the Bradbury Base's dome separates it from the rust of landscape.

I am actually on track, thank God. I keep the base centered on the grid of lines that were etched into the inside of the window. Horizon level. Dropping speed, but not so fast that I don't land us off the mark.

"Two hundred twenty-nine meters. Coming down at 7.6 meters per second."

A little fast yet. I ease off further, and below us the landscape takes on texture, with rough peaks and smooth sand dunes. The transmission tower at the Bradbury beckons, but the landing pad was hidden below dust. It had been too much to hope that it would stay clear.

The landscape scrolls beneath us, and a dark shape runs over its contours. I grin, feeling like I'm seeing an old friend. "We have a shadow."

"Thirty point five meters, down .9, three forward."

Wetting my lips, I edge us ahead until we are over where the landing pad should be. At the bottom of the window, ocher dust swirls, as if Mars is reaching up to say hello.

"Twelve point two meters, down .73. Picking up some dust." Leonard's voice is as steady as if he did this every day. "There's the pad."

Sure enough, the ship's exhaust had blown the dust away,

leaving a beautiful flat square, as ruddy as the rest of the landscape. I ease off the throttle and Set.

Us.

Down.

The feet of the lander bump and the g-forces shift. A light flashes on the dashboard, as if our status isn't clear. "Contact light."

"Shutdown." I pull my hands off the control stick and set it to neutral. I also start to breathe again. Four switches on the control panel later, I get to say two beautiful words. "Engine stop."

There is still a whole checklist to get through, but we are alive. We are on Mars. Behind me, the passengers let out a collective exclamation of glee. Nathaniel's voice carries clear through all of them. "*Baruch ata Adonai, Eloheinu . . .*"

And he says he's a terrible Jew . . .

Grinning, I let myself have a full second of looking out the window at the dust blowing across the landscape under the smoky orange sky, and then duty calls. I toggle on my microphone and call the mothership. "*Goddard*, Bradbury Base. The *Esther* has landed."

"Congratulations, Bradbury." Halim Malouf's voice has a giant grin built into it. "Perfect landing."

"Thanks." It was. "Happy to be down."

My face hurts as I unbuckle my belt. Because I am grinning like an idiot. Mars. I am on Mars. Leonard is already out of his seat, and claps me on the shoulder. "Nicely done, Elma."

"Thanks." I swivel out of my chair, awkward in my Mars suit.

Helen leans forward in her seat, one hand still holding the belt buckle. Her mouth hangs open a little as she stares out the window. As I stand, she shakes her head, blinking back tears. Catching me looking at her, she shrugs sheepishly and pats her binder of calculations. "I was looking down the whole way in."

I bend over her chair and give her a hug. "You've got time. Mission Control built in fifteen minutes for gawking."

Fifteen minutes for kissing . . . I still don't like that song, but it offers some good suggestions. I head to the back, where the colonists are getting out of their couches and running through their own checklists. Nathaniel looks up as I come down the aisle, helmet in his hands.

His smile could power the entire planet. Granted, there are only twenty humans on it at the moment, but still. "Nice flying, Dr. York."

"Why, thank you, Dr. York. Before you put that on . . ." I rest one hand on his wrist to keep the helmet down, and lean forward to kiss my husband.

Honestly, I don't care that everyone on the planet is watching.

We are not the only married couple on the ship, and I may have sparked a bit of smooching in other colonists. Helen and Reynard are pretty adorable. I'm not sure that kissing is what Mission Control had in mind for this break, but they should have. At least they recognized that, after traveling millions of kilometers to get here, we needed fifteen minutes to be human.

And then, we all get back to work, like the professionals we are. In short order, we have the lander secured, luggage ready to offload, and all of our suits sealed and triple-checked.

Leonard stands at the hatch and undogs it. "Ladies and gentlemen . . . welcome to the Bradbury Base."

He swings the hatch open, and a breeze pushes amber

dust into the room. I wish I could smell it. Slipping my hand into Nathaniel's, I squeeze his glove.

He leans over so his helmet rests against mine. With his mic off, so only I can hear him, he says, "My suit is suddenly not fitting in a specific way. I may need your help later."

At that, the thermostatic controls on my suit appear to fail, and heat floods it. "I will do my best, as a scientist and your wife, to resolve that issue."

"Elma?" Leonard waves me forward. "Want to do the honors?"

"Oh—" My face is still red from Nathaniel's . . . trouble. "But you're the mission commander."

He winks. "I've already been the first. And you are the Lady Astronaut of Mars."

Blinking against tears, which have enough weight to trickle down my cheeks, I duck through the hatch and balance on the top of the ladder. Mars. As far as the eye can see, the landscape rolls in dusty salmon, ochers, pinks, and flecks of deep purplish blue. Three steps down the ladder. The fourth puts my right foot on Mars.

My feet are standing on the surface of Mars. I am on Mars.

I am on Mars.

And there are other people waiting to also be on Mars. I shuffle away from the ladder to make space. Somehow, a part of me had expected it to be like walking on the moon, but there's more gravity here. The dust kicks up in clouds, held by the atmosphere, instead of just arcing in a frictionless vacuum. As much as I want to stand and just stare, there is work to be done.

There is work to be done, on Mars.

I head around to the side of the lander, where the cargo

bay is. Reynard joins me, and we start the process of un-dogging the hatch. Nathaniel waves as he walks past carrying a crate toward the Bradbury Base, but that is all the time we have together for the rest of the afternoon.

Space always sounds glamorous when I talk about it on television or the radio, but the truth is that we spend most of our time cleaning and doing maintenance. Today, we are doing that on Mars.

We are carrying crates on Mars. We are securing tie-down straps on Mars. We are waking a base that has been dormant for four years on Mars.

The sun creeps over the horizon as we stow the last of the crates inside the small dome of the Bradbury. Nathaniel's team has blueprints and plans for expanding the base, but for now it is comfortably cozy for twenty. Our first order of business will be to build the second habitat so that the colonists aboard the *Goddard* can come down to join us.

My work has been about getting us to the surface of Mars. Tomorrow, Nathaniel's work begins in earnest. We have this one night where our careers are balanced against each other.

I clamber into the *Esther* to make certain everything is locked down. She stands silent and empty around me. This is her first trip, but I'll be flying her up and down at least five more times to get everyone to the surface. I rest my hand on the pilot's seat with a sappy grin still on my face.

Patting the seat, as if I were saying good night to my aunt, I head toward the hatch. An astronaut is standing on the surface of Mars waiting for me. The sun has vanished beneath the horizon and I can't see his face, but I recognize Nathaniel's posture.

Eager as I am, I take my time dogging the hatch in place, following procedure to the letter. Five pumps of the handle to seat all fifteen latches. Wait for the delta pressure gauge to indicate a good seal. Only then do I let myself down the three rungs and set foot on Mars again.

On Mars. At some point, I will stop recognizing the wonder of where I am, but not today. I am on Mars.

We are on Mars. Nathaniel holds out both hands. I take them, still grinning, and lean in as if I were going to kiss him, but just tap my helmet against his. "I love you."

Yes, we could use the suit radios, but then anyone who wanted could hear us.

"I love you, too." His cheeks are streaked with tears. "Have you looked up yet?"

"No, I—" I glance up, and my words drop away.

Stars.

Above the undulating horizon of Mars, the night sky twinkles. The stars do not blaze in crystalline perfection the way they did in space. They sparkle through the atmosphere. Blue and red, silver and gold, dance against a deep purple. Across that dancing backdrop, the blinking light of the *Goddard* traces an arc across the heavens. "Oh dear God, I hadn't . . ." I hadn't seen the stars from the surface of a planet since March 3rd, 1952.

Do you remember where you were when the stars came out? I was with my husband, on Mars.

ACKNOWLEDGMENTS

First of all, thank you to Mom and Dad, who woke me up and set me in front of the television in 1969 so that I could say that I watched when the first human set foot on the Moon. I was six months old. I don't remember it, but the narrative of the fact that I did watch it is something that my parents have always reminded me of. I think that it sparked an early love for space and space travel.

Since then, I've watched footage of those early flights. I've seen a shuttle launch in person. I've gone to NASA every chance I get and so I would be remiss if I did not thank NASA and all the people who work there. Everyone I've talked with at NASA, from the folks at #NASAsocial to suit techs to astronauts to accountants, have been the nicest people. All of them seem to know that they have one of the coolest jobs in the world and are excited to share that wonder with you. Specifically, I need to thank Benjamin Hewitt, Tom Marshburn, Kjell Lindgren, and the staff of the Neutral Buoyancy Laboratory. Their help runs all through this book.

Robin Fergason is a scientist who studies the surface of Mars. She's helped select the landing sites for the *Phoenix* lander, the Mars Exploration Rovers, the Mars Science Laboratory rover, the *InSight* lander, and the Mars 2020 rover. Her dataset and interpretations are required to certify landing sites for Mars—and she helped me with getting Elma and her team down to Mars. She also provided really useful information about finding water on

Mars to give me better ideas of what Leonard would be doing.

Derek "Wizard" Benkoski kept my characters seated in air-force mentality. He's a fighter pilot and was great about giving me insights into characterization for his namesake and for Parker.

Stephen Granade is a real rocket scientist. He kept the science of navigating through space as accurate as he could and often wound up playing orbital mechanics Mad Libs. I would send him things like, "I registered Alkaid and Spica spun down to sight on Earth and presto-chango, I had the coordinates I needed to confirm our state vector. '[Jargon]'"

And then he would send back, "What if she rattles off the state vector like the *Apollo* astronauts gave numbers: no decimal points or units? 'Plus 0771145, plus 2085346, minus 0116167, minus 15115, plus 04514, minus 19587.'" For the record, those were the x/y/z position in feet and x-dot/y-dot/z-dot velocity in feet per second, with the precision limited, from the ISS's state M50 Cartesian vector on the day I asked the question.

Sheyna Gifford is my flight surgeon AND she also spent a year in a simulated Mars habitat. She gave me the vector for the illness with loads of delightfully graphic details. You can thank her for the floating spheres of diarrhea, although *thank* may not be the right word. . . . She also gave me details about life on "Mars" that I stole liberally, including the raisin wine experiment and what it's like to have an argument on a twenty-minute delay.

Kjell Lindgren not only arranged for me to watch a full run of a simulated spacewalk at the Neutral Buoyancy Lab, he and Cady Coleman also helped me dramatically rework the NBL scene and the spacewalk scenes. They are astronauts. Which, you know, is kind of a cool job. Kjell has actually done an ammonia repair on the ISS and I had watched video of that when I was working on the book before we met. But there's a big difference between watching a video and actually doing the thing. If not for him I would not have known that the lines are rigid when under pressure or that the tether pulls you slightly toward the ship in space. Cady gave me all the amazing details about the air bubble that occurs when you're in a spacesuit built for a larger person. Both of them were endlessly patient and generous with their time. All the cool stuff is theirs. The mistakes are mine.

Kari Love is a spacesuit designer and she spotted some errors as well as giving me all sorts of insight into construction choices. Broadly paraphrasing, spacesuit design is influenced by past disasters, so the American suits are focused on being fire resistant, while the Russian ones tend to focus on avoiding punctures.

I got some help on Portuguese from Amorena Noblis, and Robin and Eric Quakenbush. Yung-Chiu Wang and Vicky Hsu (and her parents) helped me with a number of things relating to Taiwan. My brother, Dr. Stephen K. Harrison—or as I like to call him, Apeface—helped with reshaping the post-Meteor global landscape.

Chanie Beckman helped me with many things related to Judaism and celebrating Passover in space. She also went above and beyond to record the Hebrew, Yiddish, and Aramaic for me to use as reference for the audiobook.

My *Writing Excuses* cohort, Brandon Sanderson, Dan Wells, and Howard Tayler, are stunningly supportive. My assistant, Alyshondra Meacham, is also a NASA Solar System Ambassador, and spotted a ton of errors on her own. My editor, Liz Gorinsky, and my agent, Jennifer Jackson, helped shape these books structurally to make them much better.

Of course, my beta readers who do yeoman's work: Alyshondra Meacham, Catherine Brennan, Chanie Beckman, Derek Benkoski, Kier Salmon, Stephen Granade, and Tracy V. Wilson.

And my husband, Robert, who does dishes, makes cocktails, and, when I am travelling, provides the balance wheel to my sidereal gyrations.

ABOUT THE HISTORY

I steal liberally from real history and you wouldn't think I could do that much with a book about going to Mars in 1963. And yet . . . the Soviets launched *Mars 2MV-3 No.1* in 1962. The rocket failed during launch and the satellite wound up in low Earth orbit, which eventually decayed and crashed. But they had the technology to send it, in the real world.

The opening scene in which Elma is listening to the broadcast of the probe landing on Mars is based on the *Viking 1* spacecraft, which launched to Mars in 1975. There were other efforts during those thirteen years, and a lot of explosions. That is probably the biggest thing that I get wrong in this alternate history—there would have been a lot more failures. Getting out of the gravity well is hard.

There are a number of places in the novel where I referenced historic transcripts of different Apollo-era missions. I say "referenced," and what I really mean is that when the First Mars Expedition is leaving Earth, I pasted in the transcript of *Apollo 8,* and wrote description to go around it with very minimal tweaking. I will be honest that I'm still hazy about what "plus Y, plus Z-direction" means. Then I handed the scene to two fighter pilots, some rocket scientists, and a couple of astronauts and told them to let me know where my edits made no sense. There were . . . a lot of notes.

The astronaut kibble, by the way, really was proposed by a nutritionist who was really a veterinarian.

Also in the horrifying-and-real category, "the bag" that Elma and Kam use with Ruby is really under development, although in the modern world, it comes with a robotic arm to handle the shaking.

The *Flash Gordon* episode that the crew performs is the actual pilot episode. I used to work in radio theater and that explosion technique, with the balloon and rice, is a real thing and surprisingly effective. Great fun!

The Tonight Show in Jack Paar's run was a very different experience to today's. The set has a *Mod Squad* sort of feel and I almost expect a Bond girl to wander through it in go-go boots. If you are curious, hit YouTube, look for "Jack Paar Tonight Show," and watch the episode with Judy Garland.

It is easy to forget, in the twenty-first century, how prevalent polio was before vaccines. The World Health Organization estimates that there are 10 to 20 million polio survivors alive today. As recently as 1988 there were 350,000 new cases of polio. In 2016, there were only 37. Thanks to vaccines, it is entirely possible that this disease will be completely eradicated. But in the 1950s and '60s, when these books are set, polio was a common and dreaded disease. There is no cure for polio. The best that one can do is address the symptoms. It strikes people differently, with some people having no more than a mild fever. At the other end of the spectrum is the iron lung. There are a handful of people alive today who have been in iron lungs since the Apollo era. These machines use a negative pressure ventilator to suck air into their lungs. There are no parts available for the machines. On YouTube, search for "iron lung interview 1956" to watch an interview with Betty Grant, a housewife with polio.

The Jewish population in Charleston is one of the oldest in North America. Much of the early population fled the Spanish Inquisition, to London and the Netherlands. From there, they migrated to the United States, and Charleston, in particular, was welcoming since the 1669 Carolina Charter expressly granted liberty of conscience to "Jews, heathens, and dissenters." Charleston resident Francis Salvador was the first Jew elected to public office in America. He was elected in 1774 and 1775 to the Provincial Congress and served until his death in 1776 in the Revolutionary War. Charleston remained the city with largest Jewish population until the mid-1800s. Elma's family would have come over in the 1780s with an influx of Ashkenazi Jews from Germany.

One of the things that gets really interesting is the intersection between traditional Southern and traditional Jewish cooking. I recommend the cookbook *Matzoh Ball Gumbo: Culinary Tales of the Jewish South* by Marcie Cohen Ferris. That said, the sour cream pound cake that Elma contemplates making is a recipe of my mother's. If you visit my website, the recipe is waiting for you. Just search for "MRK's mom's pound cake recipe."

When Elma says that she doesn't really speak Yiddish, she's downplaying her fluency because it is a language she only used with her family. This is, by the way, why I chose not to italicize it in the text but did italicize the languages that other characters speak. It is a heart language for her, so as familiar to her as English. That said, as happens with many bilingual people who don't speak the language outside the home, her sentence structure and vocabulary is still that of her childhood. I based her background on a friend from Chattanooga, whose grandparents spoke Yiddish in the home with a Southern accent.

The majority of the newspaper articles are real and often from the date that is shown in the paper. I've adjusted them for the post-Meteor timeline, but the riots, the tornadoes, and the social concerns were real. I did move one significant event though, and that's Martin Luther King, Jr.'s Nobel Prize. In our timeline, he does not win that until 1964. My rationale for moving it two years earlier is that his March on Washington—or in this case, his March on Kansas—also takes place two years earlier because of the Meteor. He received it, in both timelines, for his nonviolent campaign against racism.

Sometimes trying to maintain the feel of a time period provides opportunities, but there's also the danger of reinforcing problems from that era. I've done that with Kam Shamoun. The first transgender organizations were begun in the 1950s and 1960s. The Cooper Do-nuts Riot in May 1959 was one of the first LGBT uprisings in the United States. Kam would have been aware of these events and . . . being in the military and wanting to go into space would not have been able to pursue that dream had he come out. It wasn't a conversation I could see him having with Elma, or really anyone on the mission, and so I am misgendering Kam all the way through the novel. But the afterword isn't in Elma's voice, so I can correctly refer to Kam as he and him here. So can you.

I want to close by talking about Miltown. It was introduced to the market in 1955 and was the first widely popular psychotropic drug in American history. By 1957, over 36 million prescriptions had been filled, just in the United States, and a third of all prescriptions written were for Miltown. It was billed as a mild tranquilizer with "miraculous effects." By 1960, 1 in 20 Americans had tried Miltown. It was the first time that Americans felt like it was okay to talk about anxiety and to medicate for it. For more information about Miltown, I recommend reading *The Age of Anxiety: A History of America's Turbulent Affair with Tranquilizers* by Andrea Tone.

But I would like to ask this of you: The conversation that Elma has with her doctor in *The Calculating Stars* is the same one I had with my doctor when I went in to discuss depression. I went in because I had begun to recognize myself in descriptions of depression in books or when friends discussed their own difficulties. I don't have the social anxiety disorder that Elma struggles with, but I have plenty of friends who do. If you recognize yourself in Elma's symptoms and have not yet talked to someone, please do. Please ask for help. It's hard to escape the gravity well on your own.

BIBLIOGRAPHY

Chaikin, Andrew. *A Man on the Moon: The Voyages of the Apollo Astronauts.* New York: Penguin Books, 2007.

Collins, Michael. *Carrying the Fire: An Astronaut's Journeys.* New York: Farrar, Straus and Giroux, 2009.

Hadfield, Chris. *An Astronaut's Guide to Life on Earth: What Going to Space Taught Me About Ingenuity, Determination, and Being Prepared for Anything.* New York: Back Bay Books, 2015.

Hardesty, Von. *Black Wings: Courageous Stories of African Americans in Aviation and Space History.* New York: Smithsonian, 2008.

Holt, Nathalia. *Rise of the Rocket Girls: The Women Who Propelled Us, from Missiles to the Moon to Mars.* New York: Back Bay Books, 2017.

Nolen, Stephanie. *Promised the Moon: The Untold Story of the First Women in the Space Race.* New York: Basic Books, 2004.

Roach, Mary. *Packing for Mars: The Curious Science of Life in the Void.* New York: W. W. Norton & Company, 2010.

Scott, David Meerman and Jurek, Richard. *Marketing the Moon: The Selling of the Apollo Lunar Program.* Cambridge: The MIT Press, 2014.

Shetterly, Margot Lee. *Hidden Figures: The American Dream and the Untold Story of the Black Women Mathematicians Who Helped Win the Space Race.* New York: William Morrow Paperbacks, 2016.

Sobel, Dava. *The Glass Universe: How the Ladies of the Harvard Observatory Took the Measure of the Stars.* New York: Penguin Books, 2017.

Teitel, Amy Shira. *Breaking the Chains of Gravity: The Story of Spaceflight before NASA.* New York: Bloomsbury Sigma, 2016.

von Braun, Dr. Wernher. *Project MARS: A Technical Tale.* Burlington, Ontario: Collector's Guide Publishing, Inc., 2006.